A FEW

Married with four[...] author of *Just Desserts*, *Off the Record* and a number of erotic novels. Unlike the heroine of *A Few Little Lies*, Sue finds that her erotic writing is one of the worst-kept secrets in East Anglia. Born on the edge of the Fens, she is perfectly placed to write about the vagaries of life in a small country town.

Sue Welfare was runner-up in the *Mail on Sunday* novel competition in 1995, and winner of the Wyrd Short Story prize in the same year. She is also a scriptwriter, and her comedy appeared in the 1999 Channel 4 Sitcom Festival.

SUE WELFARE

A Few Little Lies

HarperCollins*Publishers*

HarperCollins*Publishers*
77–85 Fulham Palace Road,
Hammersmith, London W6 8JB

The HarperCollins website address is:
www.**fire**and**water**.com

This paperback edition 2000
3 5 7 9 8 6 4 2

First published in Great Britain by
HarperCollins*Publishers* 1998

ISBN 0 00 651431 6

Set in Meridien

Printed and bound in Great Britain by
Omnia Books Limited, Glasgow

This book is dedicated, with fondest memories, to the late Mr C. A. Woolley and Mr Glyn Howells, dedicated educators, who encouraged my enthusiasm for books and words and who, at different times, both offered the sage advice: 'Work more and talk less.'

1

'Letitia strode into the room, naked except for her bull whip and boots.

"I've come for you, Tony," she murmured between full pouting carmine lips.

On the leather sofa, bound hand and foot, Tony Vincetti trembled.

"Oh, please don't hurt me, Letitia," he whispered, the sweat rising in glistening beads on his top lip.

They both froze as they heard the doorbell ring.'

'Not in my book, they didn't,' Dora Hall whispered, pushing her glasses back up onto her nose. She erased the final sentence from the computer screen, then stretched, waiting for the machine to digest the latest morsel before leaning forward to switch it off.

Beside her, the intercom buzzed more insistently, followed closely by a thin, high-pitched voice through the speaker.

'Dora, are you up there?'

Dora pushed the swivel chair away from the desk and yawned. It was extremely tempting to say no. Instead she pressed the call button.

'Come up, Sheila, door's unlocked.'

She padded into the kitchen, scratching and yawning deliciously with every step. Oscar, the resident ginger tom, mewled the lament of the wildly over-indulged and leapt onto the cooker, while she plugged in the kettle and lit a cigarette. Opening the fridge, Dora prised a carton of milk off the shelf and sniffed it speculatively.

A few seconds later Sheila, her sister, pushed open the

kitchen door. She peered around and sniffed, looking rushed. Sheila inevitably looked rushed.

'Oh, you're in here, are you? I thought you told me you'd stopped smoking? You've left the street door on the latch again. Don't know why you've bought that security thing, anyone can just walk up – '

Dora hunted around for the teapot. 'I nipped across to the shop first thing.'

Sheila's eyes narrowed. 'Not like that, surely? You're not ill are you?' She picked her way across the kitchen and stood a wicker basket on the table amongst the debris of breakfast, letters and open books. Oscar headed towards the cat litter tray.

Dora glanced down at the grey dressing gown she was wearing and shook her head.

'No, I'm fine. I've been up for hours. I've been working on the computer this morning. Would you like a cup of tea?'

'You said quarter past ten,' Sheila said flatly, tapping her watch for emphasis. She looked wounded, tipping her head accusingly to one side.

'I did? I can't remember saying quarter past ten. What was supposed to happen at quarter past ten?'

Sheila sniffed again. 'I've been hanging around outside the post office for ages. Anything could have happened.' She paused and pulled her suit jacket straight. 'Absolutely anything.'

'What was it I missed this time?' asked Dora, noncommittally. 'Tea?'

Sheila sighed, picking at a small dry stain on her lapel. 'Just a quick one and then I've really got to get on. I told the vicar we'd go to his coffee morning today. Oh, and I've brought you these for that cat.' She pulled a neatly tied bundle of newspapers out of the basket and added it to the chaos on the breakfast table. 'I'd put us down for the washing up.' Sheila ran her tongue over her teeth. 'Too late now, of course. I'll have to ring up and apologise when I get back.'

Dora fished two mugs out of the cold water in the sink.

'I didn't realise you'd promised anybody. I thought you said we were just going to raid the cake stall and rootle through the bring and buy. Why don't you go into the sitting-room? I'll bring the tea through.' As she spoke she ran hot water over the remaining plates in the sink and added a squirt of washing-up liquid. It bubbled instantly and hid the debris of last night's supper under a reassuring explosion of suds.

Sheila nodded, pointedly ignoring the grubby tea towel Dora had tucked over her arm, and the miasma emanating from Oscar as he strained triumphantly over the cat litter.

Obtusely Sheila stepped across the little hall into the adjoining room, barely bigger than a broom cupboard, that Dora used as her office. Dora scrubbed the rings off the cups, watching as her sister peered myopically at the blank computer screen.

'So, how's the translation coming along?' Sheila's high-pitched voice betrayed a rich mosaic of resentments.

Dora dropped two tea bags into the pot.

'So-so, it's a bit slow at the moment. How are the kids?' She could see Sheila running a finger along her book shelves.

'Not too bad, Jason's getting his grommets next month,' Sheila said distractedly. 'Do you really read all these books?'

Dora carried the tray through and balanced it on a little table wedged between her desk and the office armchair.

'Why don't we go in the sitting-room, Sheila? You hate that armchair.'

Sheila shook her head, finger still working along the spines of the books arranged from floor to ceiling on the wall near Dora's desk.

'I prefer it in here, it's the only room you keep tidy. There's cat's hairs everywhere on that settee.' She paused. 'We're having a fund raiser next week, maybe you could sort out some of these you've finished with.' Her stubby finger tapped on one spine. 'I read about her in the paper. She's going to be in Smith's.'

Dora picked up her mug, gathering her dressing gown around her knees as she folded herself onto the swivel chair.

'Who is?'

'This Catiana Moran woman, she's doing a book signing. I saw a bit about it in the *Fairbeach Gazette*. I think it's one of the ones I brought –'

Sheila hurried back into the kitchen, reappeared carrying a newspaper, and began to thumb through the pages. She turned the paper back on itself and handed it to Dora.

'There we are. What's on in Fairbeach, half way down –'

Dora stared at a small grainy photograph.

'Oh, yes,' she said, swallowing down her surprise, and folded the paper alongside the tray. There was a familiar face on the front page. 'My God,' she whispered, scanning the headline. 'I didn't know Jack Rees had died.'

Sheila pulled a face. 'Who?'

Dora slipped on her glasses. 'Jack Rees, the MP?' She glanced down the column.

'Oh, him.' Sheila's face registered her disapproval. 'Jumped-up nobody, him. His dad was a fishmonger in Railway Road, mum used to work in the Co-op.' She sniffed dismissively and turned her attention back to Dora's shelves.

Dora stared at the picture of Fairbeach's famous son. There were few modern political giants from the fens, which had made Jack Rees all the more special – a true Fen tiger, a local hero who had dedicated his life to improving things in his home town. His features were so familiar that it felt as if she was looking at an old friend. She felt a peculiar little flurry of loss, while, across the room, Sheila pulled out one of the books.

'You've got an awful lot of that woman's stuff here,' she observed, peering at the photograph of a lascivious wet-lipped nymphet draped provocatively across the front cover. 'Do you read a lot of this sort of thing?' she whispered, turning it over so she could read the jacket.

'No, and I don't think it's really your sort of thing either,' Dora said. Leaning forward, she prised the novel gently from between her sister's fingers and slipped it back into the bookcase with the others. 'And they're definitely not suitable for a church bring and buy. Here, why don't you have your tea? How about if I get dressed? I was going into town later anyway, we could go out for some lunch if you like. I'm sorry we missed your coffee morning.'

Sheila gazed back at the unbroken spines of Dora's Catiana Moran collection.

'No thanks, I ought to be getting back. I don't see why you've got so many. There's two of some. Three of this one, *Passion in Paris*.'

Dora nodded. 'I get them sent to me by the publisher,' she said casually, handing Sheila the sugar.

'Oh, not one of those awful book club things?' Her sister rolled her eyes heavenwards. 'You really should write and get them to cancel your membership. Do you remember when Dad ordered that boat-building thing out of the Sunday colour supplement . . .'

As Sheila spoke, Dora surreptitiously slid her notes for the latest Catiana Moran novel under a pile of magazines and sat back to listen to her sister railing against the temptations of a mail-order culture.

Climbing the stone steps to Calvin Roberts' office, Dora thought fleetingly about his strong jutting chin, his rippling muscles – and sighed – only in her dreams. Her agent was small, round, with a penchant for cheap cigars, Labradors he perpetually called Dido, and propagating geraniums. His office on Northquay, an elegant Georgian crescent that overlooked the tidal waters of the Western Ouse, smelt of all three, and was a brisk ten-minute walk from Dora's flat in Gunners Terrace.

The girl behind the reception desk grinned at her. 'Hello, Dora, how are you?'

Dora pulled a wry face. 'Perfect. Is his lordship in?'

The girl nodded. 'Just got back from walking the dog. He's gone upstairs to read his horoscope. Do you want me to buzz him to let him know you're here?'

'Yes, you'd better. Can't have our lord and master caught on the cusp –'

Calvin's corner office was on the first floor. The opaque glass door bore the legend 'Calvin Roberts, Literary Agent' in faded gilt lettering arranged in a semicircle. Dora smiled as she turned the door handle. Calvin cheerfully embraced life's clichés. His office always reminded her of something out of a Bogart movie.

Calvin was sitting at the desk in his shirt sleeves, his feet up on the windowsill, flicking through an impressive bundle of papers. Apparently deep in thought, he waved her in.

In a basket near the coat stand, the latest incarnation of Dido looked up with world-weary eyes and licked her lips. There was a rolled-up tabloid in the pocket of Calvin's trench coat. It was still turned to the horoscope page.

'Hello,' Dora said, throwing her string bag onto his desk. 'I hear you've found someone then?'

Calvin grinned, and swung round to face her. 'Yes, yes, yes. She's starting a promotion tour for the latest book next week.'

'Calvin, I don't think it's supposed to work like this – I would really like to have seen this girl *before* you hired her.'

Calvin looked hurt. 'You told me you didn't want to be involved.'

Dora sighed. 'I meant with all the admin, not who you picked. I don't suppose it matters now, does it – the deed is done. Is she any good?'

Calvin grinned. 'I think so. Just wait till you see her at work.'

Dora lifted an eyebrow. 'At Smith's in the High Street.'

'You know about that?' said Calvin, feigning surprise as he lit another fat little cigar.

'I'm amongst the last by the looks of it. How did you manage to get her in there so quickly?'

Calvin tapped his nose. 'It's all to do with contacts, it's not what you know – the manager owes me a favour.'

'Better not tell me what. Have you got the kettle on yet?'

Calvin pressed the button on his phone. 'Gena, can you bring up a pot of tea for myself and Mrs Hall?'

Dora leant over the desk, pushing her finger firmly down on top of his.

'And if you've got any digestives in the tin, Gena, be a dear and bring them up.' She paused. 'Have you got a microwave in the office?'

The disembodied voice sounded surprised. 'Yes, why?'

'They've got some really good profiteroles in the freezer place in the precinct. If you nip out and get a couple of boxes I'll treat you.'

Calvin extricated his finger and the line went dead.

'Actually, I'm really glad you dropped in, I was coming to see you on my way home. Have you had the proofs of the latest book to correct yet? The guy at Bayers sent me the new covers over this morning.' He pulled his in tray closer and scuffled through the heap of envelopes. 'I've got them here somewhere. They're not bad at all.'

Dora screwed up her nose. 'Oh, please, Calvin, don't bother. Wet-lipped lovelies with "Come up and see my etchings" eyes? They're always the same. And no, I haven't had the proofs yet.' She paused. 'Did you hear about Jack Rees?'

Calvin nodded. 'Saw it on TV yesterday. Bloody shame, he was a good bloke. I nipped down to the Con Club, lunch time.' He rolled his eyes heavenwards. 'Total bloody chaos down there. Everyone running round like headless chickens. Jack's a hard act to follow. We're going to have a helluva job finding someone to fill his boots.' He took a thoughtful puff on his cigar.

Dora snorted. 'We? What's with this "we" business? Have the Con Club finally given you sergeant's stripes?'

Calvin deadpanned her. 'Father-in-law's on the selection committee. Anyway, about Catiana –'

Dora grinned and fished in her coat pocket for a roll of mints. 'Smith's next week,' she said, waving the packet at Calvin.

He declined as she palmed a mint into her mouth. 'Off the fags again? You'll get fat.'

Dora threw herself onto the leather chesterfield under one of the windows and laughed. 'Rubbish, I'm built like a ragman's whippet. Besides, it won't matter now that we've got a stand-in, will it? What's she like? That picture in the *Gazette* was dreadful.'

Calvin grinned. 'Pure twenty-four carat silicone.' He held his hands out in an impressive gesture of size. 'Teeth from ear to ear, big hair. She's absolutely perfect. I've already sent some photographs off to the agony column in that dodgy magazine we signed you up for.'

Dora nodded ruefully. 'Wonderful.'

'Oh, and wait,' said Calvin, warming to his subject. 'Better yet. I may've got her on Steve Morley's TV show.'

Dora screwed up her face. 'That magazine thing they do from Norwich at tea time? How the hell can she pull that one off? She writes porn, for God's sake.'

'Wait, wait,' said Calvin enthusiastically, clenching his fists. 'A stroke of pure genius. As the subject is a bit risqué I've told them we need a list of questions up-front. They always pre-record some of it anyway. So, you can write the answers and Catiana can learn them.'

Dora sucked her teeth thoughtfully. 'She can read as well, can she, Calvin? Good choice, good choice. And how exactly did you arrange this one off? Don't tell me the manager owes you a favour.'

Calvin grinned, leaning back smugly in his swivel chair. 'I've led young Steve to believe that I can get him one or two big names to give his show a bit of clout. The lad's hungry, this is his first big break.'

At that moment there was a knock on the door. Calvin called Gena in and then looked across at Dora.

'I've got you a ticket for the recording. You'll get a chance to judge for yourself first hand. You're a real stunner.'

Dora raised her eyebrows. 'I can hardly wait,' she said, as Gena stood the tray on Calvin's desk.

Steam rose from a stack of sad-looking profiteroles. Gena blushed.

'The defrost on the machine down there doesn't seem to work, so I've given them a couple of minutes on full,' she explained, hovering nervously.

Dora took a side plate from the tray and prised a dripping cake from the heap with a teaspoon – the chocolate bubbled ominously.

'I'm sure they'll be just fine,' she said, ignoring the hiss as the cake landed on the plate.

Parking in Norwich was a complete bitch. Dora arrived late, feeling ruffled after the drive, and slid into a seat at the end of the aisle beside a large woman wearing a duffel coat. The lights in the television studio were already dimming. On the stage below the tiered seating, a small oily-looking man in a checked suit was running through a selection of extremely old jokes. He waved his arms towards the studio audience with gusto, as if he might be able to incite laughter by friction.

The woman in the duffel coat sniffed disapprovingly and began to rummage through her handbag. Further along the row a group of students sniggered, while on the studio floor, the camera crew stalked backwards and forwards around the set, hooked up to their cables and moving like bored fish. The warm-up man faded rather than finished and a polite flurry of sympathetic applause broke out amongst the audience.

A man with a clipboard, finger in his ear, stepped into a spotlight, his face fixed in a rictal grin.

'Well, good evening, ladies and gentlemen,' he smirked with genuine plastic warmth. 'It's a real pleasure to welcome you to . . .' he glanced fleetingly at his clipboard '. . . tonight's recording of "Steve Morley Moments". Now, when Mr Morley comes on I'd like you to give him a really rousing welcome. The cameras will pan around the audience as the music comes on, so we want lots of smiles.' He pulled his face into an even more exaggerated grimace. 'Let the people at home know you're really happy to be here.'

The woman next to Dora sniffed again and then unexpectedly offered her a mint humbug. Dora sucked her way through Steve Morley interviewing a poet with a lisp, a drum majorette troop, a mime artist . . .

She stifled a yawn. It was the first time she had been to see a television recording and she decided it would probably be the last. The mime artist left to a crackle of applause and a few bars of 'The Entertainer' played over the PA.

'And finally, ladies and gentlemen . . .' the unctuous tones of Steve Morley oozed through the loudspeakers from his mock, mock Tudor living room. He stepped forwards, lifting his arms as if he were bestowing a benediction on the audience.

'. . . I'd like you to give a really warm Steve Morley welcome to Catiana Moran, the babe of the bed chamber, the first lady of lust . . .' Over the PA came the antiquated bumps and grinds of 'The Stripper'.

Dora leant forwards and let out a little hiss of admiration as Catiana Moran chasséd gracefully across the small stage. There was a flurry of applause that grew into a roar of approval as Catiana stepped into the spotlight.

The woman oozed sexual possibilities. Calvin had been spot-on with his description: she was statuesque with a great mane of tussled strawberry-blonde hair. Her little black dress, barely reaching mid-thigh, glistened over every curve, as if it had been sprayed on. Dora held her breath, while below her Catiana Moran curled herself provocatively onto Steve Morley's leather sofa and crossed her impossibly long legs.

'Good evening, Steve,' she purred, in a voice that seemed to trickle, rich as pure caramel, from somewhere just below her navel.

Steve Morley flushed crimson and began to stutter.

'Cut, cut,' snapped the little man with the clipboard. 'If we can take it from you saying, "Good evening, Steve"?'

Around Dora, the audience seemed to have woken up – all eyes firmly fixed on the reclining form of Catiana Moran.

'Why not?' the blonde whispered and repeated her opening line with – if anything – more sexual emphasis.

Steve Morley adjusted his tie and leant forwards, extending his hand. 'Very nice to have you with us, Catiana. My first question is, can you tell us how you got started writing the books you're so famous for?'

Catiana shifted position, rolling over on the sofa so that her chin was resting on her hands – the effect was devastating.

'Oh, Steve, darling, everyone always wants to know that. Haven't you got anything more interesting written down on your little clipboard?'

Dora mouthed the answers she had written, while the stunning strawberry blonde on the stage recited them. Catiana added extra emphasis to the word 'clipboard', imbuing it with a heady erotic *frisson*.

Steve Morley shuddered nervously and loosened his tie. 'What about this latest book? Am I right in thinking that you've finally decided to go public and promote what the papers are calling "the hottest hot novel since time began"?'

Catiana ran her tongue around her scarlet lips. 'Oh, yes,' she whispered huskily. 'Oh, yes . . .'

The audience, to a man, craned forwards to see how Steve Morley would cope with this siren.

Dora smiled and picked up her handbag before slipping silently into the aisle. She had to ring Calvin to tell him – for once – he'd got everything just about right. As she got to the exit she glanced back at the stage. Catiana Moran had slipped off her high heels and was stroking one foot over her long, long leg. Every eye in the house was on her. Steve Morley was practically drooling.

'You said you didn't even read her books.' Sheila bustled along the shopping precinct in Fairbeach, clutching her brolly like a quarterstaff.

Close behind, head bowed against the scathing wind, Dora pulled her raincoat tighter.

'Just call it curiosity,' she said between gritted teeth, wondering what on earth had possessed her to ask Sheila to go with her to Smith's.

Sheila snorted. 'You're not going to buy anything, are you?'

Dora pushed open the shop door and was struck by the heady aroma of new paper and warm damp bodies.

'I might do. It depends,' she said, over her shoulder.

She looked around, expecting to see Calvin Roberts lurking somewhere. Instead Catiana Moran was sitting alone at a trestle table near the book section, cradling a gold pen. Her nail varnish and the swathes of silk ribbon pinned around the table matched exactly.

In daylight, Catiana Moran was paler, slimmer – if anything more stunning – dressed in an impossibly tight copper dress that emphasised every electric curve. Against the backdrop of browsers and shoppers, wrapped up in their macs and sensible shoes, she looked like an exotic refugee from a night club, caught travelling home in her party clothes.

Several shoppers stopped to take surreptitious glances in her direction, a few ventured closer to be rewarded by her huge carnivorous smile. She worked through the little scrum around her with aplomb, flirting, teasing, tipping her head provocatively to listen to their messages and their dedications. She was a sequinned shark amongst a shoal of minnows. It was very difficult not to be impressed.

Sheila stepped closer to Dora, who was hovering, undercover, near the video section.

'She looks a right tart,' Sheila hissed. 'She won't sell a lot of that kind of thing in Fairbeach, you know. It was packed in here last week when that cookery woman came. She gave everyone bits of broccoli quiche.'

But Dora had already stepped towards the table. Catiana Moran looked up as Dora made her way to the front of the queue, and beamed, eyes glittering like bright shards of broken glass. Dora pointed towards the pile of novels stacked beside her.

'Hello, are they going well?' she asked unsteadily.

Her alter ego nodded. 'Oh, yes. My books are ever so popular,' she said in the same toffee-brown voice Dora had heard during the TV recording. 'Have you read any of them?' Catiana's eyes were blue-green with tiny flecks of gold which glittered in the shop lights – she was truly beautiful.

Dora reddened as she felt Sheila approaching. 'Yes,' she said quietly, 'every one of them.'

Catiana's smile widened. 'Oh, wonderful. Then you're going to love the latest one. It's really good.'

Dora took a book from the pile and slid it across the table. Behind them, Sheila sniffed as Catiana Moran opened the pages with carmine fingertips.

'Would you like me to sign it for you?' she purred.

Dora nodded. 'Yes, please.'

She rolled the gold pen between her fingers. 'Who would you like me to dedicate it to?'

'Dora,' Dora whispered in an undertone, 'Dora Hall.'

Catiana whipped the pen across the fly leaf and pressed the book into Dora's hand. 'Enjoy,' she murmured.

Reddening, Dora nodded and scuttled towards the cash desk. At her shoulder she could feel Sheila's embarrassment throbbing like toothache. When Dora glanced back towards Catiana, the beautiful, predatory blonde was surrounded by a group of young men; she threw back her head and laughed as she pulled another book off the stack.

Dora laid her copy on the cash desk. The shop assistant slid it into a bag.

'Do yer like her then?' the woman asked, nodding towards the back of the store, as she handed Dora the change.

Dora smiled broadly. 'Yes,' she said softly, 'I think I do.'

2

Lawrence Rawlings looked out of the window in his study. He could hear the bells of All Saints ringing in The Close. The panelled room was sparsely furnished with elegant pieces of antique furniture, so familiar that Lawrence barely noticed them. Nothing was out of place, which was how he preferred it. The spring sunlight picked out his distinctive features and then moved on to the family photographs and paintings on the wall, echoes of his past and present. Arms folded behind his back, he stretched up onto his toes. He didn't turn round as the door opened, nor when the man he had invited settled himself into the chair on the far side of the ornate mahogany desk.

'My family have lived in this house for seven generations,' Lawrence said, in a voice that barely rose above a whisper – he could almost have been talking to himself. 'We have been merchants, mayors, councillors, pillars of the establishment – centre stage in Fairbeach's long and illustrious history.'

Behind him the man shuffled the chair closer to the desk. Lawrence paused.

'I want you to find out everything you can about this young woman who calls herself Catiana Moran. Her real name is Lillian Bliss. I don't need to explain the need for discretion. I want everything you can get your hands on. Is that perfectly clear?'

His guest made a noise, a low guttural sound that may or may not have been an answer.

'There is an envelope on the desk with what details I already have, and your first cheque,' continued Lawrence.

There were two magpies cavorting on the lawn near the

orchard. One hopped up onto a low branch amongst the blossoms. Two for joy. Lawrence allowed himself a thin smile.

'You know, my father planted that apple tree on the day I was born.'

His silent companion coughed. Lawrence Rawlings slipped his hands into the pockets of his tweed jacket and fingered the business card the man had sent with his brochure. 'I think that will be all for the time being. I expect to hear from you soon. I'd like to make it clear that I am not used to this kind of thing; you are the first private detective I have ever felt the need to engage. Your card says Safeguard Associates. What should I call you?'

'Milo,' said his visitor. 'Just call me Milo.'

When the door closed behind his visitor, Lawrence carefully opened the window and took his garden gun from the umbrella stand.

'One for sorrow,' he said wryly, closing one eye and taking aim. The 4.10 cracked out across the still morning. There was a flurry of feathers, black and white on the dewy grass. In The Close the five-minute bell rang. Lawrence checked his watch – he would just have time to get to Communion with his daughter Sarah, Calvin and the girls, if he hurried.

In her flat in Gunners Terrace, Dora was spooning tuna chunks onto a saucer, while something vaguely musical rattled around inside the radio. Oscar insisted she work faster, his thoughts so loud that she glared at him furiously.

'Pack it in, I hear you, I hear you. Talk to the guys who decided tuna should be sold in second-hand submarines, it's knackered my tin opener.'

The cat narrowed his eyes and his thoughts became unrepeatable.

Sunday mornings were quiet. Once a month Dora put flowers on an unmarked grave and then went for a girls-only lunch at Sheila's, while her brother-in-law and their two children went fishing. On the draining board, in a milk bottle, stood a single cream rose: a fitting floral tribute.

From the office she heard the sound of the phone and hurried to get to it before the answering machine cut in.

At the far end of the line Calvin Roberts chuckled.

'Morning, Dora. Got your message. Sorry I didn't get back to you sooner. I'm glad you liked Catiana. I got the page proofs for *One Hundred and One Hot Nights* yesterday. Would you mind if I popped round for a few minutes and dropped them off?'

Dora sighed. 'Six days shalt thou labour, Calvin. Surely a good High Church boy like you has got that tattooed somewhere significant. Haven't you got a regular Sunday morning assignation with the Almighty?'

Calvin snorted. 'It's the wife who's the God-botherer, Dora, not me. I'm firmly aligned with Mammon, and trust me she's not tattooed, I would have noticed. So, what shall we say? Ten minutes?'

Dora sighed. 'Calvin. It's Sunday. I'm just about to go out for lunch.'

'Don't tell me – roast chicken with Sheila?' said Calvin flatly. 'I bet you can hardly wait.'

Dora rolled her eyes heavenwards. Calvin definitely knew too much about her private life.

'Ten minutes,' she said, and hung up.

Dora heard the doorbell ring just after she'd convinced herself Calvin wasn't coming after all. She pressed the security button and was about to call him up when she heard another voice over the speaker – a low, throaty chuckle alongside Calvin's cheerful greeting.

'Have you got someone with you?' Dora demanded, as the downstairs door opened. She waited apprehensively in the hall. Calvin, cigar in hand, pushed open the landing door. Just ahead of him, nestled in the crook of his arm, was Catiana Moran. She was wearing a pair of navy pedal pushers, cream high-heeled mules and a matching angora sweater, all wrapped around in a fake-fur jacket.

There was a peculiar time-defying moment when Dora stared at Catiana and Catiana stared back.

Catiana nibbled her beautifully painted lips. 'Hello, Mrs Hall,' she said, offering her hand. 'Pleased to meet you.'

Calvin steered the girl into the hall before Dora had chance to reply or protest.

'Dora, may I present Miss Lillian Bliss or, should I say, Miss Catiana Moran.'

Dora shook the girl's hand, knowing full well she had her mouth open but feeling completely powerless to close it. Finally, she forced a smile and in a tight, uneven voice suggested they might be more comfortable in the sitting room.

As Lillian shimmied through the door, Dora beaded Calvin and with a curled finger invited him to follow her into the kitchen. Still smiling he did as he was told.

'I've got your page proofs. *One Hundred and One Hot Nights*, straight off the press,' he said, clutching a padded envelope in front of his rotund little belly like a shield. Dora pushed the door to behind him.

'Page proofs?' she hissed.

Calvin took a healthy chug on his cigar and shrugged. 'Lillian said she'd like to see where you worked, give her a sense of her life, her background.'

Dora stared at him. 'Her background? What background? She doesn't have a background, Calvin. She's a model. You wind her up, pay her her money and send her home. We hired her so that I could keep my background to myself –' Dora knew she was fast running out of words, they were all jammed up behind by a little scarlet flare of indignation.

Behind them Lillian pushed the kitchen door open.

'Sorry, Mrs Hall,' she said tentatively, peering into the room. 'I hope I'm not interrupting anything, I just wondered if I could use your loo?'

Before Dora could answer, Calvin smiled. 'Sure thing, sweetheart. It's the second door on the right. Dora was just saying how nice it was to meet you. She was about to put the kettle on.'

Dora groaned and Lillian slipped away, tip-tapping in her mules across the lino.

'Sweetheart?' Dora hissed.

Calvin shrugged. 'She's a nice girl. She just wanted to come up and see where you worked. It'll make her more real, more convincing – like method acting.'

Dora slammed the kettle under the taps. 'We're talking about a model signing a few books here, Calvin, not Brando.'

Calvin pouted. 'Actually, that's what I wanted to discuss.'

Dora had a sense of foreboding. 'Sorry?'

Calvin dropped the envelope onto the kitchen table. 'My phone's been ringing off the hook since Lillian did the Steve Morley show. Regional TV want her to do a late-night slot on the Tuesday arts programme.' He paused. 'We just need another script. I've put the questions in there, they faxed them through first thing this morning.'

Dora threw two bags into the teapot.

'Another script,' she repeated. 'When are they going to record the programme?'

Calvin puffed out his cheeks. 'It's going out live on Tuesday night.'

Dora was about to speak but Calvin hurried on.

'Lillian's a natural, Dora, she learns really quickly, all she needs to swing it is your script.'

Dora licked her lips. 'I see. So when do you need this work of literary genius?'

Calvin smiled. 'By tomorrow afternoon. Won't be a problem, will it?'

It was not the easiest social event Dora had ever hosted. Lillian Bliss perched on the edge of the settee, looking around, taking in everything with her bottle-blue eyes, unsure quite what to say. Calvin hid behind a cloud of cigar smoke and Dora played mother.

'Do you live locally?' she asked, trying to fill the choking silence.

Lillian smiled. 'I do now. I've just got a new flat.'

From the corner of her eye Dora noticed Calvin wince slightly, and played the advantage.

18

'Really,' she said, handing the girl a cup of tea. 'That's nice. Whereabouts?'

Lillian simpered in the general direction of Calvin Roberts. 'Calvin's found me a really nice place down by the river. One of those new warehouse conversions?' She wrinkled up her nose. 'It's funny, me getting a nice place like that and you living here . . .' She stopped, and glanced round the room, blushing furiously. 'Well, it is small, isn't it? Not like I imagined at all, really. Not that it's not nice, I mean, I'm not saying . . .' She stopped dead, tripping over her own embarrassment, then took a deep breath and started again. 'I saw a film about this famous American writer once, she'd got this big house on the beach. And a little fluffy white dog. Calvin said . . .'

Calvin coughed theatrically before Lillian got a chance to share what it was he'd said. He tugged at his waistcoat.

'Er, right, I think we ought to be going now. Maybe Dora could just show you her office and then we can get on our way.'

Dora suppressed a smile and picked at the cat's hairs on the arm of the chair.

Lillian pouted. 'I haven't finished my tea yet, Bunny,' she protested in a little-girl-lost voice.

Calvin waved her to her feet. 'Don't worry about the tea,' he said briskly. 'Let's look at the office. We'll get some lunch on the way home.'

Lillian beamed. 'Oh, all right,' she said enthusiastically and turned her piranha smile on Dora. 'I wanted to know where I write all that stuff. That's why I wanted to come.' She stopped and buffed her smile up. 'And to meet you, of course.'

Dora lifted an eyebrow and stared pointedly at Calvin, who coughed again.

'Come on then,' he blustered. 'We'll take a look at the office and then we'll be off.' ·

There was barely room for two in the office. Dora hung back while Lillian looked around, running a painted fingernail over the books and shelves. Calvin stood in the doorway.

Dora grinned at him. 'Bunny, eh?' she whispered in an undertone.

'She's just naturally affectionate,' hissed her agent.

Dora suppressed a smile. 'You surprise me.'

Satisfied, Lillian looked up. 'Okay, all done,' she said cheerfully. She glanced at Dora. 'Calvin said you were going out to lunch, would you like to come with us?'

Dora felt Calvin bristle. She smiled and shook her head. 'That's really very kind, Lillian, but no thanks, actually I've been invited to my sister's.'

'We could drop you off on the way,' continued Lillian. 'It wouldn't be any trouble, would it, Bunny?'

In spite of herself, Dora felt a rush of affection for her alter ego. She shook her head again, Calvin shuffling uncomfortably beside her.

'That's very nice of you, Lillian, but it's not far and I enjoy the walk.'

At the top of the stairs, Lillian thanked her for tea, buttoned up her jacket and was gone. Calvin adjusted his crombie.

'Nice girl,' he said, teeth closing on his cigar.

Dora grinned. 'I hope you've got a licence.'

'Uh?'

'Dangerous animals act, you're supposed to apply for a licence.'

Calvin snorted. 'Are you sure you don't want to be dropped off anywhere?'

Dora shook her head. 'No thanks, Calvin, just make sure, between the pair of you, you don't drop me in it.'

Calvin squared his shoulders. 'Have I ever let you down?' he murmured and lifted a hand in farewell.

Dora didn't feel he deserved an answer.

On a corner plot in the newly, dismally developed Harvest Meadows, Sheila was already busy in the kitchen, slipping a tray of gold-tinted roast potatoes back into the oven.

Dora hung her coat in the hall cupboard. 'Everyone out?'

Sheila wiped the steam from her glasses.

'Uh huh. You're late. Have you taken your shoes off? That Axminster's new. Lunch will be ready in half an hour.' She peered at Dora. 'I don't know how you stay so slim, all the rubbish you eat. Doesn't seem right. I only have to look at a cream cake and I put on half a stone.' Sheila tugged her apron down over her ample hips. 'Is that the dress we got from Marks?'

After the cool sharp air outside, the kitchen seemed uncomfortably hot. Dora glanced round at Sheila's immaculate work surfaces, and sighed. 'It was the only thing I'd got left that was clean. I've had company this morning –' And on reflection the company had left her with a disturbing sense of unease.

Sheila was oblivious, setting out gleaming cups and saucers on a doily-covered tray.

'You ought to take more care of yourself. I've told you I'll come and give you a hand with your housework if you like; two fifty an hour. Cash of course.'

Dora grinned. 'Pinkerton's going rate?'

Sheila shook her head and wiped up an imaginary sugar spill. 'Never heard of them. An agency, are they?'

'It was a joke. Can I help you with anything?'

Sheila sniffed. 'It's all done now. You didn't come through the Milburn Estate again, did you?' she demanded, arranging bourbons on a small silver plate.

'Never miss.' Dora leant over and prised a broken biscuit from the crinkly red plastic packaging before Sheila could consign it to the swingbin. 'It's a really pretty walk through those new little designer houses round the back. They've landscaped the parking bays now. Weeping willows and red hot pokers, very Sunday supplement.'

'It's sick. You didn't put flowers down again?'

'A single cream rose.'

Sheila sighed. 'People talk, you know.'

'It seems very fitting to mark the place where my husband died.'

'That would be all very well if he was dead.'

Dora crunched the biscuit, hoovering wayward crumbs into

21

her mouth with her tongue. 'He might as well be. I like to mark the spot where our marriage finally passed away.' She lifted her hands to add dramatic emphasis. 'One final, fatal collision between magnolia and sage-green emulsion that changed two lives irrevocably.'

Sheila pursed her lips and picked up the tray. 'Sick.'

'I'm much happier now.'

'People do not get divorced over emulsion.'

'It was the final straw.'

Sheila sniffed. 'Twenty years.'

'Do we always have to talk about this? You always bring it up, it's over, gone, dead.'

Sheila stood to one side while Dora opened the sitting-room door for her. 'Talking about dead. Did you see they're having Jack Rees' funeral next week? Taken their time to get it organised. I suppose it's getting all those bigwigs down here. It's all over the *Gazette*. They did a special pull-out bit. You'd think he was royalty, the fuss they're making.' She took a newspaper out of the magazine rack. 'I kept it for you.'

Dora stared down again at the familiar stranger's face. Jack Rees was a local legend, a heroic tribal warrior woven into the fabric of Fairbeach history. She scanned the article – he'd been in his sixties. The report said it was his heart.

A small pain formed in her chest which she recognised as grief. It took her by surprise, though she knew the pain wasn't personal, but an abstract, unexpected sense of loss for the passing of someone of worth.

The pain, mixed with her earlier unease, made her feel faint. She stood very, very still, aware of Sheila's voice like a distant echo over the roar of the wind. The sitting room suddenly seemed as if it were a bright patchwork quilt of colours and light, all sewn together by Sheila's insistent running-stitch voice.

Sheila rearranged the tray on a coffee table and picked up the newspaper, glancing over the same front page, talking all the time. She stepped closer, into sharp focus, every last stitch of her best Sunday dress and her best Sunday face caught in a spotlight's glare in Dora's mind. Sheila, Calvin and Lillian Bliss were just too much for anyone on a quiet Sunday morning. She suddenly felt sick.

'. . . I used to see him in town sometimes in that big car of his.' Sheila leant forward to pick up her reading glasses, her tone cruelly derisive. 'Coronary it says here, too much fancy living, if you ask me, "found dead on Saturday morning in his home in Parkway by his housekeeper." The rest is all stuff about how much he will be missed . . .' Sheila flicked the glasses off the bridge of her nose and dropped the paper back onto the coffee table. 'Well, I won't miss him. They're all the same if you ask me. Out for what they can get, all of them.' She sniffed again. 'Housekeeper, I ask you –'

Dora smiled, trying not to let Sheila infuriate her; it was an uphill struggle.

Sheila peered at her. 'What are you looking at?'

Dora forced another smile. 'I don't feel very well,' she said quickly, suddenly dizzy. 'Would you mind if I gave lunch a miss today?'

Sheila grimaced. 'You might have rung and said something. Do you want me to call a taxi? You've gone really white.'

Dora shook her head. 'No, no. I think the fresh air might do me good.'

Sheila fetched her coat and shoes, lips pressed tight together with a mixture of concern and pique. From the kitchen came the hot, greasy smells of lunch cooking. It was all Dora could do to stop herself from retching. Slipping on her coat, she smiled unsteadily.

'I'll ring you later when I get home.'

Sheila nodded, shaking Dora into her coat as if she were a child. 'Hormones,' she observed sagely, 'that's what I put it down to, it's your age. I should go home and have a nice rest if I were you, put your feet up. Are you sure you don't want me to ring you a cab?'

Dora shook her head and let herself out.

Outside spring had painted everything with great daubs of sunlight and impressionist daffodils. Dora smiled and pulled

23

her coat tighter. Whatever it was, the pain had gone. She cut through the garages, back towards the town centre.

'Would-you-like-to-tell-us-a-little-bit-about-your background?' Safely back at her flat, Dora read aloud, typing in the words as she recited them. Relieved to be excused the ritual of Sheila's Sunday lunch, she took a bite out of a sandwich, and scanned the rest of the questions scheduled for Catiana's interview. Sunday afternoon, away from Sheila's pink paper napkins, and everywhere was blessedly quiet. Dora stretched, lifted her glasses to pinch the bridge of her nose, and then reread Calvin's fax.

The Fenland Arts production team certainly hadn't stretched themselves, but then again maybe Calvin had warned them off. Dora stared up at the ceiling, screwing up her nose as she tried to get a fix on Catiana Moran's fictitious origins.

'I did think about being a nun,' she typed slowly, searching for a punchline. 'But . . .'

'. . . But I look awful in black. And those house rules –' Catiana Moran rolled her eyes heavenwards. On the TV screen, she ran her tongue around her beautifully painted mouth.

Dora shifted Oscar off her lap and lit another cigarette before turning up the volume on her ageing TV. Lillian Bliss was good – just give her the words and she delivered them with faultless comic timing. Dora glanced down at the draft copy of the script, following the lines she had written with her finger.

On screen, Rodney Grey from 'Fenland Arts Tonight', reclining in his black leather chair, laughed. His amused expression couldn't quite hide his disdain. It was obvious he thought the interview was beneath him.

'So when did you start writing seriously? Most people would like to know whether you're writing from personal experience. In your latest book . . .'

On the set, Lillian was waiting for her next cue. The interviewer, still talking, touched the microphone in his ear and smiled wolfishly. For some reason the gesture and his expression made Dora shiver. She sensed something was happening but wasn't sure what it was.

Rodney Grey leaned forward onto his elbows, turning a pen slowly between his long fingers.

'Why don't you tell us the truth, Miss Moran? I mean, this stuff you churn out is hardly great literature, is it? It's upmarket porn. Cheap titillation for the masses –'

Dora tensed; that wasn't in the script. Lillian pouted and stared at him blankly. He hadn't fed her the cue line. She was completely lost.

The interviewer's smile hardened. 'Well?' He slapped the front of the novel on the little table between them. 'How can you justify this kind of cheap smut?'

Dora leapt off the sofa. 'What are you doing?' she hissed impotently at the TV. Oscar took the hint and scrambled for cover.

Lillian Bliss gnawed at her lip – there seemed to be an agonising, bottomless silence. After a few seconds, Lillian leant forward, eyes glittering, and very, very slowly the camera followed.

'You horrible stuck-up little bastard. I knew you didn't like me the minute I laid eyes on you,' she snapped with suprising venom. 'I wasn't taken in by all that smarming round me in the dressing room – if I spoke with a plum in my mouth it would be different, wouldn't it? Have you ever read one of the Catiana Moran books? Just because they're dirty you think they can't be any good. The latest one's brilliant –'

Dora stared open-mouthed at the TV. She was stunned. She couldn't have said it better herself.

Lillian Bliss took a deep breath. 'I got into writing because I wanted to, and they say write about what you know – so I did.' Lillian reached across the carefully arranged coffee table and plucked the novel out of Grey's hands. 'I've got this horrible poky little flat in Fairbeach, above the shoe shop in Gunners Terrace . . .'

Dora felt her colour draining. 'No,' she said to the girl on camera, as it moved in for a close-up. Lillian's face filled the screen, her bottle-blue eyes locked fast on Rodney Grey.

'You wouldn't believe the things I've had to do to make ends meet. You're all the same, you lot. There was this bloke, just like you, he was. Got a degree, talked all la-di-da. I'll think of his name in a minute. He liked me to –'

'No,' Dora repeated more forcefully, barely able to watch.

Rodney Grey's face was a picture. He glanced at the clipboard on his lap and, with remarkable presence of mind, began to speak.

'So, Catiana, why don't you tell us all about this new promotion tour of yours?' he asked quickly, reverting to the script, stretching the words in front of Lillian like a trip wire.

Lillian looked up at him, blinked, gathered herself together, and cheerfully recited Dora's answer as if nothing had happened.

Dora, who suddenly realised she hadn't taken a breath for a very long time, let out a long, throaty sob.

'Oh, my God,' she murmured and slumped back onto the sofa.

Dora hurried into the office and banged in Calvin's home number. In the sitting room, the credits for 'Fenland Arts Tonight' were rolling slowly up the screen. Behind them, Rodney Grey and Lillian Bliss were reduced to razor-sharp silhouettes.

Calvin picked up the phone on the second ring. Dora stared blankly at the TV, and realised she didn't know what she wanted to say, or at least, didn't know what she wanted to say first. There were so many things, the words clumped together in her throat in a log jam.

Calvin was ahead of her. 'Hello, Dora, I was just going to ring you. Don't worry –'

'Don't worry?' Her voice sounded like fingernails on glass.

'I know exactly what you're going to say.'

'You do? Well, in that case I don't need to tell you I've just torn up our contract, do I? Or that thanks to you and your little friend, every pervert in East Anglia – including my sister – now knows where I live, or that . . .'

'Whoa, whoa,' soothed Calvin. 'Your sister doesn't watch the arts programmes, she told me . . .'

'Calvin! Your protegée has just announced my address to the nation.'

Calvin coughed uncomfortably. 'Not the nation, Dora, just East Anglia.' He puffed thoughtfully. 'Late Tuesday night? Good film on BBC2? God, hardly anybody's watching. Look, I'm sorry. What else can I say? That bastard Grey set her up. He tricked her.'

'What's to trick?' Dora hissed. 'That girl is dangerous. She called Rodney Grey a horrible little bastard, on TV, to his face –' As she said it she giggled, which surprised both of them. Hysteria, it had to be.

Whatever it was, Calvin suddenly choked and then drew in a long snorting breath.

'I know,' he chuckled. 'Brilliant, wasn't it? I mean, the guy's such a complete and utter prick. Did you see his face when she started to tell him about the man with the degree?' He was wheezing now, almost unable to breathe for laughing.

'Stop it, Calvin, this isn't funny. This really won't do, you've got to talk to her,' Dora snapped. 'I live here. Muzzle her.'

'I will, I will,' Calvin giggled, and hung up.

The phone rang before Dora had a chance to turn around. She bit her lip and picked it up on the third ring.

'Hello,' said Sheila. 'That writer woman you like is on the telly. I just caught the end bit – were you watching it?'

Dora groaned, wondering how much of Lillian's interview Sheila had seen. Taking a deep breath, she jerked the phone plug out of the wall.

3

The flat above the shoe shop in Gunners Terrace looked small and shabby – an easy target. The man watched a small, plump woman ring the bell, waited for a few minutes more in his car, watching to see if she got an answer until he was certain there was no-one at home.

As she walked away, rounding the corner, he climbed out of the car and flicked up his collar. They did that in all the films, and on the telly. He crossed the road, slipping his hand into his jacket pocket. The lining was split so he could carry a jemmy tucked up under his armpit. It felt good, familiar, like part of him. It was warm from his body heat. Under his parka he stroked the grooves and the small rough patch where some-one had scratched their initials.

Rain dripped off the gutters, and now off him too. Stepping off the kerb he swore as he stepped into a deep pothole, soaking his feet inside his trainers. Bloody weather, bloody roads. He walked slowly towards the door, glancing left and right. He rang the bell to double check. No answer.

Probably Catiana had moved out now she was famous, now she'd got a bit of money. Maybe the other woman was just a cleaner or a Jehovah's Witness. He grinned, then stepped back and looked up at the grimy first floor windows. At one of them, a large ginger cat pressed his face against the glass. Someone had to be taking care of the cat; perhaps he had struck lucky after all.

Glancing around once more to make sure no-one was look-ing, the man slipped into the alley beside the shoe shop. Rub-bish bins and soggy cardboard boxes were stacked two high. Here, the gutters had failed completely; glistening waterfalls of rain cut swathes into the muddy, weed-choked path.

The alley dog-legged around a flat-roofed, single-storey extension. A crumbling brick wall divided the pathway from the fringes of the recreation ground behind.

The man looked at the wall thoughtfully; it wouldn't take too much to get up onto the roof. The extension joined on to the flat. He stood for a minute or two considering whether he ought to risk climbing up in broad daylight. From the roof he'd be able to get inside the flat, no problem. In, have a snout around for the stuff he was after, and then out. Maybe twenty minutes, tops. Inside his other pocket was an aerosol can of paint. Good way to confuse the Old Bill. He grinned. Only trouble was the little ball in the can made a helluva noise if you ran, kept banging about, rattling.

'Are you the builder?'

Startled, the man swung around. A teenage girl, arms wrapped defensively around her chest, peered at him through the rain. Her face was screwed up with cold.

He nodded dumbly, trying to gather his thoughts.

'Not before bloody time. The manager says to tell you that the damp's coming in through the brickwork in the store room now. Do you want to come in and look?' She stepped aside and indicated the open door into the shoe shop.

The man shook his head, still thinking.

'Er no, I've just come to look at the outside today.'

The girl, her hair now dripping, rolled her eyes heavenwards.

'Bloody typical. Well, I'm not hanging about out here watching you wandering about with a tape measure. If you want anything you'll have to knock or come round the front.'

'Wait,' said the man. 'You don't happen to have a key for the flat upstairs, do you? I'd like to take a look at them gutters.'

The girl pulled a face. 'Nah, it's completely separate. Didn't you come last time? The woman who lives up there is out all day today, she told me this morning.' The girl looked down at her watch. 'I'm going to go and get me dinner.' Sniffing, she stepped back into the shop, closing the door smartly behind her.

*　　*　　*

29

'Wednesday is shopping-day, Tuesday is egg-n-chips, Monday is s-o-u-p.' Dora alternated between singing and humming as she drove back along the bypass into Fairbeach town centre. She smiled at her reflection in the rear-view mirror. If she wasn't careful she would have turned into a crazy old lady before anyone realised it.

Dora had been out to Ely, trying to fill her head with window-shopping as an antidote to Lillian Bliss's virtuoso performance on the 'Fenland Arts' programme. She'd been to the supermarket first, which on reflection was a mistake. The full-cream jersey milk had probably already turned to yoghurt and the meat was no doubt busy defrosting itself all over the custard doughnuts. She turned off the main road into Gunners Terrace, slowing and easing forward as she reached the corner, trying to catch out the blind spot.

There was a car parked outside the street door to her flat – a small white car with a blue light on top. With a peculiar sense of resignation, Dora pulled in behind it. Before she had a chance to lock the car doors, Sheila appeared, and from a nearby hatchback, a slim ginger-haired girl hurried towards her clutching a notepad. They both began speaking at the same time.

'There you are. I wondered where you'd got to. You don't want to go upstairs, it's an awful mess,' said Sheila.

The ginger girl took a deep breath, pen poised above her pad. 'I'm Josephine Hammond from the *Fairbeach Gazette*. I wonder if we could have a word with Miss Moran? Why *are* the police here?'

Dora stared blankly at the two women and then pushed past them.

Upstairs, there was a young police officer in uniform standing in her kitchen – what was left of her kitchen.

'Mrs Hall?' he said pleasantly, turning round to face her.

Dora nodded. The kitchen window was smashed and everywhere seemed to be covered in cups and cornflakes and washing and newspapers and books and plates – cupboards open, milk puddling around an overturned bottle on the lino – on the wall, in spray paint someone had written 'SLAG' in huge fluorescent green letters.

Dora stared at the policeman and blinked. She struggled to find something to say but was stunned to discover that there were no words in her mouth.

Sheila launched herself manfully into the breach. 'You've been burgled.'

The policeman looked at his notes. 'Mrs Shepherd here said she came round at just after twelve o'clock today to see if you were in.'

Sheila sniffed. 'I was round at nine but you weren't here, so I nipped back.'

The man consulted his notes again. 'Twice?'

Sheila nodded, colouring slightly. 'I've been worried about her.'

'And on the last occasion Mrs Shepherd found the street door open downstairs.' The officer looked up and pointed at the broken window with his pen. 'I reckon they must have come in over the flat roof, broken that, and then let themselves out by the front door when they'd finished. Kids, most likely.'

Dora took a deep breath, but Sheila was ahead of her.

'What are their parents doing? Why aren't they in school, that's what I want to know? It's disgraceful.'

Dora turned round, stepping on crackles of broken crockery. She coughed to clear her mind. 'I've been to Ely. My cat . . .' she began.

Sheila snorted. 'Never mind about the bloody cat. Look at the mess.' She bent down to pick up the remains of a mug. 'I bought you these last Christmas – ruined.'

Dora wandered through the little flat. It looked as if a huge malevolent child had been playing hunt the thimble – drawers were upturned, books strewn everywhere, endless sheets of paper curled into snow drifts against the skirting boards.

The policeman followed in Dora's wake, Sheila skittering along behind.

'Anything obviously been stolen?' he asked, still clutching his notebook. 'Money, valuables? Your sister said the TV and video are still here.'

'Nothing seems to be missing,' said Dora, finally finding her voice. 'I don't keep a lot of cash in the house. I won't really know if anything's been taken until I've tidied up.'

In the office there were computer disks strewn all over the floor, books, notes, pens, ink – a multi-coloured archipelago of chaos nosing its way out into the hall. Dora suddenly felt as if someone was sitting on her chest, and slumped down in the swivel chair, the pulse in her ears banging out a calypso rhythm.

'Your sister mentioned your address was broadcast on TV last night.'

Dora glanced up at the young man and then Sheila. Somewhere low in the pit of her stomach she had a nasty sense of being caught out. 'Yes –'

Sheila stared at Dora. 'It's all right, I already told him about that woman on the telly. Common, if you ask me, and no more brains than she was born with. Said she lived here, but she doesn't, Dora does. She must have had the flat before. There were students in here, weren't there? All the same, students. How long have you been here? Three years? Four?' She glanced at Dora for some kind of confirmation, but Dora said nothing, deciding it was better just to let Sheila carry on – she was doing a fine job of pushing the skeletons neatly back into the cupboard. 'But fancy telling everyone the address, and on TV too.'

Before anyone could pass comment there was a funny strangled mewling sound from close by.

Dora sprang to her feet. 'Oscar,' she whispered and hurried back into the hall.

He was in the sitting room, camped out under an upturned armchair. When he saw her he lifted a feline eyebrow.

'The day I've had,' he mewled. She stroked his broad gingery skull and was rewarded with a guttural purr. He deigned to let her pick him up and nosed miserably against her chest.

With narrowed pupils, he reassured her that the chaos had nothing whatsoever to do with him.

'Spur of the moment, I reckon,' pronounced the policeman. 'Could be that they saw the TV programme – arts thing, like your sister said – but I very much doubt it. They're like magpies, these kids. Trouble is, if they don't find any money or anything they can sell quickly, they smash the place up. They reckon it's the frustration.'

Sheila made a dark unpleasant sound in her throat. 'Frustration? I'd give the little buggers frustration. So what happens now?'

The policeman shrugged. 'Fingerprint lads are on their way, but I wouldn't hold your breath. There's an awful lot of this kind of thing goes on.'

Sheila sniffed. 'What about that woman on TV?'

The man shrugged before returning to a solution he understood. 'School's just across the back from here. Maybe they saw Mrs Hall go out this morning. Maybe they climbed up on the roof for a dare. Who knows?'

Dora glanced up at the wall above the fireplace. 'At least they weren't totally illiterate,' she mumbled, reading the arc of obscenities sprayed on the chimney breast. She looked around, swallowing hard. 'I really ought to ring Kate.'

'Her daughter,' Sheila informed the policeman. 'Lovely girl, she's an estate agent, works in Banbury, you know, near Oxford? Got married last year.'

The policeman nodded and then scribbled something on a sheet of paper which he handed to Dora. 'If you give these people a ring they'll come and sort your window out,' he said in a reassuring voice.

Sheila squared her shoulders. 'I'll just nip home and get my overall. I think we've got some magnolia emulsion left in the shed. Get that wall done in no time.'

Dora was too overwhelmed to protest.

'What do you want me to say to that girl down there?' said Sheila, pulling on her coat.

Dora took a deep breath and went into the office. From the

window she could see the reporter from the *Fairbeach Gazette*, Josephine Hammond, still sitting in her car.

'Nothing,' Dora replied flatly.

Maybe the girl would get bored and go away. Dora picked up a fan of paper from the office floor. Wishful thinking.

It looked much worse than it really was, or at least that's what Sheila said at least two hundred times, as she bagged up the broken remnants of Dora's life. It was like a mantra. Plumping and straightening with uncanny zeal she cut a swathe of order through the chaos. Dora would have been immeasurably grateful, if only Sheila could have managed her act of compassion in silence.

'I don't know . . .' Sheila said, for the umpteenth time, dropping a broken plant pot into a black bag, '. . . what is the world coming to? Look at this . . .'

Dora followed her, cradling Oscar. She felt as if she was walking around inside somebody else's body.

Finally, hours later, Sheila emptied the sink, stripped off her rubber gloves and tucked them up into a neat ball.

'There we are,' she said briskly, claiming another personal triumph. 'Now don't touch that emulsion in the living room. I'll nip round tomorrow and put another coat on.' She arranged the clean brush and roller back in the paint tray. 'Might be a good idea to do the rest of the room while we're at it.' She looked round thoughtfully. 'Whole place could do with a bit of brightening up. I've got three quarters of a can of nice sunshine yellow if you want it. What are you going to do about the office?'

'I'll start in there tomorrow.'

Sheila took her coat off the back of the door. 'Are you sure you'll be all right? You can come home with me if you like. It wouldn't be any trouble.'

Dora stared at the shadowy ghosts of the graffiti on the kitchen wall. She wasn't sure whether she could bear to stay in the flat another minute and at the same time couldn't bear the idea of leaving. Even the air felt raw and hurt. She wanted

Sheila gone so that she could start to make everything better again.

'I'll be fine,' she said. 'Really.'

Sheila nodded. 'Good. Funny thing about that Catiana Moran woman, bit of a coincidence you liking her and it turning out she used to live here. Did you know about that?'

Dora hurried across to the door. 'Thank you for all your help, Sheila. I really don't know what I would have done without you.'

'You ought to ring the TV programme up and complain though, I would. I'd give them a real piece of my mind, if I were you.' She sniffed. 'Have you rung Kate yet?'

Dora shook her head. 'Not yet. I'll see you tomorrow. Thanks for everything you've done. I won't be here in the morning, I'm going to Jack Rees' funeral.'

Her sister pulled a face but said nothing.

When Sheila finally went home, Dora left a message for Calvin on his machine, then unplugged the phone and crawled into bed. Oscar claimed the lion's share, which was strangely comforting – not everything had changed.

Alicia Markham, chair of Fairbeach Conservative Association, adjusted her hat, tugging down the veil over the discreet brim so it emphasised her eyes. She smiled at her reflection; she had always looked good in a hat, and her carefully composed expression, from long practice, conveyed a perfect balance of interest and unapproachability.

'Guy really ought to travel in one of the main funeral cars. After all, he is our new candidate.'

Beside her, Harry Dobbs, the party secretary, coughed. 'It really wouldn't be right, Alicia. It's not official yet. Let's at least get Jack Rees decently buried.'

Alicia turned away in exasperation. Across the oak-panelled function room in the local party headquarters she caught Guy Phelps' eye and found herself smiling. He was sitting with his wife and two members of the selection committee. She lifted her glass in a silent salute. Charming man. He should do them very well. She turned her attention back to her reflection in the mirror above the fireplace and tipped her hat a little further forward.

'We have to wait for the official announcement,' continued Harry in his unfortunate monotone.

Alicia Markham snorted and glanced at her watch. Time for another sherry before Edwin Halliday arrived from Westminster with his entourage. She was pleased that they had sent one of the more popular cabinet ministers to represent the government. The Fairbeach by-election was crucial. The PM had sent his condolences. She ran a smoothing finger over her eyebrows. Pity he couldn't have made the effort to come himself, but then again that might look like an act of desperation, so this, presumably, was his idea of a double bluff.

Just inside the door the tables had been set for the buffet lunch. Two pubescent waitresses were arranging glasses on trays for the sherry. She pouted; best remind them that the good bottles near the bust of Churchill were for the VIPs.

Alicia would have preferred some of the more senior party ladies to have officiated, but she could hardly expect them to don pinafores today, though there were at least half a dozen who would willingly have thrown themselves on the sword for party honour. The girls shuffled backwards and forwards with trays of vol-au-vents and smoked salmon canapés. Alicia fought the temptation to tell them to pull their shoulders back. The large blonde one had the most appalling skin – where did the agency get these girls?

'Besides, I've already arranged for Guy to go with Lawrence Rawlings. A discreet statement of intent,' said Harry, to her reflection.

Alicia had quite forgotten about Harry Dobbs. He was now wringing his hands with considerable conviction. Presumably the gnashing of teeth came later.

'Every newspaper in the country has leaked Guy's name, Harry. What do you propose we do, unveil him at a fête?' she snapped. She stared at Jack Rees' wreath-topped coffin. 'At least Guy Phelps has some degree of decorum. We won't have

36

to show him which knife and fork to use.' She sucked her teeth. 'And I'm hoping we've finally seen the end of our MP ignoring a three-line whip because he's pissed, and then having to try to convince everyone it was a point of principle.' She shuddered. 'What we need to consider now is who the other parties have got lining up against us.'

Across the room, the club steward, resplendent in his morning coat, opened the double doors for Jack's widow, Caroline. Alicia tidied her jacket and glided across the parquet to greet her. She took Caroline's hand in hers and pressed an inaccurate airy kiss to each cheek.

'Caroline, my dear. How are you?'

Caroline snorted. 'Cut the crap, Alicia, and no, before you offer, I don't want a bloody sherry. Can we go to your office? Jack told me you keep a decent single malt stashed away for big occasions.'

Alicia glanced around to ensure no-one had overheard the grieving widow's outburst. 'Of course, my dear,' she said, in a carefully stage-managed voice, and led Caroline to the inner sanctum. They were no sooner inside than Caroline Rees dragged off her hat and threw it onto the desk.

'My daughter, Lucy, wants to sing "*Pie Jesu*" during the service.'

Alicia smiled benignly. 'That will be nice, dear,' she said, in her most soothing voice, pouring two stiff scotches.

Caroline grimaced. 'Don't be ridiculous. Mawkish little cow.' She took a long pull on the glass Alicia offered her. 'You know, when I first met Jack, everyone said he'd make the cabinet. Tipped for a top job. And the honours list – selfish little bastard – awkward to his last breath. Trust him to die before he picked up his knighthood.' She paused for a second or two, staring unfocused into the middle distance. 'He was tipped for one, you know – they always give them to the mavericks.' She gathered up her lips with a drawstring of old resentments. 'But he didn't know how to say yes sir or kiss arses, did he, Alicia? Our Jack, good old Jack, was born without an arse-licking gene in his entire body.'

Alicia wondered how many scotches Caroline Rees had had before she left home.

'Have you met Guy Phelps yet?' Alicia asked, trying hard to steer the conversation back to safer ground.

Caroline Rees rounded on her. 'We're going to lose the seat you know, Alicia.'

Alicia Markham reddened and squared her shoulders. 'Guy Phelps –'

Caroline sighed. 'Is a complete and utter dickhead. Everyone knows you've selected Phelps because he's a yes man. Do you think you're going to be able to persuade people that he's Jack reincarnated just because he's a local boy? Come on, Alicia, get a grip. People loved Jack Rees because he was a complete rogue. Bastard.' She smiled ruefully. 'He must have been the most unsuitable Conservative MP in living history.' A sad, single hot tear ran down her elegant face. She sniffed, pulling herself upright. 'Can I have another scotch?'

Alicia swallowed hard. 'I rather think you've had enough, Caroline. Everyone will be here soon.'

Caroline lifted an eyebrow. 'They'll find out about Jack, you know, splash his little indiscretions all over the front page. Probably do something on BBC2, fallen heroes.' She sniffed again and wiped her nose with the back of her hand. 'Nothing people like better than shooting a folk hero down, once they're dead, of course. The dead are fair game –'

There was a knock at the door. Alicia was relieved and hurried across to answer it. The steward nodded. 'Mr Edwin Halliday is here, Mrs Markham.'

Alicia sighed. 'Thank God for that,' she muttered in an undertone. She nodded to Caroline. 'If you'll excuse me, my dear.' She indicated the grieving widow to the steward. 'Get Mrs Rees a cup of coffee will you,' she said quietly. 'Make it black.'

Alicia glided back out into the main room, painting on her party smile. Caroline Rees disturbed her deeply. In some ways, although Alicia was loath to admit it, she had preferred Jack. At the very least he didn't pretend – what you saw was what you got. Caroline Rees, by stunning unsettling contrast, was a delightful woman when she was on show, the perfect politician's wife, but in private ... Alicia shivered as she approached Edwin Halliday. She almost felt sorry for Jack.

'My dear Mrs Markham, how very nice to see you again,' Edwin Halliday said, engulfing her tiny hand in both of his. 'It's a terrible shame that we have to renew our acquaintance under such tragic circumstances.'

Guy Phelps was already on his feet, as was to be expected, nosing his way into the edge of the group. Alicia stared at him for a few seconds. Caroline Rees was right about Guy, of course, that's why Alicia had been at such great pains to ensure his selection. Finally, a man at Westminster she would be able to control. But the memory of the decision she had engineered was dissipated the instant Edwin Halliday turned his smile on her.

'Man that is born of woman has but a short time to live . . .'

Dora Hall glanced up at the vicar by the graveside in Fairbeach's cemetery and suppressed a Sheila-style sniff of disapproval. His voice rose dramatically.

There was a large crowd huddled around the graveside for Jack Rees' funeral, including a bevy of local party supporters – and their chairwoman, Alicia Markham, surrounded by her initiates. Dora peered at them. Presumably one of the men in overcoats was the new Conservative candidate. The king is dead, long live the king.

Dora recognised the Labour candidate, the Lib Dem man – her concentration slipped a notch and moved on until she spotted Calvin Roberts standing in the shelter of a yew tree. She lifted a hand in greeting. He frowned miserably in her direction.

The press had been penned up in a special area. Dora glimpsed the face of Josephine Hammond from the *Fairbeach Gazette* amongst the huddle, but presumably, today, Dora was no more than a minnow amongst a shoal of far bigger fish. If the girl noticed her, she gave no indication.

Jack's widow and his two step-daughters stood by the graveside, very stiff and upright. The newly bereaved Mrs Jack Rees was wearing a very chic little black suit and a pillbox hat with a veil. At regular intervals she dabbed one eye with a stunningly white handkerchief and looked tastefully grief-stricken.

Dora tried very hard to be sad and not cynical.

'Ashes to ashes . . .'

Dora glanced around the faces of the other mourners. She knew most of them. Amongst the dignitaries – the mayor and his wife, the chairman of the local chamber of trade, councillors and businessmen – were an awful lot of ordinary Fairbeach people. The groups were interspersed with other unknown faces, presumably from London. Strangers, who, for a little while, were united in their love and respect for Jack Rees.

Across the grave, a single, beautifully stage-managed tear trickled down the face of Jack Rees' widow as she sprinkled a handful of soil on the coffin. There was a lightning strike of flashbulbs.

Disgusted, Dora turned away and huffed out a long breath. Calvin eased his way through the crowd towards her. He looked decidedly unhappy.

'Good turnout,' said Dora conversationally. Calvin made a small tight noise in his throat.

Dora stared up at him. 'What's the matter? Are you all right? Did you get my message on your machine?'

'I did. I'm sorry to hear about the burglary.' He sniffed and then a cacophony of angry words tumbled out. 'You're not going to believe this – someone broke into my office as well. I can't bloody well believe it. Makes you wonder what the damned police are up to. Kids running riot all over the place – bloody disgusting.' His heavy features reddened dramatically as he drew in a sharp breath.

Dora stared at him in astonishment. 'You were burgled?'

Calvin wrinkled up his nose. Dora wasn't sure whether he was hurt, angry or shaken. She felt very much the same.

'When?'

'Last night. Little bastards. Went through every office in the bloody building. Nicked the petty cash and smashed everything else to smithereens. You would not believe the mess.' He smiled grimly. 'Or maybe you would. Police came round first thing this morning. Said there wasn't much hope of catching the little sods.' He peered at her. 'How are you, anyway?'

Dora shrugged. 'I really don't know. Sheila's been round to give me a hand to clear up. I'm not sure which is worse really, her or the vandals. The police told me there wasn't much chance they'd catch the culprits either.'

'Bloody typical, they haven't got to deal with the mess – files everywhere, drawers emptied – the insurance will cover the damage, but that isn't the point, is it?' He took a vicious puff on his cigar and lifted his hands in resignation. 'What can you do?'

Dora fixed him with a long cool stare. 'You really want my advice, Calvin? I'd seriously reconsider muzzling Lillian Bliss.'

'Don't be ridiculous. You don't think she had anything to do with this, do you?'

'Seems a bit of a coincidence to me. One night my address is broadcast to the nation and the next day I'm burgled. Your address is all over my office and the same night someone does your place as well. Bit fishy –'

'The whole of the building was done,' Calvin protested. 'Lillian had nothing to do with it. What did the police say to you?'

'It was magpies, apparently. By the way, where *is* Lillian this morning, Bunny?'

Calvin frowned. 'Stop it, Dora. We have a purely professional relationship.'

'She makes you pay for it, does she?'

Calvin glared at her. 'Lillian's in Cambridge doing a book signing. I thought I'd already told you about that. Then later today we're holding a short press conference, more of a photo call really. You ought to be more grateful. She's generated an awful lot of interest, pre-publication sales for the new book are really creeping up.'

Dora lifted her eyebrows. 'Well, that makes it all right then, doesn't it? If you'll excuse me, I've got to get back to the clearing up.'

'Still on for lunch tomorrow?'

Dora snorted. 'Too right, I haven't got a single unbroken plate left in the house.'

'Need a lift home?' He tugged at his sleeves and then pulled a cheroot from his inside pocket. 'I'm going back through town, wouldn't take me too far out of my way –'

Dora shook her head. 'No thanks.'

The mourners were beginning to disperse. Dora headed away from the main group towards the side gate which would take her onto a short cut.

'Dora?'

Instinctively, she turned round at the sound of her name.

Hurrying across the grass was a man in a long black coat. She stopped and tried to focus on his face.

'My God,' she hissed under her breath, as a name formed in her mind. As soon as the thought hardened her stomach performed a dramatic back flip.

Chief Inspector Jonathan Melrose. Jon Melrose – the man she had left her husband for. Not that Jon knew, not that she would ever tell him. She had never so much as kissed him, but it had been the awful, ice-cold certainty that she could and would, if the offer ever came up, that had made her look at her marriage with different eyes.

Jon Melrose had unknowingly changed her life forever, and now he was standing with his hands stuffed in the pockets of his good funeral coat not more than an arm's length away.

He grinned at her. 'Hi, I thought it was you. Long time no see.'

Dora smiled. 'How are you?'

'Not bad. Look, I'm on duty at the moment, all these bigwigs need a bit of sheep-dogging by the local plod. I just wanted to say, I saw the report on your burglary first thing this morning. I was going to give you a ring.' He stopped and smiled. 'Saved me a phone call meeting you here. I wonder if you'd mind me dropping by later?'

Dora opened her mouth; too many times recently no words had come out. To her relief there was an answer all ready and waiting.

'Sure. Why not?' she said lightly. 'Do you know where I live?'

'It's on the incident report. Don't worry, I'll find it.' He glanced over his shoulder. 'I've got to be getting back. Can't keep the VIPs waiting. Once they've stopped shaking hands they start to get twitchy and wandering off on their own. I'll see you later.'

Dora watched him jog back towards a group of distinguished-looking men, wondering why it felt as if she had become a passenger in her own life.

The intercom bell rang briefly. It was later that same day and Dora was sitting in her office looking at the computer screen. Outside, the street light's glow announced the coming evening, though Dora had no sense of the time. Catiana Moran's latest, unfinished novel scrolled up slowly, line by line. She could see the words but her mind didn't seem to be able to decipher them.

The furniture had all been replaced and tidied, books rearranged, cupboards repacked, papers sorted, but the sense of calm and stillness was absent, as if the atmosphere had been ransacked along with the rest of the flat. She'd left the phone unconnected. The last thing she needed was more frantic voices to stir the slowly settling dust. She glanced at the receiver with its cord all neatly bound around, tying the words in. She really ought to ring Kate.

Her mind was butterflying. Lillian Bliss looked very much how she had fantasised her alter ego might look. Taller, bigger hair – far bigger mouth. She winced and stroked the scrolling words thoughtfully with her finger. The screen was cold.

Beside her keyboard was the novel Catiana had autographed.

The doorbell rang again. It sounded very distant. Dora shook herself as if she was trying to slough off fatigue. The bell rang more insistently. She leant across and pressed the button.

'Hello?'

'Hello, Dora, it's me.'

Dora blinked. Four simple words in a voice from the past that made her gut contract.

'Jon?'

'Would you mind if I come up?'

'Two minutes, I'm just changing,' Dora lied and clambered to her feet.

She flitted around the room in desperation, turning off the computer, tidying away Catiana's unexpurgated thoughts. Hurrying into the sitting room, she bundled the debris of the day into the cupboard near the fireplace, plumped cushions, straightened curtains and switched on a table lamp, while a nagging internal voice told her how ridiculous it was. After all, Jon Melrose had just dropped by to talk about the burglary.

Which made her wonder, if that were the case, why the sound of his voice had left an odd tingling glow in the pit of her stomach and her pulse had shifted up a gear? Glancing into the mirror above the fireplace, humorous grey eyes peered back from behind wire-rimmed glasses. She pulled them off, folded them on the mantel shelf, licked her finger and scrubbed at the spot of magnolia emulsion on the end of her nose – noting ruefully as she did that there was paint all over her hair as well.

Reflected in the mirror's dusty eye, the sitting room looked soft and homely. Taking a final swipe at the cat's hairs on the arms of the sofa, Dora hurried back into the office, letting a finger hover above the entry button. The kitchen –

Turning quickly, she threw open the door, scrumbled lunchtime's fish and chip wrappers into a ball and slam-dunked them into the bin. It was really too late to do anything about the rest of the room.

One deep breath, two deep breaths, after all she wasn't a child. Struggling to regain her composure, she stepped back into the office and pressed the button.

'Come up. It's open.'

She heard the street door close and then the sound of footsteps on the stairs. Dora licked her lips, counting the footfalls and for a second all she could think of was how gorgeous Jon Melrose had looked in black.

4

Lawrence Rawlings, cradling the remains of a large brandy, settled himself back in an armchair by the fire to watch his fellow guests. The function room at Fairbeach's Conservative Club was packed. Alicia Markham had buttonholed Edwin Halliday. The look on the cabinet minister's face was a delight. Lawrence smiled – damned woman, rattling on about the effects of agricultural policy on Fairbeach farmers, while Halliday, the worse for several glasses of wine and a rather good port, was blinking, affecting rapt interest.

Little brackets of animated conversation had formed around the function room.

Jack Rees' memorial supper for the Fairbeach Conservative inner circle had proved surprisingly successful, though Lawrence suspected Alicia had planned it to ensure Edwin Halliday MP felt obligated to stay overnight. Lawrence had seen the look in her eyes – agricultural policy was not the only thing on her mind.

His concentration moved on. To his surprise Guy Phelps was no more than a yard away, on his blind side, staring at him. Lawrence, a little nonplussed at being trumped at his own game, lifted his glass.

'Went off rather well, wouldn't you say?' remarked Guy. 'Alicia says we have to call a council of war now Jack's safely buried.'

Lawrence Rawlings said nothing.

Guy glanced back into the room. 'Marvellous to see everyone together like this. I'm sure good old Jack would really have approved.'

Lawrence snorted and indicated the chair on the other side of the hearth. 'Take my advice, Guy, save the sentimentality for the hustings. Jack Rees would have stuck his nose round the door, found a damned good excuse why he had to leave early, and then gone off to shag one of the waitresses.'

Guy coloured slightly.

Lawrence rolled the dregs of brandy round in his glass. He couldn't help wondering why Guy wasn't snuggled up along-side Alicia and Edwin. He wasn't sure he had the patience for the long trawl through the social niceties to find out. Guy was about to speak when Lawrence got to his feet.

'If you'll excuse me, my daughter and son-in-law are having a drink downstairs in the club bar. I promised them I'd go down and meet them after the dinner.'

Guy swallowed down his prepared sentence. 'You're leaving, Lawrence?' he said in astonishment. 'But, I thought –'

'Not leaving, think of it as a short sabbatical.'

'I've been thinking –' Guy began again.

Lawrence beaded him with ice-blue eyes. 'I wouldn't make a habit of it, Guy. Leave it to those of us who have the knack. Alicia, I'm sure, will handle all your serious thinking for you.' He stood the brandy balloon down on a side table. 'I'm sur-prised they haven't ordered up a circle of simpering acolytes for you yet.'

Phelps looked uneasy. 'My wife is over there with Mrs Hewitt and the other ladies. Jack Rees was a loner, I prefer to model myself –'

Lawrence leant forward and patted Phelps gently on the shoulder.

'Jack Rees was a man in a million, Guy. If he hadn't been, he'd have been Prime Minister years ago. Take my advice, take all the sycophants and hangers-on Alicia can dig up for you. And make sure they find you a good political agent. Politics is a lonely business, you can do with all the support you can buy. Now, if you'll excuse me I really have to go downstairs and talk to Sarah and Calvin. Why don't you have another brandy?'

Lawrence was pleased to be outside on the landing; the air was cool and surprisingly clear. Our Lady Margaret, rendered in oils by a member of the local art club, stared down at him from the oak-panelled wall. In certain lights she appeared to have very long canine teeth peeking provocatively from under her top lip. Tonight she wore a Mona Lisa smile.

Lawrence slipped a hand casually into the pocket of his dinner jacket. He had no great desire to see either his daughter, Sarah, or Calvin Roberts, but he had even less inclination to spend any time with Guy Phelps. He walked slowly down the stairs. He had seen the selection lists from party headquarters. There were at least four stronger candidates than Mr Phelps.

He could still hear Alicia Markham's insistent voice at the selection meeting. She'd railroaded the rest of the committee.

'What we need is another local man, someone who understands the Fens,' she'd snapped waspishly as the other names were offered up.

Lawrence shook his head; what they needed was Jack Rees. Alicia had thrown Phelps' CV onto the table.

'Guy comes from a well-known local family, he's happily married, his children all go to local schools. His interview went very well.'

They'd fallen like skittles – Harry Dobbs, Celia Heath, Elizabeth Hewitt . . .

The noise of the club bar rose up the stairwell like smoke, breaking Lawrence's train of thought.

Calvin Roberts was in the foyer hanging the phone back into its cradle. He smiled up at Lawrence as he descended. 'Evening, Lawrence, just a quick business call. No peace anywhere these days, you know what it's like.' Calvin spoke far too defensively for there to be any truth in what he said. 'How are you this evening?'

Lawrence nodded. 'Fine. Sarah in the bar?' He didn't wait for an answer. Calvin fell into step beside him and they walked in through the double doors, shoulder to shoulder like a pair of gunslingers.

Sarah Roberts smiled when she saw them both and got to her feet.

'Daddy, I'm so glad you came down. How did the dinner go? Did Calvin tell you his office was broken into?'

The two men stood either side of Sarah, eyeing each other up like dogs contesting territory. It was an old battlefield, the lines well drawn. Sarah slipped her arm through Lawrence's.

'I wanted to thank you again for a lovely day on Sunday. Lunch was wonderful, as always. The girls had a super time. I was saying to Calvin it was a shame he had to miss it.'

Lawrence wasn't looking at his daughter, but at Calvin, who in turn held Lawrence's gaze. Sarah talked on and on, her voice a delicate silken thread that bound both men together.

'Would you like a drink?' said Calvin, cutting across her.

Lawrence nodded. 'Brandy.'

Calvin was the first to turn away. Sarah guided her father to a table. Instantly, the atmosphere lightened and he smiled down at his precious child.

'So,' he said, 'what are those girls of yours doing tonight?'

Sarah leant closer and rested her head affectionately on her father's shoulder.

'I'm hoping that they're sound asleep by now. We've got a new au pair, she . . .' Lawrence listened with half an ear, comforted by trivia.

Across the room, Calvin was sharing a joke with the barman.

In her flat in Gunners Terrace, Dora took one final deep breath and opened the door for Jon Melrose. He stood on the dimly lit landing, hands stuffed in the pockets of his casual jacket. His hair was longer, it suited him. She smiled, feeling a peculiar little flutter of excitement in her stomach.

'Hello, why don't you come in, I've just put the kettle on.'

He stepped into the little hallway and grinned, running his fingers through his hair. 'I hope you didn't mind me dropping in. I recognised your name on one of the report sheets –'

'No, not at all. It's really nice to see you after –' Dora stopped, not daring to count up how many years. 'I heard you'd been transferred.'

Jon nodded. 'That's right. Sold down the river. But only as

far as Keelside. Rationalisation, they call it. What it really means is that all our officers and most of the crime reports end up sitting on a desk half way across the county.'

Silence closed over the two of them like a heavy fog. Dora rubbed her hands uneasily on her sweater. 'Why don't you go into the sitting room, I'll bring the tea in.'

Jon nodded. 'No sugar for me.' He paused. 'You've been painting.'

Dora grinned, tugging at a magnolia streak in her hair. 'I didn't like the design job my uninvited interior decorator did. Bit radical for my tastes. I've just given it another coat, mind you, if you squint you can still read most of it. Who said the youth of today are illiterate?'

The silence dropped again; neither moved. Dora laughed, thinking how ridiculous it was. She lifted her hand in invitation. 'If you'd like to go through –'

Jon looked at her. 'Things have changed a bit since I last saw you.'

Dora nodded, as Jon, like everyone else who ever visited her, stepped straight into her office. She sighed and went into the kitchen.

His disembodied voice followed her. 'So how's the writing coming along?'

'Not so bad –'

'Ever write that book we planned?'

Dora peered round the office door. 'Some of it. I just couldn't sell the idea to anyone else. Seems like a long time ago now.'

He had pulled out a copy of a Catiana novel and was squatting on his haunches in front of the book cases, letting the pages of print flicker open. Sensing her standing in the doorway he held it out towards her.

'Do you read much of this stuff?'

Dora blushed crimson. 'Er, no, actually I was going to ring the police about that.'

Jon lifted an eyebrow.

'I couldn't tell the officer who came round after the burglary because my sister was here.' Dora bit her lip, marshalling her thoughts into neat crisp lines. 'I don't read them, I write them. I'm Catiana Moran.'

Jon pulled a face. 'I've lost this somewhere.'

'My agent, Calvin Roberts, hired someone to represent me – to pretend to be me, to promote my books. That was the girl who was on TV.'

'He mentioned you were a client of his.' Jon looked up and closed the book. 'You've picked an interesting way to make a living.'

Dora blushed even more. 'It pays the bills,' she said defensively.

His face had settled into a flat landscape that told her nothing about what he was thinking. 'I wouldn't have thought it was your sort of thing.'

'I'm not sure it is really, but it sells well.'

Jon looked at her levelly. 'And, apparently, gets you burgled.'

Dora felt an unexpected crystal shard of pain in her throat, with tears pressing up fast behind it.

'I wondered if it might be a coincidence,' she said slowly, trying to steady each word before it came out.

Casually, Jon slipped the book back amongst the others. 'Maybe. This sort of break-in is very common, but it seems odd after what you've just told me that they did over Calvin Roberts' place on the same night.'

Dora leant against the door frame, trying hard to fight back the compulsion to ask Jon the next question. 'Do you think,' she began unsteadily, 'that I was burgled because of the TV programme?'

Jon pursed his lips, and stood up slowly. 'No idea, but I don't think we can rule out the possibility.' He spoke on a long outward breath, holding her gaze. His eyes were very dark, like Whitby jet.

Dora looked away first. 'I think I just heard the kettle. What about Calvin Roberts? Why did they go there?'

Jon shook his head. 'The local police think it's probably just kids. There was no money on the premises. A few quid in petty cash. It seems pretty senseless, unless of course they were looking for something and it wasn't here –'

Dora hovered between the hall and the office. 'Is that what you think?'

Jon shrugged. 'I don't know. Weekday nights are usually quiet – that's why I noticed the reports. If it had been Friday night you'd have been lost in the rush.'

A little flurry of something dark and cold had bubbled up from just below Dora's navel. She leant back against the cool panels of her office door.

Jon pursed his lips and exhaled slowly. 'Have you got any idea why someone would want to break in here?'

'I've got nothing of any value.' Dora paused. For a moment she imagined a figure creeping through the flat, his face in shadow. She shivered, a trickle of fear running down her spine like iced water. 'Maybe we should ask Lillian.'

Jon looked confused. 'Lillian?'

Dora nodded, working hard to keep her voice even. 'She's the girl we hired, the one who was on TV the other night. Her real name is Lillian Bliss. If someone thought she lived here . . .' Dora's voice faded. She didn't want to talk about Lillian Bliss. She wanted things to be normal. 'I think I ought to make the tea.'

Dora closed the kitchen door quietly behind her. If only Jon could have called for another reason – any other reason. He'd looked so impassive when she'd told him about the books; a policeman's face. She took two mugs off the draining board, trying to shepherd her thoughts back onto simple things. As she picked up the teapot, fear, red raw and completely unexpected, boiled up through her like a rising tide. Hands shaking, she grabbed hold of the kitchen sink and fought to regain her composure. It felt as if her mind could easily slip and race away from her if she didn't keep a tight grip on it.

When she came back, a few minutes later, Jon had found his way into the sitting room and was folded comfortably on the settee. On his lap, Oscar curled and simpered, purring with delight. Dora stood the tray on the coffee table.

'You really shouldn't encourage that cat, he's a complete tart.'

Jon grinned, stroking the cat's ears. 'I don't mind.'

She thought he looked very at home on her battered sofa. The soft lamp light picked out the laughter lines round his eyes. Dora swallowed hard. She wished she'd had the courage to ring him years before.

'Can you tell me what happened?' he asked, glancing round the room. 'Do you mind if I smoke? I don't remember . . .'

Dora nodded. 'Not at all, in fact if you've got a spare I'll cadge one.'

He shook out a packet and offered his lighter. Dora stood an ashtray between the mugs.

'So, what else can you tell me?'

'Nothing very much. Calvin Roberts hired Lillian Bliss to promote the Catiana Moran novels. I scripted her interviews and she learnt them.'

Jon leant forward. 'And you very thoughtfully included your address?'

Dora shook her head. 'Not exactly, she got caught on the hop and started ad-libbing. Anyway, I went out shopping the day after the broadcast and when I came back the place was wrecked. Nothing taken, just one hell of a mess.'

Jon took a long thoughtful pull on his cigarette. 'Anyone know you were going to be out?'

'No, nobody.'

Jon pulled out a small notebook. 'Several people rang your agent to find out about Lillian. The TV station gave out his number to anyone who was interested, so that might explain how they found him. Perhaps they were looking for something. They couldn't find it here so they went to Calvin Roberts' place.' He leant forward as if waiting for her to say something.

Dora remembered sitting in a café with Jon, drinking coffee. She had contacted the local police to get some background for a book she wanted to write and Jon had been volunteered to talk to her. They'd met in Lacey's coffee shop creating scenarios, spinning workable plots. This one sounded no different, except, of course, it was real.

'But what about all the damage?'

Jon shrugged. 'Covering their tracks? I should warn you, I don't think there will be much of an investigation into this. Nothing's been taken – the CID have got bigger fish to fry.' He paused. 'Divorced now?'

Dora smiled. 'I'm afraid so, Ray didn't take too kindly to me picking up off-duty policemen.'

Jon laughed, holding her gaze. 'My wife felt the same about stray writers,' he said softly.

Dora wondered exactly what he was telling her.

'What do you think they were looking for?' she asked evenly.

She'd always sensed Jon's interest was more than professional. She'd seen it in his eyes, heard in his teasing when they'd sat together in Lacey's. Hunched over her notebook, listening to his deep, lyrical voice, she had used her husband to fend him off then, bringing her marriage into the conversation like a tank trap. Now it was the burglary.

'I was hoping you could tell me. Is that tea brewed yet?'

Dora leant forward to pour it. 'By the way, what were you doing at Jack's funeral this morning?'

'Show of respect. They sent Edwin Halliday, the cabinet minister, down to represent the government. Had to keep an eye on him. He could easily have got lost once he was off the M25, you know what MPs are like.'

Dora handed him a mug. 'You're a bodyguard these days?'

Jon snorted. 'Not really, they wanted a couple of senior officers there to represent the force. I volunteered. I'd met Jack a few times, he was a nice guy.'

Looking away, Dora stroked the ash off her cigarette around the edge of the ashtray. 'What's going to happen about the burglary?'

'You want me to be honest? Not a lot. By the way, who else knows you're really Catiana Moran?'

Dora bit her lip. 'No-one, just Calvin and now Lillian. The

publishers know because of the contracts but no-one else locally.'

Jon nodded. 'Family?'

Dora shook her head. 'Good God, no, they have got no idea.'

'That's fine, try and keep it that way.' He downed the rest of his tea. 'You should be fine now, but don't quote me on it.'

'If my mystery caller decides to come back for a second look, you mean?' she said.

'Exactly. Look, I've really got to be going. At the moment there's no way of knowing what's going on. It might be nothing at all, but be careful. Check your locks and think about getting a security grille for the kitchen window.'

Dora looked around her familiar shabby sitting room. Oscar stretched and mewled. She shook her head. 'Maybe it was just kids.'

Jon lifted his hands in resignation. 'Maybe. I've asked the local plod to keep an eye on the flat while they're out on their rounds.'

Dora snorted. 'That's very reassuring.'

Jon slowly got to his feet. 'It's the best I can do at the moment.' He'd reached the hallway, hands back in his jacket. 'Thanks for the tea.'

She didn't want him to go. The realisation surprised her. It had nothing to do with the burglary, but a sudden awareness of how many years it had taken them to get back to this point.

'You know, I've really missed you,' she muttered thickly, feeling herself blush as she said it.

He didn't seem to notice. 'Funny, I was just thinking the same thing. Can I ring you, I mean, maybe we could go out somewhere, or something?'

Dora nodded. 'Yes, I'd like that.'

He was moving reluctantly towards the door. 'I know it's a bit pushy but are you doing anything tomorrow night?'

She smiled. 'Pushy I can cope with. What had you got in mind?'

'I've got the night off, maybe we could go out for a meal?'

Dora nodded. 'I'd like that. What time?'

'Eight-ish?'

'Fine.'

'I'll pick you up here.'

After she closed the door behind him, Dora pressed her forehead against the cool woodwork and wondered exactly what had happened to all the years since she had last seen him, and why they had never kissed. Behind her, Oscar mewled malevolently and scrambled into the kitchen. She went back into the office and plugged the phone in. Her daughter, Kate, answered on the third ring.

Dora barely had a chance to get past hello.

'Mum, is that you? Aunty Sheila rang me to say you'd been burgled. I've been ringing and ringing –'

'I unplugged the phone,' Dora said.

Kate sniffed, sounding uncannily like Sheila. Concern was rapidly being displaced by indignation. 'Why on earth did you do that? I've been so worried. Are you all right? Did they take much?'

Dora took a breath to reassure her she was fine, but Kate continued. 'Have you rung Dad yet? I said to Mike that maybe we ought to ring Dad and let him know.'

Dora stared at the receiver. Some part of Kate had never been reconciled to the fact that she and Ray were divorced. Marriage, even if legally dead, somehow meant you were permanently, irreversibly joined at the hip.

'No,' she said slowly. 'No, I haven't rung your father.'

Kate sniffed again. 'Do you want me to ring him? Do you want me and Mike to drive up? I mean, it's only a couple of hours. Or you could come and stay down here for a while with us. We've got the spare room done now, we're out at work all day but –'

Dora sighed, and dropped her voice into the tone she had once used to reassure Kate that she was more than a match for any monsters that lurked, fangs dripping, under her bed.

'Really, love, I'm absolutely fine, how's everything with you? How's Mike?'

Kate sucked in a long breath, determined not to be side-tracked into conversations about her marriage. 'I've been really worried.'

When Dora finally hung up she felt drained dry.

As she switched off the office light, in the darkness something caught her eye in the street below. Parked just outside the arc of a street lamp was a small dark car; inside was a man looking up at her window. A featureless moon-white face stared up at the flat. Dora smiled; the local plod. Jon had been as good as his word.

In her house in a select avenue overlooking Fairbeach park gardens, Alicia Markham waited for the fluorescent light to stop flickering. She let her eyes adjust to the glare and then slipped on her spectacles. The rest of the kitchen was in darkness, everywhere still and quiet.

Carefully, she lifted a box down from the shelf in the pantry. Inside, a diary and a filofax were neatly wrapped up in a curl of tissue paper. Her man had delivered two, or so her resident house boy had informed her. She glanced up at the other box, not that there was really time to look in that either now.

They had been delivered while she was out at Jack's memorial supper. She stood the box on the butcher's block and thumbed through the contents. No photographs, nothing that she could use. Alicia knew exactly what she hoped to turn up, and of course there might be other things too that could be of value, one could never be certain what would be trawled up. All she needed was one positive piece of evidence and Guy Phelps would be on his way to Westminster.

'Alicia, darling, are you down there?' Edwin Halliday MP's silky-smooth orator's voice followed her down the back stairs. Alicia glanced over her shoulder as she slipped the lid back on the cake box.

'I won't be a moment, Edwin, go back to bed, darling.'

They went back a long way, Alicia and Edwin, even if their links and the liaisons had always been very tenuous. Neither had any long-term plans for the other. They met at party conferences, weekend think tanks, networking retreats and funerals. She undid the top two buttons of her negligee and folded her spectacles back into their case.

'Just getting another bottle of Krug,' she called, snapping off the pantry light. 'I won't be a minute.'

If Edwin hadn't been so bloody honest she might have recruited him to help her win Fairbeach for Guy. She hurried back upstairs to bed. Perhaps the man she had hired would be able to turn up something else. They had a little more time.

5

'Post for you, Mrs Hall,' said a disembodied voice over the security speaker.

Dora glanced out of the office window. The new morning looked uninvitingly grim, but at least there was no sign of the reporter from the *Gazette*. She stood her cereal bowl beside the computer and pressed the call button, swallowing down a mouthful of cornflakes.

'Morning, Javid, just stick it through the letter box, will you? Or do you need me to sign something?'

The postman coughed. 'Do you think you could come down?'

Dora yawned and tied the belt of her robe tighter, before hurrying downstairs. Javid stood on the doorstep, grinning sheepishly, rain dripping off the peak of his cap. In his arms, he was holding a large damp cardboard box. She waved him inside out of the downpour.

'Don't tell me, let me guess. I've finally come up on the Reader's Digest prize draw?'

'Not exactly. Are you taking mail in for someone called Catiana Moran? The address is the same, I think.'

Dora pulled open the flaps of the box and took a letter from the pile inside.

'Catiana Moran, above the shoe shop, Gunners Terrace, Fairbeach.' She held out her arms. 'Sounds like that's meant for here, Javid. Better pass them over.'

He screwed up his nose. 'Have you taken in a lodger, Mrs Hall?'

Dora shook her head. 'Not exactly, Javid.' She gave him a tight smile and struggled back upstairs.

She tipped the box out onto the kitchen table and picked up a knife. 'Dear Catiana . . .' the first letter began.

Just after one o'clock, Dora shook out her umbrella and stepped from the biting, driving rain into the warmth and subdued social noises of Filbert's Restaurant.

The maitre d' smiled warmly in her direction. 'Hello, Mrs Hall. How very nice to see you again.'

Dora smiled. 'How are you, George? How's the family?'

'Very well, thank you, and yourself?'

Dora nodded her reply.

'Mr Roberts is already here. Would you like me to take your coat?'

Dora shook her head and headed towards the rotund figure of Calvin Roberts, who was sitting at a corner table, watching the rain trickle down the French windows. He turned as she approached him and frowned. 'Christ, you look rough.'

Dora pulled out a chair and slipped her coat over the back.

'Well, how very nice of you to notice, Calvin. Actually I feel a lot worse than I look. Maybe you'd like to cast your eyes over these.' She took a bundle of envelopes out of her handbag. 'Just a small selection of this morning's post.'

Calvin opened the first one. ' "Beloved Catiana, I have read all your books, I think . . ." ' He reddened, hastily scanning the rest of the first page. 'Sweet Jesus, this guy is wasted writing fan letters, maybe I should fix him up with a contract.'

Dora glared at him and pulled a sheet of paper out of another envelope.

' ". . . You should be ashamed of yourself, you painted Jezebel. Tar and feathers aren't good enough for perverts like you," ' she read in an undertone. 'Then there's the religious ones, the ones who want to take me away from all this, marry me, make mad passionate love to me, tie me to a bed and cover me in honey and whipped cream –'

Calvin grinned.

Angrily, Dora grabbed the first letter out of his hand and

stuffed it back in the envelope. 'Well, what are you going to do about these?'

Calvin puffed out his cheeks. 'You know what they say about publicity. I mean, it shows interest, people have taken the time to write.'

Dora snorted and pulled a copy of the local paper out of her handbag.

'In that case you'll probably be interested in this as well. I picked it up this morning to read the report on Jack's funeral. Page three.' She shook the paper into submission. 'Here we are: "Home of Local Porn Queen Broken Into by Vandals."'

There was a picture of Lillian Bliss above several column inches credited to one Josephine Hammond. Lillian's picture was obviously a studio shot, a pouting master class photographed against a luxurious backdrop of foliage.

Calvin shrugged, leaning forward to light a cigar from the candle in the centre of the table. 'The girl at the *Gazette* rang me for a few comments. She must have picked the call up on the police radio.'

A waiter handed them their menus.

'I'm not sure I want to eat,' Dora said.

Calvin feigned astonishment. 'Good God, now I really am shocked. I've heard the profiteroles are very good here. Surely you can be tempted?'

Dora snorted and jiffled the chair closer to the table. 'Be serious. How would you feel?' she snapped brusquely.

Calvin's face settled into an expression of concern. 'Don't be so melodramatic, you've had a break-in and a few fan letters, that's all.'

Dora let out a long shuddering sigh. 'I told you she was dangerous. You're going to have to get rid of her, Calvin.'

Calvin stared at Dora incredulously. 'Fire Lillian? Don't be ridiculous. She's a pussy cat. Okay, so she made one slip, but she'll be fine, trust me.' He narrowed his eyes. 'They could have come round to Gunners Terrace for a quote, you know.'

Dora picked at the posy on the table. 'They did, but I was out all day after the TV interview –' She stopped, letting her mind toy with the chain of events. 'Josephine Hammond was prowling around on the doorstep when I got home, looking for Catiana. What I don't understand is why she didn't come back –' Comprehension dawned. 'You rang her up, didn't you, Calvin?' she hissed. 'You rang the papers and fed them this entire story.'

Calvin lifted his hands. 'I thought I'd defuse the situation. I knew you were upset, so I set up an interview at my office, so they wouldn't come a-huntin'. I told you about it at the funeral, remember? Everyone is very curious about Lillian. And there's no such thing as bad publicity. I just gave them a brief statement before they started to sniff for something bigger. I mean, isn't that what we hired Lillian for? She's paid to take your flak.'

Dora glanced down at the interview Lillian had given. 'So, who wrote her script this time?'

Calvin looked uncomfortable. 'I didn't think you'd want to do it –' he began.

Dora slapped the paper down in front of him and pointed to a line half way down the second column. '"I really love living in Fairbeach. My agent, Calvin Roberts, has got me this lovely little flat on Anchor Quay now I'm getting successful."'

Calvin choked and grabbed the paper out of her hands. 'Where does it say that?' He read it and looked up at Dora apologetically, struggling to regain his composure. 'She likes people to like her. She just wants to be helpful. She tells them what she thinks they want to hear.'

Dora gave him an icy stare. 'That's exactly why she has got to go, Calvin. She looks right but –' Dora shivered, thinking about Catiana Moran sitting in Smith's, surrounded by all those ordinary, dull people, in her sleek copper dress, lips drawn back in a carnivorous smile. She should have guessed that something so beautiful might well be dangerous. 'Hiring Lillian was a bad move. I want my life back.'

Calvin beckoned the wine waiter over and ordered two brandies.

'Look, Dora, you really can't let this faze you.' He shook out his napkin and arranged it across his lap. 'Let's change the subject, shall we? How's the latest book coming along?'

Dora snorted. As far as Calvin was concerned, the matter was already closed. How could she make him understand that Lillian Bliss' arrival had been like a hand-grenade exploding in her life? Calvin looked at her, expecting an answer. 'Is this some sort of therapeutic attempt to make light conversation? I haven't written a single word since the break-in.'

He blew a silvery plume of cigar smoke across the table. 'It's understandable you're a bit upset but it'll pass. Trust me. The publishers are desperate for the next one. July you said, but if you can get it to them early –'

'Oh, right, so they've got plans for a best seller, have they, now we've got Lillian to push the books? I don't think so. I really don't think I can do it.' She took a deep pull from the brandy balloon, feeling a flutter of annoyance settle alongside her sense of ill-ease as the alcohol hit her empty stomach.

Calvin leant forward and rested his fingers lightly on her arm.

'Don't get so touchy. I'm just pointing out you have contractual commitments. You're losing sight of reality here.' His voice dropped to a conspiratorial whisper. 'You and I both know Lillian's just an actress. Catiana Moran isn't real. This will all blow over.'

Dora shook her head to clear it, feeling the warm glow of the brandy easing into her bloodstream. 'Not if you keep wheeling Lillian out into the spotlight,' she said softly, 'she's trouble.'

Calvin groaned and swirled his brandy. When the waiter stepped up to the table he ordered for them both while Dora sat staring out of the rain-streaked windows.

Jon Melrose had advised her to check her security – and that was before the letters had arrived. He'd looked very good, hadn't he? She'd always thought he had beautiful eyes. She encouraged his face and the sound of his voice to float up inside her head as an antidote to Calvin's indifference and found it as effective as Novocain. It surprised her just how much detail her memory had stored. Just as she was thinking about how Jon's hair curled into the curve of his neck, she realised that Calvin was still speaking, and she struggled to snap back to catch the words.

'I'm totally bloody lost without it . . .'

Dora reluctantly shook away the compelling image of Jon Melrose sitting on her sofa. 'I'm sorry, Calvin. I was miles away. What did you say?'

Calvin's face clouded. 'Oh, for God's sake. You've really got to get a grip, Dora. I was saying, the bastards who broke into the office stole my filofax, off my bloody desk. The only thing they took, I mean, it's my lifeline, that thing.'

Dora stared at him. She hadn't seen her diary recently either. Maybe Sheila had tidied it away; she would check when she got home.

'Never mind your filofax, what are you going to do about Lillian Bliss?'

Calvin groaned. 'Look, I didn't invite you to lunch to have this conversation over and over again. I wanted to see how you were. I understand that you're upset – I'm upset – but there's the bigger picture to consider. I've been talking to the commissioning editor this morning. As far as he's concerned we've hit pay dirt.' He paused thoughtfully. 'Shame you can't get the new book done more quickly. There's an awful lot of interest.'

Dora turned the brandy balloon round in her fingers. 'I'm not sure I really want to do any more.'

Calvin sighed theatrically. 'You'll feel differently when I show you the new draft contract. Why don't you come round and take a look at it?'

Dora shook her head. 'I don't know,' she muttered.

Stealthily, the waiter slipped their plates onto the table.

Calvin picked up his fork. 'Stop sulking. Let's try and talk about something else shall we?'

Jon Melrose had looked better than Dora remembered him, threads of laughter lines gathering around his dark eyes, broad shoulders – she shivered and glanced up at the restaurant clock. Eight o'clock, seven or so more hours to go.

Calvin's mouth was opening and closing rhythmically. Between words he pushed slivers of salmon into it.

'. . . What a bastard I thought, what a smug, self-satisfied bastard.'

'Who?'

'What?' Calvin stopped mid-chew, his face flushed. 'Guy Phelps, the guy they've chosen to stand for Jack's seat in the by-election. I met him at the Con Club last night.' He picked a stray piece of lettuce out of his teeth. 'You're spending too much time on your own with that bloody cat. It was all over the breakfast news this morning.'

'Guy Phelps?'

Calvin snorted. 'Oh, come on. You must know him. Lay preacher, all family values, white starch and grey suit.'

Dora pulled a face. 'I don't think so. Mind you, whoever they choose will have a hard job.'

Calvin lifted an eyebrow. 'Not this bloke, he's pure twenty-four carat arsehole.'

Dora picked at the fish on her plate; the fennel garnish filled the air with the pungent aroma of aniseed. 'You don't like him, then?'

Calvin held up his hand in mock surrender. 'Like? What's to like? He's another local boy, but he's no Jack Rees. Phelps is perfect for politics, Jack was good because he wasn't – square peg battling for the rights of round holes everywhere. No, this guy's got no bloody soul, one hundred per cent party man. Surely you must know him?'

Dora pressed the fennel into pulp. 'No, the name doesn't ring a bell.' She paused and looked out into the rain. 'By the way, where is Lillian today?'

'Got the decorators in. Getting her new flat organised. But she's booked solid all next week.'

Dora smiled without humour. 'She could prove to be a very expensive hobby, Calvin.'

He bristled and turned his attention back to his fish.

*　　*　　*

Dora left Calvin, still ruminating over coffee and liqueurs, at just after two, and was almost grateful to be back out in the rain. The water ran like a river in the gutters; not a taxi in sight. She glanced down at the clutch of letters in her hand; the raindrops were gently transforming Catiana's makeshift address into a soft unreadable blur. If only it could stay that way. The envelopes felt like fragments of shrapnel. She stuffed them in her bag, opened her umbrella and set off stoically towards Gunners Terrace.

Dora hurried along the pavement, skirting the puddles; the wind buffeted the canvas. Filbert's Restaurant was in a sedate Georgian crescent that, with the help of its neighbour and a master stroke of town planning, held the Fairbeach museum, the new library and the market square in parentheses. Perhaps it was the same fluke that created the vortex of air currents. At the corner of Green Street, a gust ran up behind her, ripping between the spokes, shredding the cover like a razor. She swore softly, backing into the wind to try and wrestle the umbrella into submission.

As she fought with the handle a car cut the corner and splashed her from head to foot. Cold water made her scream out in protest.

'You miserable bastard,' she snapped, hurling the brolly down onto the pavement. 'You total and utter miserable *shit*!'

Eventually, soaked, cold and miserable, Dora let herself into the little ground-floor lobby of her flat. She had barely time to close the door before the girl from the shoe shop was tapping on the glass.

'Hello. Mrs Hall?'

Dora forced a smile. 'Hello, how are you today?'

The girl snorted. 'Fed up with this weather, all this rain is driving me nuts, and the shop is really slow, no-one in their right mind wants to come out in this.' She looked Dora up and down. 'I just came to tell you we've got a builder coming round to look at the building. He called a couple of days ago, I'd forgot all about it –'

Dora grinned. 'Not before time.'

The girl nodded. 'Yeah, that's what I said to him. He wanted to get into the flat. He came round after you'd gone out the other day. I told him we hadn't got a key. He said he'd be back, all right?'

From upstairs Dora could hear her phone ringing. She looked at the girl and shrugged.

'Sorry, duty calls. Thanks for the message. I'll keep an eye out for him.'

Abandoning the girl, her dripping mac and ruined umbrella, Dora hurried up the stairs. Oscar bleated as she stepped over him on her way to the office and meowed in disgust as she ignored him and snatched up the receiver.

'Hello?' she gasped breathlessly.

'Afternoon.' Jon Melrose's soft voice. 'Didn't mean to make you run.'

Dora slumped down into her chair, and smiled. 'No problem, I've only just got in. How are you?'

'I rang you this morning. Are you all right?'

Dora glanced around. 'I think so, how about you?'

'Fine. I wondered if you like fried chicken?'

Dora grinned. 'Yes.'

'Good, is around eight-ish still all right tonight?'

Dora nodded. 'Fine.'

'Great. I've got to go, I'll see you later then.'

'I'll look forward to it.'

As she hung up, Oscar leapt into her lap and stared soulfully into her eyes, demanding she played fast and loose with the tin opener.

Dora spent all afternoon hoovering and cleaning right the way through the flat.

Fried chicken wasn't exactly an explicit indication of what Jon had in mind. The more she thought about it the more complex it got. Was fried chicken an invitation to go out or had he planned that they stay in with a bucket of something greasy?

She glanced at the clock and then back at the bedroom mirror. What exactly did a woman wear for fried chicken in or out? The days of dates seemed long gone, and conjured up self-conscious memories of hours spent in front of the mirror, agonising over what to wear, panicking over what to talk about. Dora opened her make-up bag and peered inside – not an awful lot had changed there.

Since leaving Ray, she realised, she hadn't actually been out with anyone. What had happened to all those years? It had never been part of her master plan not to have another relationship. It was simply that her freedom had cost too much to go looking for a compromise candidate to fill the gap Ray left in her life. After a while the gap had simply healed over.

Ironic really, she thought, tipping the lipsticks, eye shadows, little jars and tubes out onto the dressing table. Her everyday life was spent exploring the fictional boundaries of wild passion, while she spent every night alone with a neutered ginger tomcat.

It felt very odd putting on serious eye make-up. Turning the little pot of eye shadow over between her fingers, Dora looked at the faded label on the bottom. God alone knows where or when she had bought it. The surface was dry and crusty from lack of use.

It had taken most of the afternoon to decide what to wear. There had been a flurry of washing and tumble drying and ironing between Jon's phone call and now. Eventually, Dora had settled on a delicate jade-green blouse, navy trousers and a long matching jacket. The jacket hung on the back of the bedroom door, on a hanger, in case fried chicken was out.

The flat, newly painted in patches, glistened unnaturally and there was a disconcerting whiff of pot-pourri spray polish in the air. She grimaced at her reflection, suddenly feeling extremely foolish. She was bound to drop grease on her best blouse. It would be hell to get out. After all, why the fuss? This was simply fried chicken with an old friend, nothing more, just a quiet meal for old times' sake. She snorted, who was she trying to kid? She slipped the freshly ironed trousers and blouse on over her best bra and matching knickers, feeling about fifteen and just as uncertain.

Finally, gilding the lily with a touch of lipstick, she looped a pretty navy, peach and jade scarf around her shoulders and checked the clock again.

Did 'about eight' mean eight? Quarter to? Quarter past? Tying the scarf in a loose knot Dora went into the sitting room, flicked on the gas fire and stood nervously looking round, plumping cushions, tweaking things into submission.

Maybe the flat would look better with a few magazines around to make it look more homely? Sheila had tidied away most of the ambient chaos.

The drawers were stuffed with bits of paper, the odd spoon, cotton reels, cassette tapes, discarded cardis . . . Glancing at the cupboard, Dora considered the merits of holding back a tower of debris while trying to find something that said, 'together woman, with contented satisfying lifestyle'. It didn't do to look too needy.

In the kitchen cupboard were some magazines Sheila had brought to line Oscar's cat litter tray, but the *People's Friend* and the local church magazine weren't exactly the image Dora had in mind. The decision was whipped away by the intercom bell ringing.

Dora glanced into the mirror one last time before hurrying into the office and pressing the call button. She stopped short of pushing the entry button – another thing she remembered about being fifteen was that it didn't do to appear too eager either.

'Hello?' she said warmly.

There was an abstracted scuffling noise through the loud-speaker.

'Is that you, Jon?' Dora suddenly felt a tiny creeping tremor of disquiet. 'Jon?'

She moved across to the office window and craned to see who was standing in the street below. In the twilight the street lights were still dull; it was impossible to see the door below, her view interrupted by the porch.

Another dark glittering thought made her gut contract – was the downstairs door locked? She desperately tried to remember. She'd arrived home soaked through to the skin, the girl from the shoe shop had followed her inside and then the phone had rung. Peering into the shadowy street below, Dora knew with a sickening certainty that the door downstairs was unlocked.

She stepped back to the intercom. 'Who is this, please?' Speaking more firmly now.

Nothing came over the speaker. She hurried into the hall and dropped the catch on the flat door, sliding the security chain on behind it. It would be simple to open it and look down the stairs but she didn't want to contemplate what might be waiting outside.

A tight sick feeling lifted into her mouth. Images of Lillian Bliss' animated handsome face filled her mind, memories of walking into the flat to find it wounded and in disarray. The sense of excited expectation trickled away like water. She shivered, letting the fear wash over her in uncomfortable shivering waves.

Back in the office, the little call button flashed brightly once more and then went dead. She hesitated for a second and hurried over to the office window, grateful she'd left the office lights off.

The twilight had leeched everything into a chilling monochrome, stripping the colour from the bricks and the hoardings. Under the street lights, a stockily built hunched figure hurried across from her side of the road, hood up, hands stuffed into his pockets. As he got to the far kerb he glanced back up at the flat. Dora stepped away from the window, but not before catching sight of his pale plump face, rendered anonymous by the light of the lamp above him.

When she looked again, he was gone, and the only thing she could hear was the manic rhythm of the pulse in her ears.

She stared into the street, wondering whether it would be better to go downstairs and lock the street door. A millisecond later, a car pulled up on the far side of the road and she sighed with relief as she recognised Jon Melrose climbing from the driver's seat.

'There was someone downstairs, a man,' Dora said far too quickly as Jon stepped into the hallway. 'Just before you arrived.'

Jon looked at her, dark eyes registering concern.

'Are you all right?' He glanced back over his shoulder into the dark stairwell. 'Would you like me to go downstairs and take a look around?'

Dora swallowed down the metallic taste of fear. 'He's gone and I'm fine now. The intercom rang and I thought it was you.'

'Did you see who it was?'

Dora shook her head. 'I couldn't see him clearly from the window. He'd got his hood up and he didn't answer me when I asked him who he was.' She laughed nervously. 'I'm overreacting, aren't I? It was probably just a mistake. He realised he'd got the wrong address and pushed off.'

Jon lifted an eyebrow. 'Well, you've got me convinced,' he said dryly.

Dora realised that it wouldn't take a lot to make her cry. She looked up at him, trying to regain a sense of control. Her mind was full of disjointed jigsaw-piece thoughts.

'The builder,' she said flatly. 'The girl downstairs from the shoe shop said the builder was coming round. It might have been him.'

So why hadn't he spoken? Dora stopped again; for some reason something Calvin had said over lunch appeared in her mind.

'I can't find my diary either –'

John grinned at her. 'Hang on a minute. Are these the cryptic clues?'

Dora frowned, sifting thoughts, looking for the straight edges, corners and bits of sky, trying to make some sort of sense of what she was feeling. 'Why don't you go through into the sitting room.'

She opened the kitchen door a fraction and then thought better of it. Her diary ought to be in the office. She turned round, ignoring Jon and threw open the office door.

Inside it was very still and unnaturally tidy. Her eyes worked along the shelves, touching spines. She looked around, eyes searching frantically for the slim maroon book, by the phone, on the directories, on the coffee table, working backwards and forwards from the doorway, coming to the same conclusion over again and over again. Her diary wasn't there.

In the kitchen? She opened drawers frantically, turning over piles of accumulated junk, while on the kitchen unit beside her the kettle clicked off the boil. She didn't notice Jon in the doorway.

'What's the matter?'

His voice surprised her. Dora stared up at him and realised with astonishment that she had forgotten he was there.

'Something Calvin said. The people who broke into his office took his filofax, nothing else. My diary's not here, either.' She opened the fridge to take out a pint of milk and glanced into the freezer compartment – stranger things had happened.

'Where was it?'

Dora pointed into the office. 'Usually I keep it by the phone, but it's not there now.'

Jon nodded. 'And what? Keep appointments, pour out your soul?'

'It's mostly "dentist, two thirty", that sort of thing. I keep them for years, so I don't have to copy out phone numbers and things like –' She stopped and headed back into the office. Above the doorway was a narrow shelf where she stacked diaries from previous years. It was a habit. Old numbers, old contacts, stacked away in Boots A5 diaries that went back to the 70s.

She wasn't certain exactly what her expression said, but it made Jon hurry into the office to join her.

'They've all gone,' she said lamely, pointing upwards. 'I kept all the old ones up there.' Something icy shivered in her belly.

The break-in wasn't random; whoever had been there had come for a reason. Dora didn't know whether that made it better or worse. Open-mouthed, she stared at Jon.

'Did the fingerprint lads come in here?'

Dora shrugged. 'I don't know, I think they did the window, the door –' She stopped, feeling dizzy. She could feel her colour draining.

Jon guided her back out into the hall. 'Tell you what, I'll arrange for someone to come and have a look at this in the morning. There's not a lot we can do now.'

Dora was still staring at him. 'I suppose not. I meant to ask you on the phone whether we were eating fried chicken in or out. Can I safely assume from the lack of chicken about your person we're going out?'

Jon grinned. 'I thought we'd go for a drink first.'

Dora nodded. 'Good idea, I think I need one.'

Dora locked the street door with exaggerated care. She glanced around as Jon went across to his car, half expecting to see the man in the hood or worse. It was darker now and part of her was angry that she felt so vulnerable. Gunners Terrace seemed very quiet, very empty, strafed by a crossfire of dark shadows and street lights. She hurried to join Jon.

As they drew off, he looked at her. 'Did you get the locks checked and ring up about a security window?'

'Yes,' she lied, and then fell silent.

Jon grinned. 'Make sure you give the bloke a ring tomorrow.'

Dora watched the countryside peel off past the car, still annoyed with herself for reacting to one late-night caller and the missing diaries with such an overwhelming rush of fear. Seeing the lights of Keelside, she realised with a start that she hadn't spoken since they'd driven out of Gunners Terrace and coughed, sorting through her thoughts to find something to say that didn't sound inane, and failing.

'At least it's not raining.'

Jon glanced across at her. 'I thought you'd gone to sleep.'

Dora grinned. 'Sorry, I was thinking. What would someone want my diaries for?'

'Information – you said they took Calvin Roberts' filofax too.'

Dora let the silence wash over her again, tacking ideas and thoughts together at random, looking for patterns that looked right stitched side by side. Time and time again the patchwork formed the same image: Lillian Bliss.

'Now what are you thinking?' asked Jon, guiding the car in and out of the evening traffic

Dora blustered an apology. 'Sorry.' She smiled, turning so that her body and her attention were focused on him. 'I think I've lost the knack of talking to people. I spend a lot of time on my own, with just the cat and a teapot for company. I don't talk out loud much any more, everything buzzes round in my head instead.' She paused. 'I was really nervous about tonight –'

'Coming out with me?'

Dora nodded, glad of the darkness. 'Sounds silly, doesn't it?'

Jon made a dismissive sound and then laughed. 'No, not really, I feel the same. Bloody awful, isn't it? You'd have thought by the time we got to our age it would be so much simpler –'

'Our age? It feels worse now than the first time around. At least when you're a teenager nobody expects you to feel confident. Now we're supposed to be worldly wise, know what we're doing.' She smiled and pulled a packet of sweets out of her handbag. 'I don't suppose you fancy a mint humbug, do you?'

They were creeping between sets of traffic lights towards the town centre. Jon guided the car into a back-street car park behind the main shopping precinct and switched off the engine.

'We can walk from here. Would you like to go for a drink before we eat? Mac's on the market place isn't too bad.'

Dora nodded. 'Yes, that would be fine.'

The tight nervous twist in her stomach still hadn't quite

gone; almost, but not quite. She couldn't remember the last time she'd been in a pub with a man and felt unbelievably gauche. Jon looked across at her and grinned. The dim light in the car park made his eyes glitter invitingly. He locked up the car and then turned around with his hand extended.

'Pleased you came, nervous or not?' he said gently.

She swallowed hard and stepped closer.

'Yes,' she murmured, feeling his fingers close over hers. His touch was warm and dry and unbelievably comforting. They stood very still, holding hands like two teenagers, for what seemed like an eternity. Dora made the decision to step into the quiet warm space around him just as he decided to lean closer. For a split second his lips brushed hers. She shivered.

'I've waited a very long time to do that,' he said, in a voice barely above a whisper. She tipped her head up towards him and he kissed her again. This time the chaste delicacy had gone. Dora gasped, feeling as if she might drown. When he pulled away he was still grinning.

'My God,' she muttered. 'It was worth the wait, though, wasn't it?'

Jon linked his arm casually through hers. 'Shall we go for that drink now, or would you prefer to stand here necking all night? Don't answer that, I think we'd better go for a drink.'

Dora shivered, relishing the little crackle of desire that arced between them.

'Necking? Where on earth did you get that from? It sounds like something out of a teenage magazine.' She hesitated. 'I never thought we'd get this far.'

'What, tonight, or all those years ago?'

Dora giggled. 'Both really.'

'Me too.'

Dora groaned with mock indignation and fell into step beside him. 'And what do you mean, *you've* waited so long? I used to think about you when . . .' She stopped abruptly, feeling the colour rise in her face.

She used to think about him when she was in bed with her husband, Ray, fantasising about Jon's lean muscular body while they . . . She stopped her thoughts as abruptly as the words, and in desperation peered into the nearest shop window.

'Go on, tell me, then,' said Jon, leaning gently against her, 'when did you think about me?'

She heard the teasing tone and smiled. 'What an egotist! All the time, if you must know. All the time from the day we first met. That's what made getting ready for tonight so hard – all that expectation all saved up and ready to be unleashed.'

And Dora had also known, after the first time they'd met, that she could very easily fall in love with him. Which would have been fine, except of course that then she had been married to Ray.

Peering into the darkened shop window, with Jon beside her, she wondered how long it had been since she'd really thought about Ray. At one time he had figured daily in her thoughts, now he was a vague abstract outline on the distant horizon. A place she'd once known well but which had gradually been reduced to a series of blurry mental photos that left a broad impression but precious little detail.

'Are we looking for something in particular?'

Jon's voice snapped Dora back to reality and she blushed, realising they were peering into a lingerie shop. 'I wasn't really looking, I was just thinking,' she spluttered.

Jon grinned. 'Really?' He touched the glass with his finger. 'I rather like that little cream silk number at the back. What do you reckon?'

'You'd look great in it, cream is most definitely your colour.'

Jon pulled her close with a sudden urgency and kissed her again. She wasn't up to offering even token resistance and kissed him with equal fervour.

When they finally parted, he said, 'We really ought to talk.'

Dora crept under his arm, relishing the sensation of his body against hers. 'What is it, obligatory these days? What do you want to talk about?' She felt rather than saw him shrug.

'Things, all those things grown ups are supposed to want to know, old things, new things, things of significance. The real grown-up stuff.' He stopped mid-stride. 'Like that cryptic little note that you sent me when you cancelled our last date at Lacey's. I kept wondering if I should ring you. Then the next thing I heard was that you'd left your husband.'

'They weren't dates and I can't remember what I wrote,' said Dora briskly, taking his hand and hurrying him along the precinct. 'I really think I need a drink.'

Ahead of them, past darkened shop fronts and the harsh geometry of the pedestrian precinct, the road opened dramatically onto a beautifully lit medieval market place. Keelside's old commercial heart, just a street away from the river, was ringed by half-timbered houses, built from local brick. The soft ochres and creams of the merchants' houses had a kind of weary splendour, as if they had long grown tired of being picturesque.

The shopping centre was almost empty; by contrast the market place was bustling with cars and people making their way to the cluster of pubs and restaurants around the edges of the square.

Jon pointed out Mac's as they walked between the cars. It stood on one corner of the square and was lit up like a Christmas tree. 'Over there. Why don't you start by telling me about what happened between you and your husband.'

Dora puffed out her cheeks. 'You go straight for the throat, don't you? Aren't we supposed to work our way through the social niceties first?'

Jon shrugged. 'Whatever. Maybe it's my police training – I just thought you might want to talk about it.'

Dora shook her head. 'I'm not sure that I do. It all happened a very long time ago now, it's done, over. I'm not that person any more.' She glanced at him, and realised she had been unnecessarily abrupt.

Jon strode towards the pub doorway, fingers still in a weave with hers.

'Okay. You're the writer – tell me a story.' He sounded slightly drunk and Dora was suddenly convinced that he really had been waiting all those years to kiss her.

Mac's was a pseudo-traditional pub with a wealth of dark stained oak, green leather and brass studs. A small gaggle of older customers stood talking around the bar, while in one corner a juke box quietly reeled off middle-of-the-road standards. At least they could hear themselves speak.

Jon found a table in a secluded alcove and went to get a drink. Dora ordered martini and lemonade, while Jon returned cradling what looked suspiciously like a glass of orange juice. He grinned and drank their good health.

'Driving,' he said, in answer to her unspoken question as they clinked glasses. 'Now tell me.'

Dora focused on the ceiling. 'I'm not sure how scintillating this will turn out to be. Remember, you've only got yourself to blame if you're bored senseless.' She took a deep breath, feeling hot and painfully self-conscious.

'Teenage girl is whisked into matrimony by an older, more sophisticated man. Once she's married to him, it turns out he's mean, foolish, insecure, overbearing, and assumes his child bride won't notice. Which of course she doesn't, not to begin with anyway. They have a daughter. By the time the wife wakes up it seems there's no way out. She writes and that lets out all the tight bitter little feelings inside. Writing helps her to feel in control and make sense of life. She waits for years, bides her time.'

Dora stopped and took a long hard pull on her drink, afraid to look at Jon but not quite sure why. 'Are you sure you really want me to go on?'

Jon nodded. 'We're bypassing the social niceties for this –'

Dora grinned. 'Okay. The little wife gets three romances published and suddenly she's earning money, feeling better about herself. She's grown up without her husband noticing and discovering the world outside is full of bright shiny possibilities. His words are no longer hewn from the living rock and he doesn't like it. He's afraid that once she's had a bite of a few more cherries she'll get bored and leave him. He starts making demands, after all she loves him, she should do what he asks. He hopes if he claws her back, shuts her back up inside his life, that everything will be the same as it was between them and she'll forget what she's seen outside. He doesn't understand that by caging her up she's more likely to think about escaping, not less.'

Dora stopped and glanced across at Jon. 'Am I boring you?'

He shook his head. 'No, not at all, what does our heroine do next?'

Dora swirled the martini thoughtfully in the tumbler. 'Well, he's made redundant and starts to talk about the restaurant he's always wanted. Of course, she won't mind giving up her writers' club and workshops, to concentrate on building up their new business. They'll finally both be doing what they really want. Their future looms with terrifying clarity. All those little things in the past she has agreed to, all those soul-destroying compromises to keep the peace, come back to haunt her. Unless she leaves him she'll end up baking buns and pasties for a living –'

Jon leant forward, watching Dora's face. 'And so she leaves him?'

Dora took a mouthful of martini and shook her head. 'Not then. It takes a while to find the courage. One day they go for a walk and talk about emulsion. Only they both know it isn't really about emulsion. If she agrees with him she'll be giving up everything she's worked for. They won't reach a compromise. She leaves him, takes their daughter. He convinces himself she is seeing someone else. It's far easier for him to understand that, he can't quite believe that she has left him just because she's had enough.' Dora stopped, hearing her voice crackle unevenly with emotion. 'And I think that's about it,' she said unsteadily. 'It's all much tidier with hindsight, at the time I couldn't tell black from white or up from down'.

'So that's the story,' Dora said, sinking the rest of her drink in a single gulp. 'A bit melodramatic for the current market.'

'You didn't mention the dashing young police officer.'

'My God, you really are an egotist, aren't you?' Dora laughed. 'He was sub-plot, a tantalising possibility.'

79

'But did she fancy him?' Jon purred mischievously, sliding closer to her, eyes alight.

Dora groaned, leaning against his shoulder. 'She was besotted with him, but afraid that if she got involved she'd be cheating herself out of a bright new beginning.'

'And now?' His voice had dropped an octave, his dark eyes flashed invitingly.

Dora stood her empty glass on the table. 'He's going to let me buy him an orange juice, and prepare himself for the fact that he may have to carry our heroine back to the car if she carries on drinking like this.'

Jon got to his feet and headed back to the bar. 'We'll have this and then eat?'

Dora nodded. She needed something to soak up the alcohol and the memories.

The fried chicken restaurant down on King's Street seemed busy for a weeknight; obviously it was *the* new place to be. Jon and Dora waited to be shown to their table, while around them a bow wave of customers cheerfully consumed huge quantities of chicken and salad.

It smelt delicious, making Dora painfully aware that she had hardly eaten all day and the alcohol was trickling mischievously through her bloodstream. The dining area had a crisp, clean brightness about it, with cheerful red-and-white checked gingham tablecloths and blonde-wood panelled walls. The waiting staff were done up in matching gingham shirts and kerchiefs, all set off by denim dungarees.

Dora leant back against the wall. 'My God, we've walked onto the set for Oklahoma,' she whispered in an undertone.

To her surprise, Jon blushed. 'Sorry about this. I got out of the habit of eating out. I didn't know where to take you, one of the lads in the office recommended this place. By the look of it he must bring his kids here at weekends.'

Before Dora could reply, a breezy blonde cow-girl with a broad Norfolk face came over, smiling cheerfully. 'Evening, folks,' she said, in a passable American accent. 'If you'd like to come with me, I'll show you to your table.'

When they were settled, the girl slapped a menu down in front of each of them and flounced off to round up the rest of the queue.

The fried chicken was good.

'Right,' said Dora, between forkfuls of coleslaw. 'What about you? Talk to me. Fair's fair. I want to hear about you now.'

Jon peeled delicate white chicken off the bone. 'Nothing much to tell really.'

Dora groaned. 'Oh, come on, I told you all my edited highlights.'

Jon played with his chicken thoughtfully. 'I love my job and I loved my wife. I tried very hard to put a lot of energy and effort into both, but sometimes – to be fair – most of the time, the job won on points. I never could strike any sort of workable balance, and by the time I realised how bad things were between us it was just too late. Nita wanted me to be at home more, be there with her and the kids. I suppose I missed one sports day too many.'

He cut a sliver of chicken breast into rough squares. 'She was right. Hindsight is great stuff. I missed out on a lot of things when the kids were small. I was never there when she needed me. But, we just couldn't get it back to how it was. Then she met Sam. He's a really nice guy, very straight up and down. She says she knows where she is with Sam. Production manager, forty hours a week, no overtime and his wife left him because he was so dull.' Jon snorted. 'Funny things, people.' A sharp persistent bleep cut through the air. 'Oh, shit. Hang on, I've got to find a phone.'

Jon slid out from the table, wiping his lips, and hurried over to the blonde cow-girl. Dora watched as the waitress directed him to the pay phone, and then set about consuming her chicken. She had a feeling that unless she ate it now she might not get a chance to eat it at all.

When Jon reappeared a few seconds later he looked uncomfortable. 'I'm sorry, but I've got to nip back to the station.'

Dora nodded, laying her knife and fork down. 'Not a problem. Do you want to get a doggy bag for yours?'

Jon shook his head and headed off to settle the bill. As he slid the notes over the cash desk, Dora wondered how she was going to get home.

Jon hurried back to the table. 'Look, this shouldn't take too long. If you want to come with me I can get you a coffee or something, if you don't mind hanging around?'

Dora nodded. 'That's fine, but I could get a taxi home if you'd rather?'

Jon held out his hand and closed his fingers around hers. 'No. It really shouldn't take very long.' His expression suggested that he was wrestling with whether to say something or not.

Dora tipped her head on one side in mute enquiry.

'It's Lillian Bliss,' he said, in a monotone. 'Her new flat has been broken into.'

6

'And now for the local news . . .' In his study, Lawrence Rawlings sat back in his armchair, cradling the remote control in one hand and a brandy and soda in the other. The room was in shadow, only the TV giving any light, one-eyed and invasive.

On screen, the reporter shuffled a sheath of papers. 'Our main story this evening. Guy Phelps has been officially named as the new Conservative candidate for Fairbeach in Norfolk. Mr Phelps, described by political commentators as being just right of centre, was selected after the tragic and unexpected death of Conservative MP, Jack Rees.'

Lawrence stifled a yawn, as the reporter continued, 'Candidates from both the other main parties, Freda Haleworthy, Labour, and Tom Fielding, for the Liberal Democrats, will be in our Norwich studio tomorrow evening, in our main six o'clock programme. Local political pundits –'

Lawrence sniffed and switched channels. He was already sick of the by-election campaign though it had barely begun. Shame Tom Fielding couldn't be persuaded to change horses. His instinct was that Fielding's enthusiasm and good humour would be ideal for Fairbeach. Certainly his unforced common touch lifted Tom Fielding head and shoulders above that little bastard Guy Phelps and that dreadful socialist woman, Haleworthy. Fielding had something of the old Jack Rees charisma about him. Lawrence allowed himself a narrow smile – a trait that might be a mixed blessing.

There was some sort of adventure film on four. He stood the brandy balloon down on a side table and snapped on the lamp. The newspaper was around somewhere.

Years before, Tom Fielding and Lawrence's daughter, Sarah,

had moved in the same social circles, though never as a couple to his knowledge. He paused; actually that would have been another ideal match. The thought surfaced unexpectedly and took him by surprise.

He glanced at the photos on his desk – Sarah and the girls and that moron she was married to. Calvin Roberts, dressed in an expensive tweed suit, grinned sheepishly for the camera, plump fingers resting on his rotund belly. He looked like a well-buffed country squire, master of all he surveyed. Lawrence's eyes narrowed.

Lawrence Rawlings would not have chosen a bastard like Calvin Roberts as a son-in-law in any of the seven levels of hell, though he could well understand his daughter's infatuation when she had first met him. Ten years older than Sarah, straight down from London, Calvin Roberts had appeared to represent something more sophisticated than Fairbeach usually had to offer.

Sarah had met Calvin at a dinner party, while he was busy trying to make the right local connections. He'd got one decent suit, a car he couldn't pay for and a good line in lip. He'd taken Sarah out a few times, and then she'd told Lawrence she was pregnant. There was no chance of a discreet trip to Harley Street, Sarah wouldn't have agreed to that. No, it was straight down the aisle in a specially tailored wedding dress, two weeks in the Seychelles and a lot of carefully engineered surprise when their firstborn arrived a month or two early.

Lawrence wished with all his heart it hadn't been that way. He sniffed. Sadly, Calvin Roberts had had other ideas. Lawrence glanced around the elegant room wondering where he'd left the damned paper.

From an oil painting above the fireplace, Lawrence's father looked down with measured disinterest. Like most of God's finer creatures, the Rawlings were not great breeders. On the whole, they produced their offspring late in life and sparingly, if at all. Frail in childhood, robust in old age seemed to be a Rawlings family motto.

Lawrence's own baby brother had died of some respiratory complaint before he was out of infancy. Sarah's mother had had to endure months of bed rest before Sarah's arrival. Sarah had had a terrible time carrying the girls – and, of course, she had been the last of the Fairbeach Rawlings.

He did have his granddaughters, angelic little creatures, Imogen and Morwenna. Both, thank God, favoured their mother, but they were Roberts not Rawlings. Lawrence often wondered, as he watched them play, what genetic bear traps lurked beneath the faces that reminded him so poignantly of their mother.

Lawrence refilled his brandy balloon.

He wouldn't see Sarah hurt for all the world. A tight little fist formed in his belly. Calvin Roberts' grinning face seemed to be a personal insult. Lawrence settled himself behind his desk, picked up the phone and banged in a local number.

'What have you got on the Bliss girl?' he said flatly to the man at the far end of the line.

There was a heavy pause. 'Not enough yet, gov,' was the infuriating reply. 'And something else. I know it sounds bloody daft, but I think I'm being watched. Have you got someone else on the job, as well?'

'Is that some sort of joke?' snapped Lawrence.

The man coughed. 'I know, it sounds paranoid, but two or three times when I've been out and about, I'm sure there's been someone else there as well.'

Lawrence sniffed. Across the desk Calvin Roberts was still grinning.

'Get a grip, man,' Lawrence snapped and hung up.

Keelside police station was quiet, though it seemed that every light in the building was on. Jon Melrose opened the door to his office, where Neil Rhodes, his detective sergeant, was hunched over the desk, cradling the phone on his shoulder. As Jon came in, Rhodes looked up in apology.

Jon snorted. 'My night off?'

Rhodes held up his hands in surrender. 'I thought you'd

like to know about this, sir.' He handed Jon a slim manila folder. 'Same MO as before. So far it looks like nothing was taken, plenty of mess though, same graffiti. The show flat was trashed at the same time, but none of the other residents heard or saw anything suspicious. Whoever's doing this doesn't fit your usual vandal profile – no messy entry, no noise, no witnesses. And no-one knows where this Lillian Bliss woman is. I've just been on the phone to her agent, trying to track her down.'

Jon looked up at Rhodes with renewed interest. 'And?'

Rhodes glanced at the pad on the desk. 'Nothing. Her agent, Calvin Roberts, said she had no bookings for appearances tonight. Says she might have gone home to her old flat – he's going to ring back with the address if he can find it, or he suggested perhaps she might be out with friends.'

'Anything else?'

Outside, Dora Hall was sitting in the little waiting area.

'That your date?' asked Rhodes, glancing in her direction.

Jon nodded as he skimmed through the incident report; no more than bare bones, it told him nothing that Rhodes hadn't already said.

Rhodes pointed his pencil towards the corridor. Behind the glass Dora was studying a poster on the wall. 'Is she the one that writes those books?'

'She is.'

Rhodes grinned. 'Using you for research is she, sir?'

Jon snorted, throwing the folder back onto the desk. 'Chance would be a fine thing. Half a chicken dinner and you page me, not really the stuff of great romance, is it, Rhodes? So what else did Mr Roberts have to say for himself?'

'I got the impression he thought it was odd that Miss Bliss wasn't at home. He got very short with me when I suggested she might be out on a date, and he sounded a bit ruffled about what we might find at her new apartment, said he could meet us down there if we wanted. I told him there was no need, our scene of the crime boys were already on their way.'

Outside in the corridor, Dora Hall was idling through a

magazine. Jon knew she couldn't see him through the obscure striped glass. At a distance she looked deceptively small, dark brown hair cut into an unruly bob framing her oval face. Here and there the odd pure white hair twinkled under the unforgiving strip light.

She was as slim as when they'd first met. Her diminutive appearance was at odds with her personality. For a second he wondered what it would be like waking up next to her. The thought surprised him. As if sensing what was on his mind, she looked up.

At the desk, Rhodes shuffled a sheaf of papers, breaking Jon's chain of thought.

'And that, as they say, is about it, gov. I've asked the scene of crime mob to call us if they turn up anything interesting, and told them you'll be dropping in. Looks as if your hunch that there's a link between these break-ins is spot on.' He pulled a photocopied sheet out of his in tray. 'And your friend Mrs Hall's right, Calvin Roberts did report his filofax was missing.'

Jon nodded. 'Right. Now all I've got to do is convince the superintendent.'

Rhodes grinned. 'Want me to write you a note?'

On the drive back to Fairbeach, Dora tried hard to settle down. She wished she knew Jon well enough for them to feel comfortable with each other. As it was, she felt as if she was on approval, slightly ill at ease, still with a prickle of tension in her stomach.

Jon pulled out into the flow of late-evening traffic.

'I'm really sorry about tonight.'

'It's all right, can't be helped, I don't mind.' Dora hesitated. 'Well, not much, anyway. I'm not very *au fait* with how dinner dates are supposed to go these days.'

He grinned. 'I think we're supposed to get a chance to eat what we've ordered. Maybe we could give it another try, some time soon?'

Dora nodded. 'I'd like that.' She watched the headlights for a few minutes before speaking again. 'Did you find out how Lillian is?'

Jon shrugged. 'Don't know yet, I've said I'll drop in and give her a look.' He grinned. 'Don't worry, I'll drop you off first.'

'You don't have to, I've always wanted to see what it is that policemen do.'

Jon laughed. 'Trust me, it's not that impressive.'

A peculiar silence dropped over the two of them. Dora wondered if it was too late to salvage the remains of the evening, and whether she had the courage to suggest he came round after he had been to Lillian Bliss' flat.

As the lights of Fairbeach glittered ahead of them on the dual carriageway, Jon said, 'Maybe now I can convince my boss that these break-ins are linked.'

Dora sighed. Safe ground. She felt the tension easing again. 'I don't understand. What do you think they're looking for?' she said. Maybe she could just slip the invitation into the conversation, quickly without dwelling on it. 'Presumably whatever it is they want, they haven't found it yet? My place, Calvin's? Now Lillian's? What is it?'

Jon made a thoughtful sound in his throat. 'No idea, but I think we should take another look into it.'

'Right,' said Dora. 'I'll ring Calvin tomorrow.'

Jon glanced across at her. 'Actually, I didn't mean you,' he smiled. 'Try and resist any temptation you might have to go snooping around. I'm supposed to be the policeman, remember? Whoever this guy is, whatever his reason, keep out of it and make sure you give that security firm a ring.'

Dora, suitably chastened, nodded.

When they pulled up outside the flat, Dora wondered if she should invite him inside. Part of her just needed the comforting presence of another person coming upstairs with her. Jon switched off the engine. 'I'll see you upstairs.'

Dora nodded dumbly. 'Thanks,' she said, suddenly daunted at the idea of going up to her flat alone. 'I've had a . . .' She stopped. 'I was going to say, I've had a lovely evening, and I have, but it sounds so corny.'

Jon grinned. 'Me too, next time I'll leave my pager at home in a drawer.'

He leant a little closer and tipped her face towards his. She didn't resist as he pressed his lips to hers. He smelt so delicious, the heat of his body made her shiver. She felt the desperate little flicker of desire igniting again and jerked away.

'I'm not used to this,' she spluttered. 'I'm very out of practice.'

His eyes were alight, like tiny, intense dark beads in the street light. Dora fought to catch her breath.

'We won't rush it then,' he said softly. 'Shall we go upstairs and see what the cat's been up to while you've been out?'

She nodded, trying to swallow down the frantic tattoo of her pulse.

Outside it seemed very dark and cold, despite the street lights. As soon as she opened the car door, Dora sensed they were being watched. It was a little raw, electric knowing, something ancient and instinctive that made the hairs on the back of her neck stand up.

'Jon,' she whispered, turning back towards him.

He looked across at her, instantly registering the anxiety in her voice. 'What is it?'

'There's someone in the alley beside the shop.' Her voice was barely more than a breath. How she knew, or why she was so certain, was beyond her.

Slowly, Jon turned, and she watched, mesmerised, as he pulled a torch out from under the seat of the car. A split second later a stunning searing beam of halogen light cut through the darkness like a solar flare. Trapped inside the spotlight's unforgiving eye, a figure cowered against the alley wall.

'Stay where you are!' snapped Jon, even though it was obvious that the person was no threat.

Dora, no longer afraid, hurried across the road towards the alley. Whoever it was had long wet hair, bare legs and was wrapped all around in an oversized raincoat. Between the person's fingers, Dora could see terrified blue-green eyes, sprinkled with distinctive gold flecks.

'Lillian?' Dora whispered in disbelief as the girl turned, blinking, eyes swollen and tearstained, into the light. She let out a long thin mewl of terror and clung to Dora like a child.

'My flat,' she wailed. 'They've written horrible things on the wall. They said I'm a slag. A slag,' she repeated, and burst into a hot explosive cascade of tears. Still clinging to Dora, she took a long deep ragged breath. 'I didn't know where else to go.'

Dora held her closer. 'It's all right now,' she said in a soothing gentle voice, stroking Lillian's damp hair. 'Let's go upstairs and you can tell us all about it.'

Fishing in her jacket pocket, Dora gave her keys to Jon.

'Did you see anybody?' Dora asked, as she handed Lillian a mug of tea. Downstairs, Jon was putting a message through to Keelside police station.

Lillian Bliss shook her head. She was so pale her eyes seemed to dwarf the rest of her face. Huddled on the sofa she looked like a Disney rabbit. Without make-up, with her slicked down wet hair, she could easily have passed for twelve.

She curled up onto the settee, knees up, arms wrapped tight around them, dragging the coat around her. Oscar, sensing a poor lost soul, curled up alongside her and made comforting, uncharacteristic small talk, rubbing his furry, wedge-shaped head against her until she was forced to take him in her arms. Once he was settled, Lillian turned her entire attention to the cat, and hummed soft noises in the back of her throat.

Dora went to find Jon. 'I think she'll be okay, she's in shock.'

'Did you ask her if she'd got a diary or a phone book at the flat?'

'She said she'd got her address book in her bag, she's got that with her.'

Jon nodded. 'Right, I'll go and take a look at the flat and then I'll come back, if you don't mind –' He stopped, reddening slightly. 'I was going to ask if I could come back anyway.'

Dora lifted her eyebrows. 'Really?' She smiled at him. 'And there was me worrying about how I could suggest you dropped by for a coffee without sounding easy.' She giggled and stepped into his arms. 'I really have had a good night. Thanks for inviting me.'

Jon's colour intensified. 'You know what makes this difficult?'

Dora felt he didn't want an answer.

'It's that I really want this to work out. You know, me and you? We wasted an awful lot of time, didn't we?'

She didn't get a chance to answer this time around, he kissed her instead and she felt her heart kick back into a tango.

'You have to go,' she said in an undertone, as she felt her whole body respond to his touch. 'You're supposed to be going to Lillian's flat. Remember?'

Jon groaned.

Behind them, the door opened slowly. Lillian Bliss, cradling Oscar, stood framed in the doorway. If anything she was paler than before, one hand lifting to her lips. She took an unsteady step over the threshold.

'I think I'm going to be –'

'Sick,' added Dora ruefully, stepping to one side as Oscar leapt into the hall and Jon sprang back. She caught hold of Lillian, who was swaying dramatically.

'Come on,' she said in a businesslike tone. 'Why don't I run you a bath, I'll get this cleared up in a minute or two. Don't worry about it.'

The smell made Dora's stomach heave. She beckoned to Jon. 'Come on, you'd better be going too.'

He looked almost as pale as Lillian as he edged towards the door.

'I'll be back in a little while,' he said.

Dora, one arm supporting Lillian, grinned. 'I was banking on it.'

'What the hell do you mean, can she stay here?' Dora hissed into the phone.

At the far end of the line, Calvin Roberts coughed uncomfortably. 'She can't go back to the flat yet. It's a complete mess.

91

And I can hardly ask Sarah if she can come round here and stay with us, now can I?'

Dora growled. It was nine o'clock the following morning. Dora had hardly slept a wink all night. Jon, on his return, had arrived wearing the role of policeman, and when he'd left, well after midnight, Dora had felt immeasurably cheated – all this, and it appeared that Oscar had defected to the enemy.

'Why can't Lillian just go back to her flat?' she snapped.

She already knew the answer. In the sitting room, still in a state of shock, wrapped in one of Dora's shapeless dressing gowns, Lillian Bliss was talking in an undertone to Oscar. She was still ashen and painfully close to tears. Even a night away hadn't quite stilled her fears from the previous evening.

Dora let out what she hoped was a long calming breath.

'Right,' she said briskly. 'I'll go and pick up some clothes for her this morning. The flat will need to be cleared up – can you arrange that?' She stopped, aware that she was struggling to sound calm. Why was she giving him any option?

'You've got two days, Calvin? *Capisce?* Two days and then you have to find a way round this. I want Lillian Bliss out of my flat, out of my life. Two days, forty-eight hours, this is not open to negotiation.' She stopped again, thinking aloud. 'Where did Lillian live before she came to Fairbeach? What about her family? Can't you arrange for her to go home for a little while?'

There was a lengthy pause, then Calvin cleared his throat. 'Leave it with me.'

Dora snorted. 'Remember, two days, Calvin,' she repeated, and hung up.

When Dora went back into the sitting room, Lillian looked up at her with fear-rimmed eyes. 'I've got a cat,' she said.

Dora nodded. 'Really, where? At home?'

'No, at the little flat I've got over in Keelside. I was going to go and pick him up once my new place was all decorated. Couldn't have him there while the men were in, leaving the doors open and that sort of thing. The girl downstairs, Carol, is looking after him at the moment.' Her voice trembled. 'I wish I'd stayed there now, no-one would ever have broken in there.'

Dora sensed the incoming tide of tears. 'Why don't we have some breakfast and then we can go down to Anchor Quay and pick up some clothes?' She glanced at the discarded raincoat on the back of the sofa. In the kitchen, rinsed out and hung over the clothes horse, was the swimsuit Lillian had been wearing under it.

Lillian sniffed, eyes widening. 'I don't think I ever want to go back there,' she whispered unevenly.

Dora painted on a bright, shiny, uncharacteristic morning smile.

'Don't worry, it'll be fine in the daylight and I'll be there with you.' Still Lillian looked uncertain, so Dora played her ace. 'Or, if you like, you can borrow my clothes until we can get you some more. I'm sure I can find something to fit you somewhere.'

Lillian stared and blinked.

'Oh,' she said, in a little voice. Composing herself, she smiled. 'You did say you'd come with me, didn't you?'

Dora nodded. 'I'll drive you down in the car after we've eaten. And the police want you to make a statement.'

Lillian screwed up her nose. 'I told that policeman all about it last night.'

Dora nodded. 'That's right, but he isn't really involved in the case, they still need an official statement.'

Lillian considered for an instant, composure rapidly returning. 'He was quite tasty.'

Dora flushed. 'Who?'

'The bloke who was here last night. Really nice eyes. I always look at their eyes.'

Dora took another deep calming breath; two days. Two days and Lillian would be gone.

7

Lillian's new flat was on the top floor of a converted Victorian warehouse. Huge arched and circular windows, an architectural happy face, looked out over grey waters of the Western Ouse. Downstairs, in the elegant flagstoned foyer, there was still a breath of new varnish hanging amongst the lush green plants and inviting, lovingly restored old timbers.

If Josephine Hammond from the *Fairbeach Gazette* was anywhere in the vicinity, Dora certainly had no desire to be seen with Lillian. Before they left Gunners Terrace, Dora had rung the caretaker to arrange for them to be let in through the fire exit, and now crept along the service road, parking at the back of the building near the rubbish bins.

Lillian climbed the stairs reluctantly. The door of the top-floor apartment was wreathed with police incident tape.

Dora slipped the key into the lock whilst Lillian hovered unhappily behind her, as if the vandals or their wraiths might still be trapped inside. Dora stood aside once the door was unlocked. The apartment was a mess. She could easily understand why Lillian hadn't wanted to stay. For some reason, the sense of violation seemed more extreme because everything in the apartment was so new. Pristine plaster work, with barely time to harden, had been ruined, gouged down to the brickwork. Aerosol obscenities on the newly stripped wood looked like open wounds. Bright new furniture, some still in its plastic wrappings, had been overturned and slashed, cast up, left like flotsam on the shoreline in the wake of an invisible destructive tide.

Dora walked around slowly, wondering why it felt so very disturbing, while Lillian scurried around behind her, stuffing things into bags and gathering things up in her arms.

Dora picked her way through the debris, unable to stand still, righting tables and standing lamps back on the shelves. She did it without thinking, aware only that she needed to re-establish calm and order. A cream leather sofa had been disembowelled, white foam entrails cascading out like snow over an oriental rug. Outside the beautiful old arched windows, the slow waters of the river glided past like dusty silk.

Dora straightened the curtains. Poor little Lillian Bliss. She had barely had time to claim the flat for her own before it had been violated and snatched away from her. She didn't have the resilience or the emotional connections to the things inside to claw the apartment back. Lillian didn't feel safe there now because she hadn't had any time to make it feel safe in the first place.

Dora arranged a flurry of pastel cushions onto the window seat. A crescent of emulsion was soaking into the new oatmeal carpets, cream on cream, self-coloured defacing.

Dora read the bile green words across the chimney breast: 'slag', three feet high, written with considerably more venom than the insults on her own walls.

Behind her, she heard the bedroom door slam shut with a dark finality. Lillian had barely been in the apartment ten minutes. She kept her eyes lowered, as if the graffiti on the champagne-coloured walls was shouting too loudly for her to cope with.

'All done,' she said in a tiny voice.

Dora turned and nodded, cradling the keys in her hands. She looked the girl up and down. Lillian was carrying a single bulging suitcase, with clothes peeping out between the fastenings.

'Is that all you want?' Dora asked gently, but Lillian had already turned to leave.

'Come on,' she said, guiding her towards the ageing Fiat. 'Let's get back home and have something to eat.'

When they drove out into the main street, Dora spotted Josephine Hammond hunched in her car, yawning, cradling a mobile phone. It had obviously been a long night for her too.

The policeman who turned up after lunch to take Lillian's statement treated her like a child.

'So, then, what did you do next?' he said very slowly, as if the stunning blonde might have trouble comprehending sentences of more than two words. After they had picked up her clothes, Lillian had gone back to Dora's flat, painted on a happy face and was now curled up on the sofa, cradling Oscar.

'I went for a swim,' she replied in her seductive breathy voice. 'There's a swimming pool in the basement at the apartments – and a gym and a sun bed. I've used them ever since I moved in. You have to book the sun bed, so I go in the evenings.'

At least that explained why Lillian had arrived in the swimsuit and her wet hair.

When the girl leant forward, the young police officer followed the progress of her chest with an impressive single-mindedness.

Dora sighed and went back into the office just in time to answer the intercom bell as it rang.

'Hello, are you up there?' asked a familiar voice.

Dora glanced heavenwards. 'Hello, Sheila. How are you?'

'Fine. I've brought the new parish magazine round for you.'

Dora flinched, visualising Sheila's reaction at meeting Lillian in her sitting room. 'Actually, I'm just on my way out.'

Sheila sniffed. 'Have you got the police there again?'

Dora, one finger still on the call button, grabbed the jacket that was hanging on the back of her chair and picked up her handbag. If she didn't head Sheila off at the pass very soon she'd be demanding to be let in.

'Are you going to open the door then? I can't stop long. There's a bring and buy at the Corn Exchange at two.'

Dora was already out in the hall. She stuck her head round

the sitting-room door. 'Excuse me, just got to pop out for a little while.' Neither Lillian nor the policeman looked up or said a word. Dora headed downstairs, taking the steps two at a time.

Sheila was outside on the path, red-faced and obviously annoyed.

'I only popped round to see how you were,' she said, peering into the dark shadow of the stairs above Dora's shoulder.

Dora forced a smile. 'I thought we'd go out for a coffee at that new place in Market Street. Unless of course you're in a hurry?'

Sheila stared at her. 'What, one pound twenty for one of those little glass jug things? It's instant, you know. They refill them out the back. Are you feeling all right?'

Dora nodded, pulling her coat closed and tidying her hair with her other hand.

'Fine. How are the kids? I wouldn't mind going to the bring and buy.'

For a split second, as Dora was about to force march Sheila down Gunners Terrace, she had an odd feeling, fleeting but distinct. She glanced back over her shoulder. This was the same feeling she had had the night before, when she and Jon had discovered Lillian Bliss in the alleyway – an icy unnerving certainty that someone was watching them.

Alicia Markham, chairwoman of the Conservative Association, fought the temptation to lean across the car and straighten Guy Phelps' tie. It showed a touching vulnerability. She took a deep breath. First really public local event, low-key, intimate, something the average man in the street could relate to, or at least his wife would.

Guy Phelps, the new Conservative candidate, would appeal to the mainstream motherly Fairbeach voter, particularly at the moment with his winsomely crooked tie. Guy Phelps, the housewives' choice. Alicia glanced at her watch. The bring and buy was due to open at two – they had plenty of time.

They had all just come back from a quiet celebratory lunch

at the Sexton and Compasses. Guy's wife had made a pretty little speech of thanks to the ladies of the selection committee, smiling demurely in her nice new Laura Ashley frock, making a joke of having to stock up on home-made cakes at the fund raiser to fill the freezer for Party Ladies' Teas.

Everyone had smiled in all the right places. At least Guy Phelps' wife, though patently vacuous, had none of the combative edge that Caroline Rees had displayed. She had even demurely accepted a suggestion that she might wear a hat at official functions from now on.

The official party car slowed dramatically as it turned along the riverfront towards The Close, down past Lawrence Rawlings' Georgian pile. The funereal pace was not through any deference to Fairbeach's illustrious family but because the road was pitted with ruts and potholes. Guy winced as the car bounced down into the gutter.

'Perhaps I ought to have a word about the state of the roads down here. I'm surprised Lawrence hasn't mentioned it to the local council,' Guy said to the driver.

The man remained silent but caught Alicia's eye in the rear-view mirror.

Guy tapped his jacket pockets. Guy's wife – her name escaped Alicia – Laura? Elspeth? – smiled.

'What have you lost now, darling?' she said, with an exaggerated air of long suffering.

Guy grinned, adding to the endearing image of boyishness. 'My speech, sweetheart. Do you remember? I jotted down a few points on some cards, this morning at breakfast.'

His wife rolled her eyes heavenwards and produced them from her handbag.

'I said they'd spoil the line of your suit. Now remember, not too long.'

Alicia turned her attention to the rolling tidal waters of the river, slightly bemused at being privy to scenes of such domestic intimacy.

She hoped Guy had taken his wife's advice. A bring and buy sale was hardly an appropriate platform from which to launch a political career. The other passenger in the car, Colin Scarisbrooke, Guy's newly appointed political agent, leaned forward and straightened Guy's tie.

'Touching, smiling, caring, confident, eye contact. Keep it short, tip your head.'

Alicia stared at Scarisbrooke. 'Is this some new version of "I pack my bag"?' she demanded, in her most imperious tone.

Colin smiled. 'Not at all, Mrs Markham, I've been talking Guy through some of the aspects of what makes for good human interaction. Studies show that this is what your electorate will respond to. Use these tactics and they will remember Guy as a good man.' He paused. 'It's called the Diana effect.'

Alicia stared at him coldly. Guy turned his smile on her. He didn't need lessons, she thought. He had it all, already. She wished Colin Scarisbrooke had left his tie alone.

The car crept over Town Bridge to join the flow of afternoon traffic. The Corn Exchange was two minutes away.

Guy ran his fingers through his long soft fringe, checking his appearance in the discreetly placed vanity mirror, then leant forward and touched Alicia's arm.

'I won't let you down,' he said in an undertone.

Alicia felt a little flurry of pleasure as he looked deep into her eyes.

'Wonderful,' snapped Colin Scarisbrooke. 'Absolutely perfect. That's it.'

Alicia swung round and glared at him, raw with indignation.

Guy Phelps coughed. 'Now, what time do we have to leave?'

Colin, caught in the black widow's gaze, didn't move, though his eyes widened.

Guy's wife opened her handbag again. 'Oh, you men,' she laughed gaily. 'What on earth would they do without us, Alicia?' She glanced down at a floral-covered notebook, running her neatly manicured finger down over the page.

'Leave by three thirty at the latest, home to pick up our car, must remember to take your new suit, and then straight on to Norwich for the recording at the TV studio. Supper with Jean and Bob . . .' She paused, reddening slightly. 'Old friends,

99

very nice people, they live near Attleborough, he's in animal feeds – and then home.'

Alicia's eyes still hadn't left Colin Scarisbrooke. 'It sounds as if you've got everything organised, my dear, maybe we ought to have taken you on instead of Mr Scarisbrooke.'

Everyone, except for Alicia, laughed.

'And what have you got in Guy's diary for tomorrow?'

The hapless woman read on. 'Church first thing, early Communion.' She plucked a matching pencil from the spine of the little book and added another note. 'Your new grey suit for that, I think. And then Mr Rawlings has invited us all over for Sunday lunch.'

Slowly, Alicia Markham turned towards Guy's wife.

'Lawrence Rawlings?' she said quietly.

Guy's wife nodded. 'Oh yes, I'm friends with his daughter, Sarah. She thought it would be lovely if we could all get together before the madness of the by-election starts. We met through the children really. Her girls go to school with our two. So we're all going, children and everything. It should be lovely. After all, we're all on the same side, aren't we?'

Alicia smiled and nodded. What was Lawrence Rawlings up to?

Beside her, relieved to be given a stay of execution, Colin Scarisbrooke sighed and mopped his forehead with a large paisley handkerchief.

The VIP parking space outside the Corn Exchange was neatly cordoned off with orange bollards. A sleek dark car eased slowly between the cones, directed by a uniformed man who moved the markers and replaced them as required.

Standing next to Dora, Sheila sniffed and pointed.

'All right for some people. That'll be that new Conservative chap. Rest of us have to park round the back behind the Empire, but not him.'

Dora stared at her. 'I thought you always voted Conservative? True Blue, and all that?'

Sheila adjusted the wicker basket on her arm. 'I do, but

voting for them doesn't necessarily mean I think they ought to have special treatment when it comes to parking.'

There was a long queue waiting for the bring and buy to open. A brightly coloured waterfall of old women, mothers and children grouped, shuffled and fidgeted down over the steps. The sun shone, and everyone was talking, chirruping, waiting expectantly for the doors to open.

Conservative dos inevitably had a decent turn-out. There was always a nice class of jumble.

Below them, on the pavement, Alicia Markham was being helped out of the car by a man in his early forties. Dora remembered seeing him at Jack's funeral. He had a soft-boned face that probably hadn't changed significantly since he was seven or eight. The impression of boyishness was enhanced as he gently slipped his arm through Alicia's, almost as if he were helping his favourite granny up the steps for tea and scones. They were followed by a thin, nervous-looking woman in a floral print dress and a small, plump, gingery man who was mopping his forehead vigorously with a hankie.

Sheila nodded in their direction. 'Local,' she said approvingly.

'Who is?'

Sheila picked off each of the car's occupants with a well-aimed finger. 'That's Guy Phelps, new Conservative candidate, his wife, Elizabeth. She's in our flower-arranging circle for the hospital. Mrs Markham, of course. I don't know who the other man is.'

Though the occasion hardly seemed to warrant it, there was a fusillade of flash bulbs as Guy Phelps made his way up the steps followed by a press of reporters. Josephine Hammond from the *Fairbeach Gazette* was among them. On the landing, at the top of the first flight, Guy Phelps lifted his hands and smiled beatifically, setting off another volley of bulbs.

'Lovely day. It's really very nice of you all to come.' He skilfully manoeuvred his wife onto his other arm, turning left and right to ensure everyone got a good look at him, and beamed.

101

'I've always firmly believed in supporting local events. Bring and buy is a British institution, a traditional family occasion. I really think there should be more of this sort of thing. Village fêtes, jumble sales, coffee mornings. Events of this kind bind a community together. We, in the Conservative party, firmly believe family life is the very cornerstone of our nation's continued success.' He spoke in a carefully modulated, musical voice, slightly louder than the questions being asked by the reporters around him.

Dora stared down from her vantage point at the top of the steps and knew, without a shadow of a doubt, that she loathed him.

Sheila glanced at her watch. 'Two o'clock, the doors ought to be open by now.'

The queue parted like the Red Sea to let Mr Phelps and his small entourage get to the ornate double doors. As he reached the top, two committee ladies in hats waved their hands for silence. Behind them, the doors of the Corn Exchange slowly opened so that Guy Phelps was framed in cavernous darkness.

The man in a uniform scuttled across the top step carrying a microphone. One of the women coughed into it and then began to speak in a high-pitched, piping voice.

'Ladies and gentlemen, as chairwoman of the local fund-raising committee, we were absolutely delighted when Mr Phelps, our new Conservative candidate, accepted our invitation to open our sale today. I'm sure you will join me in wishing him every success in the forthcoming by-election. No doubt you're all terribly keen to get inside, so, without further ado, here is Mr Guy Phelps to say a few words.' There was a polite flurry of applause.

Guy Phelps smiled again and nodded his thanks to the blushing woman.

As he turned towards the crowd, Dora thought for one wonderful moment that Guy Phelps might break into song. He dipped one shoulder forward and angled his body so his face was caught in three-quarter profile. He smiled, looking up from under his eyebrows, while surreptitiously sliding a slim bundle of cards from his jacket pocket.

'Thank you for those kind words, Mrs Hillier. Ladies and gentlemen, I am delighted to have been asked to open the spring bring and buy today. Over the years, my wife and I . . .'

'It's past two o'clock already,' said a disgruntled woman at the foot of the steps. Sheila nodded her agreement.

'Nearly five past by my watch,' added another. A grumble of discontent from the crowd rolled forwards and up towards the Corn Exchange doors.

There was a slight, uneasy pause, but Guy Phelps' smile held firm. He took a deep breath and held up his hands.

'So, with no more ado, it gives me the greatest pleasure to declare this spring bring and buy sale open,' he said, and instantly stepped aside.

There was a muted cheer, a fragment of applause and then the crowd moved up the steps as a single body. Dora was carried along on the tide, Sheila at her shoulder. As they reached the line of tables across the entrance, the front runners already had their admission fee ready. Sheila pressed forty pence into the hand of a capable Conservative and steered Dora inside.

For a split second Dora was aware of how big, how high and how empty the hall was, with its colourful outcrops of trestle tables and bright stalls. The impression was lost as the crowd poured in around them, like waves of bright water, flowing and rolling out along the aisles.

They were barely past the first table before Sheila made a break for the cake stall on the far side of the hall. Dora knew she wasn't that quick or that determined, and instead let herself drift along on the current, carried this way and that by the swirling eddies of bargain hunters.

In a quiet backwater she bought a box of home-made Turkish delight and a bag of fudge. The fudge was wonderful, creamy, soft –

'Had any good break-ins recently?'

Dora, still with her mouth full, looked up in astonishment.

Josephine Hammond was standing beside her, fingering a rather nice cream cotton sweater on the Nearly New table.

Dora took a deep breath, swallowing the fudge down in an unwieldy lump. 'Shouldn't you be over there with the rest of the news hounds, waiting for Guy Phelps to say something infinitely wise and quotable?'

Josephine grinned. 'Probably, but I'm not sure I've got that many years left in me. Besides, I never could resist a bargain. I've left Gary, my photographer, over there to keep an eye on him. What's he going to say ? "Nice sponge, what a lovely baby. I think the cake weighs four pounds twelve ounces"?'

Dora pulled a face. 'You're very cynical for one so young,' she observed wryly.

Josephine snorted. 'So would you be, it comes with the job. NUJ stands for naturally unimpressed and jaded. I've had about six hours' sleep in three days and no prospect of a let up.' She grinned. 'So, do you want to tell me all about this Catiana Moran thing, or have I got to beat it out of you?'

Dora lifted an eyebrow.

Josephine Hammond offered the woman behind the stall a pound for the cream sweater. The woman wanted two, they settled on one fifty.

Dora realised she hadn't moved and wondered why. Maybe, she thought, it was because she might like Josephine Hammond. Two snap character assessments in one afternoon. She offered Josephine the bag of fudge.

'Here, why don't you try this. Your dentist can settle up with me later.'

Josephine grinned and teased a large square off the top. 'Well?'

'Well, what?'

Josephine pressed on despite having her mouth full.

'This Catiana Moran thing? We know there was another break-in last night. At her new place, down by the river. My bat senses tell me something big is on the boil.'

Dora resisted the temptation to tell Josephine she'd already seen her camped outside the front door of Lillian's flat, and instead palmed another piece of fudge into her mouth.

'Really?' She lifted her eyebrows again to imply a wider question.

Josephine nodded. 'There's something very fishy about all this. I've left a message with her agent, Calvin Roberts. I got the last interview with her through him.' She paused as if trying to puzzle out a connection. 'And who is Lillian Bliss? Her name is on the lease –'

Dora swallowed back a choke, as Josephine suddenly spotted a Next sweater on the table with a two-pound price tag.

At the adjoining table, Sarah Roberts, Calvin's wife, was holding up a white silk Windsmoor blouse against her chest. She and Dora made eye contact and recognised each other just as Calvin, red-faced and obviously bored senseless, appeared at Sarah's shoulder with their two daughters in tow.

It felt uncannily like an ambush.

Calvin spotted Dora and grinned.

'Hello, Dora. How's it going? Lillian okay? I'll –' He stopped, as Josephine Hammond looked up and a flash of recognition ricocheted across the Nearly New. It was followed by wonderful, awe-inspiring, breath-stopping silence.

Josephine looked first at Dora and then at Calvin, quickly weighed up her options, then edged her way purposefully around the table, still clutching the Next sweater.

'Mr Roberts, I've been trying to get hold of you since the break-in last night. About Catiana Moran. I wondered if you might be able . . .'

Dora didn't wait for Josephine to figure that maybe she'd made the wrong choice, and headed instead towards the cake stall and Sheila.

Sheila was triumphant. 'Lemon drizzle cake, two packets of those madeleine-things the kids like, and I got a nice little stainless steel sieve, thirty pence.'

Dora, one eye on the crowd, smiled. 'That's wonderful. I'm sorry but I've really got to be going now. You don't mind if I leave you here on your own, do you?'

Sheila rolled her eyes heavenwards. 'I've just asked the lady tc put a pineapple upside-down cake and some flapjacks on one side for you.'

Dora nodded distractedly. She watched Josephine Hammond's striking red hair as she made her way through the crowd of bargain hunters, scanning left and right like ginger radar.

'Would you get them for me? I'll pay you later, I really have got to be going,' Dora said hastily.

Sheila puffed out her cheeks. 'All right, I'll bring them round to yours on my way home.'

'No, don't worry, I'll . . .'

Dora started to protest when she saw Miss Hammond break cover over by the bottled preserves and mixed pickles.

'I'll ring you when I get home,' she said, with a forced smile and hurried towards the exit.

Outside, the bright sunshine made her blink. Although it was market day and the market place was full of more stalls and even more bargain hunters, Dora let out a long sigh of relief, pulled her jacket around her and hurried down the steps. The sense of having escaped didn't last – where could she go? Narrow streets radiated off from the main square, down to the river, up towards the library, back towards the shops. She hesitated – they all looked remarkably like ideal places for another ambush.

Lillian Bliss was still holding court at Gunners Terrace, Sheila and Josephine Hammond were loose in Fairbeach and they would both be looking for her, if not now, then very soon. She opened her handbag – she'd left her car keys back at the flat.

Taking a quick glance back over her shoulder to make sure Josephine Hammond hadn't seen her leave, Dora headed off down between the rows of market stalls to the shopping precinct, out through the bus station, to a rank of telephone boxes.

She pulled a piece of paper out of her purse and tapped in Jon Melrose's Keelside number and listened to the distant ringing sound with some trepidation. What if he didn't want to talk to her?

'Hello, Jon? Is that you?'

'Dora?'

She was relieved and pleased to hear a genuine note of pleasure in his voice.

'I'm really glad you rang. I've been trying to ring you. Did you get my message?' he continued.

'No.' Dora had left the answering machine on in case Lillian might take it upon herself to answer the phone.

'Oh, I rang you about an hour ago.'

Dora sighed. 'I haven't been home yet. I'm in town.'

'Is everything all right? You sound tense.'

She could hear the concern in his voice and was touched. Instinctively, she glanced over her shoulder again.

'I'm fine – I think. It feels as if someone has hijacked my life at the moment. No, not some-one: everyone.' She paused. 'I don't want to go home right now and I don't want to be out, but don't mind me, I'm just rambling. What was it you wanted to talk about?'

Jon coughed. 'Lillian Bliss. Sorry.'

Dora groaned. 'Did you have to say that? You might have had the decency to lie.'

Jon laughed. 'I did say I was sorry. Whereabouts are you now?'

'Hiding out in Fairbeach bus station. I'm seriously considering running away. Want to try talking me out of it?'

She could hear Jon smiling when he replied. 'I could be with you in about twenty minutes, maybe half an hour if you can hang on that long. Why don't you find the nearest coffee shop and wait for me? Maybe we could run away together?'

A queue, forming for the bus that had just pulled up near the phone box, caught Dora's eye.

'No need. There's a bus leaving for Keelside any minute now. If you meet me at the bus station your end I'll buy you a doughnut.'

Jon laughed. 'Right. Okay, I'll be there. See you soon.'

Dora grinned and hung up. It had been years since she'd taken a bus ride anywhere.

* * *

In his cool, tidy kitchen, Lawrence Rawlings glared at his daughter, Sarah, across the scrub-top table.

'We're fresh out of backsides to lick and babies to kiss,' he snapped, as Sarah slipped the cakes she had bought from the bring and buy sale into the freezer. 'I can't believe you invited Guy Phelps and his family for lunch.' Sarah's high heels tapped anxiously across the flagstone floor.

Through the open back door, Lawrence could hear his granddaughters playing in the garden. Calvin had dropped them off on the way back to his office. Sarah said Calvin had to nip in to check the answer machine and the fax. Lawrence had already prepared himself to drive Sarah and the girls home – no doubt something important would come up that would detain Calvin for the rest of the day. Lawrence could feel a phone call from his son-in-law coming on, which did nothing to improve his mood.

Across the kitchen, Sarah glanced up at him. Her eyes were bright. She bit her lips and looked away. Lawrence knew he had upset her and was cross with himself for being unnecessarily sharp.

'You should have told me that you didn't like him, Daddy. I wouldn't have invited them if I'd known. Would you like me to ring up and suggest Calvin and I take them out for lunch instead?'

Lawrence shook his head. 'A little too late now, isn't it? Besides, we'd have had to have him to lunch sooner or later, I suppose.'

He glanced at his housekeeper, who had already begun preparations for the following day's lunch. A trussed sumo-sized cockerel was crouched in a roasting dish on the marble slab next to the stove. Its gaping sage-and-onion-stuffed backside wore an expression that he knew was much like his own – sulky and hard done by. He certainly wasn't going to be deprived of his daughter's company for the sake of a moron like Guy Phelps.

'When you said you'd invited a few friends I thought you meant that nice girl from Ludworth and her husband, charming man, GP, wasn't he? Or the Bibbys from Parson's Drove – they are wonderfully good company.'

Lawrence's Sunday lunches were an institution. Every week, Calvin, Sarah and the girls arrived in time for church and stayed to eat, though Calvin had been absent several times just recently, blaming pressure of work.

Old family friends had a standing invitation, ringing only to tell Lawrence if they weren't coming. There was Vic Hill, the mayor, Bob Preston, former mayor and ex-chairman of the Chamber of Trade, who had come almost every Sunday since he'd been widowed, Joan Peters, the Plowrights, Harry Morton and his wife, Norma – usually around a dozen sat down to lunch plus the children.

They were all members of a self-selected inner circle, all from good families, all friends who had grown up together in Fairbeach. Bob Preston had played as a fullback in the Fairbeach Rugby Club when Lawrence had played at flyhalf and been captain. Vic Hill had been a terrific spin bowler, Lawrence a fine batsman. Harry Morton and Lawrence still played the occasional round of golf. Old friends. Good friends.

Jack Rees had been a regular visitor for years when Sarah was small, and Lawrence's wife was still alive. Later, when he could find the time and was able to disentangle himself from the bitch he was married to, Jack would gatecrash, grinning, shamefaced at not having rung first, clutching a bottle of something very good and very, very drinkable.

Lawrence sniffed and stared at the pale, pimpled pink corpse in the roasting tin. He would really miss Jack Rees.

Sarah was very quiet, tidying away the carrier bags, tucking them, neatly folded, into the drawer of the Welsh dresser.

Lawrence forced a smile. 'Don't look so glum, darling. It'll be fine, take no notice of me. You know what a grumpy old devil I can be. Here.' He slipped his arm around her waist and kissed her forehead, then held her at arm's length and with all the comic, pompous, overworked indignation he could muster added, 'Just make sure you don't ever invite the conniving little bastard again.'

Sarah laughed.

It was worth it to make her happy, even if it did spoil one of his precious Sundays.

'Why don't we have a pot of tea, Daddy, and a slice of this sponge?'

'Wonderful.' Lawrence adjusted his cuffs, glancing surreptitiously at his watch. He thought Calvin would have rung by now to make some excuse why he couldn't pick up Sarah and the girls. Sarah plugged in the kettle.

This Sunday would be doubly unpleasant; Calvin Roberts would undoubtedly be there. Lawrence much preferred it when his son-in-law didn't turn up, however lame the excuse. He hated sharing his daughter with that greasy little social climber, though he understood Calvin's absences upset Sarah. It meant Lawrence was constantly torn between being pleased for himself and annoyed for her. But this Sunday would be different, nothing short of an earthquake would keep Calvin Roberts away. He certainly wouldn't want to miss the chance to suck up to Guy Phelps. They would make a good pair.

Lawrence smiled, accepted the slice of cake his daughter offered him and settled himself in a Windsor chair beside the Aga. In the distance the phone began to ring. His housekeeper dried her hands on her apron as she strode purposefully across the kitchen towards the hall. Lawrence noticed that his daughter avoided meeting his eyes as she made the tea, while her hands betrayed the slightest tremor.

'That was Mr Roberts,' the housekeeper said, as she came back in. 'He says something has come up and he won't be back until later this evening. He wanted to know if it would be possible for you to run Miss Sarah home?'

Lawrence lifted an eyebrow. 'Is Mr Roberts still on the line?' he asked slowly.

His housekeeper shook her head. 'No, he said he was very sorry but he had to dash.'

Lawrence sniffed. Hardly any point Calvin framing his request as a question, he thought. He smiled up at Sarah, whose concentration appeared to be centred on stirring the tea leaves.

'Why don't you and the girls stay to supper?' he suggested brightly. 'I'm sure we can whip up something, and then I'll run you home later. No reason why you should be in that great big house all on your own waiting for . . .' He hesitated, his mind carefully stepping over the words he used to describe Calvin Roberts in his private thoughts. '. . . Calvin,' he concluded.

Sarah's face brightened. 'That would be lovely. I'll go and tell the girls.'

8

Dora was shaken awake and for a few seconds had absolutely no idea where she was. She blinked, fishing around for the thoughts that would give her the answer. The bus from Fairbeach lumbered down another gear and juddered over a second sleeping policeman before creeping across the tarmac into a parking bay. The diesel engine shuddered to a halt. Dora, staring out of the mud-streaked windows, realised the bus was in Keelside station and for some reason she was on it, and had been asleep.

The inside of her mouth felt like an old sock. She licked her lips and sucked experimentally at her tongue. Her neck ached and one arm had gone to sleep where she had been leaning against the window. It was not exactly the arrival Dora would have planned. She knew instinctively, even without a mirror, that her hair had scrunched up on one side into a guinea-pig quiff. Worse still, Jon Melrose was standing just outside the window peering in at her with a great big grin on his face. He looked gorgeous and immaculate.

She sniffed and rootled in her handbag, trying to track down a mint and her composure. From the corner of her eye she could see Jon climbing aboard the bus.

'Hello, madam. Before you say anything, I should warn you I'm an off-duty police officer – are you the woman who's planning to run away?'

Dora looked up. 'That's me.'

She wasn't sure what to do. Did they shake hands, kiss? He solved the problem for her by leaning forward and kissing her on the lips, very softly.

'Hello,' he murmured. 'Nice to see you,' and kissed her again.

She grinned, Jon reddened slightly. 'Do you mind?' he asked. Dora shook her head. 'Not at all. I owe you a doughnut.'

He took her hand, and Dora was suddenly very glad she had telephoned him.

'I wondered, as you're on the run, whether you might like to come back to my place? We can pick up doughnuts or maybe a take-away on the way there,' said Jon casually, as they walked hand-in-hand towards the shopping precinct that adjoined the bus station.

Dora lifted an eyebrow. 'Are you propositioning me?'

Jon grinned. 'Could be. I'd be a liar if I said the thought hadn't crossed my mind. Want to tell me why you want to run away?'

'Not another confessional? Are you sure you want to hear?' Jon nodded.

'Well, Lillian Bliss is still in residence in my flat. I've just been to a bring and buy with my sister – which reminds me, I've got some fudge and Turkish delight here, somewhere – going anywhere with Sheila is always an experience, and to top it all I was accosted by a reporter from the *Fairbeach Gazette* looking for Catiana Moran. She wanted to know about Lillian Bliss. Just as I was about to sidestep the question, Calvin Roberts turned up. You get the picture? I'd understand if you didn't, it looks pretty murky from this side.' She paused. 'It's been an odd sort of day, really. Do you think I might be overreacting?'

They were sauntering through the shopping arcade. The day was slowing down. Crowds had broken up into couples and families meandering along in the spring sunshine, window shopping.

Jon was still holding her hand. 'So you thought you'd ring me?'

Dora nodded. 'I was brought up to believe if you've got a problem, ask a policeman. Or was it if you wanted to know the time, ask a policeman?' She grinned up at him. 'I wanted to talk to you. I needed to say something sensible to someone sane.'

Jon didn't seem to have noticed that she looked like a sleepy guinea pig. Instead he turned and smiled at her.

'I'm glad you called, whatever the reason,' he said, with a pleasantly intense look in his eyes. His fingers tightened a fraction and Dora had a peculiar sense of being part of something complete. His hand in hers felt so wonderful that it made her heart go tight and bubbly, and she knew she ought to shut up, because this much euphoria would probably make her say something incredibly stupid. She knew a sure-fire cure for all this romanticism.

'But you rang me up to talk about Lillian Bliss?' she asked.

Jon groaned theatrically. 'Are you sure you need anything else to think about? We can talk about it another time, if you like. After you hear this you might consider running a bit further.'

Dora shrugged. 'I'm from the generation that thinks it's better to get the bad things over first. So, tell me, what did you ring about?'

Jon lifted his shoulders, as if offering her an apology before he said anything. 'On a hunch I ran Lillian's details and the fingerprints we picked up from her flat through our computer.' He paused, and then hurried on as if he was concerned his courage might evaporate. 'She's got a record for soliciting that goes back to before she left school. She was in care from the time she was a little kid, comes from near Norwich, and has been working fairly recently. She does the odd modelling and promotion jobs as well but . . .' His voice faded.

Dora turned and stared at him, letting go of his hand, mouth open. '"Working"? That delicate little euphemism for being on the game? Are you telling me Lillian Bliss is . . .' She couldn't bring herself to find the word.

Jon supplied it. 'Lillian Bliss is a known prostitute. She's done a little bit of club work here and there, hostessing –' He stopped again. 'Last time she was busted was last summer in Yarmouth during a Wildfowlers convention.'

Dora couldn't quite find any words or thoughts that fitted.

She stared at him. 'Are you telling me that Calvin hired a hooker to promote my books?'

Jon nodded.

'And that at this moment she is staying in my flat?'

Jon nodded again.

Dora opened her handbag and started to trawl through the contents.

Jon stared at her. 'What on earth are you doing?'

Dora snorted. 'Looking for that fudge. I'm trying to give up smoking. In moments of dire emergency I take to comfort foods and need a lot of understanding.'

Jon pulled a cigarette packet out of his jacket pocket. 'Want one?'

Dora stared at his open hand and then sighed. 'Okay, why not.'

They found a café behind the church and Jon ordered two coffees, while Dora stared thoughtfully at the fancy continental half-mast nets in the window.

'I've got to convince Calvin that he has to get rid of her,' Dora said, drawing a line across the froth on the top of her cup with a spoon. 'I've got no idea what sort of contract he's got her on.'

Jon nodded. 'I think it's a good idea – and really, the sooner the better.' He stopped. 'I also think it may explain why you, Calvin and then Lillian were burgled.'

'Meaning?'

Jon shrugged. 'We have got no way of knowing who Lillian has links with, who she's slept with, what she's done. She goes on TV and someone recognises her. And let's face it, she isn't exactly tight-lipped.' He stopped again. 'That's my policeman's instinct, but there are other possibilities.'

Dora stared at him. 'Such as?'

'Think about the letters you got. Feminists, Evangelists, perverts? Could be any one of them, someone who is interested in what Catiana Moran is up to, never mind what Lillian's done in real life.'

Dora could feel her colour draining. 'And there was me

thinking I was just paranoid. Would you mind if I had another one of those cigarettes?' she said in a small voice.

Jon shook one out of the packet and handed her the lighter. Dora took a deep pull on the cigarette.

'This afternoon, when I was leaving the flat, I'm certain someone was watching me.'

Jon nodded without comment.

Dora rolled the ash off the end of the cigarette. 'I want my life back, Jon.'

'It might be a good idea, once Lillian has left, to take a holiday. Have a few days away.'

Dora grinned. 'Is that an invitation?'

Jon stirred his coffee. 'I'm serious. People like that reporter from the *Gazette* might lose interest if there's no-one around to answer her questions. She'll get bored.'

Dora looked at him sceptically. 'I don't think so. Josephine Hammond's got her sights set on something better than the *Fairbeach Gazette*. She smells a big story, and I think she'll hang on until she gets what she wants.'

Outside the light was beginning to fade. Jon drained his coffee cup. 'Would you like to come back and eat?'

Dora smiled. 'You cook?'

'After a fashion.' He ran a finger across the back of her hand. 'I'm afraid my place isn't very spectacular.'

'You've seen my flat.'

Jon pulled a face. 'That is true. You'll feel right at home.' He waved the waitress over to settle the bill. 'It isn't far. We can walk from here.'

Dora stubbed out her cigarette. A little flutter of panic glowed low down in her stomach. It was mixed with a flickering sense of desire. She wasn't sure which would win and realised that she didn't much care.

Jon indicated the door. 'Would you mind if we just nipped to Sainsbury's? I need to get a French stick and some salad.'

Dora stood to one side and waved him through. 'I'm very impressed. After you. Far be it from me to stand between a man and his shopping.'

Jon's house was tucked away in a little back street, ten minutes' walk from the town centre, and from the outside looked old, dusty and not particularly inviting. Dora had bought wine; Jon, bread, cheese and grapes and the makings of a decent salad. Dora realised as Jon fumbled with the lock that getting wine implied drinking, which meant that Jon wouldn't be able to drive her home, which could mean anything.

She shuffled nervously from foot to foot, glancing up and down the street.

'Come on in,' said Jon, hanging his jacket over the newel post at the bottom of the stairs just inside the door. Beside the staircase, the hall stretched back into shadow. He held out his hand to take her jacket.

The hall was decorated in sage green wallpaper with tiny cream flowers. Dora assumed it had been there when Jon moved in. The floors were stripped varnished boards, with a cluster of dust bunnies nestling up against the skirting. The house smelt of men.

Jon pointed into the gloom. 'Sitting room here on the left. Dining room, next door. Down the bottom is the kitchen. Loo out through the back. Shall we go and dump the shopping?'

Carrier bags in hand, Dora followed him into the shadows. The kitchen seemed pleasantly familiar: battered pine units, a row of crockery, washed but not dried, standing on the draining board. A kitchen table with an ashtray, letters, newspapers – all of which looked as if they had been quickly shuffled into tidiness before Dora had arrived. The room had a sense of being made up of mismatched oddments. And Jon was right, Dora felt totally at home. She pulled out a chair near the kitchen table while Jon packed away the odds and ends of shopping.

'Do you want me to help you cook whatever it is we're going to eat?'

Jon grinned. 'Er, no, I don't think I do. I'm not sure how I'm going to get on with someone watching me.'

'I could close my eyes if you like.'

Jon shook the kettle experimentally. 'Would you like some more coffee?'

Dora nodded then shook her head. 'No, not really, but we have to keep this conversation going somehow.' She stood up and thrust her hands into her trouser pockets, looking out of the dusty windows into the little courtyard beyond.

'We're supposed to make small talk now, aren't we. I'm supposed to say what a nice place you've got here, and you are supposed to make humble but happy noises, and offer to show me the rest of the house and –' She turned. 'Would you mind very much if we cut that out and went hammer and tongs at a few real conversations? And the other thing is, would you mind very much if I had a cuddle?'

Jon stood the carrier bag back on the unit and stepped towards her. He slid his arms around her and she lay her head on his chest. She could hear his heart beating and smell the soft masculine smell of his body under the aftershave he was wearing. He felt warm and strong and she shivered as he held her tight against him.

Dora realised, with an intense wave of pain, that it had been far too long since she had held anyone in her arms. The thought solidified into a lump in the back of her throat. While her mind was full of excuses and anxieties and random thoughts, her body moved instinctively against Jon's and she struggled to hold back the tears.

Desire mingled with tenderness; she took a deep breath as the feeling grabbed hold. Surely this was supposed to happen far more slowly, when she felt calmer, and had thought it all through. She couldn't let herself free fall into something she wasn't ready for – whatever her body said it wanted.

She looked up into Jon's eyes. 'That feels so much better,' she murmured, in an undertone and pulled away quickly.

Jon grinned. 'Do you know, you're absolutely terrifying?'

Dora pulled a face. 'Really?'

He nodded and then kissed her, softly, mouth working against hers, sliding his tongue between her lips in an exquisite electrifying enquiry.

Dora felt her stomach back flip and every cell, every molecule, seemed to be alight and tingling. She struggled to breathe. It felt as though her whole consciousness centred on the places where their bodies touched. Returning his kiss with equal fervour, she thought she might just drown.

The phone rang as Dora slid her hand up under Jon's tee shirt. Touching his muscular warm back made her mouth water. It rang just as his kiss had become more insistent and she felt his hands sliding to caress her spine, tugging gently at her shirt. It rang just as she felt that there was nothing that could stop them – and it kept on ringing.

Jon stepped back, gasping. 'I really ought to get that.'

Dora nodded, afraid to speak. She turned away as he hurried out into the hall, and stared out of the windows. Outside was a little sunlit courtyard built with soft golden bricks around urns and a wooden bench and table. Her mind drank in the details instantly, almost like ballast, as if taking in the greens and gold of the variegated ivy would help her regain her equilibrium.

She swallowed hard and clutched at the edge of the kitchen sink. Wasn't the strong voice of reason and morality supposed to make itself heard about now? Didn't she ought to be asking herself what the hell she was doing? Dora plugged the kettle in and took two mugs off the rack. Morality and reason seemed to be remarkably quiet; perhaps they had Saturdays off.

Out in the hall, Jon tucked the phone under his chin.

'Hello, Jon Melrose?'

He expected to hear Rhodes, his detective sergeant, or someone from the station.

'Hello, Jon, it's me.' His ex-wife Nita's voice hit him in the solar plexus like a clenched fist.

'Nita?' he said, struggling to sound normal.

'I'm really sorry to ring, Jon. I tried to ring you at the station, they told me you were at home.'

He'd felt his gut contract. 'What is it? Is anything wrong?' He knew by the tone of her voice there was.

Nita had taken a deep unsteady breath. 'It's Joe, he's been knocked off his bike and broken his arm. We're over at the hospital. I thought you would want to know.'

'Is he all right?' Jon tried hard to swallow down the dizzy coppery taste of fear as he waited for more information about his son.

Nita's voice cracked. 'Yes, yes, just broken his arm and got a lot of cuts and bruises.' Her fear had started to gain momentum. 'Oh, Jon, he frightened the life out of me. We're at the General in Keelside. They're going to set his arm under anaesthetic. He's in theatre at the moment.' The tears bubbled up behind the words. 'Oh, Jon. Please come –'

Jon made soft comforting noises, trying very hard to be the strong one. As he spoke, all he could imagine was Joe's small muscular body lying on a stretcher. 'Where's Sam?'

Nita groaned. 'It's so crazy,' she snuffled miserably. 'For the first time since we've been together he's had to go in to work this afternoon. They had a breakdown at the factory. I've been trying to ring him, but there's no-one on the switchboard at weekends.'

Jon nodded. 'It's all right, don't worry. I can get someone from the station to go over there and pick him up for you. Where's Anna?' An image of his daughter, a bright shiny clone of Nita, flashed momentarily in front of his eyes.

'I left her with the people next door. I thought you ought to know, Jon –'

He spoke gently. 'You're right. I can be there in a few minutes. Is that okay?'

Nita's voice finally gave way under the emotion. 'I'm so sorry,' she sobbed.

When he finally laid the phone down, he glanced back into the kitchen. Dora Hall was making coffee, her small frame neatly arranged in a soft cream shirt and corn-coloured cords. She looked incredibly desirable. He moaned softly, with a head full of paradox.

*   *   *

When Jon came back through the door he looked distracted and, Dora thought, almost surprised that she was still there. He was clutching his jacket in one hand.

Dora stared at him. 'What is it?'

Jon seemed to struggle to find any words. 'It's my son, Joe, he's been in a car accident. I've got to get over to the hospital and meet Nita there. She couldn't get hold of Sam, he's at work. She came over in the ambulance –'

He looked at her, and then the remnants of the shopping still in bags on the table. 'I . . . what about?'

Dora held up her hands. 'You just go. Will you be all right to drive? '

Jon nodded, patting his pockets to find the car keys.

Dora smiled. 'Right, you go. I can pack the rest of these things away.'

Jon returned the smile gratefully. 'I've got no idea how long I'll be.'

But Dora was already guiding him out of the door. 'It really doesn't matter. Ring me when you get back, it doesn't matter what time it is.'

At the front door he turned towards her. 'I'm really sorry about this –'

Dora waved him away. 'Don't be so daft. I'll drop the catch when I leave. Have you got your house keys?'

He nodded and then stroked her cheek. Dora felt her heart soft-shoe a couple of beats. He leant closer and brushed her lips again.

'Thank you,' he said softly, and hurried across the road to his car. Dora watched until the car had turned out of the end of the road before she went back inside again.

She packed away the cheese, and the wine, and the grapes, and stacked the salad in the crisper box in the bottom of the fridge, then picked up her bag, and her jacket, and walked back to the bus station. Who needed the voice of reason and morality when you had fate on hand to protect you from yourself?

*　　*　　*

Jon was relieved that the traffic was in its early-evening lull. He drew into the police parking bay by the main door of Keelside General and hurried inside. He saw Nita sitting, cradling a plastic cup, in the waiting area. In the same instant she looked up and saw him. Her face was bleached white by anxiety, eyes framed raw red. He felt something lurch inside him, and hurried towards her.

'Jon?'

He opened his arms instinctively.

'Oh, Jon. I'm so glad you could come.' She sounded breathless and he felt her tears through his shirt. As she held him tight, he tried to convince himself that the immediate gut-wrenching pain of seeing her, and knowing that she was sleeping with someone else, had long since faded to a silvery scar that only ached in wet weather.

'I've sent a car to pick Sam up. How's Joe doing?'

She looked up at him, still smelling of her favourite perfume that he remembered the name of. Jon bit his lip – sometimes the scar gave him a twinge even when it was dry.

'He's doing really well, considering what he's been through. He's still in theatre. They told me he'll be a while yet. The nurse said I ought to get a cup of something.'

'Right,' said Jon, guiding her back towards the tables. 'How did it happen?'

Nita sniffed, and managed a grin. 'Always on duty?'

Jon felt a stab of annoyance. 'No,' he said quietly.

'There was a whole gang of them out for a bike ride. Joe didn't look what he was doing and went out between two parked cars. The chap driving didn't stand a chance. Fortunately he was looking for a house along the avenue and was going really slowly.' She stopped and pushed a strand of blonde hair back behind her ears. 'Would you like a cup of tea?'

Jon nodded, and watched as the woman whose body he knew nearly as well as his own hurried across to the serving area. When she came back she looked more composed.

'We'll go back up in a minute if you like.'

Jon thanked her for the drink. He felt awkward. 'How are things, then?'

Nita smiled, wiping her face with the back of her hand.

'Not so bad until today.' She paused. 'I'm not sure whether this is quite the place to tell you, but I suppose it's as good as anywhere.' She took a deep breath, exhaling slowly. 'Sam has asked me to marry him. I was going to ring to tell you myself, before you heard it on the grapevine.' She paused for a split second, her face flushing with excitement in the way he remembered.

Jon nodded dumbly. What was there to say? He glanced down at the table and then across at her. Her face was still unfortunately familiar.

'Congratulations,' he said, as warmly as he could manage. 'Tell Sam from me that he's a very lucky man.'

Nita suddenly smiled and grabbed hold of his hand. 'Thank you, thank you. I knew you'd be pleased for us.'

The expression of delight and happiness was short-lived. As it faded, she ran her fingers back through her hair. He knew she was itching for a cigarette, and almost suggested they went out into the crisp spring air to share one, then remembered she'd given up because Sam didn't smoke.

'Oh, Jon,' she cried abruptly, in a thick, tear-soaked voice. 'It's been the most terrible day. I am really glad you're here.'

Jon Melrose coughed uncomfortably, pushing himself away from the table.

'It's all right,' he blustered, trying to hide the mixed bag of emotions that threatened to drive away the veneer of reasonableness he had cultivated. He was surprised how hard it was to take his eyes off her, trying to fight the shadow images of taking her in his arms, trying to forget the way her body smelt when she was warm and soft and his.

'Shall we go up to the ward?' he asked in a carefully controlled voice.

Nita glanced at the table. 'You haven't touched your drink.'
Jon shrugged.

Dora Hall wasn't the only one who felt that their life had run away from them.

They were wheeling Joe back from the operating room at the same moment as Sam arrived. Jon felt awkward, but no more awkward than Sam, who bustled in frantically, still dressed in his dirty overalls. He smiled at Jon and thanked him profusely. His hands dropped to Nita's shoulders. Their easy familiarity made Jon flinch. Beside them, Joe lay asleep, an angel with freckles amongst the pure white bed linen.

Jon wanted to be there for Joe and yet be gone. The conflict made him uncomfortable. He finally compromised by making a great show of promising to be back when Joe woke up and finished with unsteady congratulations to Sam and Nita.

Backing away from the bed, feeling like an idiot, he suddenly wanted to say something about Dora. He felt a need to show them that love wasn't their unique experience, but now wasn't the time, and he knew he would be saying it spitefully, tit for tat. As he looked back from the ward door, Sam had his arms around Nita. His ex-wife was hunched over the bed, stroking Joe's curls back from his pallid face. Jon was touched and at the same time annoyed and couldn't reconcile either emotion.

Downstairs, he bought another drink in the café and then glanced at the phone, wondering whether he should ring Dora. Jon pressed his fingers to his aching temples and then dialled his home number first, just in case she had decided to stay and wait for him.

After twenty rings he tapped in the Fairbeach number. The answering machine took him by surprise, and he was half way through his first warm hello before the metallic recorded voice announced that no-one was at home, and if he'd like to leave a message he knew what to do after the tone.

Jon wasn't sure what it was he wanted to say so he stammered another shaky hello, before adding, 'Joe is okay. I'll ring you soon.' He wanted to add that he needed to hear the sound of her voice but it sounded so idiotic he stopped himself and hung up.

He was about to leave when Sam came over to the table.

'I'm really glad you're still here, Jon. I'm just nipping home to see that Anna is okay.' Sam spoke flatly and then extended his hand. 'Thanks for coming so quickly and getting the message to me, mate. We're both really grateful.'

Jon forced a smile. The 'we' Sam used so casually brushed another tiny splinter of pain. It wouldn't do to tell someone as nice as Sam that his welfare had had nothing to do with it. Jon had wanted to make sure Joe was okay, and Joe needed Nita to be okay too.

Sam smiled. 'Joe's awake now if you'd like to go up and see him.'

Jon nodded his thanks, and waited until Sam disappeared through the double doors before he headed back upstairs to the ward.

He watched Nita from the door. He was relieved to see her looking relieved. She glanced up as he made his way to the bed. Joe grinned at him, eyes unfocused from the effects of the anaèsthetic.

Coyly, Nita dropped her gaze. 'I think I'll just nip downstairs for a little while, Joe. It'll give you a chance to talk to your dad,' she said, rooting for her purse in her handbag.

Jon pulled up another chair alongside the bed of his only son and grinned.

'So, how's it going, Joe? How are you feeling?'

The boy reached up unsteadily to take Jon's hands with his unplastered fingers, and then sighed. 'I didn't mean to do it, Dad,' he said, watching Nita's retreating form. 'It was an accident. Mum said I can't ride my bike any more.'

Jon was about to say he would have a word with her, but Joe was still talking, sounding slightly drunk. 'Sam said he'd speak to her about it. He said women are like that, they worry a lot. You know they're getting married, don't you? Sam said accidents are just part of growing up. Sam said . . .'

Jon tucked his chair in tighter to the bedside and listened while his son demolished the last remaining fragments of his life with Nita.

9

By the time Dora got back to Gunners Terrace her feet ached, she was tired, and it was dark. The bus had stopped at every single bus stop on the way from Keelside to Fairbeach and taken in every back lane, backwater and back of beyond village en route.

Grimly fantasising about soaking in a long, hot bath, Dora hurried past the dry cleaners and the corner shop, slowing under the street light to get her keys out of her jacket pocket before crossing into the terrace.

As she rounded the corner and stepped into the road, the sensation that someone was watching her progress crept over her like a chilling mist. She resisted the temptation to look round and instead swallowed down the bubble of panic, slid the key into the door and stepped in the lobby, locking the door behind her and sliding the bolt across.

It had been so long since the bolt had been moved it groaned unhappily as she struggled to push it into place. In the darkness out beyond the street light was a shiver of movement. Dora pressed herself up against the far wall in the deepest shadow and stared into the gloom.

Jon had asked the local police to keep an eye on the flat; perhaps it was them. She kept looking, willing herself to see into the shadows. Whoever it was stayed tucked back against a wall where one of the houses stepped forward to form a niche.

After a few seconds Dora took a deep breath and felt the tension begin to ease. She must have been mistaken – there was no-one there. Turning and about to climb the stairs, there was a tiny flash of light on the periphery of her vision. She swung round, staring down its origins. Across the street, in the angle of the wall, she could just make out the glow of a cigarette tip. She watched for a few seconds, hypnotised by the way the tiny devil's eye of red light grew more intense as the watcher watched, taking deep pulls on his cigarette.

Dora closed her eyes, breaking the spell, and walked slowly up the stairs, not looking back again, trying hard not to think about anything except for getting the flat door open, and stepping safely inside.

She called out as she unlocked the door.

'Hello? Lillian?'

There was no reply, just the slightest smell of cigar smoke and from the kitchen an unhappy mewling. Dora slipped off her jacket and called again.

'Lillian, are you there?'

She opened the kitchen door first. Oscar shot out like a furry bullet, complaining bitterly, furious at having been shut in.

Dora felt the hairs on her neck lifting. From the hall stand she picked up an umbrella and opened the office door. Inside, nothing stirred except the flashing light on the answering machine, announcing a message. From outside, the glow of the street light peered in through the tiny window.

She resisted the temptation to look down into the terrace below or press the playback button, and stepped out into the hall.

Walking with calm, deliberate steps she opened the sitting-room door, backing away so that she was prepared for whatever might be inside.

On the sofa, looking angelic and sound asleep, Lillian Bliss lay curled up under a duvet, her red-blonde hair spun into a halo around her face. Dora sighed, feeling the tension dropping away.

In the corner of the sitting room the TV was on, with the volume turned down, colours like lightning flashes illuminating the sleeping girl's perfect features.

Dora scooped Oscar up into her arms. The smell of cigar smoke was more intense in the sitting room. Dora picked up the ashtray on the coffee table. There was only one person she knew who regularly smoked cigars and from the number of butts in the ashtray, Calvin Roberts had stayed some time.

The door opening must have disturbed Lillian. She sat up slowly, stretching, blinking. She painted on a beautiful smile and looked at Dora.

'Hello, did you bring something nice home too?'

Dora stared at her, wondering if Lillian had been dreaming. 'Sorry?'

Lillian stretched again. She looked like an erotic Goldilocks. 'A lady came round this afternoon and left some home-made cakes, then Calvin came round and brought fish and chips.' She looked expectantly at Dora.

'I've got some fudge.'

Lillian's eyes lit up. 'Oh, I love fudge.'

Dora lifted an eyebrow. 'What a surprise. Would you like a cup of tea?'

Lillian smiled her reply.

Dora was relieved to be in the kitchen, bossed around by Oscar. She opened a can of cat food and switched on the little black-and-white TV for company. Its flickering images might just take her mind off the man watching her in the street, the messages on the answer machine and Lillian Bliss – a known prostitute – dozing in the sitting room. She plugged in the kettle and then stretched across to turn up the volume on the TV.

'Good evening,' said the presenter. 'Tonight we have a really exciting programme lined up for you.'

Dora yawned. She doubted it was anywhere near as exciting as her life.

'In our studio with Gary Ellis we've got Fairbeach by-election candidates Freda Haleworthy, Guy Phelps and Tom Fielding lined up for a debate, and from our outside broadcast team . . .'

Dora looked away, interest fading. On the kitchen table was the cold greasy corpse of a fish supper and several cellophane and paper bags with remains of cakes in them. Sheila – Dora didn't even want to think about it. She cut herself a slice of pineapple upside-down cake and pulled out a chair. She needed a chance to catch her breath.

On the little screen they were showing a close-up of Guy Phelps' boyish features. 'I firmly believe in a return to old-fashioned morality,' he said, with great emphasis.

Across the debating table one of the other candidates, the Lib Dem man, Tom Fielding, tried to interrupt. Guy Phelps held up his hand and pressed on. 'No, no, let me finish, Tom, I know it's not a fashionable stance, and I'm certain there will be people at home who say . . .'

Tom Fielding managed to interrupt him with a rumble of good-natured laughter.

'There'll be a lot of people, Guy, who'll rightly say it's all been done before. It's an old tub to thump. Surely the Tories have to be very careful about standing on a morality platform. Remember Back to Basics? That was a complete farce. Look what happened when . . .'

Before he had a chance to finish his sentence the woman candidate leapt in. 'Do we have to rake through the past yet again? Surely we ought to be considering the issues. I want to talk about the things that genuinely concern the rural elec-torate of Fairbeach. New Labour . . .'

Bored, Dora made the tea and went into the office to listen to her messages while it brewed.

Jon's message asking her to call him was first.

Kate, her daughter, was next. 'Hello, Mum? I was a bit worried that we hadn't heard from you. I rang Dad. I know you said not to, but I thought . . .' Dora groaned.

Her ex-husband, Ray, was next. He sounded crisp and uneasy, as if she might just reach down the line and grab him.

'Ray here. Kate said you were having a few problems. Er, if you want to ring me . . .' Dora rolled her eyes heavenwards. 'I just rang to say that if you want anything, well, you know.'

She did, and fought the temptation to turn the machine off. It had been such a long time since she had heard Ray's voice that it was almost like hearing the dead speak. She hadn't seen him since Kate's wedding, but by that time, Dora had moved on so far that when she first saw Ray, standing outside the church, she hadn't recognised him for a few seconds.

It had shocked her so much that she couldn't concentrate on the service. Instead she had stared fixedly at the pulpit, trying to visualise the time when every curl, every line of his face had been etched on her retina like a bad case of arc eye.

She had sat in the front pew, watching the congregation from one corner of her eye as Ray had slid in beside her, assuming that he would have brought someone to emphasise their separation, and play step-mother of the bride. To her surprise he had arrived alone, very stiff, very upright in a dreadful checked suit. He'd told her at the reception – when he'd had several scotches – that he had never found anyone quite like her. She had smiled and sipped her orange juice.

When her daughter, Kate, was small, she had played a game, 'You are my most favourite little Kate in the whole wide world,' until the time Kate got the joke, and realised that as there was only one, she could only ever be the best and the most favourite. Ray's stilted drunken speech had sounded incredibly reminiscent of their game.

Kate would never tell Dora if Ray was seeing someone else, which made Dora think he was (and that Kate was trying to hide it from her) or that he wasn't (and that Kate didn't want Dora to feel sorry for him) by turns. Now she realised, hearing his voice, she didn't really care. He'd bought a house near Kate, but last time she'd heard he was working in Dubai. Rich now, no doubt, she thought treacherously.

Sheila's message was preceded by an imperious sniff. 'I left the cakes. You owe me two pounds sixty. The girl there didn't offer to give me the money, so I didn't ask –' There was a weighty pause. 'I didn't know you'd got a lodger. Student, is she? I didn't like to come in.'

Dora's stomach tightened. She couldn't believe that Sheila hadn't recognised Lillian Bliss as Catiana Moran, it was completely out of character. Sheila didn't usually miss a trick. Dora considered it a very lucky break, and then a miracle, and then a total impossibility. Something was wrong.

Sheila's message was followed by Jon again. He sounded tense and very alone.

Calvin next, abrupt and to the point. 'Dora, sorry I missed you. Will you remind Lillian that she's due in Peterborough tomorrow morning. I've arranged for a car to pick her up at eight thirty.' His was the last message.

Dora picked up the receiver to ring Jon back when she remembered the tea. No harm in making her lodger sing for her supper. 'Lillian?'

A few seconds later, a pale wide-eyed face appeared around the door. 'Yes?'

'Would you mind pouring the tea? Oh, and Calvin rang to say you're being picked up at eight thirty tomorrow.' As Dora was speaking the phone clicked once, twice and then burred. Dora glanced at the receiver and then tapped it against the desk.

'I've been asked to open a mucky book shop,' Lillian said, with a cherubic grin.

Dora stared at her. 'On a Sunday morning?' she said incredulously.

Lillian nodded. 'Yeah, apparently they do a lot of trade when people go to get their papers.' She pointed to the phone. 'Is it still making a funny sort of humming noise?' As she spoke, she tied the belt of her silk dressing gown a little tighter.

Dora was about to nod, when she realised that Lillian was wearing blood-red stilettos and black silk stockings. The robe was so sheer that the outline of her suspenders was clearly visible through the silk. Dora had a fleeting and very intense vision of Sheila's face, Sheila's voice and a pineapple upside-down sponge . . .

'Were you dressed like that when the lady with the cakes arrived?' Dora asked, as lightly as she could.

Lillian pouted and pulled her features into a thoughtful expression. Dora wondered if every thought she had was accompanied by such effort. 'No, I'd just had a bath and washed my hair. I'd got that robe on you lent me, you know,

131

the fluffy one? And my hair up in a topknot. I wondered who it was kept ringing like that.'

Dora nodded. Sheila saw every closed door as a personal challenge. 'And what did you say to her?'

'I didn't get a chance to say anything.'

It had been a miracle after all.

Lillian twisted a tendril of blonde hair into a corkscrew. 'Did you say the tea was made?'

Dora nodded. 'Would you mind pouring it? I've just got to make a phone call.'

Lillian agreed happily. 'Do you take sugar?'

Dora closed the office door after Lillian brought in the tea and tapped in Jon's home number. As she waited for Jon to answer she wondered why Calvin was ringing her to arrange for Lillian to be picked up? Hadn't he been there during the afternoon – and anyway, didn't Lillian's forty-eight hour deadline expire on Sunday?

Jon answered on the fourth ring.

'Hiya. How are you?' she said.

'Dora?'

She heard the pleasure in his voice and felt a little flurry of delight. 'I've just listened to your messages. How's your little boy getting on?'

Jon sighed. 'Fine, they've set his arm and other than that he's just got a few cuts and bruises. Amazing really, and incredibly lucky. Mind you, Joe's like that. The hospital are keeping him in overnight for observation but they think he's going to be fine.'

There was very little relief in Jon's voice; if anything, he sounded as if he was in great pain.

'Are you okay?' she asked in a soft voice. 'You don't sound too good.'

Jon snorted. 'No, you're right. It's been a rough afternoon.' He paused, his tone lifting a little. 'I was hoping you might still be here when I got back.'

Dora glanced up at the clock on her office wall. 'I did think about staying, but I thought you might feel pressured if you

knew I was hanging around. Would you like to come over –'
She hesitated, suddenly remembering Lillian in the sitting
room.

Jon was ahead of her. 'No, that's really kind, but I'd better
stay here in case Nita phones.'

Dora wondered if she ought to suggest driving over to see
him instead. Her car was in a lock-up five minutes' walk away,
but the idea of going back out into the dark was more than
she could bear. She had a sudden image of the single glowing
red eye in the street below.

She bit her lip. 'You ought to get an early night. You sound
incredibly tired.' She didn't like to add that he also sounded
really sad.

'Maybe you're right.' He stopped. Dora could imagine his
face and almost read his expression as he added in a soft voice,
'Thanks for ringing. It was great to see you today.'

Dora smiled. 'Nice to see you too. Dare we risk arranging
to meet up again?'

There was a wry laugh at the other end of the line.

'Why not, what do you suggest?'

Dora glanced towards the hall door. Lillian should have left
by Monday at the latest. 'Why don't you come over for a meal
at my place?'

'Sounds like a great idea. When?'

Dora pulled a face. 'How about Monday night? Let me just
see when Lillian's leaving. Would it be all right if I rang you?'

'Great. I'm on duty in the afternoon but you can always
leave a message for me at the station or on the answer machine
at home.'

When he had gone, Dora sat for a while, cradling the phone.
It still clicked and hummed almost as if it was alive. She wondered whether she ought to ring Kate or, come to that, Ray.
After a few minutes she laid the phone back in its cradle. The
day had been all together too complicated already.

Across the hallway, in the sitting room, Lillian Bliss was
curled on the sofa watching TV with the sound down. In front
of her was a tray arranged with the remains of Dora's cakes,

133

a bowl of Turkish delight and another of cornflakes. Oscar lay beside her, curled into the arc of her body, purring contentedly.

Dora smiled and sat down in the armchair by the fire.

'What have you arranged with Calvin about moving back into your flat?'

Lillian stared at her. Her expression didn't change, almost as if Dora hadn't spoken.

Dora took a deep breath. 'It can't be that tricky, Lillian. I've already asked Calvin to have your new flat cleaned and tidied up –' Still Lillian didn't move.

Dora sighed. 'I've told him that you'll have to move back in tomorrow.'

Lillian smiled and offered her the bowl of Turkish delight.

'I really like it here with you,' she said. 'I mean, you've got a cat and all that. And Calvin lives quite near. It's really handy for the shops too.'

Dora stared at her with a growing sense of unease. 'Just wait here a minute,' she said, and went back into the office. Calvin answered on the eleventh ring.

'Hellooo?' he said, cheerfully.

'Calvin, it's Dora.' She tried hard to sound brisk and businesslike. 'What's happening about Lillian's flat?'

There was a slight pause. Calvin coughed. 'Very hard to get cleaners in over the weekend, Dora. The company said they could be there first thing Monday morning.'

'Which means?' Dora snapped.

'That Lillian can be out of your place by Monday tea time.'

Dora doodled a small intense knot on her telephone pad. 'That's nearly seventy-two hours. I did say forty-eight.'

Calvin laughed. 'Come on, Dora, be reasonable.'

Dora was struggling to find a reply when she heard Lillian scream.

'Quick, Dora, quick!'

Dora threw the receiver down, and ran into the sitting room, not knowing what on earth she would find. Lillian, crouched on the end of the sofa, was pointing at the mute TV screen. Dora swung round in time to catch a pouting studio portrait of Lillian flashing across the screen. 'Look, it's me, it's me,' shrieked Lillian.

Dora pushed the volume button to catch the voice-over.

'And finally tonight, students at the Fairbeach College of Further Education have awarded local writer and celebrity Catiana Moran an honorary award, as part of their Festival Week celebrations. A spokesman for the union said they will be inviting Miss Moran to collect her award, for outstanding services to English Literature, at a charity ball to be held on Saturday evening. And now for the local weather . . .'

Dora stared at Lillian, who was totally transfixed. She threw the remote control onto the sofa and headed back into the office. 'Calvin?'

'Uh huh.' He sounded as if he might be dropping off to sleep.

'Monday tea time.'

'Right,' said Calvin and hung up.

Alicia Markham, chair of the local Conservative Association, pressed fast forward on the video recorder until she reached the debate segment of the 'Anglia Live Tonight' programme, when she slowed the tape down to normal speed.

The studio set of pale ochre and mauve did nothing for the Labour candidate Freda Haleworthy's rather liverish complexion. She had a moustache and a very mannish haircut, neither of which endeared her to Alicia, who firmly believed that an uneducated electorate could easily be swayed by personal appearance.

Tom Fielding, the Liberal Democrat candidate, was a very different kettle of fish. She had known his family for years – the Fieldings were local agricultural merchants. What she hadn't realised was what a natural political animal Tom was. Fellow members of the committee had warned her he was the man to watch and they were right.

Alicia leant forward to gauge his performance. He was comfortable, understated, with an easy manner. He laughed a lot. Worse still, his unforced good humour detracted from Guy's very polished performance. He made Guy look pompous. Alicia sucked her teeth. If he was this good on TV, he would be unstoppable on the hustings.

Tom Fielding was credible, warm, and above all, he had the kind of face which people trusted – slightly weather-beaten with crinkly lines round the eyes. She had to get rid of Tom Fielding if Guy was to have any hope of retaining the seat.

Alicia glanced at the open cake boxes on the coffee table. On her lap was Calvin Roberts' filofax. Folded neatly beside the boxes was a photocopy of Lillian Bliss' contract from Calvin's agency. Sensible of her man to get that and the rest of the Catiana Moran file all carefully photocopied on Calvin's own machine, before the papers were slipped back into the filing cabinet. Alicia sighed. Lillian's old address was there too. There was bound to be something there, surely? What Alicia really needed were the photographs that would assure Guy's success – they had to be somewhere. He had told her they offered them the perfect winning ticket, but had been guarded about how he knew they existed. It might be interesting to ask him.

Thoughtfully she turned the filofax over in her fingers, and then looked back at Calvin's handwritten list of Catiana Moran's schedule. Wherever had the man gone to school? Calvin Roberts' writing was barely legible. The diaries from the flat in Gunners Terrace weren't much better, although the author had a far better grasp of syntax.

On the TV screen the camera pulled into a tight close-up of Tom Fielding and Guy Phelps, head to head, slogging it out. Whatever the pollsters might say later, Tom Fielding was Guy's main rival. Alicia leant forward and rewound the tape. As the figures – rendered ridiculous, moving backwards at speed – slowed again, Alicia, with one eye on Lillian's old address on the contract, picked up her mobile phone and tapped in the home number of Guy's political agent, Colin Scarisbrooke. She hadn't forgiven him for humiliating her on the way to the bring and buy. Let the little gingery weasel earn his crust.

*　　*　　*

'You really do have to go back to your flat,' said Dora, handing Lillian another mug of coffee. It was seven thirty the next morning and Dora had woken Lillian in time to get her car to Peterborough. Sunday sunshine was oozing between the putty smears on Dora's new kitchen window.

The strawberry blonde wrinkled her nose and ran her tongue around her teeth. 'I'm not usually up this early. I do like it here, though. It's homely. I thought when I came here with Calvin that it was little, but it's ever so cosy really, isn't it?'

Dora looked heavenwards.

Lillian stirred another sugar into her coffee. 'And Gibson would –' Her beautifully manicured fingers flew to her mouth. 'Oh, no.'

'What is it?'

Lillian got to her feet. 'Gibson. I said I would go and pick him up.'

'I'm not with you,' said Dora. She'd lost the plot somewhere.

'Gibson, my cat. I said I'd go and get him today.'

Dora decided to say nothing; none of the questions she had asked so far had made things any clearer. Lillian appeared to be struggling her way around a complicated series of thoughts. Her face contorted for a few seconds more, and then she said, 'I really need to go back to the flat and get the rest of my things.'

Dora shook her head firmly. 'No need, Lillian. You're moving out of here tomorrow, remember. You won't need any more things.'

Lillian giggled. 'No, no, you're not following me, are you? The stuff from my old flat in Keelside. Gibson is still there. I asked Carol, the girl downstairs, to keep an eye on him and feed him and that, until I got the new flat decorated.'

Dora nodded. 'And?'

'I said I'd go over and get him, and pick up all me gear this weekend. The landlord gave me until the end of this week. I was going to get a taxi or ask Calvin to do it.'

Lillian looked at Oscar, who was doing Charles Atlas impressions on the windowsill in the sunlight.

'Thing is, if you've got a pet you're never really on your own, are you? A proper pet I mean, not like a goldfish or a hamster or anything. That's why I got Gibson in the first place. I wouldn't mind being in my flat with the cat around for company.'

Dora smiled, wheels grinding. 'You've got to go to Peterborough today, haven't you? I'll tell you what, why don't you tell me where you used to live. I could go and fetch your things and your cat?'

Lillian nodded, but Dora sensed that there was no real comprehension, so she carried on, 'And then tomorrow we could take Gibson and all your things to the new flat. Down at Anchor Quay. There's loads of room for him there. I'm sure he'd really love it – all that space.'

Lillian looked sceptical, but at least this time she hadn't turned Dora down flat.

Finally, Lillian smiled and leaned forward. 'I'll write it down for you. I live in Belleview Terrace.' She drew a swirl through a spill of coffee with one of her fingernails. 'How well do you know Keelside? Have you got a bit of paper? I'll draw you a map if you like.'

Later that morning, Lawrence Rawlings sat in his office, examining the photographs on his desk. He arranged them sequentially, creating a story board, then looked up at the man he had hired.

'I'm not sure that this is enough but it's a credible start.'

Milo grinned. 'Matter of time now. We've got Mr Roberts arriving at Gunners Terrace, we've got her letting him in. We've got them together. Trust me, it doesn't take a lot to make shit stick. Depends on what you'd got in mind.'

Lawrence could already smell lunch cooking downstairs. He glanced at his watch. What he had in mind was a bargaining chip that would give him control over Calvin Roberts, but he would have preferred more than just these few grainy photographs. After all, Lillian was Calvin's client. It would be so easy for his son-in-law, with his slick sugary tongue, to explain it all away.

Lawrence sniffed. And at the same time he had to be extremely careful his plan didn't backfire. He nodded to the heavily set private investigator. 'Keep on it and make sure you keep in touch.'

Milo turned as if to leave and then swung back. 'One more thing, gov. I think you ought to know. You know I said I thought I wasn't the only one watching Gunners Terrace for a bit of hanky panky?'

Lawrence sucked his teeth. 'I remember. Spit it out.'

The man slid another handful of prints out of his jacket pocket and arranged them on the desk. He leant over and pointed to the first picture.

'See here? This car and that bloke. Either him or that car have been in Gunners Terrace every time either me or my mate's been there. And here, I think that's got to be a camera he's holding.'

Lawrence peered at the grainy enlargements. 'Which proves what, exactly?'

The man pulled a face. 'Maybe something, maybe nothing. I just think it's bloody odd, that's all I'm saying.'

Lawrence stared at the story board of photographs. Who else might be interested in Calvin and Lillian – and more to the point, why? He needed to find out who the other watcher was. And he had to be so very careful; it wouldn't do for Sarah and the girls to find out what he was doing. They had to be protected.

He glanced at the photographs again. Catiana Moran, alias Lillian Bliss, was really quite exquisite, beautiful, tempting . . . he stared at her face. He could see why Calvin was attracted to her, but at the same time was furious that he was.

Lawrence pointed to the photo of the man in the car.

'See if you can find out who he is.'

10

By the time Dora could see the silos of Keelside sugar-beet factory glinting in the distance, her stomach was twisted up into a tight little plait. Keelside clung to the shoreline on the western rim of the Wash, fifteen miles from Fairbeach, along the dual carriageway from hell. The road's long slow curves encouraged boy-racers to execute dramatic feats of brinkmanship that made Dora flinch.

Besides the pleasures of being cut up or coming head to head with a series of latter-day charioteers, tractors meandered around blind bends at walking pace. It was a lovely sunny Sunday morning and to add extra seasoning to the mix there were roadworks on the stretch between Manley All Saints and Tydd-Hall and the bypass was the only route to the coast.

Dora gritted her teeth and repeated her reasons for coming. 'I'll pick up Lillian's cat,' she murmured, glancing at Lillian's cryptic map on the passenger seat. 'Collect Lillian's things and then Lillian will move out.' It didn't sound any more convincing for being said aloud.

She dropped the car down a gear and pulled into the right lane for exiting the roundabout. Three huge roundabouts cut Keelside off from all but the most determined. There was meant to be a flyover but it had died somewhere between conception and construction, leaving weary travellers with an unnerving selection of slip roads.

Dora eased forward on amber and waited for someone to pip her for being tardy. To remedy the lack of flyover someone had bought a job lot of traffic lights. They had been installed at the first roundabout and then cheerfully peppered the road every fifty yards after that, right the way through Keelside.

Dora pulled away on green, was pipped for having the audacity to be in the correct lane, and for the next mile and a half stopped, hopped, mirrored and signalled her ancient Fiat into the town centre.

Despite Lillian's directions and the map, Dora wasn't sure where Belleview Terrace was. She had to ask directions twice before she was certain where she was headed. Finally, with a picture of her destination in her head, she drew away into the traffic and doubled back through the old docks. She watched the town centre shops and prim town apartments give way to street after street of tidy town houses and tight-lipped terraces. Out, under the remains of the town's ancient wall, down past the tattooist and the sex shop, shuttered with heavy-duty grilles even in the day time, Dora followed the scenic route out to West Keelside along another stretch of bleak dual carriageway. Belleview Terrace was squeezed out onto the wild colonial edge of town, and had been pointedly overlooked by first-time buyers.

Dora bumped up onto a wide weedy verge and pulled the car to a halt. The little row of terraced houses had been named by someone with a very dark sense of humour. The austere red-brick frontage stared out over corrugated iron and chain-link fencing that backed a new warehouse complex. It certainly couldn't ever have had anything approaching a Belleview, even in the days when the gas works stood on the site.

Rusting chain link bowed here and there, curling back in places into convenient boy-sized openings. Festooned with faded wind-borne offerings wound into the little crusty diamonds, it looked like a wailing wall, hung with supplications to the gods of bubble wrap and fast food. Sun-bleached weeds clustered in the gutters. Elderly cars huddled along the pavement.

Dora sniffed and pulled up her collar, conscious of Sheila's disapproving voice in her head.

Lillian's flat was midway along the terrace just past a skip half full of household rubbish. Dora stepped up into the tiny bald front garden and peered at the two names in a card holder, one above the other, with bells beneath.

'L. Bliss, Flat A, C. Hayes, Flat B,' she murmured. This had to be the place.

Before Dora had a chance to decide exactly what she was going to do, the front door swung open. A tiny, bleached-blonde girl barely out of her teens, dressed in a huge sweater and tight leggings, glanced up at Dora with anxious dark-rimmed eyes. From behind her came a barrage of rock music. The girl peered up and down the street and then wrapped her arms across her chest.

'I've already got him in his box,' she said, her voice trembling slightly. 'I do love him, but I just can't keep him. I've tried ringing her again at the number she gave me, but there still isn't anyone there.'

Dora frowned slightly. 'I'm sorry?'

'Cats Protection League? I rang up yesterday to have you come and collect Gibson. The cat?'

Dora shook her head. 'I think you must have made a mistake. My name is Dora Hall, I've come to collect Lillian's things and pick up the cat as well.'

The girl bit her lip. 'You're not from the papers, are you?' she said, eyeing Dora suspiciously. 'I wondered how long it would be before you lot turned up here to get all the gossip. I saw her on the telly, you know. Lillian loves that cat but I really can't keep him. I said I'd just have him until this weekend.'

Confused, Dora nodded. 'No, I'm a friend of Lillian's, she's staying with me for a day or two. She asked me to come over and collect her things. She said you'd have a key for her flat.'

The blonde girl stepped back inside the gloomy hallway. There was no let-up in the music.

'All right, you'd better come in then,' she said.

The hallway was tiny, barely more than a couple of yards square. Just inside the door, the stairs rose steeply up towards another glass-panelled door. Tucked tight against the banister was a partition wall that cut the house in two. Standing on a table against the partition was a wicker cat basket. Inside, a beautiful grey-and-white cat circled miserably, pushing his face against the mesh. Instinctively, Dora stopped to stroke his nose through the bars.

'Is this Lillian's cat?'

The girl nodded. 'Yeah, she calls him Gibson, after Mel Gibson. Do you like cats?'

'I've got one of my own,' Dora told her.

The girl chewed her lip. 'I don't want him to go, but I don't want to keep him. I'm out a lot, it doesn't seem fair on him really.'

Inside the basket, the cat purred and rubbed his face against Dora's fingers.

'He seems to like you.' The girl looked up at Dora. 'I don't suppose you'd keep him, would you? Keep him instead of letting Lillian have him back? She loves him but she's never about to look after him. If it weren't for me I think he'd have starved by now.'

Dora paused, looking into the cat's storm-grey eyes as Gibson renewed his chorus of approval.

The girl was already by the door to her flat. 'You can go straight up. The door's open, your mate's already up there.'

Dora stared at her. Perhaps she'd misheard.

'My mate?' she repeated.

The girl nodded. 'Yeah, he must have got here about half an hour ago. He said someone sent him over to collect her furniture. Something to do with her new flat. Mind you, he didn't seem to know anything about her cat.'

Dora stared up at the door to Lillian's flat, as the girl continued. 'You'll let me know when you're done, won't you?'

Dora turned round and slowly climbed the stairs. Maybe it was Calvin, but something told her it wasn't. And if it wasn't Calvin, it was probably whoever had broken into her flat, and Calvin's office, and Lillian's apartment.

Dora wasn't certain why she was going up or what she thought she was going to achieve when she got there. Twelve steep steps, covered by a threadbare runner – she climbed them with great deliberation to the accompaniment of a thumping disco beat. The door at the top of the stairs was unlocked.

Dora pushed it open very, very slowly, revealing a giant pale pink teddy-bear, sitting on a stool in the hall. The music from the stairwell seemed to ooze up around her and push its way into the flat.

The door opposite was ajar. Dora could easily see inside. Standing with his back to her was a short stocky man in a pull-on woollen hat, heavy dark jacket, and leather gloves. Dora absorbed the details almost as if she was watching him on a film.

What could have taken no more than a few seconds seemed to go on and on, each detail blindingly sharp in Dora's mind. The man was sorting through the contents of a cardboard box on a table. As Dora stepped into the room, he swung round, eyes alight with a mixture of fear and complete surprise. He jumped and then swallowed hard.

'Can I help you?' said Dora, in her most controlled, even voice.

The man's eyes widened, his colour drained, and before Dora could frame the next thought, he was charging towards her, clutching a bundle of papers under one arm. She fought the impulse to step aside, out of his way, and leapt forward to try to stop him, but too late. With an unpleasant grunt he swung round sharply and gave her a hefty push.

Dora staggered backwards and fell heavily over the arm of a chair. She had no chance to regain her balance and rolled over, cracking her head on a side table. Outside, the landing door slammed shut.

'Bastard,' Dora hissed as she struggled to get back to her feet. Her head hurt. She rubbed it vigorously, trying to ignore the star-studded spinning walls. 'Bastard, bastard, bastard.'

Unsteadily, she headed out onto the little landing and jerked at the door handle. The door was locked. She slammed her fists against the frame.

'Let me out!' she shouted furiously. 'Let me out! Can you hear me?'

A second or two later, there were footsteps on the stairs and the door swung open. Lillian's neighbour stared at her.

'Is there something the matter?'

Dora nodded. 'Would you get on the phone and call the police? I think the man who was here just now was a burglar.'

The girl's jaw dropped. 'He told me he knew Lillian. I . . .'

Dora pushed past her, taking the stairs two at a time. Outside, Belleview Terrace was empty. Whoever he was, he'd already gone.

The girl, still standing outside Lillian's door, stared down at Dora.

'We haven't got a phone,' she said. 'But there's one down the bottom of the road. Would you like a cup of tea?'

Dora nodded. 'I'm going to call the police first.'

She asked for Jon Melrose by name.

'I'm afraid he's not here at the moment, madam. Would you care to leave a message?'

Dora sighed. 'No, but I would like to report a burglary, I think I may have just disturbed the man who was breaking in.' Dora wrinkled up her nose and looked at her reflection in a little mirror that had been wedged above the phone. What was she saying? She *had* disturbed the burglar, there was no thought about it. She leant closer to the mirror to see if there were any bruises or bumps that showed.

The man at the far end of the phone line coughed.

'I see, madam. Now, let me get some of this information down. You are?'

Dora gave him her details and said she would wait for the police car to arrive. After hanging up, she tapped in Jon's home number and felt disproportionately cheated when she got his answering machine.

By the time Dora had walked back to the flat, she had started to shake. The tiny blonde girl was waiting for her on the doorstep.

'You will still take the cat with you, won't you?' she asked, guiding Dora into the hall. At least the rock music had stopped.

Dora nodded, taking a deep breath to calm herself, then picked up the cat basket and followed the girl.

The tiny ground-floor flat was cramped, over-populated with ill-matched furniture. Some must have come with the flat and other pieces had been added by its diminutive occupant.

A huge chintz armchair struck an uneasy alliance with a bright blue PVC settee. The wood-chip walls were hung with photos and cheap prints. There were bright cushions strewn over every chair. Dora concentrated hard on the decor, trying to still the unsteady beat of her heart.

'I'm Carol Hayes,' the girl volunteered, as she indicated that Dora should sit down. 'Lillian's maybe told you about me?'

Dora smiled. 'I don't know Lillian very well, really. I'm just helping her out. But I'm pleased to meet you,' she added, still hovering by the chintz chair, standing the cat basket at her feet. Gibson made one more circuit of his wicker prison and then curled into contented sleep.

Carol smiled and waved again at Dora to sit. 'Do you take sugar?'

Dora shook her head and glanced around the busy colourful room. 'You'll need to tell the police about the man when they come,' she said gently, watching Carol Hayes as she stepped into the adjoining kitchen.

Carol pulled a face. 'If you say so. But I don't really know anything much, and I never did like coppers. That bloke just said he was a friend who'd come to get some of Lillian's stuff. I'd been half expecting someone to turn up, you know, to collect the cat and everything.' She paused. 'What do you think he wanted, anyway? Do you think he'll come back? I wouldn't have thought Lillian had got anything worth nicking.'

Dora shrugged. Her pulse was slowing now. 'I've got no idea.'

Carol shivered. 'What'll I do if he comes back? I never used to mind living here on me own. But it feels different since Lillian's left. I keep hearing funny noises. I didn't notice them, before.' She glanced down at the cat. 'That's one of the reasons

I want Gibson to go. He jumped through the kitchen window last night and frightened the bloody life out of me.' She paused. 'I'm going to look around for somewhere else, I think.'

Dora nodded.

Carol stepped forward and picked up a gilt-framed picture from one of the little tables.

'I'm getting married next year,' she said, as if that would make everything all right. She held the photo out for Dora to look at. A very young uniformed man looked back with a mixture of amusement and affection from behind the glass.

Dora smiled. 'He's very handsome.'

Carol, reddening, nodded. 'He's in the Navy.' She set the photo down amongst a cluster of others. 'I'm photo mad, me, it's my hobby. Take me camera everywhere – hang on, let me just make this tea.' She scurried back into the kitchen.

On the wall, above the mantelpiece, was a huge picture frame full of photos arranged one on top of the other like a collage. Dora got up to look at the bright sea of unknown faces and places.

As Carol reappeared, carrying two mugs, Dora turned and smiled. 'Did you take all these? You're very talented.'

For the first time since opening the front door, Carol Hayes smiled warmly.

'Not really, they're mostly all the rejects in there. The good ones are in the albums. I did this course at tech'. The best stuff had to go in for my assessment.' She stood the mugs on the coffee table and stepped up to join Dora.

'There's Lillian,' she said, pointing to a cropped photo of a handsome young woman with brown hair and glittering eyes.

Dora looked closer. 'She's got different hair in this.'

Carol laughed. 'I know, she hates that picture. That's her natural colour. She calls it Minnie-mouse brown. She dyed it blonde just after that. I did some of her once with no make-up on.' Carol snorted. 'She went light when she saw the prints.'

Dora stepped back. 'She's a redhead at the moment, sort of strawberry blonde.'

Carol grinned. 'Yes, I know. I told you, I saw her on the telly. Got a fancy new name as well. She loves dressing up. You never know what she's going to look like from one day to the next. I walked right past her once, in the precinct, when she was doing a promotion for fags. She was all done up like a cowgirl, looked brilliant.' Carol paused thoughtfully. 'She looks really nice when she's all done up.'

Dora sat down and took the mug from the coffee table. 'Have you known Lillian for very long?'

Carol's guarded expression returned slowly, like a mask slipping down over her sharp features.

'I don't know her very well at all really. She moved in a couple of months after me. Neither of us are what you'd call mixers. Keep ourselves to ourselves, though she's not stuck up or anything but . . .' She hesitated. 'It's the cat that made us friends.' Carol curled up onto the settee, folding her legs under her and twisted a tendril of blonde hair around her fingers. 'Lillian's different from people round here. More glamorous.' She screwed up her mouth thoughtfully. 'I don't understand how she's ended up in Keelside. She's done shows, modelling, all that sort of thing. It seems funny her ending up here. You'd have thought she'd have gone down to London or something. She said it was a family thing.'

Dora stared at her. 'Do Lillian's family come from round here?'

Carol shrugged. 'I don't know. She's been really good to me though. Me and her have been to a lot of parties together. Really nice dos.' She coloured slightly and Dora decided not to ask whether they had been paid to go.

Carol shifted her weight and peered at the photo collage above the fireplace.

'It's lovely she's got famous though, isn't it? Fancy me knowing someone famous. I never knew she was writing up there, you know. I didn't think she was the writing sort. I'm going to miss her. I've seen her on the telly a couple of times already. Don't seem possible, really, that she's famous. Maybe that's why that bloke wanted to get upstairs. Maybe he wanted to look at her things, you know. I've read about them sort of people in the Sunday papers.'

Dora nodded. Maybe Carol was right, except there was something about the man's face that was vaguely familiar. She turned back to Carol. 'Do you know where Lillian came from?'

Carol hesitated. 'I don't know much about her at all. You ought to ask her, really. She did say she worked in Yarmouth last summer.' The girl laughed. 'Can't see the appeal myself. Yarmouth is a right dead hole, but I suppose it's a job.'

Dora sipped her tea. Jon had mentioned Lillian had been picked up for soliciting in Yarmouth. Yarmouth to Keelside seemed like an odd move; there had to be a very good reason. 'Did she have a lot of work here?'

Carol nodded, linking her fingers around her mug. 'Yeah, she's always off somewhere or other, doing hostessing, modelling. Hang on a minute, I'll show you.'

Carol clambered to her feet and opened a cupboard in the sideboard. 'I did these for her just after Christmas.' From inside she produced two sleek black photo albums and passed them to Dora. 'She wanted something to tout around the agencies so I mounted up some old photos for her, redid a few, I took quite a lot myself. I made the classy ones up into a folio and mounted the rest up in these.'

Dora's fingers rested lightly on the crisp shiny black covers. 'Don't open them now,' Carol said. 'Take them back for Lillian. There's a whole box of her stuff in there that she asked me to keep an eye on.' She slid a crisp box out from the cupboard. 'I should think she'll want all this as well.'

From outside came the sound of a car pulling up. 'That's probably the police,' said Dora.

Carol didn't look very enthusiastic.

Dora smiled. 'Would you like me to go and show them in?'

Carol nodded.

Dora laid the albums on top of the crisp box, wanting to say something that would put Carol Hayes at ease, something of comfort – but nothing seemed appropriate.

Finally, she looked down at the sleeping cat. 'I'll look after him for you,' she said flatly.

Carol nodded. 'Thanks.' She glanced at her watch. 'Look, I've got to be at work in about an hour. How long do you think the police are going to be?'

Dora got to her feet, the mug of tea still half finished on the coffee table. 'I don't know, but the sooner we let them in the sooner they'll be done.'

Jon Melrose arrived minutes after the uniformed officer had finished taking Dora's statement. When she first saw him through the net curtains his face was tight with anxiety. She got to her feet and headed out into the hall. They met at the door.

Dora felt the shakes coming back. Seeing him there was such a relief. As their eyes met, she struggled to remember that he was there in an official capacity. Her first instinct was to curl up in his arms. As if reading her mind, his expression softened.

'I thought I told you not to go playing Miss Marple.'

Dora snorted. 'That was days ago. Besides, I wasn't playing super sleuth, honest injun. I'd only come here to pick up Lillian's things for her.' There was the slightest tremor in her voice.

Jon lifted his eyebrows.

'Don't look at me like that,' Dora protested. 'It's perfectly true, I've got to do something to get Lillian out of my flat.'

He lifted a hand and stroked her fringe away. 'They said you'd been knocked over, are you all right?'

Dora nodded. 'Fine, a bit shaky at the moment, but I'm made of tough stuff.' She forced a lopsided grin. 'Anyway, besides that, how's Joe doing?'

'Mending fast. They're going to discharge him some time this afternoon.' Around them the policemen were preparing to leave. 'I'd ask you out to lunch but I'm on duty.'

Dora grinned. 'Don't worry. I've had just about as much excitement as I can handle today. Do you think you'll be able to make dinner tomorrow night?'

Jon nodded. 'I should think so, what time?'

Dora shrugged, grinning still. 'How does eight-ish sound? I've just got to put this box in my car and get the other things Lillian wanted from upstairs. All her stuff is packed in boxes ready to be picked up.'

Jon shook his head. 'You'll have to leave the things upstairs until the fingerprint mob have done their business. I'll arrange to have it brought over to Fairbeach if you like.'

'Suits me. So there's just this box, then, and Gibson.'

She hesitated and took a step towards the door. Carol Hayes hovered, pacing from one foot to the other.

Dora smiled at her. 'I'll give you my telephone number, maybe you'd like to ring me some time and check up on Lillian and Gibson?' She pulled a piece of paper out of her handbag and scribbled down the number. Carol took it without a second glance as Dora stooped to pick up the cat basket.

'Let me help you with the door,' the girl offered, as Dora struggled to balance her handbag, the cat basket and the albums.

Jon bent down to pick up the crisp box. 'Lead on, and don't tell me you're parked half a mile away.' He winced as he realised the box was a lot heavier than he'd anticipated.

'I'm parked just across the road,' said Dora, over her shoulder. She smiled back at Carol. 'You get yourself organised for work now.'

Carol opened the doors for them, while Gibson, shaken rudely from sleep, began to complain, prowling around in the basket, making it impossible to judge the sway or the weight.

Outside Belleview Terrace, Dora tucked Lillian Bliss's photo albums up under her arm. As she crossed the main road it began to spit with rain. Gibson growled crossly. Jon, walking beside her, hefted the box a little higher. Dora fished the car keys out of her bag and popped the boot, dropping the photo albums in beside the spare wheel. Jon stood the crisp box alongside them.

Dora rested her forehead against the cool boot lid.

'Rough day?' Jon said, softly resting a hand on her shoulder. 'Still considering the possibility of running away?'

Dora laughed. 'That was Saturday. Today it seems like the only feasible solution.' She looked up at him, eyes widening. 'What in God's name am I doing disturbing burglars at my age? He could have killed me –'

Jon turned slowly and took her in his arms. Dora felt a wisp of pure fear slither up from somewhere low in her belly followed by a geyser of tears. Snuggled up against him, revelling in the security and warmth, she pressed her fists hard against her eyes.

'What on earth are you doing?' asked Jon, peering down at her.

Dora took a long shuddering breath. 'Trying to stop myself from crying,' she snorted. 'I end up looking like a snotty were-wolf if I cry.'

Jon sighed and held her closer. 'I've seen women cry before, you know, and lived. You don't have to pretend everything is all right, with me. I don't mind if it isn't.'

Dora felt the first red-hot tear burn down her face. Jon brushed it away with a fingertip. 'That wasn't so hard, was it?'

Dora snorted again, feeling the tide rising behind her eyes. 'You asked for this,' she gasped, forcing another smile. 'On your own head be it.'

Alicia Markham took a deep breath, her fingers tightening on the telephone receiver.

'What do you mean, you were seen?' she hissed furiously.

'I would have thought it was bloody obvious what I mean, Alicia. I was caught at the flat by some woman,' Colin Scaris-brooke snapped. 'And I haven't got much change, so when the pips go, that's it. This is not my sort of business, you know. Not my sort of business at all. You said all I had to do was go in and pick up any photos that were there. I should never have been asked to do this kind of thing. You've got other people to do this kind of work for you.'

Alicia drummed her fingers on her desk. 'And what did you do when this woman saw you?'

Scarisbrooke snorted. 'Cleared off, of course. I'd got no idea who she was, she sounded as if she had permission to be up there.'

'Did you find anything worth having?'

'No idea, yet,' said Scarisbrooke evasively. 'I'll let you know once I've sorted through the things I've got.'

'We need to talk to Guy as soon as possible,' Alicia told him.

'Council of war?' said Scarisbrooke.

Alicia sighed. 'Schoolboy talk. This is politics, not *Swallows and Amazons*. What we need to do is sit round and decide where we're going from here. Guy needs to be in on this.' She sighed again. 'Council of war.' And hung up.

At Lawrence Rawlings' house, the guests were being served aperitifs before Sunday lunch. Guy Phelps helped himself to another sherry from the tray and lifted his glass in a toast.

'I really must thank you for inviting us, Lawrence. Elizabeth and I were saying how very kind it was of you to ask us all.' He smiled benignly at his wife, who was sat sprung tight and uncomfortable on the edge of the sofa in Lawrence's sitting room. She had half an eye on their son and daughter, who were fighting a muted battle on the hearth rug. Guy's gaze moved around the room as if he was holding court.

'Old-fashioned family Sundays, everyone together after church. It's the very heart of our nation, where would we be without traditional family values? Sunday lunch, the whole family together.' He sighed as if he had just said something of great weight and immeasurable importance.

Calvin Roberts and Lawrence Rawlings glanced at each other, for once in complete agreement. Lawrence knew that Calvin had only put in an appearance because it was in his best interests to align himself with Guy Phelps. It might be in Calvin's best interests but it didn't mean he had to enjoy it.

Lawrence swallowed back a smile, as Guy turned his attention to Calvin. 'Wouldn't you agree?'

Calvin was now obligated to follow one inane comment with another. 'Couldn't agree more, Guy,' he murmured. 'Family is right at the heart of the – of the . . .' He stopped as Sarah came in, carrying a tray of hors d'oeuvres.

Guy leapt across the room to take one, as if they had been brought in especially for him. 'Wonderful,' he murmured and then looked at his wife. 'You really must ask Sarah for the recipes for these.'

Elizabeth Phelps nodded. 'Of course, dear.'

The atmosphere was stretched so tight in the sitting room that you could almost pick out a tune on it. Lawrence nodded to Vic and Bob, the only members of the inner circle to have appeared for lunch once his usual guests found out Guy Phelps had been invited. Lawrence had taken the precaution of ringing round to warn everyone.

'Calvin,' Lawrence said, turning towards his son-in-law, 'perhaps you'd like to show Guy and his family around the garden. Rather nice out there this morning, and I'm sure the children would like to have a run around in the orchard before lunch?'

Elizabeth Phelps sprang to her feet. 'That would be really lovely,' she said quickly, and hurried to drag her squabbling offspring to their feet. She pulled her son up by his arm.

Calvin Roberts' expression hardened. He knew that Lawrence was excluding him.

Guy Phelps, by contrast, smiled beatifically. 'What a simply wonderful idea. I've always thought this was a wonderful house. A proper family home.' He glanced across at Calvin and Sarah. 'How old is it?'

Sarah skilfully guided the Phelps family out of the French windows, with a rueful glance towards her father, while Lawrence indicated his friends should follow him upstairs into his study.

With the study door closed, Vic Hill let out a long shuddering sigh. 'Sweet Jesus, how the hell did we end up selecting that arsehole?'

Lawrence pulled the stopper out of the whisky decanter. 'Alicia Markham railroaded the committee. Sarah invited Phelps and his spawn to lunch today. Social good form – we'd have had to invite him sooner or later.'

Bob Preston blew out his lips thoughtfully. 'Are we seriously expecting to retain the Fairbeach seat with Guy Phelps as our candidate?'

Lawrence indicated the leather fireside chairs while he busied himself with the drinks tray.

'Alicia has some notion that our friend Mr Phelps will be totally controllable. Write him a speech and every syllable will be delivered with total sincerity. He believes every single word.'

Vic nodded, accepting the proffered tumbler of Scotch. 'Unlike the late, great Jack Rees.'

Lawrence nodded. 'Unlike Jack Rees, who ran our dear Alicia ragged.' He poured himself a drink.

'A situation she is hoping to avoid with Mr Phelps?' Bob suggested. 'The whole family are the same, you've met old man Phelps, haven't you? Vic, you must remember him. He was on that committee with you over at Loughbrooke . . .'

Vic looked up again, trying to recall the details. 'Oh yes, I remember. Young Farmers' thing, years ago –'

Lawrence patted his old friend on the shoulder. 'Don't worry. I know the whole family and they're all morons, no need to come up with any examples. I'll take your word for it.'

Bob took the soda off the tray. 'This family values thing, I'm surprised he's got the bloody nerve. Someone's bound to shoot him down sooner or later, all guts and feathers. Always makes a nasty mess, that sort of thing.'

Vic and Lawrence turned to look at him. 'What do you mean?'

Bob grinned. 'Well, you were at Ben Frierman's stag do last Christmas, weren't you?'

Lawrence pulled a face. 'Frierman's?'

Vic smiled. 'I remember, just, but I can't remember Phelps

being there. Jack was there, and the Lib Dem chap, and that son-in-law of yours.'

Lawrence held his face in a carefully controlled expression. He wasn't certain exactly how Calvin had found his way onto Ben Frierman's prestigious guest list.

Across the room, Bob was nodding. 'The Lib Dem chap, Fielding, Tom Fielding, that's his name. Bloody good chap, got totally rat-arsed.' He grinned. 'Shame he's not standing as a Conservative, much more the calibre of man we're looking for.'

Vic chuckled. 'At least that brass-knickered Labour bitch didn't show up. Mind you, I'd like to have seen the look on her face when that stripper popped out of Santa's sack.'

Lawrence glanced out of the window. He tried to remember Guy Phelps' face from the Christmas party, but failed. There were other faces he recalled very clearly. In his desk, hidden in the drawer, was one of them – Catiana Moran, Lillian Bliss. That's where he had met her for the first time. Her face was indelibly etched on his mind. He took a deep breath. Below the study window, he could see Calvin Roberts deep in conversation with Guy Phelps.

Lawrence looked at his watch. Ten minutes and his housekeeper would ring the gong for lunch. He sighed. It might be a good idea to have a quiet word with Bob Preston about exactly what Guy Phelps had been doing at Frierman's Christmas party.

11

When Dora got back from Keelside, Gunners Terrace was quiet, awash with Sunday-afternoon stillness. The sun shone. Dora parked right outside her door, let herself into the hallway and stood Gibson and the photo albums down on the first step. She slipped off her jacket. Upstairs she could hear Oscar bleating and complaining. It felt an age since she had had the flat to herself.

Dora stretched – a few quiet, restful hours, a hot, deep bath, a long, long soak, then she would ring Jon. She didn't look into the street to see if the watcher was still there. She felt numb, frozen over, as if she hadn't got any more fear or emotion left to burn up.

Yawning, carrying cat basket, jacket and books, Dora climbed the stairs. She decided to take the car to the lock-up later. Maybe she would have a siesta. She wriggled and jiggled, shifting weight and load so that she could unlock the top door. She had no sooner stepped into the hall than Oscar, who had been waiting by the kitchen door, let out a furious squeal of indignation, echoed a split second later by Gibson from his wicker prison.

Oscar hissed furiously, every hair on his sinuous gingery body standing up on end.

'What in God's name have you got in that basket?' he snarled, arching up onto tiptoe.

Dora stood the cat basket, which was now rocking and rolling and creaking dramatically, down on the hall floor.

Jon Melrose picked up the file he'd just received from Yarmouth: Lillian Bliss. Soliciting, shoplifting, a string of minor convictions, cautions, fines, two months inside . . . He glanced at her arrest photo. Lillian Bliss was strikingly handsome, with a mane of wild hair caught back in a pony tail – no false contrition here, no modestly averted eyes. Her face betrayed a Mona Lisa smile, glittering eyes bright and flirtatious. The face was very different from the one he had seen as she had cowered in the alley beside Dora's flat.

Jon sniffed and laid the folder alongside the other reports of the break-ins in Fairbeach and that morning's incident in Keelside. His superintendent was rarely in at weekends unless there was a major reason – one more smalltime burglary didn't count. But Jon knew that, added together, there was something here, something that linked the incidents together, and Lillian's latest robbery added weight to his argument.

The sooner Lillian Bliss was out of Dora's life the better. He stretched and looked out of the office window, willing the phone to ring and wanting it to be Dora. The thought took him by surprise. He glanced back down at the files on his desk. He had had the same momentary, gut-wrenching fear when he'd got the call about Dora as he had when Nita had rung him about Joe; that came as a surprise too.

Seeing her well, unhurt, grinning at him, had given him such a sense of pleasure and relief that he found it hard to find the words to describe it. He could still feel her body curled up against him, see her painting a smile on over her fear with a broad brush. The sensations of tenderness and concern were things he had almost forgotten existed since his marriage had ended. Until he'd met Dora, he had resigned himself to never feeling them again.

Lillian Bliss' bright eyes stared back at him from the arrest photo, moving his thoughts on. It was simpler to weigh names and reasons than the nebulous things Dora had left inside his head.

Surely the bright lights of London – almost any city – would have been a better option for a girl like her than a small sleepy Fenland town? Before Jon could tug at the tenuous thread of ideas that had started to form, Rhodes, his detective sergeant, came in.

'Just got a shout for the uniformed lads, gov. That guy you wanted to see down at the docks has turned up in a brand new Merc. Not bad for a guy with no visible means of support, eh?'

Jon picked up his jacket, his mind reluctantly letting go of Dora Hall and Lillian Bliss; time to get back to the thoughts he was being paid to have.

There was an awful moment when Dora first got out of the bath, in which she thought someone had burgled the flat again. As she stepped into the hall there was a stunning crash from somewhere close by. By some dark nightmarish twist of fate, while she had been soaking, they had been there again –

Dora froze, standing with a towel up against her face. For a moment she felt completely and utterly empty, no fear, no surprise, and then a surging tidal wave of panic rushed through her, filling her right to the brim.

It solidified in her stomach. She felt her colour draining and was about to step into the office to grab the phone when she heard a furious yowling and a mewling.

'Shit,' she snorted, the panic popping and fragmenting into ripped pieces like a burst balloon. With an overwhelming sense of relief, Dora threw the towel down and hurried into the kitchen.

She had forgotten to shut the cats in. Oscar was sitting on the table, snaking his tail angrily from side to side. The room had been thoroughly cat-attacked. A spiralling maze of feline tracks wheeled and turned, recording a running battle across the top of the kitchen units. Two mugs lay smashed on the floor, lapped by fruit juice running in a river into the over-turned laundry basket – an orange tidal surge.

Oscar eyed her with total white-hot fury and hissed, 'It's got nothing to do with me, it was him,' in a most aggressive and articulate defence.

In the sitting room, the cats had upturned a plant and two lamps; both were surrounded by a gavotte of peaty pawprints.

159

A newspaper had exploded all over the settee. Despite the mess, Dora puffed out a short sigh of relief. From under the sofa, Gibson regarded her with narrow angry eyes.

'Sorry, Gibson,' she whispered in an undertone, 'I thought I was doing you a favour bringing you here. Just hang on in there, Oscar will get used to the idea, you won't be staying very long. Why don't you try and humour him?'

She made herself a sandwich and then went into the office. The answer machine blinked its Cyclops eye, but she ignored it and tapped in Jon's home number. The phone clicked and hissed noisily as the bell rang at the other end of the line. It would be the machine but it was still good just to hear his voice.

She waited for the omnipresent bleep: 'Hi, this is Dora, I know you're out, hope you're okay and that Joe is doing well. I thought I'd ring you while everything is quiet. It was wonderful to see you today. Good to know that the cavalry still shows up –' She paused. 'Don't bring your pager tomorrow night. If you change your mind about coming, can you give me a ring? . . .' She hesitated, wondering how to finish the call. It sounded like a verbal postcard. Did she now say, 'Wish you were here, weather lovely. Lots of love?' and add three kisses? The thought made her grin, which she knew Jon would hear in her voice as she wished him goodbye.

After she had put the phone back in its cradle Dora slipped off her mules. Siesta, a few hours of undisturbed, dreamless sleep, was what she needed.

Later that evening, as the street lights began to glow jaundiced yellow, a man, keeping to the shadows, made his way to the car parked alongside the boarded-up chemist's at the end of Gunners Terrace. Diagonally opposite the flat, it gave an uninterrupted view of the comings and goings. He pulled the ignition key from his pocket and slipped inside.

He lit a cigarette, dropped the flap of the glove compartment and pulled out a tape recorder. The little light on the control panel was fading. He grimaced. It was plugged into the cigarette lighter. If this surveillance job went on for much longer he'd need to have the bleeding car towed away or get a jump start.

He pulled the earpiece out of its case, screwed it into his ear, rewound the tape, and started to listen to the recording from the little bug he'd slipped into the phone in the flat above the shoe shop. No-one seemed to have noticed it was there after the break-in, which was a stroke of luck. Probably far too busy scrubbing walls to go looking for surveillance devices.

He pressed 'play' and was greeted by a deafening burst of mind-numbing static. He winced in pain – bloody cheap eastern European imports. He turned the volume down and tried again.

He'd done the PI course. Most people came into surveillance through the services, that's what he'd read in the brochure he'd sent away for. But he had come to it by a more practical, hands-on, direct route: several counts of burglary, breaking and entering, aggravated assault, a few months as a guest of Her Majesty as a juvenile on a short sharp shock course. And then he'd seen this ad in *Exchange and Mart* for a private detective course. Correspondence, of course, twenty-four easy parts and a collection of attractive text books which had been his to keep. He'd got his girlfriend to fill in the form and do most of the course work, but even so, he'd got his certificate. He had had it framed and hung in the back bedroom he used as an office.

Bit of luck getting a cash-in-hand decorating job for that old girl, Alicia Markham. She was something high up in Fairbeach politics and that.

He smiled and screwed the earpiece in a little harder, trying to pick out the words amongst the white noise.

He'd handled it very well. 'Actually, I'm a private detective,' he'd said one day when she'd come into the kitchen to see how they were getting on. He'd seen her little eyes light up. She hadn't even haggled about his rates.

Finally, the tape was beginning to clear – well, almost. He sniffed and strained to decipher the words behind the hisses and snorts. He was concentrating so hard he didn't hear the car door open until it was too late.

A funny little grunt of indignation formed in his mind and he was about to swing round, when he felt something long, cold and metallic press against the curve of his throat and he swiftly decided, on balance, not to look round at all.

'I think we need to talk, chummy,' said a low male voice. 'Why don't you just slide across into the passenger seat, make yourself comfortable and then we can have a nice friendly little chat.'

Dora stretched and yawned, and liked the way it felt so much that she did it again. The light through the bedroom window had faded from springtime blue to street-light amber. There were no thumps, no bangs, no raucous mewlings. She eased herself off the bed like a conscientious nurse handling a frail patient. No crashes, no burglars, no Lillian. No Lillian?

Dora peered through the gloom at the bedroom clock. It was nearly ten o'clock. How long did it take to open a bloody dirty book shop for God's sake? The relief she had felt on waking hardened back up into a knot of tension. Surely Lillian ought to be home by now? Dora screwed up her face in frustration – and surely she wasn't supposed to worry about her? Hadn't Calvin's idea been that Lillian would be a quiet invisible force for the common good, promoting, smiling, signing, posing, making Dora and Calvin's life infinitely more profitable and far easier?

Dora took a deep breath and switched on the bedside lamp. Did she now ring Calvin and witter on like a worried mother hen? Stay by the phone? Call Jon? The last possibility sounded tempting, but Dora had no desire to introduce Lillian as the reason for the call. She sighed, got dressed and decided to go to see what the cats had made of each other in her absence.

They were asleep, one on either end of the sofa, which was no help whatsoever. She made up her mind to ring Calvin if Lillian wasn't back by eleven, revised that to twelve, and sat by the TV watching the programmes come and go like moving wallpaper, with no awareness whatsoever of what it was she was watching.

Just as Dora had made up her mind to ring Calvin, she heard the intercom bell ring and hurried into her office.

'Hello?' said a breathy blonde voice.

'Lillian?' Dora snapped. 'Is that you?'

'Hello?' said Lillian again, but more brightly this time.

'Where the hell have you been? I've been worried sick. What time do you call this?' Dora demanded, and then groaned. She sounded like somebody's mother.

Pushing the open button, she tried hard to get a grip. She wasn't responsible for Lillian Bliss. And she would be gone tomorrow. Why was it that the thought held no comfort? She opened the hall door.

Lillian smiled up at her from the stairwell. She was wearing a black rubber microdress and thigh-high shiny boots. Her blonde hair had been teased up into a waterfall of glistening curls.

'Hello, Dora,' she said, sounding genuinely pleased to see her. 'I've had a lovely day. Look what the man in the shop gave me.' She executed a perfect pirouette between one step and the next. 'And there was people there who wanted my autograph.'

Dora groaned softly. 'Why don't you come in?' she suggested, in as even a tone as she could muster.

Lillian's voice must have disturbed the cats because, a millisecond after she crested the stairs, Oscar and Gibson hurtled towards her, mewling, purring and fighting each other for her undivided adoration. With some difficulty, Lillian squatted down to pick them both up.

'Oh, you lovely, lovely boys,' she whispered and then looked up at Dora. 'You went and got Gibson?' Her voice was tight with emotion. 'Thank you. I missed him so much. Isn't he a lovely, lovely boy?'

Dora stared at the adoring simpering cats – perhaps Lillian rubbed herself down in cat nip or sardines.

They headed for the kitchen, because Dora didn't think that

Lillian in her rubber dress would be able to sit down on one of the armchairs in the sitting room.

She made tea and a sandwich for her resident bondage Cinderella, while Lillian, eyes bright with excitement, talked and talked and talked.

'You should have come with me, Dora, you'd have loved it, it was wonderful. They had photographers and pink champagne and lots of little things to eat on sticks and on trays, pink things mostly. And there were loads of reporters there. And then this man, Geoff – he owns the shop – said it would be nice if I wore one of the dresses that they sell, so I got changed in his flat and there was this huge pink ribbon right across the door to the shop. And then they gave me this enormous pair of scissors and I cut the ribbon and then Geoff – he was quite big – picked me up, and carried me across the threshold and . . .'

Dora listened in awed silence. Lillian seemed to have perfected a technique of speaking without needing to draw breath.

Lillian pressed on oblivious. '. . . I signed loads of autographs and hundreds of my books. Geoff wanted to take me out, but his wife said no. Then this reporter asked if I'd like to go out to dinner. Well, I could hardly say no, could I? He said he wanted to know the real me, and that he'd seen me on the telly and he'd got this lovely room at a really nice hotel and –' She paused, reddening slightly.

Dora stared at her. 'He wanted an interview?'

Lillian nodded. 'That's right. He said –'

'And he had a really nice room? Are you telling me you –' She stopped. 'You slept with him, didn't you?'

Lillian blushed. 'Not slept exactly.'

Dora took a deep breath, gathering her thoughts back into a tidy heap. 'And what exactly did you tell him during this interview? You have to be careful what you say, let alone what you do.'

Lillian squared her shoulders. 'I am, I'm always careful. I just try to tell the truth,' she said, with a slight edge of indignation in her tone.

Dora forced a smile, afraid to ask what the truth might consist of. 'Never mind the truth – what we really need, Lillian, are a few little lies.'

Lillian wrinkled up her nose.

Dora handed her a sandwich. 'I think maybe I ought to write a fictional past for you, you know, a story that you can tell people when they ask you about Catiana Moran's life.'

Lillian nodded. 'Right,' she said, and took a huge bite out of the sandwich. With her mouth full, she glanced around the kitchen. 'Did you bring the rest of my things back from the flat?'

Dora stopped. Lillian had no idea about the man in her flat, the man rifling through her things, the man who had pushed Dora over.

'No,' Dora said quickly, taking a deep breath. 'But don't worry, I've arranged for them all to be delivered to the new flat.' She didn't add that they were coming via the police, and for some reason, she didn't want to tell Lillian. Not yet, not tonight, when Lillian was so obviously happy and excited. And besides, another darker thought bubbled up in Dora's mind, if Lillian knew that someone was still interested in her possessions, still interested in this mysterious something that she had, it would be far more difficult to persuade her to go back to the flat at Anchor Quay.

Across the street, tucked away out of the street light's eye, two men sat side by side in the front seats of the car parked near the boarded-up chemist's shop. The atmosphere was not quite friendly, but it had got past the stage where the driver, now in the passenger seat, had seen his whole life flash before him.

His uninvited guest was dressed in black leather and had an air of subdued menace. He said his code name was Milo, which the passenger thought was daft, but didn't feel it was appropriate to say so.

He had responded with what he hoped was a macho grunt of approval and said he had a code name too, of course. Glancing round to try and come up with something quick, no creative thoughts presented themselves, though he did have a series of very vivid regrets and flashbacks. As his mind filled up with things he really wished he'd done, and things he should have done more of, and would now do, if he ever got the chance – he spotted the corner shop.

'Spar,' he managed to stutter. 'My code name is Spar.'

Milo lit a cigarette. 'Nice name.'

They had sat there for hours now, Spar with the earpiece still wedged firmly in his ear, Milo whittling matches into smaller and smaller pieces with a fucking great commando knife, until all that was left was a pile of very sharp splinters. They had watched the lights go on in the flat above the shop, watched the taxi arrive to bring the blonde bit home.

Spar sighed. The man, Milo, had said he wanted to talk, but so far he had said precious little. When the lights in the flat above the shoe shop finally went out, Milo turned to him.

'So, who are you working for, matey?'

Spar coughed. 'Professional confidence. I don't have to tell you that, do I?'

Milo shrugged. 'Seems to me, chummy, there are too many of us sniffing round on this penny-ante little job.'

Spar swallowed hard, the street light glinted malevolently on the blade of Milo's commando knife. 'Really?' he said, trying to keep the falsetto of fear out of his tone.

His companion nodded. 'Too many men and resources on the ground to cover what is, after all, a very small job.' He nodded towards Spar's tape recorder. 'Wiretap's a nice move, though. Wish I'd thought of that. Getting a lot through, are you?'

Spar pulled a face that he hoped would convey something and nothing.

Milo leant back, running his thumb speculatively along the blade of his knife.

'Using the same motor all the time wasn't so smart, though. I picked you up straight away.' He paused, leaning a little closer to Spar. 'I'd like to make a suggestion.'

Spar nodded. He would have agreed to almost anything.

Milo continued. 'Why don't we pool what we know? It would cut down the hours we are out and about if we shared what we know, it makes sense. Still pick up our fee, but for half the hours put in, whadd'ya reckon?'

Spar stared at him. 'Share the job?' he said incredulously. Relief did not half way describe what he was feeling.

Milo lifted his hands. 'If you don't want to –' he began.

Spar shook his head quickly. 'No, no, it sounds like a great idea to me.'

Milo grinned and slipped the knife back into his shoulder holster. 'Yeah, it is, isn't it. Fancy a beer?'

Spar was about to mention it was a long walk to the pub when Milo hoisted a backpack onto his lap. 'Here,' he said, pulling an icy-cold can out from under one of the flaps. 'Got a cool bag in there, nothing worse than warm beer, is there?'

Spar thought about the sensation of the icy-cold blade of the commando knife snuggled up against his jugular.

'No,' he agreed quickly. 'Nothing worse than warm beer.'

Milo took a great swig from his can and then wiped the froth off his top lip with the back of a meaty fist. 'Why don't we go down to the café at the bus station and have a cup of tea and a decent fry-up? We could have a nice long chat, you and me. I don't reckon a lot is going to happen here tonight.' He glanced at his watch. 'My oppo is going to relieve me in about half an hour. What time does your shift finish?'

Spar blew out his lips thoughtfully. 'About the same time,' he lied.

'Great,' said Milo, and eased himself into a more comfortable position in the driver's seat. 'Have I ever told you about when I was in the Falklands?'

Spar stared across at him, not wanting to point out that they had only just met.

'No, no, you haven't,' he said quickly.

Milo closed his eyes. 'We were yomping out across towards Goose Green, the bloody weather was really closing in on us . . .'

Spar pulled the earpiece from his ear and let out a long silent sigh of relief. Above them, the flat was in darkness, and over the rooftops the moon cracked through the clouds in a Cheshire Cat grin.

12

Dora was woken the following morning by the sound of the phone ringing. She stretched. The machine would get it, and sure enough, a few seconds later the ringing stopped, only to begin again almost immediately. She rolled over and peered at the clock. Eight fifteen, Monday morning and she was being attacked by a telephonic sadist. She groaned and pulled on her dressing gown. The ringing stopped for an instant then began again, just before the machine had a chance to cut in – pure torture.

'All right. All right,' she snuffled miserably.

Outside the bedroom door, Gibson and Oscar noisily suggested that breakfast was in order and wound themselves around her legs, trying very hard to plait her into submission.

Shooing them away, Dora picked up the phone on the fourth round of ringing.

'Yes?' she hissed.

'Dora, hello. Lovely morning, lovely morning.' Calvin's cheerful tone hit her like cold water.

'What do you mean, "Lovely morning"?' she snorted furiously. 'I'm certain if you check our contract, half way down page two, it says no phone calls before ten, and if it doesn't, it bloody well ought to. What do you want?'

Calvin coughed. 'Mornings aren't your best time, are they, Dora? Actually it wasn't you I wanted to speak to. Is Lillian about?'

Dora let out a short shriek of indignation. 'You've got a bloody nerve. She isn't up yet. What time are you coming round to move her out?'

'It's all in hand, all in hand. I just wanted to tell her that she made a cracking impression in Peterborough yesterday.

My answering machine is chock-a-block with messages.'

Dora poured herself into the armchair. 'And you got me out of bed to tell me this?'

'Not exactly, a chap from the *Fenland Post and Echo* was there. They want her to promote their latest bingo game. Sun, sex, and sand for second-time-around lovers. It's a syndicated holiday game thing. Anyway, they're really pushed for time and want to know if Lillian can go to lunch today, to talk it over. So, I'll be round to pick her up at around half past ten.'

Dora licked her lips, tracing the boundaries of a sleepy mouth. 'She is supposed to be moving out today.'

'And she will, she will. Can I have a word with her now?'

Dora snorted. 'You seriously think she might be up? She arrived home last night dressed up like a bondage version of Cinderella.' Dora felt spiteful. 'And you realise when she's not cutting ribbons and signing books, she's off turning tricks.'

There was a short but impressive silence at the far end of the line.

'Sorry?' Calvin said after a few seconds.

Dora sighed, immediately regretting that the words were already uncorked and spilt. She shouldn't talk to people in the mornings, but could hardly backtrack now.

'You heard me, Calvin. Lillian is sleeping with anyone who offers her dinner and a winning smile. Some chap told her he was a reporter. I always thought they swore a journalistic oath to make their excuses and leave when it came to the crunch? Anyway, please let me say this again, and I mean it with no malice whatsoever, Calvin, however much it sounds that way. Lillian really has got to go. You have got to fire her. This was a bad idea – how much notice do you have to give her?'

Calvin coughed and ignored her question. 'You really are a perfect cow in the mornings. You must have misunderstood. She's a lovely girl.'

'You're right, lovely, vulnerable, likeable, and bloody dangerous. She has to go, Calvin, how many times have I got to say this to you? Surely I have got to have the casting vote in this. Trust me, I have a real nose for trouble, it's probably genetic.' Dora struggled to hold back the sarcasm.

Calvin made a thick snuffling sound. 'She was only supposed to open the shop, sign a few books. Smile a bit.'

'I'm sure she did all that as well. The trouble is she is capable of independent thought. She's like a landslide gathering momentum. Why don't you stop it before it goes any further? I'm surprised you've let her go to these dos on her own. Why didn't you go with her?'

'I had to attend a very important Sunday lunch.' Calvin sounded defensive.

Dora sighed. 'Father-in-law's again?'

Calvin coughed uncomfortably.

Dora pressed on. 'Whipping the prodigal back into the fold, are they? I'm surprised they dare let you out of their sight.'

'Not at all,' Calvin protested. 'In fact, I was invited to meet Guy Phelps, the new Conservative candidate, and his family. He needs to make connections with the right sort of people to help with his campaign. Very nice chap, charming wife.'

Dora burst out laughing. 'Oh, Calvin, you two-faced creep. You were really rude about him when I met you for lunch, said he was a complete arsehole. Now here you are sucking up – what did he promise you?'

Calvin sniffed. 'We're all entitled to change our minds. He's very credible, good man, good man.'

Dora shook her head. 'Oh, for God's sake.' She could almost see him throwing out his chest, bristling at her accusation. 'Look, I'll give Lillian your message. What time are you coming to collect her things to take round to the flat?'

Back on safe ground, Calvin quickly regained his composure. 'After we've done the *Post and Echo* lunch, and I'll have a quiet word with her about her – her – behaviour.'

Dora smiled. 'Right, but I shouldn't hold my breath waiting for the results. I suggested last night that I'd write her a potted Catiana Moran autobiography in case anyone else decides to try and chase up her past history before you give her the push.'

'Good idea,' said Calvin. 'See you later.'

Alicia Markham, dressed in her favourite cream silk peignoir, leant across the breakfast table and poured herself a tumbler of freshly squeezed orange juice. Glass in hand, she indicated the chair opposite to her private investigator, lately Spar, who was standing, unshaven and hollow-eyed, in the door-way.

'Can I assume, from the fact that you're here at this time of the morning, that you have something important for me?'

Spar puffed out his cheeks. 'Yes and no,' he said, eyeing the contents of the table covetously.

Alicia sighed. 'It's far too early in the morning for con-undrums and riddles, and stop ogling my croissants.' She picked up a little bell beside her coffee cup and rang for the Filipino house boy. When he came in she barely looked up. 'Would you please bring another cup?' she said, in a crisp voice, before dismissing the boy with a regal wave of her hand.

She turned her attention back to Spar. 'Now, tell me, what have you discovered?'

'Lawrence Rawlings.'

Alicia smiled without humour. 'Really? Have you never noticed him before?'

Spar looked heavenwards, apparently composing his thoughts.

Alicia's expression hardened. 'Oh, for goodness' sake, out with it, man, I haven't got the time or the patience to tease this out of you word by word.'

'Someone else is watching Catiana Moran, the Lillian Bliss girl. His name's Milo and he's working for Lawrence Rawlings.'

Alicia sniffed. The house boy arrived with the extra cup and saucer and made much of pouring coffee for her spy. When he was gone, Alicia leant forward. She had suspected Lawrence was up to something, inviting Guy Phelps to lunch.

'And?'

Spar smiled. 'I'm still working on it, but don't worry, I've got my sources.' He tapped the side of his nose with his finger.

Alicia sighed; hiring this buffoon was almost as bad as expecting that the stupid political agent, Colin Scarisbrooke, might be able to break into Lillian Bliss' flat with a modicum of success. She narrowed her eyes.

'Have you or have you not found anything I can use to help Guy Phelps?' she hissed.

Spar looked surprised. 'What?'

'You are supposed to be helping locate and collect certain items that will assist Guy Phelps' campaign.' She peered at him for a split second, then leant forward again and cracked him sharply on the forehead with her grapefruit spoon. 'Is there anybody in there?'

Spar jumped, winced and then rubbed his head.

'That really hurt,' he whined miserably.

'Yes, but did it do any good? What is it that Lawrence Rawlings is looking for?'

Still rubbing his head, Spar said, 'Seems to me his bloke is getting divorce stuff. You know, who slept with who, where and when, and here's the photo to prove it.' He paused and screwed up his face. 'Mind you. There might be something more to it than that. He wanted to know – I mean – my source seemed very keen to know, if I'd turned up any certificates or any documents, anything legal – '

Alicia let the ideas form and reform in her mind. Lawrence Rawlings had to be gathering evidence against his son-in-law, that was the only divorce he would be interested in. Lawrence wanted to prove that Calvin Roberts had, or was, sleeping with Lillian Bliss. Alicia couldn't say that she blamed him, she certainly wouldn't want a daughter of hers married to a man like Roberts. Alicia stirred her coffee. Unfortunately, photos of Calvin Roberts with his cavalry twills round his ankles really wouldn't help her at all – but what if Lawrence's man inadvertently turned up something that she could use?

She smiled at Spar, who eyed her with some trepidation, as if she might lean forward and hit him again. Picking up a linen napkin, she pressed it to her lips.

'Well done,' she said softly. 'Now hurry along, dear, drink your coffee and get back to work.'

After the man had left, Alicia went into her sitting room and picked up the phone. It was answered after the second ring.

'Good morning, Lawrence,' Alicia said, in her most neutral tone. 'I wonder whether it would be possible for us to have lunch together some time very soon? There are things I think we need to discuss before we get the by-election campaign underway.'

She noted the few seconds' pause at the far end of the line and smiled triumphantly.

'Of course,' said Lawrence Rawlings. 'Why don't we get together at the end of the week. Friday be convenient?'

Alicia grimaced. She had hoped it might be sooner, but then again, better Friday than not at all.

'Fine,' she agreed briskly. 'Why don't I pick you up in my car, say twelve thirty? We can go to the Lodge out at Helm St Andrew, they do a marvellous entrée there. I'll book a table for one o'clock.'

She heard Lawrence smiling as he spoke again. 'Thank you, Alicia, but I think I'd prefer to meet you there,' he said softly, and hung up.

Back at Gunners Terrace, Dora made tea for Lillian and woke her up with the news that she had two hours to get ready. At the sound of her name, Lillian sat bolt upright. Dora groaned. The strawberry blonde nymphet looked just as stunning without make-up when she woke up as when she was done up like a Hollywood starlet ready to go out.

'Calvin is coming to collect you for some sort of lunch. Then when you get back, he's going to help you move back into your flat.'

Lillian smiled her reply, giggled and then burrowed back under the bedclothes. Dora, feeling unpleasantly frail, sighed and went off to get dressed.

Let Lillian sort it out herself. Dora needed to go shopping

for her dinner with Jon, romantic dinners for two didn't just make themselves, and Jon hadn't rung to say he wouldn't be coming – although perhaps she ought to check the machine to make sure. Maybe she ought to be grateful to Calvin for dragging her out of bed so early. Maybe.

She pulled on a sweater and leggings and stared at her reflection. She would look better by lunch time. Outside the bedroom door she heard Lillian moving about and then the cats renewing their discontent at having been overlooked re: breakfast. Apparently Lillian's love for things feline didn't extend to tricks with can openers.

Or, Dora thought, a few minutes later, screwing up her nose as she went into the kitchen, anything to do with the cat litter tray.

She tidied away the remains of Lillian's supper, washed up, hoping that all the activity might kick-start her circulatory system. When the cats were fed and the kitchen looked tidy, she pulled on her coat.

She heard Lillian lock the bathroom door and smiled. A few more hours and she would be blissfully alone, well on the way to salvaging her nice quiet life from the skip Calvin and Lillian had cheerfully dumped it in.

'I'm going out,' Dora called through the closed door over the sound of the shower. 'I probably won't be back by the time you leave so just pull the door to, downstairs.'

From the bathroom came a burst of 'Unchained Melody' sung high and sharp by way of a reply.

Outside, Dora climbed into her battered car and drove into town. She felt remarkably cheerful, considering, and managed to sustain the feeling all the way round the supermarket.

In the indoor market, Dora wound her way between the brightly coloured stalls and stopped just long enough to buy a huge pot plant. She wasn't good with plants, but this one was a splendid monolith of verdant excess, and would cover up the coffee stain on the sitting room carpet very nicely.

She glanced up at the clock above Boots – ten past eleven. Lillian should be long gone to her newspaper luncheon. It was going to be a good day after all. Now all Dora had to do was go home and whip up a culinary masterpiece.

Back in Gunners Terrace, sunlit and familiar, any residual menace dissipated by the light, she unpacked the car, making a final trip downstairs to bring up the plant. She was half way across the pavement when Sheila blustered around the corner and eyed her accusingly.

'Morning,' said Sheila brusquely. 'I've been really worried about you. You said you'd ring. I've left dozens of messages on that machine of yours. Did you get the cakes?'

Dora let out a little sigh of frustration. She hadn't checked the machine to see whether Jon had changed his mind about her invitation either. She backed towards the door and gave it a hefty shove.

'Sorry,' she said, without a shred of sincerity.

Sheila tried to wrestle the plant pot out of Dora's hands. 'You're getting very unreliable. It's not like you at all. So, are you all right, then? I thought maybe you'd have thought about going to the doctor's.'

Dora stood to one side and let Sheila bustle into the hall then dropped the door latch with her chin.

'No, I'm fine, really. I'll get you the money for the cakes when we get inside.'

Sheila stopped mid-stride. 'What about all this burglary business, have you heard anything else from the police?'

'No, here, just give me a hand with this plant, will you?' She struggled upstairs with Sheila, executing an impressive turn on the landing so that she could get the foliage through the door without ripping half the leaves off.

Inside, Dora's kitchen was bright, light and she knew, as far as Sheila was concerned, suspiciously tidy.

Sheila's face immediately betrayed her curiosity. 'Expecting someone, are you?' she demanded, as she peeled off her coat.

Dora hefted the plant up onto the table. 'Yes, funnily enough I am . . .' She hesitated, looking down the corridor at the closed spare bedroom door, hoping Lillian had already left.

Sheila sniffed, waiting for the opportunity to turn her curiosity into words.

Dora glanced at the clock. 'Actually I've got quite a lot to do today.'

Sheila sucked her teeth thoughtfully and looked round the kitchen, gathering up question marks like silver bullets.

'There's something the matter, isn't there? I thought that the other day when you left the Corn Exchange in such a hurry. Something's going on.'

Dora pulled out a chair and slung her coat over it. 'No, there's nothing, really,' she assured her briskly. 'I'll just find my purse and pay you for the cakes.'

Sheila didn't look convinced. 'Nerves, I'd go and see the doctor, if I were you. Bound to shake you up, being broken into like that. He'll give you something, help you cope. Is that why you've taken a lodger in? Makes sense – someone else about the place.' She paused, redeploying her questions. 'So, who are you expecting, then?'

There had been a wildlife programme Dora had once watched, in which a shoal of piranhas had stripped the carcass of an ox, bite by bite, until only the bones were left. Sheila had the same tenacity; little questions, like barbed teeth, bit into her mind.

Dora held up her hands in resignation. 'No-one special. A friend,' she said, wondering how much of the truth she could escape with.

'What, one of your writer friends? Jill, is it, or that girl you were at school with? I saw her last week in Freeman Hardy and Willis. She said she hadn't seen you in ages. She said she'd give you a ring.'

More tiny teeth, another little bite.

Dora sighed. 'No, it's not a school friend.'

Sheila's eyes lit up like flares. 'Not a man?' she gasped incredulously.

Another bite – snip snap.

'Yes, a man.'

Sheila smiled and leant back. 'Anyone I know?'

Teeth close to the bone now.

'No, I don't think so.'

Sheila squared her shoulders and eyed Dora. 'And he's coming here?'

Dora nodded and slammed the kettle under the tap. 'Yes, he's coming here. He's coming here tonight for dinner.'

Sheila drew her lips together into a little rosebud of deep contemplation. 'Brave of him, has he ever tasted your cooking?' She paused. 'I'm surprised you're bothering with men after all this time, at your age.'

Dora swung round, trying to swallow her indignation.

'What do you mean? He's a good friend, he –' She stopped herself. If she wasn't very careful she would end up letting Sheila strip the ox right down to the white gleaming bones. She plugged the kettle in.

'We'll have a quick cup of tea and then I'm afraid I'll have to ask you to go,' she said coolly.

Sheila watched Dora's face. 'There's a lot more to this than you're telling me, isn't there, Dora?' It wasn't really a question, more of a statement.

Dora blew out a slow steady stream of air, trying to catch back hold of her life. A few seconds later the intercom bell rang. Sheila clambered to her feet.

Dora shook her head. 'No, no, stay where you are. I'll get it. You just make the tea, I'll go and see who it is.' She pulled the office door to behind her while she pressed the call button.

'Morning, Dora. As I was in the neighbourhood, I thought I'd drop in. Are you feeling okay after yesterday?' Jon Melrose's deep voice echoed around the office.

Dora sighed. 'Almost.'

'Do you mind if I come up?'

Dora glanced back over her shoulder towards the kitchen door.

'If you must,' she sighed, and pushed the entry button.

She heard Jon jogging up the stairs and jerked the door open before he had a chance to knock. He stepped inside, looking unnervingly gorgeous, and grinned.

'Morning. My excuse is, I've come to check on what time we're having dinner.'

'Eight-ish. Would you like a cup of tea while you're here?'

Jon shook his head. 'Afraid not. I can't stop long, we've come to see someone in Fairbeach. I just wanted to make sure you were okay. By the way, after Lillian's break-in I think we may have some movement on the breaking and entering. I wondered if you'd come to the station and take a look at some mug shots we've got. How's it going with –'

As he spoke, from the corner of her eye Dora could see Sheila getting to her feet.

'Hello,' said Sheila, stepping into the hall, eyes taking down every tiny detail in shorthand.

'Hi,' said Jon pleasantly.

Sheila extended a limp, ladylike hand. 'I'm Sheila, Dora's sister. And you are?'

Jon smiled, shaking her hand. 'Jon Melrose, I'm a friend of Dora's.'

Sheila sniffed. 'Having tea, are you?' She was using her best telephone voice.

Dora tried to suppress the desire to throttle her. She had held the forced smile on her face so long it felt as if rigor mortis had set in.

Jon held up his hands. 'Thanks, but no thanks, I've really got to be on my way.'

'Right,' said Sheila briskly, adding a dot to every i on her mental notes. 'Well, if you'll excuse me, I think I just heard the kettle click. Nice to have met you, Jon.'

She retreated, leaving the kitchen door open just a fraction. Dora imagined her pressed against the other side, straining to hear every last word, and grinned in spite of her discomfort.

'I just wondered if there was anything you wanted me to bring tonight?' Jon asked softly, moving a fraction closer.

Dora felt her heart flutter – he was planning to kiss her. She struggled to catch a breath but without success as fleetingly his lips touched hers. She looked up at him in astonishment.

'I've driven all the way over here just to do that,' he said mischievously. 'So, anything else you want?'

Dora, her mind doing a series of erotic back flips, flushed crimson. 'No, that'll do just fine. Come here, I'd like to do it again.'

Jon laughed and kissed her less gently. 'I promise not to bring my pager.'

There was a quiet intense silence where Dora tried hard to marshal her thoughts back into a nice neat heap.

'What about if I bring a dessert and the wine?'

Dora nodded, the pulse still fluttering in her throat. 'That will be fine, bring something sweet, sickly and wildly over-indulgent,' she said, struggling to sound normal.

Jon glanced again at his watch. 'About eight-ish then?'

'I'll look forward to it,' she muttered unsteadily, guiding him hurriedly back out onto the landing.

His fingers closed around her shoulders and this time he held her close to him. He kissed her hard, tipping her face towards his. She shivered as she felt the beat of his heart through her clothes.

'Please,' she whispered, glancing back into the flat, 'not now.'

He looked down at her with bright shiny eyes and kissed her on the end of the nose.

'Soon though,' he murmured, and loped off down the stairs. At the bottom he hesitated and then lifted a hand in farewell.

Trembling, Dora closed the door behind him.

Sheila was out of the kitchen like a featherweight boxer closing in on the final round.

'Was that him?' she hissed.

'Yes,' said Dora, trying to make it sound as if she had nothing else to add. 'He's a policeman.'

'Is he sorting out this burglary thing for you?'

Dora nodded. 'Yes, I think so.'

'I suppose he must meet a lot of women that way,' Sheila observed.

Dora sighed. 'Have you made that tea yet?'

* * *

On the other side of Fairbeach, while Dora drank tea with Sheila and finally paid her for the cakes, Lawrence Rawlings was alone in his dining room. He was standing beside an oak table, resting his hands on its smooth cool surface and looking, without seeing, into the garden.

The table had been made by a master cabinet maker, Arran van Bellsin, in the summer of 1820. It had been delivered to Fairbeach on 7 September of the same year, and had stood beneath the window for as long as Lawrence could remember. He stroked the grain of the timber with something that felt uncannily close to love.

In the cupboard, in his study, was the original bill of sale, signed by a venerable ancestor, his great-great-grandfather perhaps? Lawrence frowned – he really ought to remember, he used to know. If he closed his eyes he could imagine every single stick of furniture in the dining room – in the entire house, come to that. Perhaps reflection on the unchanging nature of some things was part of the ageing process; he certainly seemed to be spending more and more of his time doing it these days.

The very idea that Calvin Roberts would one day run his hands over the little table and not consider its provenance but its worth, chilled Lawrence down to the very marrow.

He could feel a groove under his fingertips. His father had told him that his father had been left in the dining room by a nanny, left to sketch a view from the window, while she went off for an assignation with the footman.

Bored, rebellious, a small ancestral Rawlings had etched a tiny furrow in the impossibly hard surface. Sarah knew where it was too, and Lawrence had found her on Sunday – while Calvin was committing political buggery with that arsehole Phelps – running her hands over the table top, unconsciously finding the shallow groove like a touchstone.

He wouldn't have it. He wouldn't stand for it. He would buy Calvin off, force him to leave Sarah. Mercenary bastard, it wouldn't take much, particularly if Lawrence had the evidence that Calvin was committing adultery.

Lawrence sighed. What an old-fashioned word adultery seemed – it would break Sarah's heart, and Lawrence wasn't altogether convinced that getting rid of Calvin was the lesser of two evils. Was it Sarah's happiness that drove him or was it something else? Wasn't it really an unpleasant glacier-cold hatred for the man, for taking something of his and using it with such disdain, such casual abandon?

Lawrence ran a fingernail across the groove. Things must have been simpler when the table had been crafted by Arran van Bellsin, much simpler. Indiscretions discreetly hidden. People who had been brought up to know their place and expect no more or less. Jack Rees would have understood how he felt. Jack always understood and always had an answer. A tiny crystal shard of grief cracked somewhere in his solar plexus.

Outside the dining room window, daffodils bobbed cheerfully in the sunlight, making fun of his pain.

And then there was Alicia Markham. He wondered what it was she wanted, but instinctively he had already guessed. What she knew was quite another matter.

His man had told him that she hoped to find something to assure Phelps' success in the by-election. Scuppering that alone would be ample reward, thought Lawrence, though exactly what Alicia hoped she might find was completely beyond him.

Lawrence straightened his jacket. Perhaps he would have what he wanted by Friday, in which case he would ring Alicia and politely decline her invitation to lunch – that would give him even greater pleasure.

When Calvin and Lillian arrived back at Gunners Terrace from their lunch at the *Echo*, Calvin refused, point blank, to take Lillian's cat in his car to Anchor Quay. It was late afternoon, and Lillian was standing in Dora's hallway, surrounded by a selection of her worldly goods, waiting to move out and pulling a tearful face.

Calvin held firm. 'No, no, no,' he said, chomping down hard on his cigar butt, 'the damned thing can't go in my car. They always piss all over everywhere. The whole bloody car will stink to high heaven. No.'

Dora stood in the kitchen door with an empty cat basket in one hand and was trying very, very hard not to speak. She just wanted them gone. Gibson had vanished, like a magician's rabbit, straight under the sofa in the sitting room, and it would take some heavy-duty stalking and tempting to get him out and into the wicker basket.

Dora leant against the door frame. After she had got rid of Sheila, the flat had been deliciously quiet. She had tidied, hoovered and polished, cut up onions, chopped tomatoes, all with one eye firmly on the clock and then, while looking for a pair of earrings, had found a face pack in the bottom of the drawer.

She instinctively knew mixing it up and slapping it on would draw Lillian and Calvin back like a magnet, and wasn't at all surprised when they proved her right. The face pack had just gone from tingly to crispy-meringue-hard when the doorbell rang. Calvin had lumbered up the stairs, in a filthy mood, with Lillian close behind, trying very hard to smile in spite of it. Neither seemed to have noticed that Dora was covered in crisp pastel-pink goo.

The frosty chill had lasted while Lillian collected her things, and now seemed to be in danger of thawing with explosive consequences as they reached an impasse over the cat.

Lillian looked up at Dora. 'Would you bring him for me?'

Dora shook her head. 'I can't at the moment,' she said between her teeth. 'I can't go out like this and it's got to stay on for another twenty minutes. After that I've got to get ready. A friend's coming round for dinner.'

Calvin wrinkled up his nose. 'I thought it looked tidy in here.' He took a long sniff. 'Food smells good though.' He appeared to be restricting his civility to Dora, which did nothing to make her feel any better.

He stared at the suitcase and bags around Lillian's feet. 'Is this all of it?'

Lillian, cowed, nodded.

Dora sighed. 'Look. I'll tell you what –' As she spoke a creamy gobbet of face pack dropped onto the freshly vacuumed floor. 'Why don't I bring Gibson round tomorrow for you?'

Lillian nodded. 'All right. I'll just go and see if I've left anything.'

Dora eyeballed Calvin. 'You've really upset her,' she whispered. 'Is this about sleeping with that reporter, yesterday?'

Calvin snorted. 'It wasn't me. When we got to the newspaper offices there was this group of women protesters outside.'

Dora stared at him. 'Because of Lillian?' she said, now oblivious to the cracking sounds from the face pack.

Calvin shook his head. 'No, sheer bloody coincidence. Apparently the *Echo* ran a story about female rights and managed to upset half the Doc-Marten-wearing feminists in the area. This group have been picketing on and off for about a week, and then Lillian arrives.' He lifted his hands, miming an explosion. 'They took one look at her as she shimmied out of my Jag and went ballistic. Threw eggs and flour all over my crombie – the stain won't come out, you know. It's completely ruined, a four-hundred-quid coat.'

Dora sighed. 'I'll go and see to Lillian.'

She went into the spare bedroom. Lillian was sitting on the bed, with her back to the door, apparently staring out of the window.

'Are you all right?'

Lillian's shoulders were trembling.

'It was really horrible. They called me a painted trollop,' Lillian gasped in a hot miserable little voice. 'And then one of them recognised me from off the telly. She said I was betraying my fellow women. Everywhere.' Lillian's shoulders were heaving up and down now.

Dora stroked her hair. 'Don't cry,' she said in a low voice. 'Think what a lovely day you had yesterday at the sex shop.'

Lillian let out a long throaty sob and turned round. Dora flinched. Even when she cried, Lillian Bliss looked beautiful. One great crystal tear was rolling down her cheek, another poised, like a glittering drop of dew, on her dark lashes.

She sniffed. 'And then they started to throw things at us. Tomatoes, eggs – ' She shivered. 'Good job I'd already changed into that new rubber dress. The man in the office was able to sponge it all off for me. He really made a good job of it.'

Dora stared at her. 'Come on,' she said gently. 'Let's get the rest of your things together. Don't worry about Gibson, I'll bring him round for you tomorrow.'

Lillian smiled her sweet shark smile. 'You know, you're such a nice person, Dora. I'm really glad you're my friend.'

What was there to say? Dora smiled ruefully, feeling the face pack break up like an ice flow. She felt a peculiar empathic sense of hurt for Lillian that she couldn't quite handle. It was the same feeling she had had once when her daughter, Kate, had been bullied at school. The sensation took her by surprise.

'Come on,' she said, stroking back a curl of red-blonde hair from Lillian's face. 'We'd better not keep Calvin waiting.'

When they'd both finally gone, she tucked away Gibson's cat basket in the kitchen. She'd put off catching him until tomorrow. She plugged in the kettle and then set about restoring the running order in her mind. The face pack appeared to have given her a rash.

13

Dora dragged the gate-leg table out from the spare bedroom and wondered if she had time to nip out to buy a tablecloth before Jon arrived – something exotic, something sophisticated – something clean. Cartwheeling the table around on one of its little dumpy legs, a drop leaf swung out and grabbed at the door frame, lifting a great curl of new paint and plaster before falling with a resounding smack on her thumb. Dora swore softly under her breath. Maybe she could find a tablecloth that covered blood stains and went with bruises.

She stuttered and hiccuped the heavy oak table across the carpet, eventually sliding it under the window so that they'd be able to look out on the street below. Somewhere she was certain she had candles. Dora glanced at the clock and then the wall, wondering if a quick dab of Copydex and a smear of emulsion would be dry by eight-ish.

Gibson dozed in the hearth, one eye closed, while Oscar perched above him on the mantel shelf, debating whether the newly installed pot plant constituted an invitation to shred.

Dora looked at him sharply. 'Don't even think about it,' she snapped, as he insinuated a questioning, chiselling nose down towards the tumble of crisp green foliage. She pulled one of the armchairs forward a little and slid a dining chair either side of the newly arranged table. It looked vaguely Parisian, she thought, bohemian. She stood back and smiled.

Gibson was not impressed. Above him, with the skill of a proctologist, Oscar leant down, clinging to the mantel shelf by a single molecule of claw and paw, and nipped a leaf off the plant. Dora hissed at him, smoothed her hands down over her shirt-tails and looked at the clock again.

The sitting room looked good. All she needed now was a

decent cloth, there was an old pair of Liberty-print curtains in the bottom of the ... As she glanced up she saw something in the street below and for an instant felt a tiny flutter of panic. What if the watcher was there again? Nervously, Dora stepped away from the window and took a deep breath.

Lillian was gone, things would get back to normal. She wouldn't give whoever it was the satisfaction of looking out, there or not. She wouldn't look, she would plan for Jon's arrival.

She'd made a curry – roghan gosht – they'd have pilau rice, poppadoms, mango chutney. She took another deep breath, letting the rich smell from the kitchen settle her nerves. She was home, she was safe, and Jon Melrose was coming to dinner.

Dora turned away and headed quickly into the hall.

The curtains were in the bottom of the airing cupboard, the candles in a box in the kitchen. There were an awful lot of other thoughts skittering through the shadowy recesses of her mind as she plunged into the drawer to find a candlestick. Something glinted in the corner of her mind – a slick little moondark puddle of desire, a ripple of expectation.

She'd already changed the sheets on the bed, whipping off the sensible striped flannelette in favour of the ones Sheila had given her for Christmas, cream things with impossible-to-iron frills on the sheet and duvet cover and fiddley broderie anglaise inserts in the pillows. There was wine in the fridge, beer, half a bottle of scotch.

She grinned, forcing the candles to stand up by ramming a ball of tin-foil into the holders with a kebab skewer. Was getting a policeman drunk an acceptable way to get him into bed? She reddened at her own thoughts – it had just been too long.

She had spent so long subverting and subjugating her physical desire into words. Her prose was a sensual masterpiece; a blissfully erotic, seamless guided tour around sexuality at its most stylised. But reality had never been so smooth, or so uncomplicated; people in real life made judgements, had opinions and independent thoughts, sulked, wore socks in bed

187

and broke wind, were self-conscious, fumbled and blushed – what if she had got it horribly wrong and Jon really didn't fancy her at all? What if . . . she straightened her shoulders and tried to strangle the little nagging voice that suggested she was maybe just about to make a complete fool of herself. Apprehension and expectation were a disturbing combination.

Carefully, she carried the curtains and candles into the sitting room and set them on the centre of the table. Maybe she had come to believe her own propaganda and along the way had forgotten the mixed emotions of doubt and uncertainty that went hand-in-hand with the rest of the cocktail. What would it be like waking up beside a man after all these years? She wondered if she drooled in her sleep and if the mirror lied and she was entirely composed of cellulite after all. Talking herself in and out of passion was almost more than she could bear.

Finally, when the table was set, Dora slumped down into the sofa and encouraged the cats onto her lap.

'You see,' she said in a conspiratorial voice, sliding her fingers along Oscar's sinuous back, 'I've forgotten how to play this game. I've been fully occupied on the sidelines writing the commentary. I don't know how it goes any more.'

There was a hint of appeal in her voice. Oscar's eyes narrowed and he began to purr.

'God,' she snorted dryly, as Gibson vied noisily for her attention. 'I wish you pair were men. I'd know exactly what to do then, slap half a can of tuna on the lino and you'd be putty in my hands.' Gibson rolled onto his back and mewled provocatively.

'You're quick off the mark tonight, sir,' said Rhodes, as Jon Melrose closed the file on his desk and threw it back into the in-tray with an unmistakable gesture of finality.

Jon tidied away the rest of the things by the blotter, sliding pens and forms casually into the drawers. 'Someone once told me there was more to life than work,' he said, eyes wandering back and forth to check his efforts. 'I've decided to investigate the possibility.'

Rhodes snorted. 'Change of tune as well. Don't tell me, another night out with Mrs Hall?'

Jon glanced at his watch. 'Dinner, actually.'

'Very nice, where are you going? Somewhere posh?'

Jon stretched and then got to his feet. 'I'm having dinner cooked for me.'

Rhodes grinned. 'Watch yourself, sounds like you're getting your feet under the table there, gov.'

Jon pointedly ignored him. He had a nervous bubble of anticipation in his stomach. It was years since he had felt like this. He pulled on his jacket, nipping in the bud the grin he felt coming on.

'So,' he said briskly. 'I'm off to Sainsbury's to buy dessert and a bottle of something half decent and very drinkable.'

'Hope you have a nice time, sir.'

Jon nodded. 'Don't ring me unless Lord Lucan turns up.'

As he closed the door, he heard Rhodes laugh good-humouredly.

Jon hit the first wave of Keelside's rush hour. The cars ahead of him were arranged along the by-pass like a child's necklace of brightly coloured beads. He ignored the tailback on the first of the roundabouts and caught himself singing at the next and every subsequent red traffic light.

On the radio, some perceptive soul was flooding the air-waves with classic love songs. Gladys Knight and the Pips caught the Midnight Train to Georgia against a backdrop of lush rural splendour. Jon sat back in the driver's seat and strained for the high notes, grinning madly. He even managed to park right up by the entrance to the store. The sun was still shining, and, from the look of it, every checkout was open. Maybe there was a god after all. Whistling, he climbed out of the car and pulled a trolley out of the stack.

'Jon?'

Two aisles from the checkout, he had a trolley full of frozen, microwavable gratification, three frozen desserts and an expensive bottle of wine. Hearing his name, Jon Melrose stopped mid-stride and looked back over his shoulder.

'Nita?' he said incredulously as his ex-wife hurried towards him, bright with smiles.

'Oh, Jon. I'm so glad to see you, I wanted to thank you for what you did the other day. I don't know what we'd have done without you.' She sounded breathless and emotional.

Jon shrugged, trying to find something to say. He wondered if she truly imagined he would abandon Joe when he needed him. Nita was talking as if he was a helpful stranger, not Joe's father.

'How is Joe?' he managed to say.

'Doing really well, maybe you'd like to pop in some time to see him? Sam wouldn't mind. You don't mind Joe not coming to yours next weekend, do you? Only I thought maybe he ought to take things a bit easy for a little while. Stay close to home until the consultant's seen him again.'

Before Jon had a chance to reply, Nita continued, 'I'm really glad I've seen you here.' Her smile grew wider still. She pushed a strand of blonde hair back behind her ears. 'It's no good, I've got to say something.' She took a deep breath, exhaling through toothpaste-white teeth. 'I'm pregnant. We only picked up the test results from the doctor's this morning, what with Joe's accident and everything – I mean, I was already more or less certain, but I wanted it to be official before we told anybody. The kids are so thrilled. We all are –'

Jon nodded dumbly; what was there to say? He glanced down into his trolley and then up at her.

'Congratulations,' he said, as warmly as he could manage. 'Looks like you've all got a lot to celebrate.'

Nita laughed. 'Thank you, thank you. I knew you'd be pleased for us. I told Sam you'd be pleased.'

Before he had time to side-step her, Nita pressed forward, closing herself around him in a delighted excited embrace. He stiffened, feeling the outline of her breasts pressing through his thin shirt and belatedly tried to pull back. Too late. She kissed him full on the mouth, her scent, the heat of her body making his mind reel.

'Oh, Jon,' she gasped, 'I'm so happy. I just can't tell you.

Oh, would you like to come round tomorrow? You could come when Joe gets home from school. I'm sure he'd be really pleased to see you. Stay to tea.'

Jon Melrose coughed uncomfortably. 'That would be great,' he said, prepared to say almost anything that meant he could extricate himself from her arms.

'Good, can you give me a ring to let me know you're definitely coming?'

Jon nodded.

As quickly as Nita had arrived she was gone, blue eyes bright with joyful tears.

Jon leant heavily against the handle of his trolley and took a deep, deep breath, as if he were recovering from a punch to the stomach.

Dora had bathed and still had a warm baby glow of cleanliness about her. She wanted to take a final look at the sitting room. She'd spread one curtain over the table, covering it in a rich festoon of pagan abundance, whilst the other hung across the back of the sofa, covering the worst of the plucks, with the cushions arranged in an inviting arc. She teased a pair of nail scissors from a jar on the mantel shelf and carefully snipped off the long white strings that peeped out over the arm, revealing the cloth's pedigree.

The intercom bell rang – it was barely half past seven. She rolled the strings into a knot and stuffed them into her pocket before heading for the office.

'Hello?'

For a little while she had forgotten about the man in the street, the burglaries, Lillian Bliss – the memories scurried back into her head like a tumble of gnawing rats. Dora had a horrible sense of *déjà vu*. She took a deep breath, not giving the caller a chance to answer.

'Who is this please?' she snapped nervously.

'It's me, are you all right? I thought I'd come over early.'

Jon's voice brought a sigh of relief.

'I'm fine, come up.' She pressed the entry button. It wasn't

191

until she was sliding the catch across on the upstairs door that she remembered she was still in her dressing gown, and immediately flushed crimson.

Jon Melrose, bearing gifts, peered around the door and grinned.

'You look wonderful. I didn't drag you out of the bath, did I? Or do you always meet men on your stairs dressed like that?'

Dora felt the colour in her cheeks intensify. 'I did say eight-ish.'

Jon looked embarrassed. 'You did, you're right. But I thought . . .' He stopped. 'Do you mind? I could go away again and come back later, if you'd prefer.'

Dora stepped back and beckoned him in. 'No, it's all right, come in.' She laughed nervously, still frightened of getting it all wrong. She puffed out her cheeks. 'Tell you what, do you fancy a drink? There is a huge pile of God-knows-what that I bought from the supermarket in the fridge. Will you pour me something strong and bracing while I go and get dressed?' She paused at the bedroom door. 'I'll have you know I cleaned the fridge out in your honour.'

'You really know how to sweet-talk a man, don't you? Shall I put my offerings in there as well?'

Dora leant back out of the door. 'It depends what you brought.'

Jon opened his large bag. 'A strawberry pavlova, some sort of frozen chocolaty something with cream and nuts on the top and . . .' He peered at the final box. 'An appley thing with ice cream.'

Dora grinned. 'I see you're a man who can take instructions, I like that. Stick them in the fridge, I'll sort them out in a minute.'

Relieved that he was there and was the same as she remembered him, Dora dressed quickly. Discarding the dress she'd so carefully ironed as too fussy, she slipped on clean black leggings and a long silky golden shirt. Barefoot, she padded back out to the kitchen, where Jon had poured two long glasses of cinzano and was topping them up with lemonade.

He had his back to her and was dressed in a soft blue chambray cotton shirt tucked into faded jeans. In the nape of his neck, dark, grey-touched hair curled against his skin. She took a deep breath. A lemon lay dissected on the table beside him – and suddenly, more than anything in the world, she wanted to touch him. Stepping forward, she slid her arms around his waist, and pressed her face into his muscular back, breathing in the soft male smell of his body. He turned slowly towards her and she wondered momentarily whether she might faint.

He looked down at her with his dark glittering eyes and smiled. 'Well, hello there, Dora Hall,' he purred, and she knew then that she hadn't forgotten as much as she'd feared.

'Hello, Jon Melrose.'

He kissed her softly, with exaggerated tenderness, as if she might break. She wondered if she would cry. Instead she wheeled away from him, fingers still caught in his.

'I'm incredibly nervous,' she said, in a low voice.

Jon held out a glass in her direction. 'Dutch courage?'

Dora laughed, and closed her fingers round the glass. 'If you insist. I've cooked a huge curry, I thought we'd eat in the sitting room –' The need to touch him was overwhelming. The desire inside her reared up, uninvited, like a cornered animal, and she hastily let go of Jon's hand and grabbed hold of the sink to steady herself.

He moved closer, brushing tender moist kisses into her neck, into the soft damp tendrils of her hair, and when she heard a low throaty moan it took her a second or two to realise the voice was hers.

'This is much, much too fast. What about the curry?' she heard herself say, as he pulled her into his arms, hands lifting to hold her closer. It seemed as if they stood there a very long time. The kiss went on and on until finally she pulled herself away breathlessly.

'Bloody hell,' she whispered thickly, looking up into his dark mischievous eyes.

He grinned. 'You say all the right things.'

Dora took a long pull on her glass. 'I think we'd better eat. Trust me, it'll be much safer if we keep a table between us. Do you want a lesson in how to cook rice?'

Jon shrugged and sat down at the kitchen table. 'I think I just want to be with you. I'll treat any cookery lesson as an added bonus.'

She moved around the kitchen slowly, aware that his eyes were on her and felt embarrassed and delighted by degrees.

As she rinsed the uncooked rice under the tap, with her back towards him so she couldn't see his face, Dora said, 'I think you ought to know something. I've never slept with anyone other than Ray. I was going to work up to telling you slowly, if . . . well . . .' She could hear the embarrassment in her voice and laughed, spinning round, red-faced, to look at him. 'God, this is so ridiculous, I keep telling myself I'm all grown up now. I flog porn to pay my rent and I still can't find the words to say this. Maybe it would have been better if I'd written it all down before you arrived and just handed you two or three pages of lovingly typed manuscript as you came through the door.'

Jon stood up slowly and took the colander out of her hands, standing it beside the glass of cinzano on the draining board.

'Would you like to go to bed with me?' he asked, in the quietest of voices.

She nodded. 'Yes, I rather think I would,' and then she grinned. 'Hang on, I'd better turn the curry off, first.' She looked at him again, feeling the colour in her face deepen a dozen shades. 'Are you like a boy scout? Always prepared?'

Jon paused for a second and then a light of comprehension dawned.

'Oh God, no – I thought it might look a bit previous to turn up here clutching a bottle of plonk, a selection of frozen desserts and a packet of three.'

They both looked at each other and burst into peals of laughter. Jon picked up his jacket from the chair. 'I'll just nip out, there's a late-night chemist on the corner of Park Street, isn't there?'

Dora grabbed hold of his hand. 'Wait a minute, let me come with you. I might change my mind if you leave me here on my own.'

He lifted an eyebrow questioningly, and Dora continued smiling. 'What I mean is, chicken out, run away, take another bus somewhere. Oh, I don't know. Just give me a minute to put some shoes on and grab my coat.'

In Jon's car, removed from the electric atmosphere of the flat, he turned and grinned at her. 'I got home from work and couldn't wait to get over here. I'd been driving round Fairbeach since just after six.'

Dora stretched back in the car seat. 'Well at least the desserts should be defrosted. I've been like a cat on hot bricks since I saw you this morning. This all seems really silly.'

... But not as silly as sitting in Jon's car, outside the late-night chemist on Buxton Crescent, after discovering the one on Park Street was closed. Dora had wondered whether to offer to go in with him, but the image of a middle-aged couple huddled self-consciously over the Durex display was more than her imagination could cope with. Instead, she sat in the car peering out into the rapidly darkening night, and picking at the leather fascia on the glove compartment. Jon seemed to be taking a very long time, and alone, dark fears and uncertainties came bubbling up unbidden and unwelcome. Part of it was the sense of shyness. She dropped the sun visor and looked at her shadowy reflection in the little mirror.

'I'm a grown-up,' she said firmly, 'I am.'

The reflection said nothing, just betrayed the wild little glint in her eyes. She looked back into the street as Jon reappeared with a carrier bag tucked under his arm. Dora laughed aloud, leaning over to open the door for him.

'What did you get? Toothpaste? Insoles? A hot water bottle?'

Jon slid into his seat and pulled a face. 'How did you guess? Actually, nothing but what we needed. God, it was tough going in there. I felt like a schoolkid. And then when I'd puckered up and paid, the assistant behind the counter decided that a carrier bag would be more discreet.'

Dora guffawed. 'More discreet than what?'

Jon turned the key in the ignition. 'God alone knows, it was her suggestion, not mine.' He turned towards her, just before the car pulled off. 'I don't know whether I ought to say this, but I think, Dora Hall, that I could very easily fall in love with you.'

Dora stopped, swallowing back her laughter. 'I know,' she said softly. 'Good, isn't it?'

When they got back to the flat, the good humour closed down to a quiet expectant pulse. Jon looked across at Dora as she fought with the front-door lock. 'How many years has it taken us to get this far?'

Dora sighed. 'Don't let's think about it.' She held up her thumb and finger with a fraction of an inch between them. 'I'm still this far from being too scared.'

Jon leant against the wall, looking puzzled. 'Do I frighten you?'

Dora shook her head, feeling the lock finally give under her frantic turning.

'No,' she said quietly. 'I frighten myself. Let's go in and eat, shall we?'

Upstairs, the lights were still on. Dora headed straight for the kitchen and began to cook the rice. Jon moved around her; both pointedly ignored the neatly folded carrier bag on the kitchen unit.

The tension ebbed and flowed over dinner. The curry was delicious. Jon ate like a condemned man, thought Dora ruefully, as she slid the partially defrosted pavlova onto a plate.

Gibson and Oscar, seeming to sense the atmosphere, had vanished under the sideboard, and peered out nervously as if they were expecting something dangerous and disturbing to happen – maybe they were right.

Jon got up when dessert was finished. 'I'll make the coffee, if you like.'

Dora, replete and lulled by good wine, pushed back her chair and smiled. 'Everything is all ready on the tray.'

Jon nodded. When he returned with the coffee, Dora was

curled up on the settee, and Sade purred her soft musical invitation over the speakers of the stereo.

Jon sat down beside her, arm slipping easily around her shoulders. 'Music to seduce policemen by?'

Dora laughed softly, resting her head against his. 'I do hope so,' she murmured. 'That was the plan.'

He moved closer and pressed his lips to hers. After a second he pulled away, eyes reduced to hypnotic pin pricks. 'I'm not sure I can live up to the performance of the guys in your books.'

Dora reddened. 'You've read my books?'

Jon shook his head. 'No.'

Dora laughed. 'I'm glad about that.' She snuggled closer. 'Do we have to keep talking?'

It was just after five when Dora awoke. She sat bolt upright, caught on the edge of a dark compelling dream. She had dreamt Jon Melrose was in her bed and that she had reached out and . . . She snapped on the bedside lamp. Jon's dark hair pooled around his handsome face beside her on the pillow. The lamp light disturbed him, he blinked and frowned, face screwed up in discomfort, sleepy eyes complaining at the brightness. She snapped the light back off almost as quickly as she'd put it on and snuggled into the warm crook of his arm.

'Morning,' he said in a tender sleepy voice.

Dora said nothing, letting her hands slide across the broad expanse of his chest. Tight-curled hairs sprung past her fingertips. It wasn't quite morning yet and there was still plenty of time to carry on dreaming.

Dora whistled while she cleaned out the cat litter tray, throwing open the windows in the flat, feeling as if something had changed irrevocably in her life. The spring sunlight kissed everything golden and the two cats, totally befuddled, sat in awe of the great burst of activity that threatened to engulf them. Jon had finally left just before eight to go to the police station, but had promised to ring later, and she knew, if he rang, he would be back.

She glanced in the sitting-room mirror – she even looked different. The intercom bell broke her reverie. Dora waltzed into the office and pressed the button. 'Hello?'

Sheila's unmistakable voice crackled through the speaker. 'Hello, you sound very cheerful today.'

Dora grinned. 'Come up, it's open.' Even from one flight down she could hear Sheila sniffing. Nothing could spoil her mood, though. She had a strange bubbling feeling in her stomach and couldn't stop smiling.

Sheila peered suspiciously around the door as if she expected to be waylaid. Dora laughed, she could feel charitable towards even Sheila today.

Sheila stood her shopping bag down amongst the remains of last night's supper. Dora had cleared most of it away; only the bottles were left.

Sheila picked up one and peered at the label. 'So, how did it go last night?' she said slowly.

'Fine, dinner was wonderful.'

Sheila sniffed, and then eased herself carefully onto a kitchen chair. 'Nice.'

Dora had already got the kettle plugged in. Sheila had two methods of attack – either she took a long time to work around to what she really wanted to say, or alternatively came straight out with it, like the thrust of a well-placed blade. Today she was working up to it slowly and Dora was not in the mood. She leant against the sink.

'Come on, Sheila, you might as well tell me. What's bugging you?'

Sheila bit her lips and then sucked her teeth. 'I just wondered how much you knew about that chap, Jon, you're seeing, that's all.'

Dora felt the bubble settle in her stomach. Sheila, like Job's comforters, was seldom the bearer of good news.

'I don't know what you mean, Sheila. He's a policeman, he . . .'

Sheila lifted a hand and a sharp-focused pair of eyes. 'He used to live in Wrights' Avenue, didn't he? Down behind the high school. Married that girl Thompson?'

Dora blustered. 'I really don't know,' she began, feeling the level of euphoria drop a degree.

Sheila stood the empty bottle back on the table. 'I saw him yesterday in Sainsbury's, with his wife. They were all over each other. I couldn't really hear what they said because I was in the aisle across the way, near the biscuits . . .'

There was more, Dora could feel it. Sheila leant forward. 'They were all over each other,' she repeated.

The bubble landed and popped with a dark sickening hiss in Dora's stomach.

'They're divorced,' she said evenly. 'Jon told me they were divorced. She lives with someone else now.'

Sheila coughed. 'They all say that. They'll tell you anything – he didn't look divorced yesterday, I can tell you.'

Dora wanted to find something concrete to say to Sheila that would shut her up, something that would strike like a body blow. Most of all, she wanted to defend what she felt. She glanced out of the kitchen window into the recreation ground beyond the alleyway at the back of the flat, focusing her thoughts.

'I don't really care whether they're divorced or not,' she said flatly, without emotion.

Behind her, Sheila made a dark choking noise. 'How on earth can you say that?' she spluttered. 'That's disgusting.'

Dora threw two tea bags into the pot and slammed it down hard on the table next to Sheila, holding her sister's astonished gaze.

'Because it's true,' she snapped, and as Dora said it, she realised to her horror it was.

Dora wasn't certain whether she should ring Jon, or whether she really wanted to. She opened the phone book and stared at the number for Keelside police station for a long time before tapping it into the phone. It was answered on the second ring by an efficient-sounding woman. In the background Dora could hear a crackle of other voices.

'I wonder whether I can speak to Chief Inspector Jon Melrose, please?'

The woman hesitated and then said pleasantly, 'If you'd like to hold, I'll try and get him for you. Who shall I say is calling?'

Dora bit her lip. 'Er, a friend, Dora Hall.'

'Just a moment, please.'

Dora heard the woman ask someone else about Jon, and then heard the reply with equal clarity, before the woman amended it for her benefit.

'I'm afraid he's not available at the moment, would you like to leave him a message?'

Dora declined politely, and dropped the receiver gently back in its cradle.

The unseen person close to the telephonist had told Dora everything she needed to know. 'No, he's already gone home to his wife, just say he's not available.'

When the phone rang a few seconds later she ignored it. Everything seemed very still, except for the insistent voice of the telephone ringing on and on. Without looking back, she hurried into the kitchen.

Gibson and Oscar were sitting on the windowsill, posing in the sunshine. Dora swept Gibson up in her arms, and before he had time to double guess her, she tumbled him into the cat basket.

'Time to go home,' she said, in a low unhappy voice, and snapped the lock shut.

14

As Sheila left, Milo and Spar were having a conference in Milo's Mini Metro. The car was parked unobtrusively by the boarded-up chemist's shop. The venue for their conference had been decided by the fact that Spar's ageing car had finally run out of juice and needed a new battery. Milo had already changed it. Job done, they compared notes after the meetings with their respective employers.

Spar lit up a cigarette. 'So what do we do now?'

With the new battery in place he had reviewed Dora Hall's most recent calls on the tape recorder. The tape confirmed what they already knew – Lillian Bliss had moved back to Anchor Quay.

Milo sighed. 'Lotta time spent doing nothing with this job. We need to tango, shake a few trees, get the players up and running.'

Spar nodded; what the hell was Milo talking about?

'Somewhere,' Milo continued, 'is the information we both need, maybe in the same place, maybe separate places.' He jabbed a finger towards the windscreen. 'The truth is out there.'

Spar stared at him. 'I thought the main thing was just to get a photo of Calvin Roberts shagging Lillian Bliss. Anything else was gravy on the taters.'

Milo let out a long soulful breath.

'Things are not always what they appear, matey. Yes, I've got to get that, and no, that ain't all I need. I've been talking to a contact of mine, owns the linen shop opposite side of the river to Anchor Quay. I reckon we should set up a surveillance post there.'

Spar nodded. There had to be more.

'Got any more of those telephone bugs on you?' asked Milo.

'Yes,' said Spar guardedly. 'I bought a job lot. Mail order.'

Milo grinned. 'Good. Have you got one on Lillian's phone over at Anchor Quay?'

Spar didn't like to say that he had, but that he hadn't managed to make it work, so he shook his head.

'Not enough time when I was trashing the place. I thought I'd been rumbled.'

Milo pulled back his lips in what might or might not have been a smile. 'We'll get one in there, stake out the flat from the shop opposite, get this thing wrapped up and done with. Blanket surveillance. I've got a low boredom threshold, me. It's time for short sharp shock tactics.'

Spar winced. His only exposure to a short sharp shock, courtesy of Her Majesty, had involved a very nasty incident with a big butch skinhead that he would prefer to forget.

In the driver's seat, Milo was still talking. '. . . Rally the rest of your team. How many men can you muster?'

Spar coughed. 'Er, all my other lads are just about to go on a package tour to Marbella, they booked it up months ago.' He lifted his hands skyward. 'You know how these things are.' He cast a sideways glance in Milo's direction, wondering if he'd pushed the bounds of credibility a little too far.

Milo snorted. 'Ain't it always the same? You just can't get the bloody staff these days, can yer? Where's their sense of loyalty? They reckon the unemployed can't find work, then you give the little bastards a job and what do they do – fuck off to Marbella when the going gets rough.' He shook his head. 'Well, in that case it looks like it'll just be you and me then. My oppo's got himself a job at the canning factory, shift work, three sixty an hour. He reckons he prefers steady hours . . . Eh up, look sharp, kettle's boiling –'

Across the street, Dora Hall, carrying a cat basket, opened the door to the flat. Her shoulders were hunched forward, her expression closed and determined. In one hand she held a set of keys.

Milo nodded. 'Game's afoot. Do you reckon it's worth giving her drum another bang? While she's out?'

Spar waited for the subtitles. Milo continued talking as Dora set off down the street. She was leaning to counterbalance the contents of the cat basket.

'We'll follow her. Maybe we can find out exactly how much she knows.'

Dora was still cradling her keys.

'Reckon she's going to get her car.' Milo turned the key in the ignition. 'Soon see. I wonder what she's got in that basket.'

Spar shook his head. 'A cat?' he suggested.

Milo snorted. 'You're new to this game, aren't you, son?' Slowly he drew away from the kerb, keeping Dora Hall in their sights. When she got to the lock-up garages they hung back at the junction, watching, waiting until she re-emerged in her Fiat.

Dora was trying hard to keep her thoughts in a small tightly bound box, right up in the front of her head between her eyes. No room for Jon Melrose, no room for Sheila, she was just going to concentrate on the immediate things, present tense thoughts. Get round this roundabout, take Gibson back to Lillian.

Ahead of her the cars crept forward. On the back seat of her car, Gibson circled miserably around the cage, yowling melodramatically.

Dora tried to get a look at him in the rear-view mirror, wriggling it so that she could see his unhappy feline face. When they made eye contact in the mirror, he hissed malevolently.

'Calm down,' she muttered. 'Lillian loves you. You're going to a nice new home. You'll be just fine.'

She was at the front of the queue of cars now, waiting for a break in the traffic. Flicking the mirror back into position, she caught a glimpse of the blue Metro behind her. Two men were hunched in the front seats.

One more car, she could go after this red one – Dora nosed forward, foot on the accelerator. Just as she pulled onto the roundabout, Gibson let out a mind-numbing, banshee shriek, making her jump, swear and brake all in the same instant.

Behind her, the blue car braked sharply and there was a nasty squeal of tyres. With her stomach neatly folded up in the back of her throat, Dora lifted a hand in apology to the men behind her and carried on, taking the next turning off towards Anchor Quay. The entrance to the residents' car park was no more than a hundred yards away from the roundabout. She glanced into her mirror just before she indicated – the blue Metro was still right behind her and indicating as well.

Dora pulled into a parking space overlooking the river, and gathered her thoughts back up.

'I'm sorry,' she practised in an undertone. 'I didn't mean to cause you any problem. The cat frightened me. I braked instinctively. Could happen to anyone. Sorry.' She glanced into the mirror and then over her shoulder. The men had found a parking space right up against the back entrance to the apartments. Where, she thought ruefully, had she had any sense, she ought to have parked.

They didn't look like residents. Dora took a deep breath. Was she going to stay in the car all day? Behind her Gibson yowled again and rattled the door of his cage.

She slipped the key out of the ignition, struggling to maintain her calm, climbed out of the car, opened the back door and swung Gibson's basket onto the gravel. She painted on a smile. She'd have to bluff it out, apologise, look winsome and inept. Grovel.

From the corner of her eye she saw the men getting out of their car and mentally measured the yardage between herself and the doors. It felt a bit like chess – as she moved, so did they, one step ahead, across the board with alarming speed towards the entrance to the flats. Maybe it might be better to get into the car and come back later after all. Maybe they were electricians, maybe it was a coincidence, maybe –

The larger of the two men, the driver, stepped in front of her just as she reached the door. He was a lot faster than he looked. She didn't need to turn round to know that his friend was a few paces behind her. Checkmate. She took a deep breath.

'I'm really sorry about the roundabout – I was . . .'

'What've you got in the basket?' the man demanded, nodding down towards her hand.

'Sorry?'

The man managed an oily grin. 'The basket. Giv'us it here.' He held out his hand in a gesture that suggested it was not an invitation.

Dora watched her arm lifting, bearing the basket and Gibson, without any conscious awareness that she was doing it. Minutes earlier she had struggled to carry it; now the basket rose up in front of her like a hot-air balloon.

What happened next seemed to take place in slow motion, although it was over in an instant. Still holding her gaze, the man snatched the basket, flipped the catch without bothering to look inside and tipped it up, giving it a violent shake as he did so.

Gibson, already bad-tempered at being imprisoned and totally out of sorts with life generally, exploded out of the lid of the cat basket like a furry grey hand-grenade and roared off up the front of the man's army fatigues, thought better of it, did a dramatic U-turn and hurtled across the car park as if jet-propelled.

Dora, open-mouthed, stared back at the man, too confused, too shocked to form any coherent thoughts. Before she had time to compose herself a familiar face loomed into view.

Josephine Hammond from the *Fairbeach Gazette* seemed to materialise from out of a clear blue sky, and said cheerfully, 'Morning, Dora Hall, isn't it? How's it going? Need any help?'

Dora turned fractionally, breaking the hold of the man's gaze and at once he threw the cat basket down and ran off towards the blue Metro, followed closely by his friend.

Dora stood staring at Josephine.

'Are you all right?'

Dora shook her head. 'Not really. I think I may just have been mugged. Would you mind helping me catch Gibson?'

Josephine Hammond shrugged. 'Anything's better than being cooped up in that car. I keep thinking that they've given me this job so I jack it in. What are you doing here? Catiana Moran? Lillian Bliss? I see Miss Moran is back upstairs this morning.' She paused. 'And what was going on with your jolly little friends? They didn't look much like veterinary nurses to me.'

Dora shook her head. It felt as if someone was squeezing her lungs. 'Look, just help me catch this bloody cat, will you, and then we can talk,' she gasped.

Josephine grinned. 'Right-oh, I've got a tuna and mayonnaise sandwich in the car, maybe we could use it as bait.'

Fifteen minutes and an awful lot of cat coaxing later, Josephine Hammond pushed the remains of a toasted teacake into her mouth. Her eyes narrowed. 'So, you're telling me that Lillian Bliss isn't really Catiana Moran? That's right, isn't it? And you are the one who writes the books. You're Catiana Moran.'

Dora topped up their teacups and nodded. 'Off the record, yes. Calvin Roberts hired Lillian to promote my novels. In my defence, I would like to add, that it seemed like a very good idea at the time.'

They were sitting in Ye Olde Cosy Tea Roome, which was across the road from Anchor Quay, facing the front entrance. Gibson was safely back in his cat basket, locked in Dora's car, mumbling over the remains of one of Josephine's tuna sandwiches – and Dora was spilling some of the beans.

The truth could surely be no more awkward or dangerous than the lies. Dora couldn't contemplate facing Lillian straight away, and hadn't protested as Josephine had guided her across the road to the café and promised to pick up the bill.

Across the table, Josephine picked a stray currant out of her teeth. 'You ought to ring the police and report those guys.'

Dora sighed. Images of Jon Melrose filled her head, touching her face, stroking her shoulders – and maybe lying to her.

She shivered. 'You're probably right.'

Josephine nodded. 'I know I am, that's why I was here this

morning. I picked up a message on the police radio saying they were delivering some boxes first thing. They'd only just gone when you arrived. I'd planned to have a sandwich and then go and re-introduce myself to Miss Moran. Shame you couldn't have had your meeting with the muggers a bit earlier. We could have called up the cavalry. Six hairy-arsed coppers all spoiling for a fight – it would have made the front page.' She paused and pulled another teacake onto her plate. 'Actually, it still might.'

Dora snorted. Her hands had just about stopped shaking, but there was a lot of tea in the saucer to testify that the tremors hadn't been gone that long.

'My place, Lillian's new flat, Calvin Roberts' office and Lillian's old flat –' Dora counted off on her fingers. 'Four burglaries and then this thing this morning, and I'm certain someone has been watching my place. I've got a . . .' She paused. What was Jon? She took another breath. 'The police think the burglars may be looking for something.'

Josephine nodded. 'And this morning's little run-in would suggest, whatever it is they're looking for, they haven't found it yet. Right? I really think you need me on your side.'

Dora sighed. 'Please don't mention this to Lillian, I want her to stay where she is.'

Josephine's expression suggested her mind was elsewhere. 'What the hell do they think it is you've got?'

'I only wish I knew,' said Dora. 'I'd give it to them to get my life back.'

Josephine pulled a pad out of her shoulder bag.

Dora frowned. 'I did say all this was off the record.'

'I know, I know, but I think better when I write things down.'

Josephine carefully wrote out a list of names: Dora's, Lillian's, and Calvin's, adding Catiana Moran's last of all.

'What is it?' she said, staring down at her list. 'There has to be some sort of a link.'

'Lillian.'

Josephine nodded. 'Yes, but surely it can't be because of

your books? What mileage would there be in that? Who cares whether you write them or Lillian does?'

Dora had to agree with her. 'No-one except perhaps my sister.'

'Right, so we're back to Lillian Bliss. What the hell has she got, or does she know, that someone else wants so badly?'

Dora shook her head. 'No idea, why don't you try asking her yourself? I've tried and got nowhere.'

Josephine clicked her tongue against the roof of her mouth, thinking hard. 'We are assuming whatever she's got, she got it since she came to Fairbeach.'

Dora felt a little shiver. 'Yes,' she said slowly, 'since she started to work for me.'

Josephine doodled a small leaf under Catiana's name. 'But where was she before? You said the girl in her old flat told you she'd moved in late last year? Where did she live before that?'

Dora shrugged. 'No idea. I know she spent some time in Yarmouth.'

Across the table Josephine was getting to her feet. 'Time, I think, that we found out some more about Miss Bliss.'

Lillian welcomed them into her new apartment as if she hadn't seen Dora or Gibson for years. The elegant sitting room was strewn with cardboard boxes in various stages of unpacking. It looked as if they had been disembowelled. Ornaments, shoes and clothes were heaped across the furniture and floor. The oversized teddy-bear that Dora had seen at the flat in West Keelside lolled drunkenly on one of the sofas.

Lillian waved them to sit down amongst the chaos and hurried off to make tea. Dora wondered whether it was possible to get tannin poisoning – she'd already had four cups at Ye Olde Tea Roome with Josephine.

'Right,' said Josephine, once they were each cradling a mug. 'Can you tell me why you decided to settle in Fairbeach?'

Lillian Bliss looked up and then took a deep breath.

'I find it very inspirational, the river coursing through, the –'

Dora held up her hand to stop her. 'No, Lillian, not the thing I wrote for you, just tell Josephine the truth.'

Lillian screwed up her nose. 'But you said I was to stop telling the truth, you said . . .'

'I know what I said, but now I'm telling you to tell us what really made you move here.'

Lillian sniffed. 'But I like what you wrote about me. I really like being Catiana Moran.'

Josephine Hammond smiled warmly. 'And you can carry on being Catiana Moran, talking to me doesn't have to change that at all. What I'm trying to do is find out about Lillian Bliss.'

Lillian looked at Dora for a sign of approval. Dora nodded. 'It's all right, really.'

Lillian licked her lips. 'I was born in Fairbeach and lived here when I was little. Then, when I was about four, me and Mum moved to Norwich.' She stopped, gathering thoughts together. 'I thought I'd come back and see if I could find my dad, my real dad, not like an uncle or anything. I'd been trying to find him for ages and then I did.'

She paused, staring down into the gaping mouth of her teacup. 'My mum and dad weren't married.' She grinned. 'Well, not to each other, anyway. I was fostered when I was about six or seven because my mum was ill. She couldn't cope with me as well, though I used to see her sometimes. She had cancer – anyway, when I was fourteen she died. So when I got to eighteen I decided to start looking for him. I had to wait to see if he would see me. You know, all that stuff.'

Dora leant forward. 'But you did find him?' she said encouragingly.

Lillian nodded. 'Yeah. He got in touch with me last October and said he'd like us to meet up. I'd stayed in Norwich until then, did a bit of work in Yarmouth during the summer season, bit of modelling – but when he said yes I got the flat in Keelside. Belleview Terrace was close, but not too close. We met up quite a few times.' She smiled. 'He was really nice and seemed pleased to see me. I thought he was a lovely man, we got on really well.'

Her eyes misted over. 'He even invited me and my flatmate, Carol, to this big Christmas party at a great big house. He laid on a car to pick us up and everything. I took a load of old photos to show him, photos of my mum and when I was a kid – you know the kind of thing. I wanted to show him all the things he'd missed, I suppose. Try to make up for lost time.' She sniffed, eyes brighter still. 'Doesn't seem fair, really. We were just getting to know each other and then he died too.'

Josephine nodded. 'It must have been awful for you.' Her tone was gentle and encouraging. Dora realised she was good because she was genuinely interested.

'He came from Keelside, did he?' Dora could feel Josephine Hammond's mind circling the things that Lillian knew, gently picking through the chaff, searching for the ears of wheat.

Lillian shook her head, twirling a stray tendril of hair into a barley-sugar twist. 'Fairbeach, though he wasn't here a lot of the time. He met my mum here though, before we moved to Norwich.'

Josephine leant forward. 'So you came here to be near him?'

Lillian grinned. 'Yeah, it was him that fixed up this place for me, said it was a belated coming-of-age present.'

Dora stared at Lillian. 'You said Calvin got the flat for you?'

'Well, he did. He did all the legal stuff, solicitors and that sort of business. I met Calvin at this party too. He said he could find me a job.' Lillian giggled. 'I thought it was a wind-up, you know how blokes are. But he's a nice man, Calvin. I really like him. I don't think my dad liked him much, but maybe he didn't know him very well.'

Dora stared. She couldn't wait for Josephine to ask the next question and so she asked it for her.

'Who is your dad, Lillian?' she said quietly.

Lillian smiled her radiant shark-toothed smile. 'Jack Rees, you know, the MP?'

'Bloody hell,' hissed Josephine Hammond.

*　　*　　*

'It still doesn't make any kind of sense,' said Josephine, glancing down at the notes she had made from her interview with Lillian.

Dora snorted. 'What does these days?'

They had said their goodbyes to Lillian and driven back to Dora's flat together. Dora wasn't sure that she could face another cup of tea, but had put the kettle on anyway. On the way back they had called in at Fairbeach police station and given the man behind the desk a potted summary of Dora's encounter with the two men at Anchor Quay. He'd made a note and assured Dora someone would call in to see her. Dora only hoped, at the moment, that the someone they sent was not Jon Melrose.

Josephine accepted the mug of tea without comment. Presumably journalists had cast-iron bladders.

'Where's the mileage?' Josephine wondered, tapping her pad. 'A single exposé about a dead politician? If he was alive it would be different. I mean, there is a story here, but not something that would call for these sort of tactics. Besides, Lillian is hardly making a secret of it, is she? All we had to do was ask. And what else did she say?'

She glanced back over her notes and read the comments. ' "My dad's name is on my birth certificate. He wasn't ashamed of me or anything. He seemed quite proud really. He'd only got step-daughters, and didn't seem to get on very well with them. He said he always wanted a kid of his own." '

Josephine rubbed the bridge of her nose. 'Sad, really. Did you know Jack?'

Dora nodded. 'Not well, not personally, but I suppose everyone in Fairbeach thought they knew him, didn't they? What about you?'

Josephine tipped her chair back against the wall. 'I liked him, he always had a quote. A couple of times he rang me up and gave me a juicy bit of gossip – and social, party things – he'd always make sure we got an invite so that we could mingle a little.' She blew out a long slow breath. 'His wife is a cow, though.' She rolled her eyes heavenwards. 'Caroline

Rees, now there is one perfect twenty-four-carat gold bitch. Only together when the party demanded. Separate houses, separate lives. He died all alone, you know. I can understand Jack being pleased to find Lillian, someone who had been looking for him, someone to love.'

Dora pulled a face. 'I've got a fridge full of defrosted dinner-party desserts, fancy a big bowl of comfort food?'

Josephine nodded. 'Why not.'

Dora cut her a large slice of strawberry pavlova.

'There is something we just aren't seeing.' Josephine glanced at Dora. 'You're the writer, what's missing in this plot?'

Dora snorted. 'Sex. I don't have to worry too much about plot with my stuff, just endless variations and permutations to get the main characters into the sack.'

Josephine, still staring at her notes, felt around for the plate of cake. 'Maybe you've got something there. I wonder who else was at this Christmas party.'

'That shouldn't be too difficult to find out. I'll ask Calvin, he'll jump at the chance to name drop.' Dora hesitated. 'The thing is, you're looking for a story, maybe he wouldn't be so keen to know everything he said was going to end up on the front page of the *Gazette*.'

Josephine grinned. 'I'm not going to write it yet. Besides, when I do, I'll say "a reliable source". Don't worry, I'm used to deflecting flak. In the office I'm the odd one out, the token carrot top, the token woman, the token vegetarian, the token Lib Dem supporter. I'm used to being out on a limb.' She glanced around Dora's kitchen. 'Actually, I always fancied being a novelist. I've got to be off, will you ring me when you find out about the party?'

Dora nodded, as Josephine fished in her handbag and pulled out a business card. 'My mobile number is on there. Any time, any place, anywhere, that's me. Oh, and thanks for the tea and cake.'

There was a sound of the doorbell ringing. Dora sighed and got to her feet: Jon? Sheila? Lillian? Guiding Josephine towards the door, she took a quick detour into the office.

'Good afternoon, is that Mrs Hall?' said the disembodied voice through the speaker. 'PC Reed here, you reported an incident at Fairbeach police station this morning? I wondered if I might come up and have a word with you about it.'

Dora gave the policeman a statement and then went to sit in the office.

An insistent ringing bell woke her.

Whoever was ringing had their finger firmly pressed on the downstairs bell. It was Jon. It had to be Jon. She would ask him about his wife quietly, calmly . . . She pressed the call button and yawned before she spoke – the gap was just long enough to let Sheila's voice in.

'Hello, it's me, I was wondering if you'd like to come to tea. We've got tinned salmon.'

Dora groaned.

'You've left your answer machine on . . .' Sheila said.

Dora heard the sentence beginning through the speaker and finishing as Sheila climbed the stairs. 'I really hate those machines. You never listen to the messages anyway.'

Sheila bustled past Dora and into the kitchen.

Watching her sister's mouth flap up and down, like a guppy out of its tank, Dora wondered who Sheila spoke to the rest of the time. She needed to provide a running commentary, a constant soundtrack. Dora held up her hands to stem the verbal tide. 'I'll get changed.'

She stepped back into her bedroom. Even through the door, Sheila's voice was clearly audible, seeping through the cracks in the woodwork. Dora groaned and quickly dragged on a clean sweater.

Detective Sergeant Rhodes handed Jon Melrose a slip of paper. 'I thought you'd be interested in this. We've just had a report in from Fairbeach about a mugging.'

Jon stared at the bald statement and felt the flutter of anxiety returning. 'Is Dora all right?'

Rhodes nodded. 'Fine, as far as we know.'

Jon picked up the phone. 'We've got to do something about

all this. I'm going to ring Dora and I want you to pull all the files on the other incidents. It's high time we got this sorted out. I need you to organise some manpower.'

Dora's number rang once, twice. He glanced at his watch – where was she? He heard the phone pick up, and was about to speak when the answer machine cut in. It was good to hear her voice but he needed it to be Dora, not a recording.

He imagined her face and couldn't help but smile. All day long he had had tiny vivid recollections of the night before. Not all of them had been about making love. He could imagine her leaning towards him across the table, eyes alight with the glow from the candles. And the way she had stretched out on the sofa, easing the cat up off her lap when he had carried the coffee in. Being with her felt so comfortable, so easy. He listened to the recorded voice asking him to say something after the tone. He wanted to leave his love, his need, but instead he said he would ring back later.

There were three phone calls from Jon on the machine when Dora finally got back from Sheila's. They sounded increasingly frustrated with each recording. Dora skimmed through the flat, turning on lamps as she listened to the tape play back; three from Jon, two empty silences punctuated with a soft wet sound that she knew were almost certainly Sheila sucking her teeth, one from Calvin saying he would be round to see her. She paused as she heard Jon's voice again and felt a bitter-sweet pain.

Tea with Sheila and her family had felt like being in the witness box, being cross-examined by the prosecution when they had whiff of a guilty verdict.

Oscar eyed her suspiciously – all this to-ing and fro-ing and homing of itinerant toms was really too much for a cat. He had vented his spleen, in her absence, by nipping the new leaves off the plant by the hearth. Soft stars of foliage lay in a fading wilted heap.

When the intercom bell rang again Dora was tempted to ignore it. She eased herself up to look out of the window. Jon

Melrose's car was parked under the street light. She pressed the call button in her office with a strange reluctance and sadness.

'Hello.' His disembodied voice made her shiver. She wasn't sure exactly what she wanted to say and let her finger hover unsteadily over the button that would undo the lock downstairs.

'Hello, Dora?' he said again, with an edge of concern.

'Hello,' she said softly.

'Hi, how are you? I saw the report this afternoon, are you okay? Can I come up?'

Dora bit her lip. Rationally she should let him in and ask him about his wife. Simple, adult, honest, bloodless rationality. She wanted to feel his arms close around her and make everything all right.

She took another slow breath and said, 'No, not tonight.' She hadn't known what the answer was going to be until her mouth formed the words, and now they were out and said she had no intention of changing them.

There was a few seconds' silence over the intercom before Jon asked softly, 'What's the matter?'

She didn't know how to answer him. 'I'm not sure,' she whispered, 'I think I need some time,' and let her finger lift off the button.

She stood up and switched off the office light before going back to the sitting room. She saw Jon cross the road, back towards his car, pausing to look up at the office window. She didn't watch him drive away, and for the first time in days, she longed for a cigarette.

15

Dora slithered out of bed in the early hours of the morning, feeling as if she had a hangover. She struggled manfully to the bathroom and turned on the shower.

Oscar, reading the weather report as stormy with sudden squalls, scurried off to the kitchen after putting in a polite request to be fed, sometime, sometime soon, if it wasn't too much trouble. Now would be good, even though he realised it was painfully early. After a few minutes he decided he was being too understanding, mewled miserably and slinked his way back around Dora's legs to be rewarded by a few words of old Anglo-Saxon.

Dora scrubbed an oval in the steamy mirror and contemplated her reflection. She ought to have let Jon in. She would have slept better, or maybe not slept at all, but at least she wouldn't have been alone with her thoughts, turning over and over, knotting the bedclothes into an escape rope. She should have let him explain, there probably wasn't even anything to explain. Why had she believed Sheila, of all people?

God, being awake was almost as bad as trying to sleep. She groaned miserably and dragged a comb through her unruly shower-damp hair.

She felt an overwhelming sense of grief and loss for something that might have been, still might be, maybe never really was. She sighed, annoyed with herself for being so pathetic. Surely, after all this time, she ought to have the knack of saying what she meant? Or was talking to men something else that had been forgotten along with the finer steps of the mating dance?

It was only four thirty but she couldn't face another hour in bed. When she hadn't been thinking about Jon she had been thinking about Lillian Bliss – which was almost as bad.

The early light made the flat seem grey and terribly empty. Finally, she fed Oscar and went into her office. Maybe she ought to tell Calvin she wouldn't do another book. She switched on the computer and waited for the machine to announce it was ready.

Sucking a pencil, Dora lay back in the swivel chair, eyes and mind idling through the contents of the computer screen in front of her. After years of practice she could easily step inside the fictional landscape, contoured in letters, mapped out in sentences. To begin with, she wandered through it as a distraction. Ran it through the spell checker, encouraging the errors to float to the surface to be scooped off.

After ten minutes she was completely absorbed by the story, wandering around, looking at the bare framework of the new book like a homesteader eyeing up newly nailed timbers. She'd already cleared the ground and laid out the foundations in nice straight lines.

Outside the office window, the day brightened, but Dora didn't notice. Writing was almost better than sleep, and infinitely better than the thoughts that had driven sleep away.

She tapped words into the keyboard without being aware that she was doing it, adding layer upon layer of little bricks, guided by whatever jinn was inside her head that drove the story on. She couldn't imagine doing anything else.

Oscar, recognising the return of a familiar obsession, curled contentedly at her feet. He understood this, knew the signs and was glad finally to have his normal life back.

Real time passed unnoticed as Dora worked. She paused only to make tea, but even then her consciousness was firmly fixed on the world inside the new book. It was comforting to have some sense of control back. Fictional passion, totally untainted by uncertainty and pain, was so very much easier to work with than the real thing. Dora's latest heroine, who didn't have a sister, and certainly wouldn't lose a night's sleep consumed by doubts over an errant lover, strode enthusiastically from bed to bed without so much as a backward glance.

217

When finally Dora looked up at the clock it was after nine. For a few minutes she sat still, totally stunned, as if she had woken up on a train at an unexpected destination. She closed the machine down reluctantly, like a miser closing the lid on his hoard, and lifted up her glasses to rub the bridge of her nose. She needed to talk to Calvin.

Calvin was very surprised to see Dora in his office first thing in the morning. He waved her towards a chair.

'I was going to come round to see you today, didn't you get my message on your answering machine?' he said.

Dora nodded.

'I didn't think you did mornings. Do you want me to ring down for some tea?'

Dora stretched. 'I didn't sleep very well and yes, I could murder a cup. I came to talk to you about Lillian.'

Calvin groaned. 'Please, can't you bear with me on this for just a little bit longer?' He pulled a sheet of paper from the in-tray and handed it to Dora. 'Here, take a look at that. I wanted to talk to you about bringing the delivery date for this new book forward by a month or so. The publishers were on the phone again yesterday. They want to cash in on Lillian's success. The punters are baying for the latest one – they've already had to do another print run. Look at the list. Lillian's scheduled to do half a dozen more signings, a bit more promotion work and then there's this presentation thing up at the college and the Spring Ball afterwards. Another month's work at the most.'

Dora lifted an eyebrow. The odour of rat was all pervading.

'Really? You told me your machine was full of messages about Lillian the other day. The publishers are frothing at the mouth for the new book and then, in the next breath, you say you'll give Lillian another month at the most?'

She saw a glint of avarice in Calvin's eyes and sighed. He was still hoping she would change her mind.

'She's really looking forward to this ball thing,' Calvin said in a cajoling voice. 'She's been out to get herself a new ball gown and everything. She's going to be so disappointed if we have to turn it down.'

'I can do without the emotional blackmail, Calvin.' Dora paused, feeling tired. Maybe she should have had a nap and tackled Calvin after lunch. 'Lillian can go to the ball – far be it from me to shoot Cinderella down in flames – and these other things on your neatly typed little list, and then that is it. I don't care what happens, or what comes up. No more, nothing, zilch. Don't take any more bookings, is that perfectly clear?'

'We had a phone call yesterday about her opening a super-market – you're getting a slice of her appearance money. What if . . .'

Dora bullseyed him with a furious glare. 'No, this list and then it's curtains.' She paused as Gena, Calvin's receptionist, came in carrying a tea tray.

All the way down to Northquay, Dora had been thinking about the things Lillian had told her and Josephine Hammond. As Gena closed the door on her way out, Dora took a deep breath.

'Calvin, I want to ask you, how much do you know about Lillian?'

Calvin stared at her. 'What's to know? She's a model, good-looking – bit loose with her favours but, then again, she wouldn't be the first girl who made her way up the ladder by using the old casting couch route.' He preened a little. 'But I've had a word with her, explained a few home truths. I don't think it'll happen again. I've arranged for one of the girls from the office downstairs to go with her from now on if I can't make it. Like a chaperone. Why do you want to know?'

Dora took the cup of tea he offered her. 'I want to know how you met her.'

Calvin reddened. 'What is this, truth or consequences?'

'I really need to know.'

Calvin snorted. 'At a party. She was there with a lot of other girls. She told me she was a model and I said maybe I could find her a bit of work. You know how these things go. We kept in touch.' His expression left Dora in no doubt what Calvin meant by 'in touch'.

He tugged self-consciously at his waistcoat and continued. 'When the Catiana Moran promotion job came up I thought she'd be absolutely perfect for it. You can't say that she hasn't been successful.'

Dora nodded. 'And, of course, she's very, very grateful to you for getting her a break?'

Calvin looked away and stirred his tea. 'Is all this any of your business?'

Dora nodded. 'Yes, I think it is. Whose party was it?'

Calvin looked uncomfortable. 'I've already said that I'm only going to keep her on the books for another month. Where exactly is all this leading?'

'Maybe nowhere at all. Whose party was it?'

'Ben Frierman's. His Christmas bash.'

Dora's blank expression made Calvin sigh.

'Oh, come on, Dora. You must know him. Ben Frierman? The big seed merchant? Lives out at the Tollbridge? He always holds a big stag do at Christmas, sort of social let-your-hair-down do for the local nobs. Dancers, good food, loads of booze. Everyone always goes. It's a tradition.' There was a hint of appeal in his voice which Dora pointedly ignored.

'Who is "everyone"?'

'Me, Lawrence Rawlings, Bob Preston. Jack Rees was there as well this year. Anyone who's anyone, really – Guy Phelps, the new Conservative chap was there and Tom Fielding, the Lib Dem guy. Chairman of the Rotary club, Lions club, rugby club committee, most of the members of the chamber of trade. Gerry Hanley the JP. It's a bit of boys'-own thing – you know, strippers, belly dancers.' He stopped as if he hoped he'd told her enough.

'And you met Lillian at this party?'

Calvin nodded. 'Yes, but there were lots of girls like Lillian there. The place was crawling with them. Ben is famous for finding a good class of –' He stopped, blushing furiously.

Dora leant forward. 'What? Tart? Hooker?'

Calvin coughed, blustering to hide his discomfort. 'No, no, that wasn't what I was going to say at all. Lillian was there with her flatmate. She told me she'd been invited specially. I thought they were really nice girls, I thought – '

Dora held up a hand to silence him. 'And when you got to know Lillian better, she asked you to help her buy somewhere to live in Fairbeach?'

Calvin stared at her in astonishment and then pulled a cigar from his top pocket. 'Who told you that?' he demanded defensively.

Dora rolled her eyes heavenwards. 'Lillian, of course, she couldn't keep a secret if her next meal depended on it. You helped her buy the flat at Anchor Quay?'

Calvin lit his cigar. 'All perfectly above board. She asked me if I would do some business for her. She said she hadn't really got a head for figures. I took a small finder's fee but nothing that could be misconstrued.'

Dora suppressed a snort. 'Didn't you wonder where she got the money from?'

Calvin sucked his cigar thoughtfully. 'It did cross my mind, but girls like Lillian have a habit of attracting . . .' He struggled to find the right word. 'Er, patrons. I thought maybe she had a sugar daddy hidden away somewhere who'd slipped her few grand.'

'Slightly more than a few, Calvin.'

Calvin turned away. 'All right, all right, slightly more than a few, but it wouldn't be the first time a girl like Lillian's used a little bit of pressure to get what she wanted out of life.'

Dora stared at him in astonishment. 'You thought Lillian was blackmailing somebody?'

Calvin nodded. 'The thought did cross my mind, until I got to know her a bit better. I mean, let's face it, she isn't the sort.'

He was right. Dora stared down at the list of bookings in her hand without taking in the words. Lillian hadn't got the guile to blackmail anyone – and she hadn't needed to. Jack Rees had given Lillian the money willingly because he believed she was his daughter, but that didn't explain why someone wanted something from Lillian now Jack Rees was dead.

Lillian said she had taken him some photographs of her as a child. Dora bit her lip. Jack Rees had loved Lillian for being his. Dora felt a tiny flutter of pain. She looked up at Calvin and then put the cup back onto his desk.

'Thanks for the tea.'

Calvin stared at her. 'What the hell do you mean, "thanks for the tea"? What was all that about?'

Dora shrugged. 'Idle curiosity.'

She slid the sheet of paper back alongside the cup.

'One more month, including the Spring Ball, and then she is off the case, Calvin. I don't care what she wants or how much you like her, or what you've promised her. She is history.'

Calvin sniffed and bit down on his cigar. 'It's not going to be easy. Lillian is a sweet girl. Sensitive.' He stopped when he realised Dora was staring at him, completely unmoved. 'What shall I tell the supermarket people?'

Dora deadpanned him.

He held up his hands in surrender. 'All right, all right, I'll tell them to get someone else. What shall I tell the publishers about the new book?'

Dora was very tempted to suggest the same solution, but instead she nodded. 'I'll see what I can do.'

When Dora got back home the phone was ringing. She picked it up before the machine had a chance to swallow the words, hoping it was Jon.

'Hi,' said Josephine Hammond. 'How's it going?'

Dora groaned. 'Please, don't ask.'

Josephine laughed. 'Tetchy, tetchy. Have you had an opportunity to speak to Calvin Roberts yet?'

'I've just come back from his office. Lillian was telling the truth. She and Jack Rees met at a Christmas party organised by someone called Ben Frierman. I'm not sure if that's any help, though. It sounds as if the world and his wife were there with Lillian and Jack. Well, no, not his wife, it was a stag do. I just wish I knew what it was these people were looking for.'

Josephine made a distracted noise.

'Are you writing this down?' snapped Dora angrily. 'This is supposed to be off the record.'

'Nope, the guy on the other desk just handed me a piece of paper. Do you fancy coming to a barbecue?'

Dora laughed. 'Sorry?'

'I've got to go and do a report on some minor royal visiting a hospital this afternoon, but I'm covering a fund raiser for Tom Fielding, the Lib Dem guy, tonight. We could talk on the way. I'd like some company, these dos are always the same.'

Dora sighed. 'Are you serious?'

'Uh huh, look, I've really got to go now. Pick you up about seven?'

Dora stared at the phone. 'Okay, why not. What do I wear?'

Josephine laughed. 'Well, you could start by trying a happy face. Gotta go, catch you later.'

Dora had barely put the phone down before it rang again. This time it was Sheila. 'You're in, then? I rang to see what you were doing.'

Dora had doodled a large succulent barbecued sausage on the pad beside the phone. 'I'm about to start work,' she lied.

'Oh, I see. I just wondered if you'd like to come round to tea again tonight? Peter is taking the kids round to see his mum.' Sheila paused. 'I thought we could talk. Doesn't do you any good, being in that flat all on your own all the time.'

Dora looked down at the plump blue biro sausage. 'I won't be on my own tonight, I'm going out.'

Sheila sniffed. 'Not the policeman?'

So much disapproval in three words.

Dora sighed. 'No, not the policeman, just a friend. I'm going out at seven and I won't be back until late.' She sounded far more decisive than she felt. 'So, thanks for the invitation but I'm already booked solid.'

She heard Sheila add a little sniff of annoyance as punctuation. Here was Sheila being considerate for a change and Dora wasn't in the least bit grateful.

223

'Right,' Sheila said briskly. 'Well, in that case I'll give you a ring tomorrow, then.'

Dora switched the answering machine on to catch the phone before it had a chance to ring again and headed off to bed. A few hours' sleep and then she'd try painting on a happy face. Jon's number was pinned to the board above the phone. She touched it for luck. Maybe she'd ring him before she went out. Maybe.

Josephine Hammond arrived early, catching Dora half dressed, half awake and still brushing her teeth.

'Are we all ready then?' she grinned as she jogged up the stairs.

Dora glared at her. 'Are you always this cheerful?'

'Almost always. I wondered whether you'd mind taking your car and following me? Only I might have to eat and run.'

'So we won't be able to talk on the way?'

Josephine giggled. 'Have you got a CB?'

Dora snorted and went off to finish getting ready.

Half an hour later they were standing inside the elegant Victorian-style conservatory of a large house on the outskirts of Fairbeach. A buffet table ran the length of the room, beyond which double doors led into the main house. The whole of the lower floor seemed to be full of people. The guests were mingling, talking, everyone waiting for a plump man, standing on the patio, to perform the ritual burning of the sacred cow, beefburger and chicken leg.

Dora took a glass of fruit juice from a tray offered by a small girl all done up in her party clothes, who giggled at her. Dora handed Josephine a glass.

'Why did you invite me?' Dora asked as she and Josephine eased their way towards a quiet corner. By the time they had left the flat Dora had repeated everything Calvin had told her.

Josephine wrinkled up her nose. 'I don't know. You seemed a bit down in the mouth. I thought you could do with a night out.' She paused long enough to lean across the untouched buffet table and pop a stuffed egg into her mouth. 'It isn't just this Lillian Bliss thing that's getting you down, is it? Or are you always this bad-tempered?'

Dora stared at her. 'I am not bad-tempered.' She stopped. 'Maybe I am. Oh, I don't know. I just can't think straight at the moment and I didn't sleep very well last night.'

Josephine handed her a plate of prawn vol-au-vents. 'Has to be a man. Only men can do that to you – although gastric flu comes a very close second.'

Dora stared at her. 'No-one else is eating yet,' she hissed in an undertone.

Josephine glanced over her shoulder. 'Someone's got to be the first, besides I missed my lunch. When they're all eating I'll be mingling and interviewing. Gary ought to be here by now, clutching his faithful box brownie. I'll just go and see if he's arrived yet.' Cradling a clutch of vol-au-vents, Josephine headed off through the press of people to look for her photographer. Dora watched her go and then scanned back and forth across the faces of the guests. She knew almost everyone in the room in some way or other. There would be no problem striking up a conversation if she felt the need. She turned back towards the table and practised smiling; it felt like a grimace. Maybe Josephine was right, maybe she was just bad-tempered after all.

Out of the corner of her eye she watched a masculine pair of hands rifling through a basket of cheese straws.

'Aha,' she said. 'No eating until they fire the starting pistol.' Looking up she grinned at a tall, good-looking man caught with a cheese straw half way to his mouth.

He laughed. 'I really love these.'

He looked familiar. Before Dora could flick through the mug shots in her mind, he offered his hand. 'Tom Fielding.'

Dora reddened as she shook the hand of Fairbeach's Liberal Democrat candidate. 'Mine host?'

Tom Fielding shook his head. 'Not exactly, Libby Calley and her husband have organised the party for me. You ought to try these, they're really delicious.'

Dora took his word for it, introduced herself, and hooked a cheese straw out of the basket.

'Aren't you supposed to be over there somewhere, kissing babies and loving old people?'

Tom snorted. 'I take it you're not a committed Liberal Democrat supporter then?'

Dora bit into the cheese straw – he was right, they were wonderful.

'Actually,' she said, through a flurry of puff pastry, 'I'm very even-handed in my political affiliations. I loathe all politicians on principle.'

He laughed and choked.

Dora continued. 'I was invited by Josephine Hammond from the *Gazette* because she thought I needed a night out, but I'm absolutely certain she's only here for the food.'

Tom grinned. 'More than likely.'

'You know Josephine?'

He nodded. 'Is there anyone who doesn't? She's famous, or maybe that should be notorious. Talk of the devil –'

Josephine was shouldering her way towards them with Gary close behind.

'Tom,' she beamed with genuine warmth and kissed him enthusiastically on both cheeks. 'I might have known you'd be over here in the wilderness trying to bring the don't knows, and don't cares, back into the fold.' She winked at Dora. 'Just don't be taken in by his little-boy-lost look.' Tom grinned. Josephine beckoned to Gary. 'I really think we ought to have a photo of this for the album.'

Dora winced as the flash bulb exploded.

Josephine Hammond made a great play of producing her notepad.

Tom Fielding leant casually against the table. 'So, what would you like me to say, Jo?'

'Something outrageous would be nice. But meanwhile would you mind going over to the barbecue so Gary can get a cheery snap of you with the bride and groom?'

Dora stared at them. 'What about me?'

Tom grinned. 'Have another cheese straw, I'll be back.' He stepped aside to let Josephine go first but she waved him on. 'Just follow the man with the camera, I'll be there in a second.' She smiled slyly at Dora. 'So, what do you think, then?'

'About what?'

Josephine sighed. 'Tom Fielding, for goodness' sake.'

Dora stared at her. 'His political views? His penchant for cheese straws? I'm not with you.'

Josephine pulled a face. 'Is he gorgeous or what?'

'Are you serious?' Dora spluttered. She hastily gazed around to try to spot him. He had emerged onto the patio and was posing beside their hosts. He was good-looking, he was tall, he was easy to talk to. Maybe she had just misplaced the device that worked out who was fanciable and who wasn't. 'Are you telling me you fancy Tom Fielding?'

Josephine laughed. 'Me and half the other women here. Who wouldn't? And he's unattached. Did you see those big brown eyes – pure gastric flu.'

Dora pushed the rest of the cheese straw into her mouth. 'He's a politician.'

'Okay, so nobody's perfect.'

Later that evening, Dora drove her car slowly into Gunners Terrace. It had been a good night. So good that she had invited Josephine back for coffee – it would be nice to have a little girl talk. They could swap notes on the effects of men and gastric flu.

As she turned in at the junction she sensed something wasn't quite right. Everywhere seemed unnaturally light and busy. She wondered whether there might be a fire. By the corner shop a small group of people had gathered under the street light and were staring in the direction of her flat.

Easing her car into first gear she crept past them. Glancing towards the shoe shop she felt her stomach contract sharply; there were two police cars, parked nose to nose, outside her street door. An officer waved the car on as she stared unblinking at the group of men heading upstairs.

There was no easy place to park, so she rounded the corner and drew up behind a delivery van. In her rear-view mirror, as she turned the corner, she saw Josephine Hammond screech to a halt alongside the police cars.

Her hands shook as she locked the car – the burglar had to have come back. He was in her flat. Someone had to have seen him. She took a deep breath, trying to get control of the rogue pulse that throbbed in her ears.

'Everything will be all right now,' she murmured in an undertone. 'They've got him. They've caught him. I'll know why all this is happening.'

On the pavement in Gunners Terrace two men stood shoulder to shoulder, looking into the open flat door. One of them was Jon Melrose. As Dora approached, he looked over his shoulder and glanced in her direction. For a second there was no recognition and then she saw the flash in his eyes and he looked again.

'Dora, I've been trying to ring you. We've had your flat under surveillance since yesterday. Are you all right?'

Before she had a chance to reply there was a bloody, chilling scream from the flat above.

Dora felt her colour drain.

'Oh, my God,' she whispered. Before the cry had finished, Jon and the other man had turned and sped inside, leaving Dora standing alone on the kerbside.

A police constable stepped towards her, hands spread. 'Best if you stand back, ma'am.'

She started to protest, 'It's my flat', but he had already taken her by the arm and was guiding her away, as a scrum of men bundled noisily out from the yawning street door. Through the jostle she could see Josephine Hammond nosing forward.

Dora froze as she heard a familiar voice shrieking out amongst the mêlée.

'Will you get your hands off me. Do you know who I am? I'll write to my MP. I'll . . .'

Dora spun round, slipping away from the PC.

'Sheila!' she yelled. 'My God!' and ran back towards the heaving knot of bodies.

Her sister, Sheila, was red-faced, struggling, sniffing imperiously, while being held firmly round the neck by a burly constable. She did not look amused. Catching sight of Dora, she whipped one arm out from the policeman's grip and waved it, bawling, 'Ask her who I am, just ask her. She'll tell you.'

At the roadside, another constable had opened the door to one of the squad cars and was waiting for the wailing, struggling Sheila to be bundled inside.

'Wait!' Dora shouted. 'Stop! Stop! That's my sister.' She tried desperately to press her way between the men.

A split second later, Jon Melrose appeared behind the scrum and lifted his hands.

'Stop,' he yelled, in a crisp authoritative voice. The scrum became a tableau. He stepped closer and shook his head. 'Let her go, please, gentlemen. Unfortunately you appear to have caught the occupant's sister.'

The men carefully and slowly disentangled their arms, looking self-conscious and ill at ease. One bent down to rub his shin, whilst a furious Sheila, her blood up, stood in the centre of them, her fists grinding into her hips.

'What the bloody hell is this?' she snapped at Dora and Jon. 'Just what do you think you're up to?'

Dora moved closer, taking her arm. 'Come back upstairs. I'll try and explain,' she said in a small quiet voice.

Sheila violently extricated herself from Dora's gentle touch. 'I will not. Don't come near me. What exactly are they doing here?'

Dora stared Sheila in the eye and in as calm a voice as she could muster said, 'What is more to the point, Sheila, is what exactly you're doing here?'

Sheila reddened. 'Er, I . . . I . . .' she blustered.

Dora closed her fingers more tightly around her sister's elbow. 'Let's go upstairs.'

Around them, the group of police officers were composing

themselves, straightening jackets and ties, tidying themselves after their misguided capture.

Jon caught Dora's eye. 'I'll be up in a minute,' he said. She nodded.

Sheila turned at the foot of the stairs, singling out the officer who was rubbing his leg, and stabbed an angry finger in his direction.

'I've got your number, mate,' she growled unpleasantly. 'You'd just better watch yourself.' She caught hold of the bottom of her jacket and tugged it straight, adopting an exaggerated air of superiority.

'Fascist,' she hissed and then bustled up the stairs.

The flat looked remarkably untouched; only the office showed any real signs of the struggle that must have taken place. Papers and magazines were strewn across the carpet, together with the contents of a large Jiffy bag. Dora squatted down to gather them up and then stopped. They were the page proofs Calvin had brought her to correct when he had first visited with Lillian. Pages and pages of *One Hundred and One Hot Nights* were spread out over the entire floor. Dora looked over her shoulder at Sheila, whose bluster had rapidly dissipated.

She stood up slowly. 'Well,' Dora said, gathering the sheaf of papers together into some sort of order, 'is there anything you'd like to tell me?'

Sheila sucked her teeth, picking uncomfortably at her sleeve, reddening furiously. 'I was going to ask you the same question.' She indicated the papers scattered all over the office floor. 'What *is* all that?'

'You've been snooping through my things,' said Dora flatly. She could feel a little bright gem of fury sparking in her belly.

Sheila sniffed again. 'You haven't been yourself lately. I wondered if there was anything I could do to help, anything . . .'

'You thought you'd come over here and snoop around while I was out for the evening?'

Sheila shifted her weight, twisting her torso, tipping one

foot so that it rested on the toes in a poor impersonation of long-gone childhood innocence.

Dora looked heavenwards. 'Well?'

Sheila looked as if she might cry. 'I'd still got the spare key you gave me when you went on holiday. I thought I'd come in and . . . and . . .' She struggled to find a plausible explanation, when both of them knew there wasn't one.

Dora stared at her, waiting for the lie.

'I thought I'd nip round and tidy up for you. A little surprise for when you got back,' she murmured quickly.

Dora snorted with exasperation and ran her fingers through her hair. 'Oh, for God's sake.' She stepped closer, her voice dropping to a dangerous purr. 'How could you? We're not kids any more, Sheila. This is my home. I'm a bloody grown-up, not some twelve-year-old who needs checking up on. We're not in bunk beds now, you know. You just can't come round here to read my diary just because the fancy takes you.' She took a long breath. 'I really can't believe you did this –'

Sheila wriggled uncomfortably under Dora's unflinching stare.

'Is that stuff yours, I mean, do you write it?' she said at last.

Dora sighed. 'Yes, and so are all the others. I wrote them. And before you get on about how disgusted or shocked you are, don't bother. I'm not interested. You shouldn't come snooping if you can't cope with what you find.' Her tone was icy.

Sheila stepped away from her. 'You're Catiana Moran, aren't you?'

Dora shook her head in disbelief.

'Hello,' said Josephine Hammond, as she breasted the top of the stairs. She smiled at Dora. 'I don't suppose you've got any of those cakes left, have you?'

Jon Melrose climbed the stairs wearily. It had been a very long day. Above him, he could almost hear the icy silence between Dora and Sheila. He stuffed his hands in his pockets. Dora was waiting for him in the hallway.

He lifted an eyebrow. 'How's your sister?'

Dora pulled a face. 'Making tea. I think she'll survive.'

On cue, Sheila poked her head around the kitchen door, waving the teapot.

'It's disgusting,' she began aggressively. 'They could've done me untold damage. What were they thinking about? I've just been telling the woman from the *Gazette*. It's an outrage.'

Jon pulled himself up to his full height, suspecting Sheila might be a formidable adversary.

'We were trying to arrest a burglar, ma'am. We had your sister's flat under surveillance.' He stopped, his expression cool and professional. He wasn't going to add that, thanks to Sheila, he probably wouldn't get the manpower to do it again.

'After tonight's farce the likelihood of anyone turning up here is pretty remote. The news will spread like wildfire.'

Sheila huffed. 'I had no idea.'

Dora groaned. 'I think that probably was the plan, Sheila.' She turned to Jon. 'Are you watching Lillian's place too?'

Jon nodded. 'Yes, and Calvin Roberts' office, but let's stick to calling her Catiana Moran for the time being. The fewer people who know you're really Catiana the better.'

In the kitchen doorway, Sheila froze. 'How many other people know about this? Why didn't you tell me before?' A bright flower of indignation blossomed in her eyes. 'We went to see that woman in Smith's . . .' She stopped again, as if she was having difficulty breathing. 'So who was she, then?'

Jon caught Dora's eyes and lifted his hands in apology. 'Sorry.'

Dora shook her head. 'It doesn't really matter.' She turned to Sheila. 'She's someone who works for me. I'm surprised you didn't guess about the books before now . . .'

Sheila sniffed. 'I didn't have a lot of time really. I'd just got myself settled down when his lot burst in.' She shivered. 'It gave me a real turn.'

Dora carefully prised the teapot from Sheila's fingers. 'Here, let me make the tea.'

*   *   *

A squad car, driven by a small blonde WPC, took Sheila home. Josephine Hammond, after getting an eye-witness account from Sheila, tactfully excused herself with a promise to phone later. Jon slumped in a chair in the sitting room. Now everyone had left, the flat was blissfully quiet.

Jon was stretched in front of the gas fire, legs out, eyes closed. He looked very relaxed. Dora crept in quietly and as she did, he opened one eye.

'I've got to go back to the station to write up a report on tonight's fiasco.' He stopped and looked up at her. 'Why wouldn't you let me in last night? I think we need to talk.'

Dora took a deep breath. 'Again?' she said with a wry smile. 'This is becoming a habit.'

'Yes,' he said softly. 'I don't understand what's going on. I put it down to shock but,' he grinned, 'I've been going crazy trying to find a way to talk to you.'

Dora sat down on the sofa. 'How long have you got?'

Jon glanced at his watch. 'Fifteen minutes, so give it your best shot.'

'Okay. The thing is, when I write there are never any surprises. There's nothing unexpected, because it's me who's doing the expecting. I sometimes feel as if my only real life is through the looking glass of the computer screen.' She paused. 'I keep forgetting that real is out here.' She could hear Jon breathing but didn't look at him.

'So what is it you weren't expecting?' he asked, in a low even voice.

Dora sighed. 'It's so hard to put into words that really mean what I want to say. At the moment, it feels as if my life is slipping through my fingers. Real life has come charging up behind me while I wasn't looking. The sense of having any control over what happens to me has gone. Lillian, the break-ins, yesterday with those men.' She stopped and took a deep breath. 'And then there's you. I just didn't think I could care so much about someone so soon.' She paused. 'Or that I could be jealous.'

She heard Jon make a small noise of surprise. 'Jealous of what?'

'This sounds so stupid, I'm not sure I can even bring myself to say it.'

She heard Jon smile as he spoke. 'Try me. You've got thirteen minutes left.'

'Someone saw you in Sainsbury's with your wife.'

Jon hissed, and then said quietly, 'And they told you about it? Don't tell me, let me guess. It had to be Sheila.'

'Pathetic, isn't it? I tried ringing you at the station, and the officer on the desk said you'd gone round to your wife's place.' She reddened, it all sounded even more ridiculous when she said it out loud. 'I've been here for twenty-four hours letting my imagination run riot. I should have let you in last night.' She paused and turned towards Jon – he was watching her. The look in his eyes made something inside her ache.

'Please tell me something true, Jon Melrose,' she whispered, close to tears. 'Tell me something to stop me drowning in all the lies my imagination keeps inventing.'

Jon crept across the rug towards her.

'All right, Nita is pregnant and she told me in Sainsbury's. It was a complete surprise.' He stopped and she heard the pain in his voice as he continued. 'She and Sam are over the moon. She'd already told me they were getting married in May when I was at the hospital. I was completely gutted. It isn't that I want her back, or anything remotely like that. It's just an ending. I don't know, I'm not really jealous, I'm just – just something else that hurts a lot.'

Dora felt the tension shiver out of her body like a heavy coat falling away.

'Then Nita invited me round to see Joe. It felt really odd, seeing them all tucked up together. Joe is so excited about having a new brother or sister. He talked about it all the time I was there with Nita dotting round making me tea. And I'm not part of their lives any more. I'm pushed right out onto the edge. Don't misunderstand me, I don't want that again, but some part of me still loves all the things we used to have between us. And now there's nothing there for me any more.' He sighed. 'When I left, I felt the same way as I did when my dad died. There was this cold sad lump in my chest.' He stopped, eyes bright with emotion. 'And that's it, all of it.'

Dora reached out and stroked a curl of hair back off his face. 'I'm really so sorry I didn't let you up last night. I could have saved us both a lot of misery.'

He caught hold of her hand and pressed it to his lips. The depth of the comfort she felt, and returned, made her shiver. She felt the tension draining away, earthed out by a single touch.

Jon sighed. 'It feels good to be here with you.'

Dora curled up against his broad chest. 'How much longer have we got before you've got to get back?'

'Eleven minutes.'

Dora grinned up at him. 'A girl can do an awful lot in eleven minutes,' she said softly, and pulled him closer.

16

Meanwhile, in a darkened room above one of the shops that lined the far side of the Western Ouse, overlooking Lillian Bliss's apartment, Milo adjusted the focus of his camera lens and pressed the shutter release. The motor drive whirred. Milo grinned.

'Here we go again. I wonder what this boy eats for breakfast. Remind me to ask him.'

Spar's mind was on other things. He'd gone to retrieve the tape from the car in Gunners Terrace. He was just fishing the thing out of the machine when all hell had broken loose. There had been flashing blue lights, sirens, coppers everywhere. He had felt a sinking terror that hadn't really dissipated even when he realised they weren't coming after him. Hunkered down in the passenger seat, his guts had turned to liquid.

Now, safely back with Milo, he'd already listened to the tape twice but still couldn't concentrate on picking out the words from the crackle of background noise. He pulled the earpiece out and stretched.

'Fancy a cup of Bovril?' he asked, taking a flask out of his sports bag.

Milo snorted. The motor drive whirred again.

'Not for me at the moment, matey. Our Mr Roberts is now in the final furlong, sweating hard and heading for the finish line.'

'Not our Mr Roberts, your Mr Roberts,' Spar huffed miserably. 'S'pose you'll jack it in now you've got what you want.'

Milo turned towards him in the gloom. 'I told you, I've still got to try and find some documents Rawlings wants. Don't sound so miserable, matey. The game's not over yet.'

Spar crouched down on a packing case. 'I'm still no nearer finding the photos my governor wants.' He sighed. 'She hit me, you know – with a spoon.'

Milo stared at him. 'Really? I wouldn't stand for that. No, I wouldn't. Anyway, don't dwell on that now. What did you get off them tapes? Anything interesting?'

Spar sniffed. 'Can't make it out, the static's too bad.'

Milo, stiff from sitting hunched by the window, uncurled slowly.

'Here, you come and have a butcher's at this pair. I'll have a listen if you like.' He took the earpiece from Spar.

Spar pointed the long telescopic lens at the window opposite and stared down the view finder. It took a few seconds for his eyes to adjust. When they did, he could see Calvin Roberts sitting on the side of a king-sized bed, pulling on his shreddies. Behind him, Lillian Bliss was curled up amongst a tumble of sheets, one breast peeping provocatively, like a plump puppy, over the creamy-white duvet.

Spar sighed – lucky bastard, at least Roberts was getting his oats. Spar's girlfriend, while not objecting to surveillance and private investigating in principle, was getting a bit miffed at staying home nights, and had asked him twice now whether he was seeing anyone else on the sly.

Through the lens Spar watched Calvin Roberts lean across the bed and nuzzle Lillian affectionately. He turned away in frustration.

'Shit,' said Milo, breaking Spar's train of thought.

'What is it?'

'Dora Hall and that ginger bitch Hammond from the *Gazette*. They're in cahoots. Some how they managed to work the Christmas party connection,' he said flatly. 'And by the sound of it they've been sharing what they know with the Lib Dem guy.'

Spar stared at him. 'Bloody wars. What are we going to do?'

Milo shrugged. 'Tell our clients and then move faster. We need to find Miss Lillian's little box of tricks, wherever she's got it stashed.'

He leant over and snatched the camera out of Spar's fingers.

'Oy,' protested Spar. 'Watch it, what d'you think you're doing?'

Milo pressed the rewind button on the camera. 'I'm going to get these pictures developed and then first thing tomorrow morning I'm off to see Mr Lawrence Rawlings.'

'What about me and Mrs Markham?' Spar whined.

Milo flipped the back of the camera open and dropped the rewound spool of film into the palm of his hand. 'I'll do you both a set of prints if you like.'

'That isn't what I mean and you know it,' snapped Spar. 'What am I going to tell Mrs Markham?'

Milo was pulling on his jacket, hastily stuffing things into his bag. 'Is she paying you by the day?'

'Yes . . .' Spar began.

'Well then, in that case tell her anything you like, but for God's sake, don't tell her the truth. The women on the tape still don't know exactly what we're looking for, they obviously haven't found anything themselves, and until they do, we've got the edge. We need to get into that flat.' He pointed towards Anchor Quay. 'And go over it with a fine tooth comb.'

'Hang on,' protested Spar, struggling to his feet. 'Don't leave me here on me own.'

Dora woke just before four thirty. This time there were no dark thoughts driving sleep away, only Jon Melrose. As she turned over, he snuggled closer, wrapping his arm around her.

'I didn't have you down as the jealous type,' he murmured sleepily, against her neck. She felt the insistent press of his body against hers and smiled.

'Me neither, until now.' She turned over again and wriggled across the bed so they were lying belly to belly.

'How long have we got?' he whispered.

She peered over his shoulder at the glowing numbers on the alarm clock. 'About three hours.'

Jon kissed her neck, lifting a hand to stroke her breast. 'Care to show me again what a girl can do with eleven minutes?'

Dora giggled. 'If you really insist.'

At just after ten that morning, Lawrence Rawlings took the brown envelope from Milo and turned it over thoughtfully in his fingers. He was relieved to see the man had had the sense to seal it.

'Finally got what you want, then,' said Milo, with a sly grin.

Lawrence sighed – if only that were true.

'What about the negatives?'

The private investigator aped offence. 'Please, Mr Rawlings, what do you think I am? They're all in there, if you'd like to count them up. I've put the whole reel in, duff shots, negatives, the whole shooting match. I'm not into funny business. Couple more days and I hope to have my hands on copies of the other items you mentioned.' As he spoke he pocketed the cheque Lawrence had written him.

Lawrence continued to stare at the brown envelope.

'Right.' Lawrence looked up. 'Just one more thing, I would like to make this perfectly clear. No strong-arm tactics. If I'd wanted bully boys I would have hired someone else.' He unfolded the *Fairbeach Gazette* and set it down next to the envelope. There was a report on the front page. 'Local woman mugged in daring daylight attack outside Anchor Quay apartments.'

He glanced at Milo. 'The description the woman gave the police makes interesting reading. I hope this has nothing to do with you?'

Milo's expression contorted into a mask of blameless-ness, but Lawrence was not convinced. He waved the man away.

'I'll be in touch,' promised Milo.

Lawrence nodded, and when Milo had closed the door behind him, he sat down at his desk to contemplate the sealed envelope. It was strange, the very things he wanted gave him no comfort whatsoever. There was a knock at the door. Hastily, Lawrence slid the envelope into a drawer and called his house-keeper in.

'Sorry to disturb you, Mr Rawlings. Mr Preston is here to see you. Shall I show him up?'

It would be a relief to speak to a friend. 'Yes, please, and would you bring us some coffee as well?'

The woman nodded and left.

Seconds later, Bob Preston pushed the door open.

'Morning, Lawrence. How's it going? I had to go and see the bank manager this morning, so I thought I'd pop by on my way back. Not disturbing you, am I?'

Lawrence shook his head. 'Not at all, come in and sit down.'

Bob Preston, a former Fairbeach mayor, was a bluff jovial man with few pretensions. Their friendship had already spanned more than half a century. Lawrence waved him towards one of the armchairs that flanked the hearth.

'It's good to see you. You'll stay for coffee, won't you? And what about lunch on Sunday? Shall I book you a seat at your usual table?'

Bob grinned. 'That arsehole Phelps isn't likely to be here again, is he?'

Lawrence grimaced. 'No, thank God. Mind you, the by-election campaign starts the week after next. If you feel you're missing him, don't fret, his face will be pasted all over every billboard and lamp post from here to Keelside.'

Bob Preston groaned. 'What a wonderful thought. Actually I wanted to talk to you about something else. I've got something here for you to take a look at –' Bob slid his hand into his jacket. 'I picked these up this morning.'

Lawrence stepped towards him and then froze, as Bob pulled out a folder of photographs from an inside pocket.

'Thought you might like to take a look at these.'

Lawrence struggled to regain his composure, glancing back towards his desk. The coincidence was almost more than he could bear.

'What are they?' he muttered uneasily.

'Here, take a look for yourself.'

Lawrence accepted the first print without really focusing. His mind was on the grainy photos of Calvin and Lillian.

'Well, what do you think?' said Bob, grinning joyfully. 'My new home. My old place isn't the same since the wife died, you must know what it's like. My boys are more or less running the business single-handed anyway. And the old arthritis is playing me up these days. All this damp fen air finally getting to me.'

Lawrence struggled to absorb the images.

'This isn't in England, is it?' he said, staring at a candyfloss-pink villa all set around with palms and exotic creepers. In front of it, glittering behind an ornate wrought-iron screen, was a swimming pool.

Bob handed him another picture, this time an interior shot taken from the room overlooking the pool. The room was painted cream and had red-tiled floors. French windows opened onto the patio and pool beyond, sunlight still glistening on the water.

Lawrence stared up at Bob. 'Not Spain?' he gasped incredulously.

'Tenerife. I've just bought that villa out there, signed the papers this morning. I'm going to retire to the sun, Lawrence. Nothing to keep me in Fairbeach now. The kids are all grown up, and besides, they won't say no to a free holiday in the sun once or twice a year. Probably see more of them out there than I do here.' He grinned. 'You can fly out yourself for a bit of mid-winter sun, if you fancy the idea. We can paint the town red, like we did in the good old days.'

Lawrence sat down heavily, dumbly accepting more photos as they were passed to him.

'You haven't mentioned this before,' he said at last, when he was surrounded by a sea of bougainvillaea and cool cream interiors, lovingly captured in photograph after photograph.

Bob shrugged. 'I know, but I didn't really make my mind up until a couple of weeks ago. Jack's funeral was the last bloody straw. Christ, he was only a couple of years older than me. I looked round all those familiar faces, feeling the cold nipping at my bones and I thought, is this all I've got to look forward to? Eh? Watching my friends die? Wearing my best

241

coat to pay my last respects? No.' He gathered the photos back like a poker hand.

'No, that's not for me. I'm going to have a few years in the sun, live it up, party till dawn, go out with a bit of a bang.'

Lawrence was so stunned that he could barely speak. 'But Tenerife?' he whispered softly.

Bob nodded. 'That's right. We had a few really good holidays out there when the wife was alive. They know how to give you a good time. Nice weather, good food, what more could you want, eh?'

Lawrence struggled to follow what his friend was saying. 'So when are you thinking of going?' he managed to ask.

Bob laughed. 'I'm not thinking about going, Lawrence, I *am* going. Six more weeks and then I'm off. That'll just about give me enough time to pack up what I want, give the kids what they'd like out of the house, sell the rest, and stick the house on the market. No, I've done my bit for Fairbeach. I'm off.'

Lawrence stared at him in disbelief. 'But we're friends,' he began, trying hard to reach down inside to find the things he wanted to say.

Bob nodded. 'I know we are, Lawrence. Good friends. The best of friends. That's why I came to tell you about it first.'

Lawrence had a rush of panic. It felt as if everything he knew, all the things that had been woven seamlessly in and out of his life, were unravelling. He was grateful when his housekeeper knocked on the door and brought in the coffee. It gave him the chance to take a breath.

On the other side of Fairbeach, Alicia Markham was getting ready to host a lunch for the workers from Central Party Office who were coming down to help during the run-up to the by-election. Local party members would be there as well – everyone all keyed up and all ready for the off. Her dining room was a froth of white linen napkins, floral arrangements and candelabra. It looked luxurious and yet at the same time quite businesslike.

When the campaign got underway there wouldn't be the

time for such niceties. Guy would be lucky if he managed a ham sandwich between all the appearances and canvassing.

In the hall, discreetly arranged on a side table, were a fan of campaign leaflets and a single framed poster, fresh and crisp from the printers.

The photo of Guy Phelps was perfect. He was shown with his wife, what's-her-name, and their children, under a banner headline that read, 'Family Matters'. Very catchy. She smiled. Perhaps Colin Scarisbrooke, Guy's political agent, wasn't such a moron as he first appeared. The new slogan had been his idea.

She checked her watch. Guy really ought to have arrived. She had told him eleven, which would have given them ample time to talk alone before the party types got their hands on him. It was already nearly half past. She still hadn't got the information she needed to make his success a certainty, but she had a strong feeling something was on its way.

Her house boy came into the dining room carrying a cordless phone on a tray.

'Mr Phelps for you, Mrs Markham.'

'Guy, where on earth are you?' she snapped, as she snatched up the phone. 'I did say eleven. People will start arriving soon. You should really be here to receive them.'

'Don't worry, Alicia. I've been busy working all morning, time just got away from me. Colin and I have been going through some ideas he has for putting a bit of snap into the campaign. Something that will show the electorate exactly the sort of chap I am.'

Alicia sniffed. 'What's this, more caring, peering, kissing and hugging? Or has Mr Scarisbrooke come up with something else?'

Guy sighed. 'No, no, it really is the most wonderful idea. We've already arranged for the press and TV to come along and cover it. We're just out looking for some homeless people.'

Alicia stared down at the phone in disbelief. 'What?' she snapped.

'Or if not, some unmarried mothers. Look, I've got to dash. Colin has just managed to corner a tramp. I'll see you in a little while.'

Alicia looked at the beautifully arranged table. Her guests were due to start arriving at twelve. How dare Guy be late? She took a deep breath. Perhaps she was just being oversensitive; after all, these were exciting times for him. She could talk to him when everyone had left. And perhaps she'd have a word or two with Mr Scarisbrooke as well and make it perfectly clear that it was she who had ensured Guy was selected as the Fairbeach's Conservative candidate. Guy owed his loyalty to her, not Scarisbrooke and his pop psychology. She smiled and laid the phone down on the sideboard. Guy was like an ancient knight who owed his allegiance to her – his queen.

She waved towards one of the waitresses hired to serve lunch.

'Go and fetch me a sherry, will you?'

The girl peered at her. 'What? One of them ones off the tray in the hall?'

Alicia nodded, and the girl scurried away. The agency who sent the waitresses hadn't taken a blind bit of notice of her request for someone more presentable. This creature's accent was so thick you could wedge doors open with it. Perhaps she ought to impose a rule of silence.

Alicia retired to her office to wait for Guy and her guests. When her sherry had been delivered she meandered through her diary. Her lunch appointment with Lawrence Rawlings was pencilled in for Friday, tomorrow. She considered ringing him and inviting him along today. There was more than enough room at the table for another place. They could all talk together after lunch, perhaps organise a mutually beneficial plan of campaign. The thought took a single breath and then died.

Lawrence Rawlings wasn't a man to put his cards on the table, nor would she respect him as much if he ever did. Besides which, she doubted that Lawrence would actively help

244

her get Guy elected. He'd understood perfectly well why she had wanted him selected in the first place.

There was a discreet tap at her office door. One of the waitresses dithered in the doorway.

'Mrs Markham, your guests from London have just arrived.'

Alicia downed her sherry in a single gulp. Damn Guy for being so late and for the London mob for being so early. She took a quick glance in the mirror to check she looked presentable and then fixed on a welcoming smile.

Just as she glided into the drawing room, preparing herself for the round of shaking hands and making sociable noises, her house boy hurried in. He jabbered something incomprehensible.

'It's all right, I'm coming now,' Alicia said. 'I know the guests are here, just take their coats, show them into the drawing room and give everyone a sherry.'

He scurried through the words again. This time she was able to pick out Guy Phelps' name from the tangle.

'He's finally here, is he? Well, that's good, get him into the hall to welcome everybody.'

'No,' stammered the boy. 'There's a bus outside. Mr Phelps has brought a bus.'

Alicia fixed him with an ice-cool stare. 'No, he has not,' she said calmly, carefully enunciating every word. 'You are mistaken.'

From outside she heard the sound of voices and followed the boy along the corridor. Mr Phelps had brought a bus. Alicia stared at the mêlée in the hall. A stream of dirty, ragged men and women were pushing their way in through Alicia's front door. Amongst them, a befuddled group of Conservative party workers in suits and neat little dresses were blinking and circling, as if they had woken up inside a bad dream.

Waitresses began to hand out glasses of sherry. Alicia struggled to close her open mouth.

Just inside the double doors, which opened onto the drive, was a TV camera crew. As she crossed the room, heading towards the door, there was a lightning strike of flash bulbs, presumably from photographers who had been carried inside on the first wave. Josephine Hammond from the *Gazette* called Alicia's name.

Alicia ignored her. She could see Guy Phelps climbing the steps, Colin Scarisbrooke at his elbow. Guy grinned and lifted a hand in salute.

'Alicia, hello! I told you we wouldn't be very long, didn't I? We had a real stroke of luck down at the Seaman's Mission on the quay. Filled the bus up in one fell swoop. Good, eh?' He gave her the thumbs-up and then lifted his hands to encompass the room. The TV camera panned round to catch him in its Cyclops stare and he began to speak.

'When we in the Conservative party say family matters we really mean family matters. And by family we mean every-body. Every member of our society. Rich or poor, black or white. Here, in Fairbeach, we are all one big family. Every . . .'

Alicia took a hasty step back from a man who smelt of rotten fish and sat down heavily on the bottom stair. Across the room she could hear the drone of Guy Phelps in full flood. Through the window she could see the first cars from the local Fairbeach Conservative Association arriving.

Colin Scarisbrooke shouldered his way between the people until he was beside her. He was carrying two sherries and a shoe box. She stared up at him in total disbelief as he handed her a glass and then dropped the box into her lap.

'There we are, Alicia,' he said cheerfully. 'A little present.'

'You complete and utter bastard,' she hissed, glancing down at the box. 'What's this?'

Colin shrugged. 'It's a media rout, my dear Alicia, they love it. I had them camped out, waiting for us at the end of your drive.' He leant a little closer, wearing a nasty self-satisfied smile and tapped the lid of the shoe box. 'And those are the things I got from Lillian Bliss's flat. Don't ask me to do your dirty work from now on, Alicia. Breaking and entering really isn't my style.'

Alicia downed her sherry in a single mouthful.

*　　*　　*

When her doorbell rang at just after two o'clock, Dora wasn't all together surprised. Before he'd left, Jon had said he would finish his shift at lunch time. She hurried into the office and pressed the call button.

Before she could speak Lillian's voice whispered up through the speaker. 'Hiya, it's me.'

Dora snorted – at least it wasn't Sheila. Unfolded on her desk was the latest edition of the *Fairbeach Gazette*. It would appear that Dora had made it as a media personality even when trying very hard not to. She monopolised the entire front page and a decent part of page two: the main headline read, 'Local woman in police stakeout fiasco' – in which Josephine had skilfully managed to avoid giving away Dora's address, and under that was the story of Dora, this time as an 'unnamed woman', who had run into daring daylight catnappers. On page two was a picture of her looking extremely surprised, standing beside Tom Fielding, clutching a handful of cheese straws.

On the letters page was a flurry of comments about Catiana Moran taking up residence in Fairbeach: for, against, and one suggesting that she might present a fire hazard to other residents should the fire services ever be called to Anchor Quay. The letter, written by a former Second World War fighter pilot, was an account of having nearly been killed as a result of sharing a hotel with Diana Dors. Dora felt morally obligated to read on. According to the correspondent the firemen had spent so long ogling Miss Dors in her night attire they had quite forgotten about everyone else, and had to be reminded, by the correspondent, their first duty was to fight fire and save lives.

Dora grinned. Much more of this and Josephine Hammond might just as well move in and save on shoe leather and petrol money.

'Can I come up?' said Lillian, over the speaker.

Dora had completely forgotten about her. 'What's the matter?'

'Nothing,' Lillian giggled. 'I've just brought you something.'

Oscar, disturbed by the bell, arched his back and gave a fretful meow. He hoped it wasn't Gibson coming back for a visit.

Dora pressed the entry button. 'I'm working so I'm afraid you can't stop long,' she lied.

'This'll only take two ticks,' said Lillian.

Dora heard the door open downstairs and went to let her in. Lillian was wearing a tiny red dress, a black leather bomber jacket, black tights and spike-heel boots. Dora groaned.

'Are you going somewhere?' she asked, stepping to one side.

Lillian shook her head. 'No, I'm just slobbing about today, but I've had to come out because the men from the council turned up to do something with rats.'

Dora glanced at the open newspaper which she could just see through the office door and fought to suppress a giggle. Perhaps Lillian ought to write to the *Gazette* about it.

Lillian opened her handbag and pulled out a long pink envelope. 'So I've been up to town and had some dinner and had a look in the shops. It was lovely, the man in the café asked for my autograph and was really nice. Here, these are for you,' she said, with a warm smile. 'A little thank-you present.'

Dora started to protest, but Lillian pressed on, 'It's all right, I didn't have to pay for them, they're complimentary, but it's the thought that counts, isn't it?'

Dora opened the envelope. Inside were two tickets for the Fairbeach College of Further Education's annual Spring Ball.

Dora stared at her. 'Tickets for the ball?'

Lillian nodded. 'I thought you'd like them, and I want you to come and see me get my award. I mean, if it weren't for you, I wouldn't be getting one, would I?' She paused and reddened slightly. 'It ought to be you getting it really. Calvin told me that you wanted me to go after this month. I don't understand. I mean, it's been good, hasn't it? I've had a lovely time, what with going to the shops and signing autographs and things. I thought me and you were getting on really well.'

Dora stared at the beautiful blonde and felt dreadful. If only Lillian could have learnt to keep her mouth shut, if only she wasn't a convicted prostitute, if only she didn't have something that somebody else wanted. If only . . . Dora coughed, fighting the temptation to justify herself out loud. She suspected Lillian wouldn't be able to understand.

'It's nothing personal,' she said quickly and scanned round her kitchen for a source of inspiration. Pinned up on her notice board was a letter from the Inland Revenue.

'It's a tax thing,' she lied and then hurried on. 'Would you like a cup of tea while you're here?'

Lillian pouted. 'I hate the bloody tax man, I don't open his letters any more.' She stopped. 'I don't want to stop you getting on if you're busy.'

Dora, feeling cruel and guilty, shook her head. 'No, you're fine. Really.'

Lillian shimmied out of her little leather bomber jacket.

'All right then. I'd love one. Have you seen the *Gazette* today?'

Dora was about to say yes, but Lillian was ahead of her. 'I didn't know there was so much crime about. Awful about that woman being mugged outside my place, wasn't it? I asked the people down in the gym if they knew who it was, but no-one was saying anything. She must be ever so upset. Fancy trying to steal a cat. There's a woman downstairs with two lovely Siameses. I reckon it must have been her.'

Dora was caught with her mouth open, and then realised with a start that Lillian didn't know the victim of the mugging was her. Somehow, in amongst Lillian's revelations, she and Josephine hadn't got around to mentioning it. Dora turned away and filled the kettle. It was probably better if Lillian didn't know.

'And that thing about Diana Dors. She was a film star, wasn't she?' Lillian continued. 'You know, I'd never thought about being a fire risk like that. It makes you think, doesn't it?'

'It certainly does,' said Dora, tucking the tickets to the Spring Ball up behind the bills on the kitchen shelf.

17

While Lillian had been out exploring Fairbeach, drinking tea with Dora Hall, and trying to remember the name of a film she had once seen Diana Dors in, Milo and Spar, a.k.a. the rat men, conducted a fingertip search of her flat down at Anchor Quay.

Milo, kneeling beside a wall unit, closed a drawer and opened the one above. Spar was extremely impressed by his new partner's speed and style. They'd already done the bedroom and the bathroom. Milo moved amongst Lillian's possessions with such grace and lightness of touch that no-one would ever guess they had been there. Grudgingly, Spar had to admit it was far better than his own Blitzkrieg approach.

Milo's fingers worked across piles of paper and old receipts like a concert pianist. Another up-front burglary was out of the question after the events in Gunners Terrace the night before. It was a sure bet, if the Plod were staking out Dora Hall's flat, they most certainly had a pair of eyes firmly fixed on Lillian's place.

Milo sat back on his heels, rubbing gloved hands over his muscular thighs. From the shelf above him, the cat watched events with a belligerent frown. Lillian Bliss might not know who Milo and Spar were, but the cat certainly did.

They'd borrowed a van from a friend of Milo's, been down the hire shop and picked up two pairs of disposable hooded overalls, a shiny new industrial hoover that looked like a spaceship, and two paper face masks. *Voilà* – rat catchers.

Milo had flashed Lillian his sports club membership card, spun her a yarn about the hoover spraying assorted toxic fumes to lay waste the fictitious rats, and she'd cleared off without a peep. She'd just got her coat and left, with explicit instructions not to come back for at least four hours. Sweet as a nut.

'How much longer have we got?' said Milo.

Spar looked at his watch. 'Ages yet. Why?'

Milo nodded towards the coffee table. 'Make a space, will you, I want to take some shots of the stuff I've found.'

'Anything dodgy there that Mrs Markham might want?'

Milo shook his head and shuffled through the snaps he'd taken out of one of the drawers.

'Nah, these are just pictures from when Lillian was a kid. My governor is really keen to get his hands on any old photos I find.'

Spar pushed a pile of magazines to one side. 'Wouldn't it be simpler just to nick them?'

'The idea is that no-one knows we've been here, nicking them would rather give the game away, don't you think? Besides, my client expects copies.'

Spar grinned. Milo was a real fount of useful information. 'So what else have you got?'

Milo's face folded miserably along well-worn lines.

'Bugger all, really, just the photos, no legal stuff, no papers, no letters.' He looked up and chewed his lip. 'Maybe there's a safe in here somewhere. Tell you what, find something and tap around the walls. Gently though, matey, too much tapping and someone's bound to start complaining. Look behind pictures. If there is a safe it'll be somewhere easy to get to but well hidden.'

Spar picked up a discarded high-heeled sandal.

'We could try the fridge,' he suggested helpfully. 'I always keep my dodgy stuff in a bit of clingfilm in with the tomatoes.'

Milo stared at him. 'We're talking about birth certificates, stocks and bonds, maybe deeds of sale, receipts, letters, and your dodgy photos – not half an ounce of Moroccan black.'

Spar was hurt. 'Worth a try though?'

Milo sighed. 'All right, go through the freezer as well while you're at it. Look for any boxes that have been opened and resealed. Mind you, if we do that, we're assuming that she wants to keep stuff hidden instead of just safe.'

251

Spar stood cradling the sandal.

'Don't just stand there, get tapping,' snapped Milo.

Spar tapped in three-four time, tapped in Samba and Rumba, tapped out all his favourite country and western tunes, tapped every wall, every floor – nothing.

The fridge was full of fruit, toffee yoghurts and bars of chocolate, though there was a suspicious number of whipped cream aerosols stacked in the door. The freezer was empty except for half a dozen tubs of Haagen-Dazs ice cream and a packet of frozen peas.

Milo's search didn't seem to have been any more successful. He stood up and stretched.

'Nothing,' he said, linking his fingers and turning them back so that the joints made a disturbing popping sound.

Spar threw the shoe back onto the carpet alongside its partner. 'Where do you think the stuff is, then?'

Milo let out a long exasperated sigh. 'If I knew that we wouldn't be doing a fingertip search of this place, would we, matey? Got another bug on you? We'll stick one in the phone while we're here, maybe we'll find out that way.' As he spoke, he crossed the room and picked up the phone. Spar hurried across to intercept him; after all, there was already a bug in there, it just didn't work.

'Here, let me,' Spar offered quickly, 'you've already done a helluva lot of work today.'

He wrenched the phone out of Milo's fingers and whipped a Phillips screwdriver out of his top pocket. 'Won't take me a tick.'

He crouched down and unscrewed the back. The original bug appeared to have melted and glued itself across the wires. Just as he was about to pick it off, the phone rang. He nearly dropped it and then instinctively picked up the receiver.

Milo glared at him, but it was too late.

'Hi, Lillian, Calvin here. Lillian?' said the voice at the far end of the line.

Spar coughed.

'Who is this?' asked the man.

'Er, it's er . . . I'm the rat catcher,' Spar stammered.

'Rat catcher?' Calvin repeated incredulously. 'What rat catcher?'

Caught up in the lie, Spar was obligated to run with it. 'From the council. The whole place is alive with rats.' He was getting the feel for this. 'Big as corgis, some of them. We've gotta spray the whole building, top to bottom, and stick poison down. Christ, it's a bloody horrible job. I said to my girlfriend the other day . . .'

'Yes, yes, all right,' snapped Calvin. 'Is Miss Bliss there with you?'

'No,' said Spar, glancing over his shoulder just to check. 'When we fumigate everyone has to leave, I –'

'Right,' said Calvin. 'Well, could I leave her a message? Ask her to call Calvin Roberts when she gets back, will you?'

'Certainly,' said Spar helpfully. 'I'll tell her the minute she gets in.'

When he hung up Milo was staring at him.

'Why didn't you just tell him he'd got the wrong number and unplug the bloody phone?'

Spar shrugged.

'Just get the bug in and let's get out of here.'

'But what about the message for Lillian?' said Spar.

Milo shook his head. 'Forget the bloody message, let's just get going.'

Jon arrived at Dora's flat just as Lillian was about to leave. As they passed in the hallway, exchanging pleasantries, he eyed the strawberry blonde suspiciously. Though Dora did think, watching them, that his eyes lingered a little too long on the vast expanse of long slim leg the girl was showing.

'Tea? A cheese sandwich?' she suggested, as Jon sat down in the kitchen and boosted Oscar up onto the chair beside him.

'Please. I didn't know Lillian was going to be here.' He stroked a finger along Oscar's back. 'I thought she was all safely settled at her new flat.' He stopped and pulled a face. 'I don't want to sound like an authoritarian husband but I'd be careful how much you have to do with Miss Bliss from now on.'

Dora snorted. 'Well, blow me down, what a surprise. Don't worry, you're not telling me anything I haven't already learnt first hand.' She leant over and kissed him. Reaching across the table she slipped the pink envelope off the kitchen shelf. 'She just popped round to bring me two tickets to the college ball on Saturday night. Want to come with me? I bet you look incredibly sexy in a dinner jacket.'

Jon grinned. 'How can I resist an invitation like that? The only thing is I'm not sure about the Lillian Bliss connection.'

Dora snorted. 'I'm not asking you to dance with her.' She paused. 'Just come with me. Besides, I'd really like to go. I've never been given an award before.'

'It is a joke,' Jon pointed out.

Dora bristled. 'I do know that. But I want to be there when she gets it. As she said, she wouldn't be there if it wasn't for me.' She leant against the kitchen unit and sighed. 'The thing is, I've got Calvin to sack her. She's got another month and then it's all over.'

'You sound as if you regret asking him to fire her. I thought you'd be relieved.'

Dora turned away and pulled a loaf of bread out of the bread bin. 'I am relieved, it's just that she can be so sweet. Dangerous but sweet. Oh, I don't know. Lillian Bliss aside, would you like to come to the ball with me?'

Jon nodded. 'I'd be delighted. The only problem is I'm working till late, eight-ish. Nita said I couldn't have the kids this weekend because of Joe's arm, so I've already swopped shifts with another guy.'

Dora pulled a face. 'Damn. What about if I go on my own and you meet me there when you've finished work?'

'Okay. I can get washed and changed at the station and be at the college by, say, nine? Would that be all right?'

'Fine. That's settled then. Would you like to eat this sandwich in here, in the sitting room or –' she grinned ' – in bed?'

Jon got to his feet, eyes alight with amusement.

'Good God, woman, you're totally insatiable.'

Dora curled into his arms. 'How very perceptive of you to notice. I'm not sure that I am really. I think my body is making up for lost time. You're not complaining, are you?' She reached out and touched him. 'I just love to feel you next to me. It seems so long since –' She bit her lip and then grinned. 'For the last few years I've spent an awful lot of time working on the theory but not much on the practical. You don't mind me lusting after your body, do you?'

Jon's reply was a kiss.

It was nearly seven when they woke up. Dora lay for a little while feeling comfortable, warm and totally at ease. Life was remarkably good, considering. A month more and Lillian would be history and she already had Jon Melrose. Beside her, he stirred into wakefulness.

'My cheese sandwich is all dry and curly,' he observed, rolling over onto his side and staring at the bedside table.

Dora laughed. 'Do you want me to make you another one?'

Jon shook his head. 'No, do you fancy going out to eat?'

'Sounds like a good idea. I'll go and run the shower. Would you like one, too?'

He wriggled closer and pressed his lips against her hip, tickling kisses over her warm skin.

'Have you ever had a shower with anyone?'

Dora grinned down at him. 'Yes, but it was so long ago now, I've forgotten how it goes.'

She felt rather than saw Jon nod. 'Don't worry, it'll all come back to you. Trust me.'

By eleven thirty the following morning, Alicia Markham had already arranged for the contract cleaners to come in and shampoo all the carpets, though she very much doubted that the stains would ever come out of the cream shag pile in the dining room. She was trying hard to blot out the memory of the previous day's fiasco.

What made it worse was that Colin Scarisbrooke had been

correct in his assessment. All the local TV stations had carried a segment about her impromptu house party for the needy on their news broadcasts, even if one had accused Guy Phelps of blatant media manipulation. She hadn't been able to bring herself to ask Guy to stay behind to talk to her. She wasn't altogether convinced she wanted to talk to him ever again.

She stared at her reflection in the dressing-table mirror. All dressed up for her lunch date with Lawrence Rawlings. She just had to clip on her earrings and add a little perfume.

It was all going wrong. Guy was supposed to do what she said, not what that arsehole Scarisbrooke told him. What would Guy be like when he got to Westminster, always assuming that he won the by-election? It disturbed her that she had misread him, or perhaps it was just that she had under-estimated the degree to which he could be manipulated.

. . . Which was exactly Lawrence Rawlings' comment when they sat head to head over an expensive lunch at the Lodge. He topped up her wine glass.

'You can't possibly control him, Alicia. He is a loose cannon. Guy Phelps has no moral centre. He'll go whichever way the wind is blowing. Hunt with the hounds, run with the hare, protest along with the hunt saboteurs. You really have to get rid of him.'

Alicia stared at Lawrence. 'You know it isn't that easy.'

Lawrence snorted. 'I thought you were Fairbeach's lady fix-it? Isn't that what all this super-sleuthing is in aid of, so you have something in the biscuit jar to keep Mr Phelps in line?'

'No, unfortunately not,' she said. How could Lawrence possibly think that she was employing her man to find something to tighten her hold on Guy? She stopped herself from saying so out loud, and began to think. Perhaps he had a point, maybe she could find something to nail Guy down. She left the wheels inside her head to grind it over and carried on speaking.

'My original idea was, finally, to have an MP at Westminster who would co-operate with me. Someone who would listen. Jack Rees was such a trial.'

Lawrence eased his knife through the butter-soft fillet steak. 'And impossible to get rid of?'

Alicia snorted dryly. 'I'm back to square one, aren't I? The reason I asked you here today was to suggest we formed an alliance, a coalition.'

Lawrence, still chewing, nodded. 'To achieve what?'

This was harder going than she had hoped. He was making her crawl every inch of the way. 'For the mutual exchange of information, though I have my suspicions that our respective private investigators may have already come to the same conclusion.'

Lawrence looked at her thoughtfully. 'Presuming I were to agree, how would I know if I came across whatever it is you want?'

Alicia glanced down at her plate. 'Rest assured, Lawrence, if you already had what I'm looking for, or happen to come across it, you would know, instinctively.'

Lawrence suppressed a smile. 'I see. What concerns me is that you are planning to use this magical something to get Mr Phelps into Parliament. I'm not sure I can agree to help you.'

Alicia grimaced. 'I'm not asking for your help or your approval, just a little co-operation.'

Lawrence leant back. 'What if I told you I'd already got what I wanted?'

'I'd say you were bluffing. If you had, you wouldn't be here having lunch with me. You may have something but not everything.'

Lawrence smiled. 'You're a very shrewd woman, Alicia. Let me make a suggestion. If I find anything that fits the description of the item you're looking for then I'll let you have it. All I ask is that you think long and hard about whether you use it to further Mr Phelps' political career. Do we have a deal?'

Alicia stared at him. Had he conceded? Surely it couldn't be this easy?

'And what is it you're looking for, Lawrence? What do you want me to find for you?' she asked quickly.

Lawrence Rawlings was looking past her, his blue eyes focused somewhere in the middle distance.

'I'm not certain any more that what I'm looking for exists,' he murmured. There was a poignancy in his tone that made Alicia reach across the table and touch his hand. The fleeting brush of her fingers snapped his concentration back onto her face.

'I've always thought business and food make a terrible combination and this steak is quite magnificent,' he said, with forced joviality.

Dora had spent Friday morning combing the shops in Fairbeach for something to wear to the Spring Ball. By eleven o'clock she had been to every clothes shop at least twice. At lunch time she had driven to Keelside, dragged round every shop there and was still gownless. Defeated, she drove home and got changed into old clothes for a full-frontal attack on the chaos in her car. It was in desperate need of transformation from pumpkin to stage coach.

When she got back downstairs, clutching a bucket and a can of spray polish, Josephine Hammond was pulling up in her car.

'Afternoon, grumpy. I was just coming to see you. How's it going? You look completely knackered. How's the man in your life?'

Dora flinched. 'I don't remember sending out for a reporter, what I really need now is a fairy godmother with wings and a wand.'

Josephine stared at her. 'Sorry?'

'The Spring Ball tomorrow night. I've got two tickets, a hot date, and haven't got a thing to wear. It's years since swanning around in frills was on my agenda.'

Josephine eyed her up thoughtfully, as Dora pulled the door to. 'Actually I might be able to help. There's a woman out at Abbotsbridge who does a very nice line in secondhand clothes

258

– all designer labels, all very discreet. You have to ring for an appointment. I've used her several times. I could give you the number, if you like.'

'Sounds promising. I don't suppose you'd consider coming with me, would you? I could do with someone to ooh and ahh in all the right places. Guide me away from things that make me look like a middle-aged meringue?'

Josephine glanced at her watch. 'Maybe. I could give her a ring on my mobile, if you like, see if we can come over now.'

Dora looked down ruefully at her working clothes. 'A couple of hours or so would be better. I'd planned to set about the car. It's full of junk, and short of a pumpkin and six white mice turning up unexpectedly, I've got to take it to the ball tomorrow night. Anyway, what are you doing here?'

'Just passing. I rang you earlier but you weren't in so I thought I'd drop by and see if you were okay. See the *Gazette* yesterday?'

Dora grinned. 'I'd never considered myself a one-woman news extravaganza.'

Josephine snorted and then looked at Dora's dilapidated Fiat. 'Why are you taking your car anyway? I thought you said the good-looking policeman was coming. I assume he's the hot date?'

Dora snorted. 'You don't miss a trick, do you? Yes, actually he is, but I'm meeting him there.' She pulled a black plastic bag out of her jacket pocket. 'How long are you staying? Long enough for me to shuffle some of the muck out? I'd offer you a cup of tea but if I don't make a start soon I'll never get it done.'

Josephine nodded and settled herself against the wall. 'Actually I'm skiving. I told my editor I was off talking to an informant. Do you want me to ring this dress woman?'

'If you wouldn't mind.' As she spoke, Dora popped the boot and started pulling things into the rubbish bag. Standing in amongst the muddle of old Wellingtons, blankets and newspapers was a crisp box whose origins she couldn't remember.

Behind her, Josephine was tapping numbers into her mobile phone.

Dora opened the lid of the box and peered inside. On the top was a photograph of a child on a beach. Confused, she pulled out an envelope. Inside was a folded birth certificate; Lillian Bliss' birth certificate. She stopped and glanced up at Josephine. Where had it come from? Random thoughts came tumbling back as memories. It was the box she had picked up the day she had gone to Lillian's old flat. Carol Hayes had had it in her sideboard, keeping it safe for Lillian, and Jon had put it in the car for her. Dora felt ice-cold certainty tickle down her spine like chilly fingers; this was the box everyone was looking for.

Behind her, Josephine Hammond was talking on the phone, arranging to view ball gowns. Dora glanced over her shoulder and then returned the photo and the certificate to the box. Carefully, she shimmied it over the lip of the boot and into the black rubbish bag. As calmly as she could, she slammed the boot down.

'She says it's okay,' said Josephine, snapping the phone shut. 'She's just had some new things in. We can go over . . .'

Dora glided past Josephine cradling the rubbish bag in her arms.

'. . . Oy! Where are you going? I thought you were going to disembowel your car.'

'Change of plan, come upstairs and help me get the hoover, will you?' Dora spoke in a slightly louder than normal voice, just in case anyone was listening.

Josephine stared at her 'Have I suddenly gone deaf?'

'Just come with me,' Dora snapped, and beckoned Josephine to follow with a nod of her head.

With a bemused expression, the reporter wheeled round and followed her. 'What had you got in mind for the ball then, something slinky? Something –'

As soon as they were inside Dora kicked the door shut.

'I think I've found it,' she hissed, lifting the box up to indicate what she meant.

Josephine screwed up her nose. 'Sorry? Have I missed something? I'm not with you.'

'I've found a box of Lillian's things. She gave it to the girl in the flat downstairs for safe keeping. I think I've just found Fairbeach's answer to the holy grail.'

Comprehension dawned on Josephine's face.

'Oh, my God,' she whispered, following Dora up the stairs. 'What are you going to do?'

Dora stopped mid-stride. She really had no idea. 'Ring Lillian,' she said quickly. 'Whatever is in here, it belongs to her.'

'But we're going to look through it first, aren't we?' said Josephine. 'Before you ring?'

Dora turned and banged the door open with her hip and stood the bag on the kitchen table. 'I don't think we ought to, it's private.'

'Oh, for God's sake. You're not in the Brownies now. Aren't you in the least bit curious? Here, let me, I'm the reporter. Private is not in my vocabulary. Pass it over.'

Josephine unrolled the bag and took out the first things from the top of the box. They were photos of Lillian as a little girl. The birth certificate confirmed what Lillian had already told them; Jack Rees was listed as her father.

It was very difficult to stand back and watch Josephine sifting through the box. Finally, unable to resist the temptation, Dora picked up a bundle of photos, trying to make something of the images. Nothing. She picked up a thick brown envelope and opened it.

'I don't understand,' said Josephine, shuffling through another pile. 'This can't be it. It's just a box of old photos, there's nothing here anyone would want to –'

The noise Dora made stopped Josephine mid-sentence.

'What is it?'

Dora handed her the envelope. 'I think you'd better take a look at these.'

'Oh, my God,' breathed Josephine, turning the first photo towards the light. 'This is Tom Fielding.'

Dora nodded. 'And Lillian Bliss, and I think in the next picture the one underneath is Carol Hayes, Lillian's flatmate.

Carol told me she was a photo freak. She must have taken a camera with her to Ben Frierman's Christmas party.'

Josephine sat down heavily on a chair.

'Bloody hell, these are amazing.'

Dora snorted. 'No wonder he wants to get them back.' She shook her head. 'How the hell could he have stood next to me at that barbecue, knowing who I was, and look me straight in the eye?'

Josephine turned the pictures over thoughtfully 'Nice buns, though. I knew he'd be gorgeous with his clothes off.'

Dora glared at her. 'For God's sake, be serious. Your precious Tom Fielding hired someone to break in here, to mug me and terrify Lillian – Jesus.' She ran her fingers through her hair. 'He's so plausible, no wonder he's in politics.'

Josephine shuffled the pictures back into a pile.'So, what are you going to do now?'

Dora sighed. 'God alone knows. I really ought to ring Jon and let him know.' She paused and strung a series of thoughts together. 'What if I rang Tom Fielding?'

'Are you mad?' hissed Josephine

Dora plucked the photos out of Josephine's hands and then looked in the envelope. The negatives all lay in a neat bundle alongside the prints.

'No, listen to this. What if I rang up and offered to give him the pictures and the negatives back?'

'Seriously?'

Dora nodded. 'Why not? It would solve everything. He gets what he wants. He calls off his trained monkeys and then we all get on with our lives. Simple.'

Josephine blew her lips out thoughtfully. 'This is going to make one helluva story.'

Dora glared at her and tightened her grip on the envelope. 'No! I don't care what you do after you leave here, but you're not having these. Is that perfectly clear? These photos are the ticket that will buy me my life back.'

Dora headed for the office, every step dogged by Josephine. She hunted through the directory and then tapped in Tom

Fielding's office number. Someone answered after the second ring.

'Good afternoon, Fielding Agriculturals, Mr Fielding's office. Can I help you?'

Dora coughed.

'Yes,' she said slowly. 'I wonder whether I could have a word with Mr Tom Fielding, please.'

The woman started to make negative noises but Dora pressed on. 'Would you please tell him I have something that might be of interest from . . .' She paused, struggling to keep the name in her head. 'Frierman, Ben Frierman's Christmas party.'

The line went dead and then, seconds later, Tom Fielding asked coolly, 'Who is this speaking, please?'

Dora took another breath. 'I've got the photos you want. You can call your heavies off now. I really don't want these pictures. Perhaps we can come to some arrangement.' The words came out in a tumbling jumbled rush.

'Sorry?' said Tom Fielding. 'Look, if this is an attempt at blackmail you've picked the wrong man. When you put the phone down my next call will be to the police.'

Dora swallowed hard. This wasn't how she had imagined it going at all.

'Blackmail? I'm not trying to blackmail you, I just want to give you these photos back so that you can stop harassing me. The burglaries? The mugging?'

To her complete astonishment Tom Fielding started to laugh.

'What burglaries?' he said incredulously. 'I don't know what you're talking about. Who is this?'

The strange thing was that Dora believed him. 'But I've been broken into, Lillian's been broken into, my agent –' She stopped. 'Are you saying you haven't been looking for these photos using a couple of strong-arm men?'

'Exactly,' said Tom Fielding. 'Are you telling me you're not a blackmailer?'

'Most certainly not. I found some photos of you and Lillian Bliss together at Ben Frierman's party. I just want to give them back with the least amount of fuss.'

Tom made a thoughtful sound. 'Look, I can't talk now. I've got to leave for London in about half an hour. I won't be back in Fairbeach until tomorrow night for the Spring Ball. Could I meet you after that?'

Dora stared at the phone in astonishment. 'What am I supposed to do with these photographs until then?'

'I suggest you put them back wherever you found them, obviously they were safe there. Look, I've really got to go. Can we meet up tomorrow after the ball?'

'I'm going as well,' Dora blurted out, without thinking.

Tom laughed. 'Well, in that case, bring them with you. What do you say we meet up under the clock tower afterwards. It's pretty out of the way there. Do you know where I mean?' He paused for a few seconds. 'I met you the other night, didn't I? Let me think, Dora Hall, that's it, isn't it?'

Dora groaned. 'Oh God, I'm afraid so,' she said, glancing over her shoulder. Josephine Hammond was so close to the receiver that they were sharing the same air. 'One thing. I ought to warn you, the press already know about the pictures.'

'Don't tell me, Josephine Hammond.' This time Tom's voice sounded despondent.

Dora nodded. 'Got it in one, she was here when I found them.'

Tom coughed. 'All right, leave it with me. I'll set things straight. And tell Josephine, if she's there, that I'll do the decent thing.'

Dora felt a little flutter of panic.

'Suicide?' she said in a low voice. 'I don't think – '

Tom laughed. 'No, not suicide. Until tomorrow then, Dora. Shall we say twelve by the clock tower. I would say come alone, but it sounds a bit melodramatic, just be careful who you bring.'

Dora dropped the phone back into its cradle and looked at Josephine. 'He said he was going to do the decent thing.'

Josephine nodded. 'I heard. I think you ought to repack all these things and put them back in the boot of your car.'

Dora stared at her. 'Are you serious?'

Josephine nodded. 'Absolutely. Then we have a nice cup of tea, and then we get off to Abbotsbridge, in your car, to get you a ball gown. Like Tom Fielding said, they've been safe enough until now. What's changed?'

Dora felt her stomach tighten. The envelope looked deceptively innocent; little dark thoughts began to surface like marsh gas. She bit her lip.

'Everything. If Tom Fielding isn't after these photos, who the hell is it? And how far are they prepared to go to get them? What if they come back here before tomorrow night?' Ice-cold eddies and ripples of fear made her voice sound uneven. 'This is crazy. I don't want to keep the pictures here. What if someone steals the car? Or –'

'Look, calm down,' said Josephine. 'No-one in their right mind is going to steal that rusty heap of yours. It'll be all right. No-one's found them so far, why should they find them now? Tomorrow night they'll be gone.'

Dora sighed. 'I wish I felt as confident. You know what these are, don't you? A noose around Tom Fielding's throat – he's ruined if they ever get out and maybe if they don't. Whoever's got these has got Tom Fielding by the balls.' She slumped back into her chair. 'It was a hell of a lot simpler when I didn't know what they were or where they were.' Another chill trickled down her spine.

Josephine stared longingly at the envelope. 'If you're really that worried I could always take them home with me.'

In spite of the tension, Dora found it impossible not to laugh. 'No thanks, Josephine, don't be offended but I just don't trust you to keep them to yourself.'

Josephine dropped a friendly hand on her shoulder. 'That's what I like about you, Dora, you're a great judge of character. Come on, let's go over to Abbotsbridge.'

18

Dora found it very hard to concentrate on choosing dresses. She had parked her Fiat so close to the window of the house at Abbotsbridge that Josephine Hammond had had to climb out over a flower bed to get to the path.

The dress woman showed them into her spare room where clothes hung neatly on rails around the walls.

'What size are you?' she said, looking Dora up and down.

Dora didn't know.

'I'll get a tape measure. I would have said ten, maybe twelve. You're lucky, we've got lots of things in that size. Finding you something really special shouldn't be a problem.'

Dora stood with her arms out like a child while the woman discovered her best kept secrets. When she'd done, she turned round and pulled a cream floor-length sheath dress out of the rack. 'This is very nice.'

Dora stared at it. 'Too low, I want something to cover up my scrawny arms, my skinny non-existent bust and my naturally ungainly stance.'

The woman nodded, working a professional finger along the rails. 'I'm fresh out of bin liners and brown paper bags. What about this instead?' She pulled out a long peacock-blue dress. It had a square neck, was cut on the bias so the skirt flowed out in a swirling arc, and it had a matching lined lace jacket.

'The jacket is lovely, hangs down to mid-thigh, perfect for hiding a multitude of sins.'

Josephine nodded her approval. 'It's nice.'

Dora had to agree.

The woman smiled. 'Why don't you try it on. Oh, one thing,

watch the lining in the jacket – it's split under the arm.'

In the changing room, Dora took a glance at the tag on the hanger. Even the beautifully handwritten italics didn't quite take the sting out of the price. There was obviously a lot of money to be made in secondhand schmutter. She slipped the dress over her head, zipped it up, and then turned to look in the mirror.

The transformation was quite remarkable. The dress fitted her perfectly, clinging comfortably over the bodice before dropping elegantly into a full skirt. Dora posed for the mirror. It did look good.

Carefully, mindful of the split lining, she pulled on the jacket and grinned at her reflection. The jacket was superb, the final touch, its slightly padded shoulders enhancing her slim silhouette. The heavy lace had been dyed to match the jacket exactly. The dress moved like liquid around her. The whole outfit whispered style. Dora stood up on tiptoe to see how it would look with heels and then backed confidently out from behind the curtains of the dressing room.

'Well, what do you think?' she said, with a self-satisfied grin.

The woman smiled at Dora and then at Josephine. 'I'd say we'd got it with the first shot.'

Dora nodded. 'Me too, I'll take it. Do you do shoes and those fiddly little bags?'

The woman laughed. 'Funnily enough we do. Let me show you what we've got.'

Dora arrived home feeling quite triumphant. It was only after Josephine had left and she drove down towards the lock-up garages that she started to feel uneasy. The cardboard box in the boot glowed in her consciousness like a fiery beacon.

What if . . . she stamped the thought out before it got a chance to form itself into something dark and nasty. The worst thing that could happen was that whoever it was found the photos before the ball, and used them for whatever it was they wanted them for. Either way, the pictures would be gone. Either way she would get her life back.

She sighed and flipped the slippery dress bag out from the back seat. She was pleased with the outfit – more than pleased – delighted.

The woman had offered to get the jacket repaired, but Dora, keen to have the dress home, had gone for a discount instead – not that it was much of a discount. It would take her ten minutes to catch the lining back together – if she could just lay her hands on a needle and thread.

Dora slung the dress, on its hanger, over her shoulder, pulled out the shoe box and little carrier with her new evening bag inside and headed home.

Oscar eyed the great sheath of white polythene with barely concealed avarice. Dora sighed. 'No shredding, no ripping, this is going straight in the wardrobe.'

The light was flashing on the answer machine. She pressed the play button and headed off to the bedroom to put the dress away.

Jon's message was first. He sounded apologetic.

'Dora, look, I'm really sorry but I don't think I'll be able to get round tonight. I'm on lates anyway, but we've just had a job come in out at Middlereach.' She heard the grin in his voice as he continued. 'If I can get round I will, but don't count on it, I'm totally bushed. See you tomorrow at the ball if I don't see you before. By the way, I've just dropped my dinner jacket off at the cleaners.'

Dora experienced an odd sense of relief. At least she wouldn't have to explain to Jon about the photos, or about her liaison with Tom Fielding. Relief was followed by a tiny flutter of unease. Wasn't she supposed to want to tell Jon? She had hardly got to know him, had barely begun something that could be called a relationship, and already she was relieved not to have to tell him the truth. How long did the truth between couples last?

The train of thought was broken by a whirr and a beep and the sound of Kate's voice on the machine.

'Mum, hello. I just thought I'd ring to see how you are. I wondered why we hadn't heard anything from you. I tried ringing Sheila but she seems a bit upset. Have you two had a row?'

The tone changed slightly, from confident to something younger and more vulnerable. 'Can you ring me? I'm at home all day today. Have you heard any more about the break-in? Are you okay? I'm worried about you.'

Dora walked back into the office. She realised she hadn't rung Kate in a week. She paused and stared down at the phone.

All the lies she had so carefully woven had given her nothing but trouble. Tucked away quietly in her flat they had grown horns and teeth, and then Lillian Bliss had brought them all out to haunt her. And not just Dora's lies. Other people's lies had homed in on her like a beacon.

She flicked the tape back and listened to Kate again. She had lied to Kate all her adult life, lied to Sheila, now she was thinking about beginning all over again and lying to Jon.

She picked up the phone. The only way to take the power away from the lies was to drag them, kicking and screaming, out into the daylight. She tapped in Kate's number and settled herself down in the armchair.

'Hello, is that Kate? It's Mum here.' It sounded very strange calling herself 'Mum'. Dora cradled the phone in her shoulder, wishing she had a cigarette.

Kate's voice was tight and guarded. 'Hello, how are you?'

Dora wondered. The bridges between them were rusty from disuse. 'Not so bad, and yourself?'

'So-so.' It felt like two tigresses moving slowly around each other, vying for position.

'I got your phone call.'

Kate made a little dark noise in her throat, not quite a growl, not quite a whine. Dora coughed. This was so hard that she was tempted to hang up and forget the whole idea. She heard Kate sniff, sniffing seemed to run in the family.

'Are you ill?' Kate asked.

Dora shook her head. 'No, love. I'm fine. Life's just been a bit strange here recently. I'm sorry, I really should have rung you sooner.'

'I rang Auntie Sheila, she said you'd got a boyfriend . . .'

Dora groaned. Trust Sheila.

'. . . And that you were very upset about something. Sheila thinks you ought to see a doctor. Are you going to tell me what this is all about? I think I ought to know.' Kate's voice was uneven, with a ragged emotional edge.

Dora sighed and took a deep breath. 'Kate,' she said flatly, 'you're right, we do need to talk. The man I'm going out with is a policeman. He's called Jon Melrose, I think you'd like him. But I'd like to explain why someone broke into my flat.'

Kate suddenly burst into tears. Her words spilt out in hot miserable little sobs. 'It's something serious, isn't it? You're really ill and you're not telling me because you're afraid of hurting me again, that's it, isn't it? Have you rung Dad? I could ring him again if you like. I know he'd have you back. He wouldn't want you to be on your own, not if you're really ill.'

Dora's jaw dropped in complete astonishment. 'What?'

'Aunt Sheila said you've been acting strangely. She said you'd been really odd recently. I don't want to hear about boyfriends. I know it's Dad you really want, isn't it? You ought to ring Dad and let him know what's going on. What is the matter, how long have you got? Can't they operate or something?'

Dora stood up stiffly, rapidly regaining her poise. Why was it that she felt as if she was inadvertently living someone else's life? 'Kate,' she said, as evenly as she could. 'Please stop this. You're working yourself up into a state about nothing. God knows what Sheila's been telling you, but take it from me, it's a pack of lies. There's nothing wrong we me. I haven't got *anything*.'

'Then why haven't you rung me?' Kate snuffled miserably.

'Why don't you sit down, Kate. There are some things I need to tell you.'

Kate let out a dark, choking, strangled sob and Dora cursed Sheila and the gift of an overactive imagination.

'Sit down, Kate,' she purred, in a comforting tender voice, straight from the cradle side. 'I'm trying to explain. First of all, I'm not ill, honestly.'

Kate sounded as if she was blowing her nose. 'You're not ill?' She sounded almost disappointed. Dora began to wonder if Kate was deaf as well as given to overreacting. Patiently she shook her head.

'No, not ill, not ill at all.'

'So what's the matter with you then?'

There was nothing left now but the truth. Dora suddenly felt tired. 'Have you ever heard of a woman called Catiana Moran?' she said slowly.

'Yes, she writes porn. There's a cut-out of her in our book shop. Sheila said you'd been to see her.'

Dora glanced around the desk for a cigarette. There had to be one somewhere. 'That's right. Well, I'm really Catiana Moran. The girl is a model I hired to promote my books. Catiana Moran is my pseudonym.'

Kate snorted. 'Don't be so ridiculous, mo–' she snapped, but something about Dora's tone stopped her mid-sentence. 'Oh, my God,' she murmured weakly. 'You're telling the truth, aren't you? My God, that is totally and utterly gross, Mother,' she whispered. 'How on earth could you?'

Dora sighed. Maybe the truth wasn't such an easy option either. She found a single crumpled cigarette in the top drawer of her desk and lit it. It tasted foul.

When she'd finished explaining to Kate, she rang Sheila, who was very quiet.

'I rang to say I'm sorry if I overreacted the other night.' Dora held out an olive branch and waited for Sheila to take a chainsaw to it.

Sheila sniffed a reply. 'You should have told me about those books before,' she said indignantly. 'I felt such a fool.'

No-one was helping.

Next, she tapped in Lillian's number, half hoping, half expecting that she would be out.

'Hello,' said Lillian in her toffee-brown voice. 'Who is this speaking?'

'It's me,' said Dora. 'I think I've found out why we are being burgled.'

'Oh, that's good,' said Lillian cheerfully. 'What is it?'

Dora looked up at the ceiling and sighed. 'Do you remember you told me you went to a Christmas party at Ben Frierman's house? You and Carol met a man called Tom Fielding there?'

There was a little squeak of comprehension from the phone. 'Oh yes, he was lovely. Do you know him too?'

Dora decided to press on. 'While you were there Carol took some photos of you and Tom in bed together. Well, that's what all this has been about. Someone has been trying to find them, but I've got them now. I've arranged with Tom to give them back. Is that all right?'

Lillian was quiet for what seemed like a long time. 'It was after my dad had gone home. Lots of the people had already left, Calvin and them. The ones who stayed had had a lot to drink – and Tom was so nice to me. I really didn't think about the pictures. Carol's photo mad, you know? I suppose I'd sort of forgotten about them. I thought maybe Carol had still got them at her place,' she said. 'Why would anyone want a few photos? You know he took us both out to his house the next day. Cooked us a big breakfast and everything. Not like Calvin, I've been thinking about Calvin a lot – Tom was so nice to me and Carol –'

Dora shook her head. How did she explain to someone like Lillian that the photographs of Tom Fielding were political dynamite?

'The thing is, Lillian, technically, I suppose the photographs are yours. I'm ringing up to ask if you mind me giving them to Tom Fielding.'

Lillian giggled. 'You mean like a souvenir? No, no, if he wants them, he can have them.'

Finally, Dora rang Jon. She had saved him up until last. In some ways it was going to be the most difficult call to make.

The receptionist said, 'I'm really sorry, ma'am, but he isn't in the station at the moment. Can I take a message?' Dora politely declined. Truth by proxy was not what she had in mind.

Oscar jumped up onto her lap and purred. For him, truth was an open can of tuna.

Spar waited until early evening before he loped down to Gunners Terrace to pick up the tape from the car outside Dora's flat. Milo had arranged with a friend who ran a garage to swap the motors round a bit, so Spar had to check the key under the street light to make sure he had the right one. This private eye business was beginning to lose its edge. The money was good but he could do without all the hanging about and the fiddly stuff.

He'd left Milo in his garage, developing the photos they had taken that morning when they had searched Lillian's flat.

Spar was a bit of an atheist, which was a good thing. He'd read a notice once, in the electronics factory where he'd worked when he come out of nick. It had said, 'God is in the details', and he knew then that he hadn't got the time or the inclination to go looking for Him. Same with all this private investigating lark. There was just too much hanging around, too much waiting for something to happen.

He glanced up at the windows of Dora Hall's flat. The lights were on in the sitting room; intermittent flashes of light through the curtains told him she was watching TV.

Probably watching 'Coronation Street' and then 'The Bill', although she looked more like a BBC2 documentary sort of woman. He adjusted his jacket and headed towards the maroon Citroën parked up against the old chemist's shop.

At least he could get the tape and then go home, maybe listen to it in front of the fire with a can of beer. He had considered inviting Milo back to share a bevy or two but, on balance, he'd decided his girlfriend would make for better company.

He slid into the driver's seat, took a new tape from his jacket pocket and popped the old one out. In the gloom he could just pick out the spools. It didn't look as if she'd been talking to that many people. Maybe it wasn't worth swapping the tapes after all. He thought it over for a few seconds. Milo had pointed out to him that listening to the tape in the car looked a bit suspicious.

He stared at the dark tape spools. Maybe his partner was right, but it had worked pretty well up until Milo had told him it wasn't kosher. Besides, new tapes cost him a quid a pop. He weighed the recorded tape in his hands for a few seconds and then slapped it back into the machine. He'd listen to what was on it, and then, if there wasn't anything interesting, he'd rewind and record over it. He picked up the earpiece and pressed 'play'.

When Spar heard Dora's call to Tom Fielding he felt a nasty little shiver of what might have been. Bloody hell, he'd very nearly decided not to listen to it at all, just rewind and set it to re-record.

Swallowing down the unpleasant sensation in his stomach, he clicked the machine off and sat back. He'd have to go and find Milo now. He slipped the cassette into its case and then his pocket. His girlfriend would be most dischuffed.

Alicia Markham listened to Spar's telephone call with a sense of relief. Finally. She smiled. They'd got Tom Fielding pinned to the canvas – or at least, as near as damn it. It wasn't until she put down the phone that she began to feel a little uneasy. With Tom Fielding out of the running, Guy Phelps' victory was almost certainly assured. She sat back and stared at the phone.

Lawrence Rawlings had suggested she might consider whether she actually wanted to help Phelps into power. His voice filled her head like a bad migraine. If Guy Phelps was in office, without her there to monitor every action, every word, every thought – she grimaced. The sense of triumph quietly faded and died. She had put herself out on a limb for Guy Phelps and for what? His election would be a disaster for Fairbeach. Without her to sheepdog him every step of the way, he would sink, and if she wasn't careful he would take her down with him. After all, everyone knew she had hand-picked him. Rawlings was right, Guy Phelps had to go. It had been Phelps who had told her about Tom Fielding in the first place, almost in passing.

'Tom's not the kind of man we want for Fairbeach,' he had said, in his marvellous, modulated voice, when she had been talking to him about the opposition after one of their first strategy meetings.

'Morally unsound,' he'd said. His tone had been self-righteous, verging on the pompous. 'I could tell you a thing or two about Mr Fielding,' he had said, his face composed into the archetypal expression of the school sneak. And he had told her, carefully edited of course, but with sufficient weighty pauses and knowing looks to make her aware of the whole scenario. She wondered again how he knew so much.

Lillian Bliss' television performances had been a gift from the gods. Alicia had fantasised about the headlines splashed across the tabloids. 'Politician in bed with porn queen. Pictures inside.'

She sighed.

Stacked under the table in her office were the handbills and posters for Guy's election campaign. She picked up the phone and tapped in Lawrence Rawlings' number.

He didn't sound at all surprised to hear from her.

'They've found what I'm looking for, presumably your man's already let you know,' she said flatly. 'I'm going to pick it up tomorrow night after the ball. Under the clock tower, at the college, at midnight, unless I can have my man sniff it out beforehand.'

She heard Lawrence's discomfort. 'A little theatrical for my tastes, Alicia. Did you think about what I said?'

Alicia nodded, even though she knew he couldn't see her.

'Yes,' she said, without emotion. 'I've thought about it a great deal. And you're right. Will you be there tomorrow to pick up the material?'

'Of course,' said Lawrence. 'If you want me there. We agreed to form an alliance, didn't we?'

Alicia sighed. 'Indeed we did. Until tomorrow then, Lawrence.'

19

Dora woke up on the morning of the ball with a peculiar sense of anticipation – in the uneasy no-man's-land between excitement and apprehension.

Outside her bedroom window, the sky was overcast and grey. Ominous twists of black cloud hung against a stormy sky like dead crows on a fence. She'd always thought God did a nice line in melodramatic touches. It matched her mood perfectly. She felt like a condemned man.

After breakfast, just when she had almost decided to go out, the doorbell rang. As she went into the office, Dora made up her mind that if it was the cat muggers they could have the photos, have the car, anything.

'Hello?' said Sheila, sounding unnaturally subdued. 'I thought I'd pop round and see how you were. After you made the effort to phone –'

'Come up,' said Dora. 'I could do with the company.' She could hardly believe she'd said it.

Sheila peered round as she came in.

'You don't look very well at all. What, no policeman? Packed you in, has he? I –' She stopped, seeing Dora's eyes flare. 'I just came to see if you're coming round to lunch tomorrow? I thought you might like a change of scenery.'

Dora snorted. 'I don't know.' It crossed her mind that an awful lot of things might happen between now and lunch time tomorrow.

Sheila sniffed. 'Got something else planned, have you?'

'I'm going to the Spring Ball tonight . . .' Dora began.

Sheila's expression squashed the rest of the sentence up in the back of Dora's throat.

'You're going to the college ball?' Sheila repeated incredu-lously.

Dora resented the suggestion that she wasn't ball material. 'I was invited,' she said waspishly. 'I'm going with Jon Melrose.'

Sheila nodded. 'I suppose, being a chief inspector, he moves in those sort of circles. Balls, dinner parties, choral recitals up at St Faith's. Bit of a turn-up for you, though, isn't it? What are you going to wear? Are you having your hair done?'

Dora didn't know whether to be angry or relieved that some things in life never change.

Sheila was hovering in the hallway.

'I've bought myself a new dress. Would you like to see it?'

Sheila nodded. 'I hope you bought something sensible that you can wear again. Such a lot of money, clothes these days, and you don't get out a lot, really, do you?'

Dora pulled the wrapping over the blue evening dress and held it up against herself for Sheila's inspection. Her sister's X-ray vision spotted the torn lining in the jacket in an instant.

'It's damaged,' Sheila pointed out indignantly. 'Someone's already worn this. I'd take it back if I were you. You've been done. How much did you pay for it?'

Dora sighed. 'It's secondhand. I was going to clean my car out, have my hair done, and then I thought I'd just stitch it up. It won't take much to put right.'

Sheila nodded. 'I could do it for you if you like. Nice colour. Where did you get it? One of the charity places? I always pop into the Barnardos shop myself, they have a lot of nice things in there.'

Tonight would be the denouement, the grand finale, Lawrence Rawlings thought reflectively, as he stood at his office window, watching the magpies playing in the orchard below. He couldn't help wondering exactly what it was that this woman, Dora Hall, had found.

His imagination shifted the discovery from a cabin trunk, to a box, to a single black-and-white photograph. How much more would anyone know after tonight? How much truth could anyone stand in a single lifetime?

Calvin would be at the ball with Sarah, Lillian Bliss would be there to accept her award – all acting, all lying. Lawrence sighed and turned away as the magpies careered through the virgin blossom like missiles.

Perhaps what he was looking for, the shreds of hard evidence he wanted, wouldn't be there. Ironic that truth could not be substantiated, while lies could and went on to a life of their own. Perhaps he ought to trust his instincts more. Could the truth be subjective? Could belief alone make something true?

Dora came back from the hairdressers to find Calvin pacing up and down outside her door, puffing angrily on a small cigar.

'Come in, come up, what on earth is the matter with you?'

Calvin chomped miserably on the butt end.

'Bloody Lillian Bliss, that's what's the matter. She's dumped me, worse than that, she's terminated our contract. Just like that.' He snapped his fingers for added emphasis. 'Tonight is her last appearance as far as she's concerned. She told me first thing this morning. One more night and then she's not doing any more work for the Catiana Moran contract.'

Dora stared at him. 'What?'

'Exactly. She said she wanted to go out on a high and the ball and the awards, apparently, are it. She said I didn't treat her properly. She said she'd been talking to you. What exactly did you say to her?'

Dora shook her head. 'Nothing, nothing at all.'

Calvin stamped his way up into the kitchen. 'She said there was nothing to keep her in Fairbeach now, asked me if I'd put the flat on the market for her. What a bloody cheek. The paint's barely dry on the walls. Jesus!' He threw himself onto one of the chairs. 'Ungrateful little bitch, after all I've done for her.'

Dora was about to say something soothing when Calvin began again. 'She said our relationship was over. Over! I just don't believe it. I said to her, "Relationship, what relationship?" and she just laughed and said, "Exactly." She said I treated her like a cheap tart. A cheap tart! And then she laughed, for God's sake! Where does this leave me? High and bloody dry, that's where. I'd got big plans for her, another month and I –' He stopped as if suddenly aware of who he was talking to. 'What I meant to say was –'

Dora held a hand up to silence him, her imagination filling in the blanks.

'Oh, don't worry, I'm ahead of you, Calvin. What you meant was, another month, a few more breaks, and Lillian would be all over the nationals. That's what you were hoping for, wasn't it? You'd have a nice big slice of a national celebrity? All that talk to me about doing that list, another month, it was pure hogwash, wasn't it? Did you think if you frightened her with the threat of the sack, she'd be so grateful when you changed your mind, she'd sign up for less money? Or were you hoping it would be me who asked you to get her back, when sales dropped off? You make me sick. Come on, Calvin, why not tell the truth and shame the devil?'

Calvin Roberts reddened visibly. 'I –'

Dora stared him down. 'The truth?'

'Yes, all right. Let's face it, Lillian's hot property at the moment. I've had a guy on the phone from one of the girlie mags, he wants her to do a centrefold. There's interest from satellite TV, a radio phone-in, even a record company, for God's sake. She could make us all a small fortune. What can I do to persuade her to come back?'

Dora shrugged. 'You could try telling her the truth?'

Calvin snorted. 'Are you totally mad? What's the truth got to do with anything?' He narrowed his eyes. 'This is all your fault – it was you who wanted to get rid of her in the first place.'

Dora sighed and opened the door onto the stairs.

'Are you going to the ball tonight?' she asked, trying hard not to let his aggression feed the little fluttering fears in her stomach.

Calvin's expression relaxed, as if he was relieved to change tack. 'Yes, what about you? Did Lillian give you the tickets I got for her?'

Dora nodded. 'I've got a lot to do between then and now. Why don't you go home and have a nap or whatever it is you do to relax, before you explode.'

In the back bedroom of his terraced house, Spar carefully buttoned up the waistcoat under the dinner jacket Milo had hired for him. He grinned at the reflection in the mirror on his wardrobe door, and slicked his hair down with a comb.

'What about that, then? What do you reckon?' he said, executing a faultless pirouette. 'Not bad, eh?'

Milo snorted. 'It'll look better when you've got your trousers on. This bleeding tie is driving me nuts. We should've got them ones that were on elastic.'

They were round at Spar's house down by the docks. Outside the dusty windows the sky was already darkening. Spar had a growing sense of expectation – this was more like it. This was the proper stuff, exciting stuff.

Milo adjusted his tie and then leant across Spar's dressing table.

'All right if I use a bit of your after-shave?'

'Sure thing,' said Spar. 'Help yourself. That Rampant is good stuff. A bloke on the market gets it for me. What's the plan for tonight?'

Milo winced as the alcohol hit his newly shaved chin. He blew for a few seconds until the stinging passed.

'Right, Dora Hall's going to bring the photos with her, so as soon as she's inside the hall I'll go over and have a shufty in her car. Which reminds me, make sure the torch has got new batteries in it. Long life, none of your bargain basement crap. When she goes inside, you make sure you find out her cloakroom ticket number. Give it a minute or two, and then go back and tell the girl behind the desk she's forgotten something, fags, hankie – use your imagination – and then you go through her pockets.'

Spar pulled a face. 'How come I get to do her coat? I wanted to help do the car with you.'

Milo puffed out his cheeks. 'All right then, but you can only come if you come as look-out. Right?'

Spar grinned triumphantly. 'Right.' He could hardly wait.

Dora couldn't quite believe the mirror in her bedroom. She turned around again just to check that she wasn't mistaken. The new blue dress was perfect, as were the shoes, the tiny evening bag and, remarkably enough, the woman who was wearing them. She grinned at the elegantly coiffured figure, and the woman in the mirror grinned back. She glanced across at the bedroom clock. A few more minutes and she would have to leave. There was just enough time to put on her jacket and add a spray of perfume before leaving.

She pulled the lacy jacket off the hanger. She hadn't sewn up the split sleeve seams. She pulled it on anyway; it wouldn't show.

Downstairs the night was already dark. She tip-tapped on her high heels to her car. She'd parked it outside the street door when she'd come back from the hairdresser, thinking it would be easier to leave it there, rather than negotiate the uneven pavements down to the lock-ups in her new high heels.

She undid the boot. Lillian's box was still there, all wrapped around in its shiny black plastic bag. She pulled down the top and looked inside. The photos of Tom Fielding were back in their envelope and pushed down the side. She took the envelope out and turned it over in her fingers before tucking it away safely.

'Well, here we go,' she murmured under her breath, closed the box flaps, pulled the plastic bag up around the sides and snapped the boot shut.

Driving in high heels was a mistake. She popped, hopped, jumped and spluttered her way across town towards the college.

The trees along the college drive were strung with chains of fairy lights. It looked quite magical. She joined the phalanx of cars creeping up towards the car park.

Away from the main building, where a crowd of party-goers was already scurrying towards the doors, was the clock tower. It stood on a slight hill, surrounded by a skeleton of scaffolding. It was built and rebuilt annually by final-year construction students. At the moment it was three-quarters complete, which told everyone that the summer term was finally on its way. Dora glanced across at it.

'See you at midnight,' she murmured under her breath and indicated left. She bumped over the sleeping policeman into the staff car park, away from the red stream of tail lights which was heading towards the main car park, alongside the function hall.

The staff car park was in darkness. She drove slowly towards the far side, well away from the buildings, so that when she turned off the headlights the Fiat was completely engulfed in a shroud of grey. Dora sat for a minute or two wondering whether it would be a better idea to hide in plain sight amongst everyone else. Her stomach was quietly tying itself up into a sheep shank with a double half-hitch.

She ought to have said something to Jon.

Dora stared out into the gloom. Here and there patches of potholed tarmac were picked out by a string of overhead lights. Rather than relieve the darkness they seemed to accentuate it.

They would be going home in Jon's car. So, tucked out on the edges of shadow, the Fiat wouldn't be in anyone's way. At least, that's what she told herself. They could pick the car up in the morning.

Easing herself out into the chilly night air she straightened her dress and jacket. Through the twilight she could hear a thread of dance music. Grabbing hold of it, she let it guide her back towards the ball.

From outside, as Dora approached, it appeared that the guests stepped from monochrome anonymity into a bright spotlight when they climbed the steps up towards the main door. There was a receiving line down in the foyer. The mayor was shaking hands with everyone, as was the principal of the college, the vice principal and the president of the students' union, who was all done out in top hat and tails. Alongside the main party were a dozen other minor somebodies and a plethora of wives.

Dora took her courage and her full-length skirt in both hands and climbed the steps. Another hour and Jon would be there too. She'd tell him all about Lillian Bliss and Tom Fielding then – it wasn't too late to put things in order. As she moved along the line, shaking hands, she saw Josephine Hammond at the top of the stairs. The reporter was dressed in a black sleeveless sheath dress and looked stunning.

Across the foyer, Alicia Markham was standing by the coat check talking to Lawrence Rawlings. Behind them, Guy Phelps was talking to his wife and Calvin Roberts and his wife, Sarah. Bob Preston, Fairbeach's former mayor, cradled a champagne glass and chatted to the chairman of the chamber of trade. Everywhere she was surrounded by familiar, respectable, comfortable faces.

Nothing can happen tonight, Dora thought, as she glanced around. The place was awash with pillars of the community. Everything was going to be all right after all. Dora let out a long low breath to ease the knot in her gut and headed towards Josephine.

'You look amazing,' she said as they met on the stairs.

Josephine grinned and struck a pose. 'Same pedigree as yours. Not bad, eh? Seen Tom Fielding yet?'

Dora winced. 'Did you have to say that? I was just thinking it was going to be all right.'

Josephine poked her playfully in the ribs. 'It is, it is. Come on, let's go and get a glass of champagne. Is Lillian here yet?'

Dora looked back over her shoulder. 'I haven't seen her.' As she spoke there was an explosion of flashbulbs.

Josephine pointed a long beautifully manicured nail. 'Talk of the devil – Gary just bagged her mugging with the mayor for the front page of the *Gazette*. Just look at her.'

Below them, Lillian Bliss was making a grand entrance. She was dressed in a fantasy scarlet ball gown. It was cut off the shoulders with a skirt like a tiered wedding cake. As she moved along the line, the president of the students' union executed a sweeping bow, plucked off his top hat and offered her his arm. Lillian fluttered an ostrich feather fan in front of her perfectly made-up face and slipped her arm through his.

Dora couldn't help but smile as a ripple of applause broke out amongst the spectators for Lillian's breathtaking entrance.

Josephine grinned. 'Well, she has most definitely arrived now. Come on, let's mingle. I'm supposed to be working.'

At the coat-check desk, Spar watched Dora Hall's progress up the main staircase. Damn, no coat. He looked round to see if he could spot Milo. His companion was over by the potted ferns talking to one of the waitresses. Spar pushed his way through the people towards him.

'Milo?' His friend smiled at the waitress and gave her his business card.

He turned to Spar. 'Just drumming up a little bit of trade. We might have ourselves a nice tidy divorce case after this. So, what did you get?'

Spar pulled a face. 'Nothing. No coat.'

Milo snorted. 'Better get out into the car park then. Where is Dora Hall?'

Spar nodded toward the staircase. 'Gone off with that reporter from the *Gazette*.'

Milo grinned. 'Off we go then, sunshine. Time to rock and roll.'

They slipped through the crowd, outside into the cold night air. Spar fought the temptation to head back in to get his parka. It was bloody nippy.

'We'll take a row of cars each,' decided Milo, pulling a fag out of a silver cigarette case. 'If you find the Fiat come and get me. Don't try anything on your own.'

Spar set off, eyes working over the line of cars in front of him. Funny how the light made them look a different colour.

He went up and back and up and back growing colder and colder as he got further away from the lights of the hall.

Milo, picked out by the single red glowing eye of his cigarette and a white rectangle of dress shirt, met him at the far end of the final line.

'She can't have brought her car,' said Spar desperately, slapping his arms up around his thin hired dress suit.

Milo sniffed. 'Well, she didn't bleeding walk, did she?'

Spar was so cold he was close to tears. 'Maybe she came in a taxi.'

Milo's eyes glittered angrily in the gloom. 'Was she carrying anything?'

Spar thought about it. 'Just a little tiny bag, no bigger than a fag packet.'

Milo threw the cigarette butt down and ground it into the tarmac. 'Then she hasn't got it on her. She must have brought her bleeding car.' He sniffed, looking left and right. 'She's stuck it out of the way somewhere.' He grinned. 'Which is a good sign. Come on, we'll have a look over the back here.'

It took them two minutes to find the Fiat tucked away in the staff car park.

'Bingo,' Milo hissed and pulled a pair of surgical gloves out of his jacket pocket. 'Get the torch out and tell me if you see anyone coming. You are about to witness a master craftsman at work.'

Out of the corner of his eye, Spar could see the torch light dancing, while he kept his attention firmly on the rolling sea of darkness around them. After a few seconds there was a reassuring click as Milo popped the lock and then the sound of him opening the door, sliding into the front seat . . . Minutes passed.

It was amazing what you could see just by listening, Spar thought, and he was about to tell Milo how he knew exactly what he was doing, when Milo swore.

'Nothing,' he snorted. 'She's cleaned the bleeding car out. It's as clean as a whistle in here, nothing.'

'What about the glove box?' Spar asked, even though he had heard it snap open a few seconds earlier.

'Just the handbook and a torch from the AA.' Milo clambered out. 'Can't see her taking out the back seat or anything like that.'

'What about the boot?' Spar suggested.

'I know, I know,' snapped Milo, 'I was going to do that next. I've done this before, I'm not half-sharp, you know.'

Spar turned his attention back to listening, as Milo circled the car on the uneven gravel.

'Shit, I reckon she must have put everything out of the bleeding front in here. It's full of rubbish; boots, ropes, crisp packets . . .' There was a pregnant pause. 'And what have we got here?' hissed Milo, with a triumphant note in his voice. 'Bingo.'

Spar spun round. 'What is it?'

Milo passed him the torch, pulled a large carrier bag out of his pocket and started to shovel photographs into it. He looked up at Spar.

'The mother lode, my old son, the mother lode.'

Back inside, Dora glanced around the hall, trying to pick out Jon's face from amongst the crowd. The clock above the door said it was nearly nine. A group of dignitaries had assembled on the stage and the music had faded to a respectful level.

The college principal tapped the microphone and murmured, 'One-two, one-two.' Satisfied it was working, he gave a broad smile of welcome.

'Ladies and gentlemen, it gives me great pleasure to be hosting our eleventh annual Spring Ball. As is our tradition, tonight we will be presenting awards which have been made by both the faculty and the student body to members of staff, the student body and members of the community alike . . .'

Dora let her attention drift back towards the main doors. Guy Phelps was standing under the balcony with a group of men in dinner jackets. Dora's eyes moved across them casually and then swung back. She recognised the man beside Phelps.

They were sharing a joke, their heads angled together. It was the man she had seen with Phelps at the bring and buy – the same man she had seen breaking into Lillian's flat in Keelside.

She poked Josephine. 'Who is that guy with Phelps?' she whispered.

Josephine looked round in surprise. 'What?'

'The man there, on his right?'

A flurry of applause broke out as the principal announced the awards would be followed by a buffet supper in the refectory.

Josephine peered round. 'That's Colin Scarisbrooke. He's Phelps' political agent. Why?'

Dora let the information sink in and then shook her head. 'I'm not sure, but I think I may just have found out who is looking for Tom Fielding's photos.'

Josephine stared at her. 'What? Are you certain?'

Dora turned to check, but the crowd had shifted, obscuring her view. 'I think he's the man I caught breaking into Lillian's flat.'

Josephine's incredulous reply was interrupted by another burst of applause.

'This year,' the principal continued, as the clapping died down, 'to present the awards, we are privileged to have local businessman and longstanding supporter of our college charity projects, Mr Lawrence Rawlings . . .' There was more applause.

Dora felt obligated to watch Lawrence Rawlings making his way to the front of the stage, but not before she saw Alicia Markham, with her tail up about something, blustering through the doors at the back of the hall.

'Good evening,' Lawrence Rawlings began. 'My association with both Fairbeach and the college has been lifelong . . .'

Alicia Markham pushed her way into the VIP ladies' washroom, followed somewhat uneasily by Spar and Milo. She waved them inside.

'For God's sake get in here, and stop drawing attention to yourselves. Everyone else will be downstairs watching the awards ceremony. Here, give me that bag.' Snatching it away from Milo she up-ended it onto the long marble counter and pawed through the landslide of photos and papers like a terrier after a rat.

The first thing that caught her eye was a buff envelope. Inside was a folded sheet of paper. It wasn't the photographs, but perhaps it might be what Lawrence was looking for. Inside was a birth certificate. She scanned it in seconds, her eyes resting on 'father's name'. What was written beneath was a revelation. She stared at Milo and Spar without focusing.

'My God,' she hissed. This had to be what Lawrence had been looking for. He was trying to protect Jack Rees. She hesitated and then reread the certificate. At the funeral hadn't Caroline, Jack's widow, said something about Jack being found out once he was dead? Alicia read it again: Jack Rees was Lillian Bliss's father.

She smiled thinly, carefully re-folded the certificate into the envelope, slipped it into her handbag and then began to search again. She sifted through swimming certificates, endless photos of the young Lillian Bliss with a mongrel on a pebbly beach . . .

It was dross. All of it. She looked up at Milo.

'Is this it?' she said murderously. 'Are you certain you looked everywhere?' There was an unpleasant acidic taste in her mouth. These men were complete morons. She could have done a better job herself.

Milo lifted his hand in apology and then sniffed. 'What you want not there, then?'

Alicia beaded him with a furious glance. 'No, it's not there.' She sucked her teeth. 'Where the hell are the photographs?'

Spar considered for a few seconds. 'Dora Hall said she was going to deliver them at midnight.'

Alicia couldn't bring herself to speak to him and instead stared into his reflected gaze.

Spar flinched.

'Well, she's got to have them, then, hasn't she?' Milo reasoned. 'We just go there at midnight and pick them up.' He squared his shoulders. 'Two of them, two of us and one of them's a woman. And anyway, we'll have the element of surprise.'

Alicia sighed. 'Right. I want you to go to the clock tower and wait.'

'Why?' said Spar. 'It's really cold out there.'

'In case she decides to get there early,' Alicia snapped. She looked at Milo. 'Then it will be one against two. One of whom will be a woman.' She snapped her handbag shut with an air of finality and then swept out of the powder room, leaving Milo and Spar staring at the pile of photos.

Spar looked uncomfortably around the pale pink interior of the ladies' toilet. 'What are we going to do, then?' he said.

Milo picked up the carrier bag and began to funnel the photos back into it.

'Do what the lady says. Maybe there's something in this lot your man Rawlings might want.'

'No,' said Spar unhappily. 'I didn't mean that. What about waiting up at the clock tower for Dora Hall? It's bloody freezing out there.'

Milo grinned. 'We'll light a little fire. Do you know any good ghost stories?'

'And finally, last, but by no means least, we have the awards given by our student body,' announced the principal. He smiled indulgently. 'As always, their choices have been a little eclectic.'

Dora was beginning to get twitchy. She wanted Jon there with her. Across the room, Lillian was preparing to climb the steps up to the stage.

'Hello, you look stunning,' purred a familiar voice, as a hand slipped around Dora's waist.

Smiling, Dora turned round, and looked up into Jon's dark eyes. 'You'll really have to get rid of those crepe-soled shoes, or is it a police thing, sneaking up on people? I've been watching out for you.' She nodded towards the main entrance.

Jon grinned. 'Perks of the job. They let me in through the side door. How's it going?'

He smelt beautiful and looked better. A flutter of desire was stamped on by the realisation that Dora now had to tell him about Tom Fielding's photos, and how she was planning to meet him at midnight. It seemed melodramatic and ridiculous.

Dora took a deep breath. No time like the present.

'I've got something I have to tell you –' She was cut short by a thunderous explosion of applause as Lillian Bliss mounted the stage. The strawberry blonde seemed to float across towards the dignitaries, blushing demurely, and acknowledging her audience with a discreet wave of the hand.

Lawrence Rawlings appeared totally overawed by her and held onto Lillian's hands far too long as he awarded her her certificate and crystal vase. Lillian rewarded him with her carnivorous smile, and a delicate peck on each cheek, before she turned towards the microphone.

'I'd just like to say thank you very much for this award. It really does mean a lot to me,' she said, in her low breathy voice. Her eyes moved across the audience until she met Dora's eyes and then she winked slowly. 'I'd really like to thank my dear friend Dora Hall, without whom none of this would have been possible. Thank you, Dora.' As she spoke she hoisted the vase up in the air to a round of tumultuous applause.

Dora groaned and tightened her grip on Jon's arm.

'Don't worry,' he said, out of the corner of his mouth. 'It'll all be over soon.'

Dora looked up at him and pulled a miserable face.

'That's what I wanted to talk to you about. I think we ought to go and find somewhere quiet. Let's go out into the corridor.'

It took two minutes to explain, which was almost exactly the same amount of time Jon stared at Dora after she had finished speaking.

Finally he opened his mouth and said, incredulously, 'Are you stark raving mad? This isn't fiction, you know. What are you playing at? Why didn't you ring me?' He glanced over his shoulder, back into the hall. 'I ought to go and find Tom Fielding.'

Dora shook her head. 'No, please don't. I did try to ring you, but you'd already gone out. And I think Colin Scarisbrooke is the burglar. He works for Guy Phelps.'

'I need to find a phone –'

Dora caught hold of his arm. 'No, Jon, please. I want Tom Fielding to have his photos back without any fuss. Nobody else involved, not the police, not the press, no-one. When it's over I'll find a way to let Guy Phelps know what I've done.'

Jon shook his head. 'So what do you want me to do?'

Dora grinned sheepishly. 'I don't suppose you'd consider coming with me to the clock tower at midnight, would you? In an unofficial capacity?'

Jon snorted and then thought better of it and put his arms round her. 'You are totally and utterly crazy.' He kissed her. 'I'll come and keep an eye on you, but next time, God forbid, that you get your hands on a bunch of incriminating photos, try telling me first.' He paused and looked down at her. 'I'm serious, Dora, I want to live a whole life with you, not just the edited highlights, pushed to the outside edge by your little lies – all of it, no omissions, no exclusions.' He paused. 'Do you understand?'

Dora nodded and then kissed him back. 'Yes, it's just that I'm not used to having someone around to lean on,' she said softly. 'Now do you want to eat or dance? Do you dance?'

Jon shrugged. 'I can do that thing where you stand close and shuffle round very slowly.'

Dora grinned. 'I know that one, too.'

Jon caught hold of her arm. 'Be careful. All joking aside, you're playing a dangerous game.'

Dora nodded. 'I know.'

20

While they waited near the clock tower, Milo told Spar some very unpleasant stories about things he'd seen when he'd been in the infantry. Spar shuffled down inside his coat, wriggling so that it covered his ears, trying hard to get as much of his body covered up as he could. He was nervous about being alone with Milo in the dark and even more so about what might happen when Dora Hall and Tom Fielding finally arrived. There was frost in the air and as he breathed, a plume of water vapour curled out in front of him like dragon's breath. Below them, the bass notes of the music from the Spring Ball filtered through the darkness like a heartbeat.

They'd found a good spot to hide though, tucked away behind a portakabin, where no-one could see them, but they could see the clock tower quite clearly.

Milo was drawing another gory story to its conclusion. 'So then, Charlie says to the MO, can you bring me leg back in a carrier bag as a souvenir? Something to put on the mantelpiece to show the kids.' Milo took a long drag of his cigarette and laughed dryly. 'What a sod, eh? Good bloke, Charlie, I miss him. Mind you, he'll never play in goal again.'

Spar nodded distractedly. 'How much longer have we got to wait?'

Milo slid his sleeve up and looked at his watch.

'Few more minutes. You'll know when it's time because they stick the outside lights on, so the drunken bastards can find their way back to their cars.'

'And what do we do when Mrs Hall and Tom Fielding show up?'

It was something that Spar, until now, had been too nervous

to contemplate. Milo laughed again. Spar really didn't like the slightly hysterical edge to his tone.

'What d'you think? We've got the element of surprise, cover of darkness – classic army ambush. God, this takes me back. Those two won't want a lot of trouble. If we're really lucky, she'll get here before him, in which case it'll be a doddle. If not, I'll grab the woman, you take Tom Fielding. Bish-bash-bosh. Thirty seconds, just like that. She'll be scared shitless, I reckon. She'll hand the photos over, don't worry – and there we are, mission accomplished. Just look like you mean business.'

Spar pulled a face. He wasn't convinced he wanted to look as if he meant business. Dora Hall was not much over five foot, it hardly seemed fair that Milo had chosen the easier option. 'What if Fielding fights back?' he asked apprehensively.

Milo grinned and flexed his shoulders. His teeth glinted like fangs in the firelight. 'Whack him one. Not too hard though – if in doubt, go for the family jewels.'

Spar, trying to suppress the big knot that was forming in his throat, looked down at the hall. He could hear the strains of the 'Last Waltz'. Now seemed a good moment to broach the subject that had been flitting in and out of his mind for several days.

'Milo, I don't reckon I'm really cut out to be a private eye,' he said. 'I can't do with all this. I've been thinking about fish. I was looking in *Exchange and Mart*. There's this bloke does a starter pack for koi carp farming. Two hundred quid a throw. He reckons you can make a lot of money if you can get the right stock. I've got that shed out the back of my place. And my girlfriend . . .'

Milo waved him into silence. 'You don't have to explain it to me, matey. If surveillance isn't in your blood you're better off getting out of it. Snipers are born, not made.' He dropped to one knee, and in the light from the fire took up a shooting position.

Spar was about to agree and then realised that in Milo's

imaginary sights, a hunched figure was making his way up the rise towards the clock tower.

'Tom Fielding?' Spar whispered, his guts quietly turning to magma.

Milo nodded. 'That's our man.' He pulled back on the imaginary trigger and imitated the report of a rifle. 'Looks like Mr Fielding is very keen to get his hands on Mrs Hall's photo album.'

Spar glanced around nervously, his gaze settling on the old tin can they had used as a makeshift brazier.

'Do you think we ought to put the fire out?'

Milo shook his head. 'It'll be all right. Just keep your voice down and keep out of sight.'

Across the car park, Spar could see two other figures heading their way. Their approach was much more determined but they stayed in the shadows. They didn't want to be seen. Spar screwed up his eyes, struggling to pick out their faces, and then realised it had to be Lawrence Rawlings and Alicia Markham. All they needed now was Dora Hall and they'd have a full house. He crouched a little lower. Where was she?

Tom Fielding climbed with a certain determination in his gait. Hands in his pockets, his head was bowed against the biting night wind. Spar had no doubt from the way he moved that Tom Fielding could handle himself in a fight if it came to it. He would have given his soul to have been anywhere else but crouched in the darkness beside Milo.

Tom Fielding was getting closer. Spar tried hard to remember to breathe. Finally, he could see Dora Hall walking briskly across the tarmac. From the way she moved he could tell she was cold too, cold and nervous. She ought to have brought a coat, he thought. She must be freezing.

While he had been watching Dora, Alicia and Lawrence had vanished into the shadows. Spar thought Dora Hall was brave to come at all, let alone by herself. He knew he wouldn't do it. His pulse quickening, he crept closer to Milo, who was hunkered down behind an unfinished brick wall, and waited.

* * *

Dora's apprehension was growing more unmanageable as she got further away from the safety of the main college buildings. What had been no more than a nervous flutter all evening was rapidly spinning itself into a dark glistening thread that tightened like a garrotte around her stomach. She glanced back towards the bright lights of the hall. It would be all right, said a voice in her head, the calm reasonable voice she used for trips to the dentist. Nothing would happen, she would be fine. Just fine. It didn't sound very convincing.

Litter cartwheeled by on the wind and made her jump, stifling the reassuring voice and opening the floodgates to a great heaving mass of doubts; what the hell did she think she was doing? Jon was right, she had been a complete idiot to agree to Tom Fielding's midnight rendezvous.

Dora looked up at the clock tower, looming ominously against the night sky. An abstract image of someone breaking into her flat scurried through her mind, followed by the faces of the men who had tried to steal the cat basket at Anchor Quay. What was to say they weren't already waiting for her in the shadows? What if they had been working for Tom Fielding after all? Anything was possible.

The calming voice was quieter now, reduced to an almost incomprehensible mumble. She took another breath, trying to throttle the life out of the fearful whine that had taken its place, the whine that was loudly encouraging her to turn and run – a few more minutes and it would all be over, whimpered the calm voice, just a few more minutes. She peered into the gloom, picking her way across the uneven concrete. One step at a time, and then another, and another, closer to the tower; it would soon all be over.

Seeing in the dark had never been Dora's strong suit and the added anxiety that she might trip helped to wind the tension tighter still. By the time she stepped into the puddle of dark at the base of the clock tower, all her senses were strung as taut as piano wire. Every molecule felt as if it was desperately straining to pick up something, some clue, some hint from the darkness. She glanced left and right, feeling horribly alone, wondering where Jon was. He'd told her he would ride shotgun, but she wished she'd asked him to stay a bit closer.

The icy wind tugged and pulled unnoticed at her evening dress. Fear had banished the biting cold to the distant edge of her consciousness. What if Jon wasn't there after all? She struggled to stamp out the thought before the implications caught hold, and focused all her attention on the shadows around the base of the tower.

In his hiding place by the portakabin, Spar felt dizzy. He could almost hear the adrenalin pumping through his veins. He was crouched like a runner on the starting blocks, swallowing down the bitter taste that flooded his mouth – a few seconds, just another few seconds, and it would all be over. His body seemed to have forgotten how to combine breathing and thinking. His palms were wet, his eyes were fixed on the darkness.

'Get ready, get ready – not long now,' Milo murmured, as Tom Fielding finally settled himself beside the clock tower. 'He's all alone.'

'And I think it would be a good idea if we kept it that way,' whispered an unfamiliar voice behind them.

Spar started so violently that both feet left the ground. The pent-up breath burst out of his chest as if he had sprung a leak. He swung round, feeling his guts do an unpleasant double somersault, and knew for certain that he was in the wrong job. He looked up straight into a torch beam and flinched. He hated violence, especially the real sort where you were likely to get hurt. He glanced round, expecting to see Milo explode like a madman out of the shadows and wondered if he would have the courage to follow him. For an instant Spar had an unnerving flashback of the commando knife and prayed that Milo had left it safe at home.

To his complete amazement, Milo took one look at the light, whimpered, and fell onto his hands and knees.

Spar looked heavenwards, offered an earnest word of thanks

and then snapped, 'Who the hell are you?' After all, someone had to say something manly.

'Chief Inspector Jon Melrose, Keelside CID. Now, if you gentlemen would like to stay calm, I think we can ensure that this goes off smoothly. What do you say to that?'

Spar put his hands up and clambered to his feet. He didn't like to contemplate what sort of sentence he might have got for helping to do over a police officer. 'We're not doing anything,' he protested weakly.

Their captor waved them closer to the portakabin.

'Good,' he said. 'Let's make sure that's how it stays. Just keep out of sight.'

Milo got up clumsily, clinging to the bag of photos like a security blanket. Jon Melrose switched off his torch, and Spar, sweating with relief, began to tremble.

'Tom?' Dora whispered into the darkness. 'Are you there?'

The words echoed around the skeletal framework of scaffolding, making the hairs on the back of her neck prickle.

Ahead of her, a torch flickered into life.

'Dora Hall, I presume?' said Tom Fielding in a low even voice. 'Is that you?'

Dora hurried towards the cone of light, aware only of desperately wanting to be somewhere else and the thump-thump-thump of a nervous pulse in her ears.

'Have you got the photos?'

She could barely see Tom's face, just the monochrome of his Burberry mac picked out in the torch light. Dora nodded, then realised he might not be able to see her face.

'Yes,' she said, struggling to keep the tremor out of her voice. Just as she moved towards him she was surprised, and then relieved, to see a figure step out of the shadows to her left.

The relief was instantly snatched away when a woman's voice said crisply: 'In that case, Mrs Hall, I think you had better give them to me. Now.'

Dora froze, while Tom Fielding instinctively turned towards

the sound, catching Alicia Markham's distinctive features in the torch beam.

Dora gasped and hissed Alicia's name. Beside her, also caught in the spotlight's glare, was Lawrence Rawlings. He winced, lifting his arms to cover his face. Alicia stared down the light towards Dora and held out her hand.

'Give me the photos.'

Dora struggled with a growing sense of astonishment. Of all the people she had expected to see under the clock tower, Alicia Markham and Lawrence Rawlings had not been amongst them. 'I haven't got them with me,' she said as evenly as she could.

Alicia stepped closer. 'Please don't lie to me. We know you have them, we had your phone tapped. I'd like you to hand them over or I shall be forced to take them.'

'No, Alicia,' said Lawrence firmly. 'I've already said no strong-arm tactics.'

Alicia snorted. 'Don't be so silly.' She looked out beyond the light as if trying to find something in the darkness. From the portakabin came a mumbled, muffled, scuffling sound.

'Get over here, you two, and get these photos,' Alicia barked. 'What the hell am I paying you for?'

'It's all right, Dora,' Jon Melrose called, from somewhere close by. 'I've got her little helpers here with me. Give the photographs to Tom and let's get out of here.'

Hearing Jon speak finally toppled Dora's carefully balanced self control. The tight bubble of fear that had been rising in her chest exploded like a mortar shell. She took a great gulp of air and, forgetting everything else, totally consumed by a volatile mix of terror and relief, ran blindly towards the comforting sound of his voice. She stumbled forwards, disoriented in the darkness and the flickering torch light. It was pure animal instinct, so strong and overwhelming that she was running before she had time to form the thought.

Alicia Markham and Lawrence Rawlings hurried after her, followed by a bemused Tom Fielding. As they rounded the corner near the portakabin, the overhead lights came on outside the main hall and, like a river flowing, lights snapped on all over the campus.

One moment Dora was in darkness; the next instant, the area behind the portakabin was flooded with light. As her eyes adjusted to the glare, she saw Jon standing over Alicia's henchmen, and instinctively took a step back – they really *had* been waiting for her in the dark. She stared at the two men, feeling her fear flutter back to life, and sucked in another breath.

'You sent them up here to ambush me,' she whispered, swinging round to face Alicia and Lawrence. 'They were waiting for me, weren't they? Who the hell do you think you are, Bonnie and Clyde?'

Alicia Markham's face contorted with fury. 'Oh, God give me strength. This is a complete and utter farce,' she hissed at Milo and Spar. 'Don't you two have guns or something? Make her give me the bloody photos.' She lunged forwards, made a grab at Spar and slapped him hard, then turned back to Dora, one fist still clenched around his collar. 'Give me those photos. I've paid for them. By rights they're mine.' She extended her free hand. 'I already know what they are, delightful Technicolor snaps of our friend Mr Fielding here. Guy's already told me about them.'

Given the circumstances, Dora thought Tom Fielding looked remarkably relaxed. He fixed Alicia with a humourless smile.

'He has, has he? I hope you don't live to regret going so far out on a limb for that bastard Phelps, Alicia. You know he was there at Ben Frierman's party, don't you? Did he tell you he likes to watch? That's how he knew about the photos in the first place. That's how your Mr Phelps gets his jollies. He sat in on the performance. Or maybe he forgot to mention that?'

Alicia, although visibly shaken, stood her ground. 'I really don't care,' she snapped, glaring at Dora. 'I want those pictures. I've paid through the nose for them and I intend to have them.'

Dora didn't move.

It was too much for Alicia; roaring with frustration, she

turned her attention back to Spar and shook him furiously. 'You and your bloody little bag of happy family snaps. Why couldn't you have done what I asked you? It was so damned simple.'

Spar whimpered and covered his head with his hands. His tormentor threw him to the ground, then hunched her shoulders and squared up to Dora.

'I'll ask you nicely, just once more. Give me the pictures, I want them now. Do you understand?' Each syllable was enunciated with icy clarity between gritted teeth.

Dora took a step back. Fairbeach's normally restrained first lady was white with rage, her fists clenched, her jaw set. For a moment Dora was convinced that Alicia was going to punch her.

Before either woman could move, Tom Fielding stepped between them. 'Calm down, Alicia, it's all over,' he said firmly, and then glanced at Dora. 'Have you really got the photos?'

Dora nodded and reluctantly slipped off her jacket, pulling the envelope of prints out of the torn sleeve lining.

Tom took them from her. 'I wondered where these had got to. I was so drunk that night – ridiculous at my age. I was flattered, I suppose. When they didn't surface I almost thought I'd got away with it. I'd got no idea that they would cause you all such trouble. Or me, come to that.' He smiled grimly at Alicia, who was still spoiling for a fight. 'But we all have to pay for our mistakes.'

Alicia growled.

He held up his hands in mock surrender. 'It's all over, Alicia. You've won. Game, set and match. I've already resigned. I did it last night after Dora rang me. Your little lapdog Phelps is home and dry. So you won't be needing the photos any more.' He paused, eyes fixed firmly on hers. Alicia Markham's bluster trickled away like melting snow.

'Fifteen years in local politics,' Tom continued in a reflective voice. 'Gone, just like that. My own fault. A big price for a little pleasure, but at least I know I've done the right thing –

I only hope when all this is over, Alicia, you feel the same way.'

Before anyone could stop him, he stepped over to the brazier and dropped the envelope into the glowing wood. It hung for a second, as if held by fingers of fire, and then surrendered and burst into a corona of flame.

Alicia let out a wail of abject misery.

Spar scrambled forward, only to be grabbed by Jon.

'Leave it,' he snapped, though it was patently too late.

Alicia stared into the blaze and then dragged her coat up around her shoulders. She glared at Spar.

'You're fired, you little bastard,' she snarled.

Lawrence Rawlings gently pulled Spar to his feet. 'What did you do with all the other pictures you found? Were there any documents with them?' He was unnaturally calm.

Spar, speechless, waved towards Milo, who had picked himself up off the floor, and was tugging at his suit and sleeves, as if straightening his clothes would help him regain his composure. In one hand he was strangling a crumpled carrier bag. 'Shell shock,' he mumbled miserably. 'Goose Green, never been the same since. Medical discharge . . .' Nobody took a bit of notice.

Beside the brazier, Alicia pulled an envelope out of her handbag. 'I assume this is what you are looking for, Lawrence? You are an old fool.' She sounded extremely tired. 'I really don't understand why you want this. You've already got the photos of Calvin Roberts and that girl in bed together. Plenty of evidence to get your daughter a nice clean divorce. I assume that was what you wanted all along, wasn't it? And as for this, I really can't see the point of trying to save Jack Rees now. He's dead, or are you just protecting fallen heroes? The old boys' network infuriates me.' She undid the envelope and pulled out a sheet of paper. 'I know Lillian Bliss was Jack's daughter. I read it on her birth certificate.' She waved the paper at him. 'It's all here in black and white for anyone to see. You can't hide it. Anyone can get a copy from the register office. There's nothing here worth having.'

With a dismissive sweep of her hand she dropped Lillian's birth certificate and the envelope into the flames alongside the curled ash of Tom Fielding's photographs. As a final gesture she snatched the carrier out of Milo's terrified hands and up-ended it. The contents slithered out. One or two pictures fluttered in the breeze, drawn towards Milo and Spar's fire in the upturned can.

To Dora's surprise, Lawrence leapt forward to rescue them. As he scrambled around in the dirt, Alicia started to walk back to the main hall with an exaggerated air of dignity. Spar trailed behind her, Milo behind him.

Tom Fielding nodded to Dora. 'Thank you,' he said softly, without a trace of rancour, tucking his hands back into his pockets.

She watched him disappear into the shadows.

By the brazier, Lawrence Rawlings was still on his hands and knees, hunched over the photographs Alicia had tipped out of Milo's bag.

In the flickering firelight he turned the prints backwards and forwards, eyes working furiously across the faded images. His face was tight with concentration. He looked a world away from the distinguished businessman of the awards ceremony. His face was smeared with ash, his hands full of photos, some charred, others folded and torn. For a moment Dora wondered if he was having some kind of breakdown.

'Tom's already burnt the photos Alicia wanted. They're gone,' she said gently.

Lawrence Rawlings blinked, tears glittering in his eyes. 'I don't want those photos,' he said unsteadily. 'I never did. I want these. The ones of Lillian when she was little. I want the photos of my daughter.'

Dora looked at him in astonishment. 'No,' she said, helping him to his feet and brushing him down. 'Jack Rees was Lillian's father.' Lawrence felt terribly frail under his heavy overcoat.

The old man shook his head. 'No, that's not true. Alicia was wrong. I knew from the minute Lillian came to see Jack that she was my daughter. At that Christmas party, she stood in the doorway of Ben's office and I knew then. And these photos.' He spread them out like a hand of cards. 'She looks just like my daughter Sarah did when she was little. There have to be some letters somewhere, something to prove Lillian really is my daughter.'

Dora stared at him. 'I don't understand.'

'Jack Rees was notorious, he used to love them and leave them. Always did. Fielding's just the same, he'll bounce back – that sort always do.' Lawrence swallowed down a sob. 'Lillian's mother was quite beautiful, you know. She deserved so much more from life than a man like Jack. I couldn't bear to see the way he treated any of them, but her most of all. So I, so I . . .' He stopped, reddening furiously.

'You went out with her too?' Dora suggested gently.

A single tear rolled down Lawrence's face, cutting a glistening path through the soot on his cheek. 'How tactfully put, Mrs Hall. Yes, I saw her for months behind his back. I don't know whether he ever knew or even whether he cared. When Jack found out she was pregnant he made some sort of financial arrangement. I don't know exactly what it was. I suppose she must have thought it was better to have an MP named as the father rather than me, more clout.' He stopped, wiping the tear away with the back of his hand.

'Then, later on, Jack met Caroline; she was the original merry widow. Played him at his own game, you know, played hard to get, turned him down, stood him up – he was completely hooked. She had already got the two girls. By that time I think Jack was keen to put down roots, have a family of his own, but nothing happened. They tried for years to have a child. She always insisted Jack had a problem. Told me he'd refused to have the tests, said he already had a daughter. That was when the rot really started between them.' Lawrence paused, visibly struggling to control his emotions.

'I suspected then, I wondered if I should go looking for them.' He stopped. 'My wife was never strong. Lillian's mother was so alive, so full of fun, so vital. I would have liked to have

304

found her and the baby. All those years wasted . . .' The words dried in his throat.

After a minute or two he straightened his shoulders, recovering some of his former poise, but with eyes firmly fixed on the harvest of photographs. 'I was hoping I might find something, some little thing that would prove what I already know is true.'

Dora put her hand on his arm. 'Come on,' she said softly. 'Let's collect the rest of the photos.'

Jon appeared from the shadows and they crouched down beside Lawrence. Between them they gathered up the remains of the pile.

As Lawrence walked away, Jon slipped his arm around Dora. 'Are you all right?'

She nodded, afraid to speak in case the tears that had gathered behind her eyes found their way out.

He leant forwards and kissed her gently. 'Good, next time maybe you'll do things my way.'

Dora laughed. 'Trust me, there isn't going to be a next time.'

Out of the corner of her eye, she saw someone hurrying towards them.

Josephine Hammond crested the little hill. 'Oh shit!' she cried breathlessly. 'Don't tell me. I've missed it all, haven't I? It's bloody Gary's fault. He's blind drunk again, you can't take him anywhere – so where's Tom Fielding? What happened?'

Dora shook her head. 'Nothing much, Jo. Believe me, it wasn't very spectacular. I gave Tom the photographs and he burnt them. Finito, the end – I can't say I'm sorry to see the back of them.'

Josephine Hammond groaned and turned back towards the hall. 'I'm going to kill Gary.'

Jon glanced at Dora, his dark eyes reflecting the last of the firelight. 'Ready to go home now?'

'More or less.' Dora's teeth had begun to chatter. 'Has your car got a decent heater?'

Jon slipped off his jacket and wrapped it round her shoulders. 'Here.'

As she pulled it tight he caught hold of the lapels and dragged her towards him, kissing her hard. 'You know you're an awful lot of trouble, don't you?'

Dora nodded. 'Always have been.' Desire, mingled with a sense of relief, made her giggle. She curled up against him, delighted to feel his arms tighten around her. She hadn't thanked him for protecting her or for the decision to let everyone involved walk free. There would be time later; at the moment she wanted to revel in the warmth of his body against hers.

Dora grinned up at him. 'Did I ever tell you that you looked really sexy in a dinner jacket?'

Jon smiled. 'I think you may have mentioned it.'

21

Spar carried the new box of fish pellets out to the pond in his back garden. He'd already got the fish in – nice they were, very peaceful. The plants looked good as well. A half-opened water lily like a brilliant lemon yellow flare reached up towards the sunlight.

Across the garden, through the shed windows, he could see the new breeding tanks, their filters plopping and hissing gently in the balmy air. A cloud of fish fry glinted and spiralled in the watery currents.

Summer was finally nudging spring aside. He stretched luxuriously, master of all he surveyed. Two rolled-gold koi broke the glittering surface of the pond and executed a perfect synchronised turn.

'Where do you want this new pond liner, then?' asked Milo, struggling up the path behind him. 'I reckon maybe we ought to have bought one of them little fountains as well. I like fountains. We could build a wall up round the back of the first pond, stick this one in behind it and have a waterfall. Buy some nice rocks and stuff. It'd look great. What d'ya reckon?'

Spar threw a handful of pellets into the crystal clear water. Hungry mouths bubbled up and snatched them off the surface.

'Not in this man's army,' he said. 'Maybe a bridge, though, and one of them little pagoda things like the Japanese have. Over there, by the wallflowers.'

Milo nodded and eased the unwieldy black plastic pond shape down onto the grass. 'Whatever you say. Do you want me to get the rest of the stuff out of the car?'

Spar nodded. 'If you don't mind.'

* * *

Alicia Markham stood on the terrace of her home, watching her gardener spray the roses for black spot. She glanced down at her watch. It was nearly twelve o'clock. From inside, through the open French windows, she could hear the tinkle of cutlery as the waitresses added the final touches to the buffet table. It appeared they had embraced her order for complete silence without question.

Very soon, Fairbeach's triumphant new Conservative MP would be arriving for lunch. Alicia was hosting a little thankyou celebration for all the campaign workers for their efforts.

Alicia turned to glance at her reflection in the glass doors, and smoothed an errant curl back into place. Perhaps some of the decisions she had made regarding Guy Phelps hadn't been altogether sound, maybe she had been misguided, but ultimately, she assured herself, she only had Fairbeach's interests at heart.

The house boy guided Parliament's newest member out onto the terrace to join Alicia for a pre-luncheon sherry. Alicia painted on a perfect smile.

'Caroline, how wonderful to see you, darling. How's Westminster treating its latest arrival? I want to hear all about it.'

Caroline Rees, Jack Rees' widow, grimaced.

'It is a complete dump. I've got to share an office and the traffic –' She peered at the tray the house boy was waving under her perfectly powdered nose. 'And no, I don't want a bloody sherry, haven't you got any scotch?'

Alicia smiled graciously. 'Of course. Why don't we all go into my office?'

Persuading Guy Phelps to resign had not been difficult, though Alicia had had to improvise about what the photos of Tom Fielding contained, inferring, hinting and then blatantly lying so that Guy believed he was in at least one of them. Ill health had been the reason he had come up with for the selection committee.

It was hardly original, but, by that time, rumours of the events at Ben Frierman's Christmas party had seeped into the ether. The committee's words of regret had been tinged with more than one sigh of relief.

Caroline's clearance through the selection procedure had been remarkably swift, and, with Tom Fielding out of the picture as well, her election victory a landslide. It appeared that the Fairbeach electorate thought being married to a local hero was recommendation enough.

Colin Scarisbrooke, Caroline's agent, hovered uneasily in the doorway, fingers wrapped tight around his sherry glass. He and Alicia had barely spoken a word more than necessary since the day he had brought a busload of tramps home for lunch.

'Hello, Alicia,' he said in a pointedly neutral tone. 'How are you?'

Alicia nodded her welcome. 'Hello, Colin. Why don't you join us?' she said, extending a conciliatory hand. 'Have a glass of something decent for a change? I'd like to talk about what we intend to do for the Fairbeach farmers during the next session. Oh, and we must sort out the times for Caroline's surgery. We've had several calls at party office already.'

Lawrence Rawlings sat at his desk and carefully removed the buttonhole from the lapel of his best suit. It had been an odd sort of day. A beginning and an ending. A whisper of confetti fluttered onto his desk alongside the photograph of Sarah, Calvin and the girls.

He didn't really like register office weddings, though Lillian had looked wonderful in a confection of cream satin and gold lace. Apparently, she had met his old friend Bob Preston on the night of the Spring Ball, introduced by the president of the students' union, who, it seemed, worked for Bob's firm as a Saturday boy.

While Lawrence had been grovelling on his knees looking for photographs and proof and an end to his pain, his old friend had been asking Miss Lillian Bliss out to lunch and she had graciously accepted.

Lawrence looked at his watch. Very soon, the happy couple would be boarding a plane for Tenerife, heading for a new life in a pale pink villa, with swimming pool, and a starburst of bougainvillaea around the patio.

Lillian, bright-eyed and ecstatically happy, had promised Lawrence she would send him some of the wedding photos. At least now he would be able to have a photograph of her and Bob alongside the others on his desk and no-one would ask him why.

He had considered sharing his thoughts with Lillian, particularly as Bob had brought her to Sunday lunch on several occasions since their first date, but in the end Lawrence had decided to leave well alone. Remarkably, Lillian genuinely did seem to be in love with Bob Preston.

When Lawrence had tactfully enquired if Bob had any idea what sort of girl Lillian was, Bob Preston had smiled beatifically.

'Does it really matter? Didn't I say I wanted to go out with a bang? Lillian makes me happy, Lawrence. Don't worry, just wish me well. I think, to be perfectly honest, she is looking for a father figure.'

The irony had not been lost on Lawrence as he had watched Lillian, snuggled up in the crook of Bob's arm, when they had cut the wedding cake.

Across the desk, Sarah smiled back at him from inside her silver frame. While on his crusade to decide whether the truth needed to be told, Lawrence had tried to broach the subject of Calvin's infidelity.

It had been on one sunny Sunday morning when Calvin had had an assignation elsewhere. Sarah had smiled and slipped her arm through his.

'Daddy, I do know what you're trying to say, but don't underestimate me, I already know about Calvin. The thing is, he really does love me and the girls – in his own way.' She looked at him pointedly. 'Just like you loved Mummy.'

Lawrence had stared at her, completely dumbfounded, wondering when he had given himself away to his daughter. At what point in her childhood had she realised that he lied too? Was the fault all his, after all?

He had reviewed his will, but what was there he could do, other than trust his canny daughter to keep Calvin's avarice in check? He'd send a handsome cheque as a wedding present to Lillian, saying it was what Jack would have done had he lived.

He picked up the confetti and stared at it before consigning the bright fluttery petals to the bin. They actually made quite a handsome couple; the ex-rugby-playing ex-mayor and his beautiful blonde bride.

That girl, the reporter, Josephine Hammond from the *Fairbeach Gazette*, had been at the wedding too. She'd taken photographs and interviewed the happy couple, though during the reception he had overheard her telling someone that she had just got a job on a national newspaper.

Stiffly, Lawrence got to his feet and looked out of the open window. Amongst the greenery in the orchard, in stunning contrast to the verdant growth and the nubile swelling apples, two magpies watched him, button-black eyes staring up towards his study.

Lawrence sighed, feeling fatigue sweep through him like a cold wind. Suddenly, out of the void, he heard a song thrush, its voice as keen and strong as a choirboy's. The bird was nowhere in sight, but it trilled and swooped defiantly through its virtuoso performance, ending on a climax of pure unadulterated pleasure.

Without a backward glance, the magpies took off in unison, rising up like smoke signals into the new blue summer sky. Lawrence smiled. Come the winter he might just fly out to see his old friend Bob and his new wife after all.

Beside Dora, the intercom buzzed more insistently, followed closely by a thin high-pitched voice through the speaker.

'Dora, are you up there?'

Dora pushed the swivel chair away from the desk and yawned.

On her desk was Calvin's latest proposal. He'd finally found a buyer for a children's story she had written when her daughter, Kate, was small. Some guy in America was very interested in securing the film rights. Would she consider flying to California to discuss it?

Dora tucked the letter back in her in-tray.

'Dora, are you up there?' Sheila repeated.

It was extremely tempting to say no. Instead she pressed the call button.

'Come up, Sheila, it's unlocked.'

She padded into the kitchen, scratching and yawning deliciously with every step. Oscar and Gibson, the resident tom cats, mewled the lament of the wildly over-indulged and leapt onto the cooker while she plugged in the kettle and lit a cigarette. Opening the fridge, Dora prised a carton of milk off the shelf and sniffed it speculatively.

A few seconds later, Sheila pushed the kitchen door open. She peered around and sniffed, looking rushed. Sheila inevitably looked rushed.

'Oh, you're in here, are you? I thought you told me you'd stopped smoking? You've left the street door on the latch again. Don't know why you've bought that security thing, anyone can just walk up –'

Dora hunted around for the teapot. 'I nipped across to the shop first thing.'

Sheila's eyes narrowed. 'Not like that, surely? You're not ill, are you?' She picked her way across the kitchen and stood a wicker basket on the table amongst the debris of breakfast, letters and open books. Oscar headed towards the cat litter tray.

Dora glanced down at the grey dressing gown she was wearing and shook her head. 'No, I'm fine. I've been up for hours. I've been working on the computer this morning. I'm working on a new book. Lillian Bliss may have gone, but Catiana Moran is still going strong.'

Sheila looked at Dora and tipped her head accusingly to one side. 'What are all those boxes doing in the hall? Are you moving out? I did wonder if you would after all the thing with the burglaries. It makes sense really.'

Behind Sheila, the kitchen door opened to reveal Jon Melrose, fetchingly attired in a white towelling bathrobe. He grinned at Sheila, whose face had frozen into a tight mask of astonishment.

'No, actually I'm moving in, until Dora and I can find a house to buy together,' he said. He glanced at Dora, hovering by the teapot. 'Any chance I can have a cup?'

Dora nodded. 'My pleasure. Why don't you sit down, Sheila, you've gone really pale.'